Praise for Candice Fox

"I can't wait to read what this talented writer does next!"
—Chevy Stevens

"Intense . . . quirky, no-nonsense characters complement the suspenseful plotting, which includes a multitude of twists. Readers will look forward to seeing more of Ted and Amanda."
—*Publishers Weekly* on *Gone by Midnight*

"*Gone by Midnight* hits terminal velocity halfway through page one and never slackens."
—*Australian Book Review*

"Fox builds tension and suffuses it with humanity. . . . A pair of protagonists [that] readers will take to their hearts."
—*Booklist* (starred review)
on *Redemption Point*

"*Crimson Lake* is a compelling read that is sure to leave an impact after the last page."
—*RT Book Reviews*

GONE BY MIDNIGHT

CANDICE FOX

A TOM DOHERTY ASSOCIATES BOOK FORGE NEW YORK

This is a work of fiction. All of the characters, organizations, and events portrayed in this novel are either products of the author's imagination or are used fictitiously.

GONE BY MIDNIGHT

Copyright © 2019 by Candice Fox

All rights reserved.

A Forge Book
Published by Tom Doherty Associates
120 Broadway
New York, NY 10271

www.tor-forge.com

Forge® is a registered trademark of Macmillan Publishing Group, LLC.

ISBN 978-1-250-31759-9

Our books may be purchased in bulk for promotional, educational, or business use. Please contact your local bookseller or the Macmillan Corporate and Premium Sales Department at 1-800-221-7945, extension 5442, or by email at MacmillanSpecialMarkets@macmillan.com.

First U.S. Edition: March 2020
First U.S. Mass Market Edition: February 2021

Printed in the United States of America

0 9 8 7 6 5 4 3 2 1

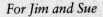

For Jim and Sue

GONE BY MIDNIGHT

The real trouble came at midnight.

Martin Askin had arrived in Cairns at five o'clock in the afternoon and checked into room 607, dumping his bags on the floor and marching to the windows to yank down the blinds. He'd stood in the room in the dim light, surveying the crisply made bed and the desk neatly arranged with the room service menu, daring there to be some sign of trouble. A forgotten bar of soap in the immaculate bathroom. An unemptied bin.

His plane had sat inexplicably on the tarmac at LAX for forty-five minutes before takeoff, and again for half an hour at Sydney Airport, adding more than an hour onto an already seventeen-hour haul in economy. A flight attendant had spilled hot tea in his lap somewhere over the Pacific, and the plane's toilets had been malfunctioning, filling the back half of the plane with a wretched stench. His taxi driver from Cairns

Airport had got lost for ten minutes on the drive to the hotel, and at the reception desk the computer had frozen just before his key could be assigned.

If one more thing went wrong, Martin Askin was going to lose it.

Everything in the room seemed fine. He'd shed his clothes, showered, and slipped, groaning, between the cool, starchy sheets.

At 5:31 p.m., the door to room 608 had slammed. Knocking, bashing sounds, the unmistakable near-hysterical laughter of overactive young boys—a bunch of them. Martin had resisted the urge to burst into tears from exhausted rage. He'd pulled the pillow over his head and gone back to sleep.

When he next looked at the clock by the bed, it was 7:07 p.m. The swirling, rising music of a movie playing too loudly in the next room reached him, but what had broken him out of his sleep was a knocking against the wall. The boys were jumping on the beds, ramming the headboards into the wall. He looked at the phone beside him and thought of calling reception and complaining, but sleep took him before he could.

At 8:03 p.m. the door to the room slammed a few times in succession. Heavy footsteps by his door. At 9:11 p.m., squealing. One of the boys screaming, "Get off! Get off! Get off!"

Martin Askin woke at 11:02 p.m. to the sound of the door slamming again and machine-gun fire in the movie. He sat up and bashed on the wall above his bed.

"Would you shut the fuck up!" he roared, sensing immediately the smallness of his voice in his own room. If he could hear every sound in 608, couldn't they hear him? "Stop slamming the goddamn door!"

No response. The movie next door played on. He thought he recognized Dwayne Johnson's voice. His eyes ached when they closed.

At midnight, an adult voice, the first he had heard, split through his dreams like a chisel, leaving a pain in his temple. He was out of the bed in a panic before consciousness had fully arrested him. Martin stumbled in the dark toward the door, shunting into the unfamiliar wall by the bathroom. Just as he opened the door to the hall, the woman in room 608 did the same. Martin had the sense, though he couldn't be sure, that the blond woman's voice had been rising and rising and now it was at fever pitch.

She didn't seem to know whether she wanted to go back into the room or stay out in the hall, holding her head and pacing. A trio of small boys, one of them already blubbering with tears, followed her movements back and forth as other hotel guests emerged from their rooms.

"How can he be gone? How can he be gone?" the woman was crying. She was panting, sweat-slick and badly sunburned. "Richie? Richie? Oh, Jesus. He's missing. He's gone!"

One of them was missing.

I snapped out of my sleep, the sweltering night materializing around me, loud through the open windows of the house. The rain had come and gone, but the reptilian and amphibian creatures that dwelled in the forest around my property kept up their barking, hoping for more to break the heat.

I threw back the sheets, sitting on the edge of the bed as the thought evolved from a panicked impulse into a clear message.

I'd put six geese away that evening. Not seven.

It was something I felt rather than knew. My geese are well-trained. They obey my commands like fat, feathered soldiers, and when I'd opened up their coop at sunset and told them to get in, I'd observed a row enter the little house without feeling the need to do a roll call. There should have been six gray, one white. I went out into the hall and through the kitchen, finding my way by the square cutouts of moonlit rainforest in each room, until I grabbed my torch and pushed through the back screen door.

My heart was beating hard. The dog, Celine, knew something was up immediately, guessed wrongly that it was her residency on the cane lounge—a terrible misdeed. She slithered guiltily off the cushions as I jogged down the stairs and through the wet grass to the goose coop.

Six heads popped up from under wings.

"Shit," I whispered, pushing on feathered chests as they came crowding at the entrance to be let out. I refastened the door of the coop and swung the torch around the property, the wire fence at the waterline, the gently lapping lake, still as pale glass in the moonlight. I braced for that terrible sight—a scattering of feathers trailing into the woods where the missing bird had been dragged by a fox or wild cat. Celine was whimpering at the edge of the porch, wagging her tail encouragingly so that it thumped the boards as she tried to work out my mission.

My geese are important to me. I had rescued the family of birds from certain death on the banks of Crimson Lake a year earlier, unaware that they would be the ones to rescue me. I'd taken comfort in caring for creatures more helpless than myself after an accusation had destroyed my life and taken away my home, my job, and my family.

Now one of them was gone.

I did a lap of the house and caught sight of a pale mound underneath the lounge Celine had been sleeping on. The bird was tucked against the wall at the very back corner of the porch. I flattened on the wooden boards and shined the torch on the bird, and she lifted her head slightly.

"Peeper," I called, reaching. "What are you doing, you silly thing?"

She wouldn't come. I jumped up and slid the couch away, and lifted the large, warm bird from the ground. I knew immediately that something wasn't right. When I picked up the geese they usually pedaled their feet in protest. Peeper's legs remained limp. I set her down and she stood for only a second before sinking again into a bundle, her head tucked against her chest.

"Oh no." I lifted her once more with shaking hands. "No, no, no."

I drove furiously. A part of my brain was already whispering placations about the bird in the box in the back of the car, trying to prepare for that awful moment when I arrived at the veterinarian's office seconds too late. Her limp body at the bottom of the plastic carrier, a wing splayed, the neck like a dropped rope. *It's a stupid bird*, I thought. *They can't live forever. You gave them the best life you could.* Though the words were easy to find, they were impossible to believe.

The headlights lit the dirt roads lined by high golden walls of cane, making fluttery embers of thousands of grasshoppers and moths disturbed by my passage. I glanced at the clock. It was three in the morning. The run-down houses and abandoned barns in the fields near my home were dark and empty.

I knew only one vet in the area. I'd taken the geese there the day I found them, when I was drunk and still ravaged by my time in prison. The veterinarian had made no effort to disguise his hatred when he discovered who I was, but he had already treated my birds. I was headed there when I saw for the first time a new, bright blue sign in the distance: *VET*.

I scanned the façade quickly for any indication that they gave twenty-four-hour emergency care, but there was none. I grabbed the box from the back of the car anyway, not daring to look inside, and ran to the glass doors.

I pounded and yelled for only a few seconds before lights began flickering on at the back of the building. Hope. The silhouette that jogged toward me through the dark was petite and lean, a woman pulling a thin dressing gown around her. She must have lived above the surgery. I lowered my eyes to the box in my hands, but I knew there was going to be no disguising who I was. Everyone in the country knew me. My trial, and its aftermath, had been a national sensation. I began speaking before she could unlock the door.

"Please don't turn me away," I said. "My bird is sick. She's really sick and needs help right now. I'll go. Just please help her. She—"

"Why would I send you away?" The woman frowned at me. Her accent was British. Northern. My mind raced. Was she new to the country? Her big, green eyes were searching mine, no sign of recognition in them.

I swallowed, shook my head.

"No reason. I meant, uh. It's just the hour. The terribly late hour."

"Come in." She held the door open and I slid past her. A wall of scent, disinfectant and animal fur, the husky smell of the bags of seed and dry dog food stacked on shelves near the counter.

In the light of the surgery room I got a better look at the doctor. Honey-colored hair falling from a hastily applied clip. Her small face was crowded with big, sumptuous features. I was prickling with emotions, relief and terror as she opened the box and peered inside.

"Oh hello, birdy," she murmured, almost to herself. Then to me: "I'll be thirty seconds." She jogged into a back room. I couldn't look into the box, did a restless lap of the surgery room instead. The certificate on the wall read Dr. Elaine Bass.

Dr. Bass came back in a minute dressed in a T-shirt and denim shorts, pulling on white latex gloves.

"I didn't catch your name," she said.

"It's Ted. Collins." One truth, one lie.

"Laney." She smiled, reaching slowly into the box. "And this is?"

"Oh." I felt heat come into my face. "Peeper. She's a year old."

"How long has she been unwell?"

"I don't know." The dread was returning. I watched as Laney lifted Peeper onto the examination table. "She didn't go into the coop with the others at sunset. I found her under a couch."

Laney took the big bird's wing in her hand and pulled it gently away from the feathery body, stretching the beautiful arc, fanning shades of gray, black, cream. She felt around the base of the bird's neck and smoothed back the feathers on her head.

"All right, Ted. I'm going to ask you to leave her with me."

"Can I please stay?" I cleared my throat. "Just, you know. Until we know something."

"Of course." Laney gestured to the door through which we'd come. "Stay as long as you like."

I heard her talking to my bird, calling her by her name, through the door to the waiting area. I read every brochure in the room, coming to the conclusion that there were far too many types of parasites in the world. When Laney fell silent, I sat on the couch and surrendered to my crushing worry.

The truth was, without my birds I might not have been able to recover from what had happened. On the side of the highway one fateful day, I'd pulled over to fix a noise in my car, not realizing that I'd parked only meters from a young girl waiting for a bus. She'd been abducted and brutally assaulted only minutes after I left her side. I was accused of the crime, charged, put on trial, and then the charges were dropped, the judiciary leaving me to be sentenced by the public when they couldn't find the evidence to do it themselves.

I'd been an ordinary man. A drug squad cop. A husband. A father. Now I was Australia's most hated man.

I'd fled to the property in the remote wetlands of Far North Queensland, and taken heart at caring for a group of birds who might have died without my help. They were a symbol of something for me. Of hope. Of worthiness.

When Laney appeared in the doorway an hour later, I realized with embarrassment that I had turned my thoughts to her to escape the tension of not knowing how Peeper was doing. I'd been wondering how long she'd been in the area. Whether she owned this shop or rented it. Why on earth she'd come from wherever it was she'd been born in England to this faraway tangle of rainforest on the edge of nowhere. It was a novelty for me to meet people who didn't know me from my time in the media spotlight.

She didn't mess around. "I'll have to wait for some tests to come back, but I'm almost certain she's got aspergillosis," Laney said.

"That sounds bad."

"It can be. But you may have brought her in just in time. *Aspergillosis* is a fungus. Gets in the lungs."

"Is it something I've done?"

"I'm sure it isn't," she said. "You seem like a pretty attentive owner. It's the Tropical North. Fungus loves it here, and poultry are susceptible to it. Is this a pet goose or do you have a farm?"

"No, no, she's a pet. But I have six others."

"Huh." She gave me an appreciative look. "The bird man of Crimson Lake."

I managed a smile.

"Go home and check the others," she said. "And keep an eye on their behavior over the coming days. Because Peeper separated herself off from the rest, the others may be fine. Empty all their water, clean out their living quarters, sterilize everything. I'm going to give you some potassium iodine drops and instructions for treating their water."

She went behind the counter and started looking through bottles and packages there.

"Is she going to be okay, do you think?"

"Look." Laney sighed, bringing a small bottle to me. "Ted, birds can be really flaky. It's very difficult to predict in the early stages how treatment will go."

I nodded, locking my eyes on the bottle in my hands, trying to keep my face hard.

"Give me your number and I'll let you know how we go. Okay?" She rubbed my bare forearm, a gesture that surprised me and, it seemed, her. Her hand fluttered at her eyebrow, embarrassed. "If she makes it, I'll have to have her here for a few days at least."

We finished up, and Laney saw me to the door. I waved, a strange tingling in my chest as I climbed into the car. I put the feeling down to nerves. It was only a matter of time before this woman found out who I was, and most likely that realization would come swiftly, when an employee asked about the bird, perhaps, and she described me. She had run my credit card and failed to notice the different surname, but that was a lucky break. In a couple of days, if Peeper survived, I'd come back in to pick the bird up and find Dr. Bass's warm smile had soured into the uncomfortable grimace I was used to seeing on the faces of most people I dealt with.

A heavy heart is best lightened by work. Though the sun was only just rising over the tips of the blue mountains across the lake, I parked beside my house and went right out the back. The birds marched out of their coop like they weren't missing one of their number. I took the grain container from the edge of the porch and poured out a handful, settling among the birds as they stabbed hungrily at my palm with their beaks, spilling grain everywhere. Woman, the mother of the geese and the only pure white bird, stood at the back and eyed me without reducing herself to the indignity of hand-feeding.

In fact, I'd already cleaned out my goose coop and their water trays with a pressure cleaner the day before, because this was an important day, one I had been counting down to.

My daughter Lillian, who was almost three, was coming to visit me in my home for the first time.

My cleaning efforts had not been so much inspired by a desire to impress her as to impress her mother, my ex-wife, Kelly. After my arrest our marriage had dissolved, and she'd since taken up with a man who worked in the fitness industry, like her. Things were serious between them, and had been for some time. I didn't know if Jett, the boyfriend, really believed the accusation against me, or if he was just a territorial dick, but I did know he was completely against leaving Lillian with me for several nights. The house needed to be clean, orderly, safe, welcoming. That meant fungus-free. I went around the side of the house to grab the pressure cleaner for a second round and stopped dead at the sight of the police car in my driveway.

I stared at the two officers as they exited the vehicle and headed toward me.

They were young patrol officers. A couple of Cairns boys, it looked like. I knew all of the cops in Crimson Lake and Holloways Beach by sight, some of them from working cases in the area as a private investigator with my partner, Amanda. A continued career in the police force had been out of the question after my arrest, but Amanda Pharrell had employed me on two murder investigations and a smattering of the private-eye jobs small towns seem to generate—poisoned family pets, cheating husbands, injury insurance fraud.

The young officers strode down the small incline toward me, and their lifted chins and smirks didn't give me much confidence that this was a friendly visit. I turned on my heel and started walking back around the side of the house.

"Hold up, Conkaffey!"

I went straight to my phone, which I'd left on the cane lounge on the porch. Celine ran over to the officers and did a tight circle of them, sniffing and barking good-naturedly.

I picked up my phone and typed a quick message to Amanda. Three letters.

SOS.

I knew it was all I had time for. And I was right. In seconds the two officers were boxing me in against the wall of the porch.

"Ted Conkaffey?" snapped one of the officers, a square-headed guy with tattoos poking up from his collar, and a name badge that read *Frisp.*

"You know who I am," I said.

"We're here to escort you to Cairns. Please hand me that phone and do not resist arrest."

This was my nightmare. The moment I had played and replayed a thousand times in my sleep, the moment that pressed into my consciousness sometimes hourly, no matter where I was or what I was doing. Fear of rearrest. It was happening. All I could hope for was that the action plan I had put in place for this very scenario would make the experience as painless as possible.

I had never been acquitted of the charges laid against me. They had simply been dropped due to a lack of evidence. When the tables started to turn in the courtroom, the state had decided they didn't want to proceed with my trial for fear of my being acquitted and them never being able to charge me again. I'd gone to bed every night since my release knowing that it might be my last free night, that a piece of evidence or a witness out of the blue might reopen my case at any time. Although recently the New South Wales police had released an official statement saying that I was no longer a "person of interest" in the abduction and rape of Claire Bingley, few news outlets had given the statement much coverage. It's hard to turn the great ship of public opinion around. Most people tend to believe an accusation as terrible as mine couldn't possibly fall on the completely innocent. If I wasn't guilty of Claire's assault, I was surely guilty of something.

I had briefed my few allies on what to do if I was ever arrested again.

Step one, Amanda would receive my distress signal. She would open an app on her mobile that traced the location of my phone. She would then call my lawyer, Sean Wilkins, who would make plans to get to where I was being held as soon as possible. Amanda would then call my friend Dr. Valerie Gratteur, who would go to my house and oversee any police searches that occurred there to make sure they were performed properly.

While all this was happening, I would say nothing of consequence to the police and try to make sure my rights weren't trampled on. It was a good plan, one I'd worked on carefully over a series of months. But of course it hinged on everyone following the script, and the two young cowboys standing before me didn't look like they planned to do that at all.

I held on to my phone and backed into the corner of the porch.

"I will not comply without an arrest warrant." I held

up the phone and turned the camera toward them as I thumbed the screen. "I'm recording this, which is my right. I want to see the warrant and—"

Gamble, Frisp's squat, long-armed partner, faked grabbing at the phone. As I swung it away from him, Frisp snatched it from my hand. My plan was already going awry. Celine stood on the edge of the porch, terror in her big black eyes, the hackles rising along her wide back. She gave a low, groaning growl, a sound I'd never heard her make. Dangerous, from the pit of her belly.

"Celine, it's okay, honey," I assured her.

"Hands on the wall." Frisp pointed.

"I want to know what I'm being arrested for. That's my right."

"If that fat fucking dog goes for me, I'm going to swat it." Gamble had a hand on his baton, Celine tracking him as he stepped back from her.

"You touch my dog and I will end you." I looked Gamble in the eyes, my whole body trembling with rage. "I mean it. I will fucking. End. You."

Gamble must have seen something in me that turned him. He glanced at Frisp for encouragement, but found none. Trying to breathe, I put my hands on the wall, still talking for the sake of the officers' body recorders, which I hoped were turned on.

"I have not been read my rights," I said. "I've seen no arrest warrant. My property has been unlawfully confiscated. I don't know where I'm being taken or why."

"Save the victim act for the courtroom, Conkaffey."

Frisp cuffed my hands behind my back, ratcheting the metal bands too tight.

My mind was crashing. I needed to stay calm, stay ahead of the game, but blood was rushing into my neck and face. I couldn't swallow. I let them lead me to the car to avoid upsetting my animals any more than was necessary. As I turned the corner at the side of the house, I saw the geese were on their feet at the end of the yard, beaks high with distress, wings splayed out from panting breasts. Celine followed us, whimpering and growling, until I stopped beside the driveway.

"Celine, it's okay. Go to your bed and stay." She took uncertain, fearful steps back toward the porch. "Good girl. On your bed."

In the car, Frisp tossed my phone into the center console, which was stuffed with cigarette butts. There was a pressure in my chest and back like hands pushing against my rib cage, squeezing the life out of me, making my eyes bulge. I sucked in air and tried to stay calm, tried to rationalize the situation. Amanda would already be putting the SOS plan into action. There was nothing I could do now to stay free, but I could do things to get free again. Time to change tactics. Gather information.

As far as I was concerned, there were three possibilities.

First, that my charges for the abduction, sexual assault, and attempted murder of Claire Bingley had been brought again. If that was the case, then I had a plan. I knew who had really assaulted Claire, and her father did, too. Months earlier, I had watched help-lessly as Dale Bingley had murdered her attacker, a young man named Kevin Driscoll, in a Sydney ware-house. To prove my innocence to him, at least, I'd helped Claire's father find the real perpetrator. And he'd enacted his brutal revenge. A diary had been found in Driscoll's car that implicated him in Claire's attack. I would use that to defend myself in a new trial. It wasn't much, but it was something.

That brought about the second possibility. The New South Wales police had questioned me extensively over Kevin Driscoll's death. They had bits and pieces to go on—my phone had been in the area of the crime scene, and I had communicated with Claire Bingley's father in the lead-up to the murder. He had come to my house, slept on my porch, drunk my whiskey, and then been found at the scene, calm but unwilling to cooperate with police inquiries. Dale was in the same position I was—no one could prove that he had done more than stumble into the warehouse where Kevin Driscoll was killed. There was no murder weapon, no physical evidence to link him to the crime. His charges were dropped, but not dismissed. Maybe things had changed. Maybe I was being arrested now because they'd found something that could definitively put me in that warehouse on that awful night.

The third possibility was that something completely new had happened. That at some time in the past twenty-four hours a child had been stolen, assaulted, or abused, and I was being brought in as a suspect. It was possible that a new accusation against me had emerged. It had happened before. If that was the case,

I needed to think about my alibi. I'd spent the whole night at home, only leaving to visit the vet at 3 a.m. But I'd sent messages and made phone calls, used the internet. I was sweating, my brain thrumming with ideas, trying to form and consolidate strategies.

I was distracted from my turmoil as the patrol car rolled toward Cairns, gliding down Kenny Street. I expected the car to turn left for the police station nestled in the heart of the tourist district, but they continued along Wharf Street, past palm-lined beaches, the newly risen sun just beginning its onslaught on the pavement. They continued past the sprawling, empty parking lot of the convention center toward the blazing-white blocks of the White Caps Hotel.

The back parking lot entrance was blocked with police cars. As we approached I caught a glimpse of a huddle of press at one of the side entrances, where more police officers stood guard, stern-faced and unaccommodating.

"What's happened?" I asked.

They ignored me.

"Hey, shitbird." I nudged the wire mesh between Frisp's seat and mine. "I asked a question. What's going on?"

"What's going on is you pushed your luck too far this time, kiddie-fucker." He glared at me in the rearview mirror. "You should have quit while you were ahead."

He went into the bathroom off the staff dining room and briefly made sure there was no one in the stalls, still trying to catch his breath. The air wouldn't come, his efforts only bringing oxygen into the top of his lungs. The supervisor's words in the men's change room only minutes earlier rang in his head like a bell being struck over and over, a blinding, painful sound.

"They're not having any luck finding the boy. Things are getting serious. The boss wants all staff in conference room eight, right now. Leave your things and go."

The man knew he should go to the staff meeting. He needed to be seen there, looking shocked and horrified with the rest of them at the child's fate. He *was* shocked and horrified, but he was not surprised. He already knew what had happened, could picture it in his mind like a video on playback. He went to the sink, bent, and gagged, but the sickness refused to rise.

What he wanted to do was go back to where it had happened. To see the awful reality for himself.

He looked at his reflection in the mirror, wiping sweat from his face with calloused hands. It was typical of him to have done this. He knew exactly how his father would have reacted if he was still alive, watching the events unfold the way he used to watch him play when he was a child: an army sergeant surveying one of his troops with his arms folded, eyes heavy lidded, lip curled with distaste. The man in the bathroom could see his father at the edge of the sand, the surf washing at his thick ankles, pointing with his impossibly big finger at his work.

"Don't put that there. It'll collapse. All right, put it there and see what happens. See? See? You don't have any understanding of structure. You've got to learn, you idiot."

He could feel the structure of his life collapsing now like the sandcastle, hand-molded edges sliding and falling under the weight of his stick and rock embellishments. All his hard work crumbling. There had been no warning, no cracks or shudders. He crouched now, holding the edge of the sink with one hand, even his legs unable to take the weight anymore. He was shaking so badly the huge ring of keys on his belt was jingling.

How could he have done this? How could he have let it happen again?

I was marched through a foyer packed with police officers standing in groups, looking at maps and talking on phones, the seating area and a huddle of tall tables completely swamped by blue uniforms. There was a queue of worried-looking people who appeared to be checking out of the hotel, but instead of doing so at the reception counter they were being taken one by one into rooms and having their suitcases opened on a large table. Every face in range turned toward me. I walked straight and tall between the cowboys as we turned left off the foyer and down a hallway into a large boardroom stuffed with the older, harder faces of non-uniformed cops. The only face I recognized was that of a visibly stressed Damien Clark, the chief superintendent of the Crimson Lake police.

"Chief, we've brought you Ted Conkaffey, as requested."

Chief Clark looked at me, his mouth slightly parted in shock.

I stared back, my jaw set. "I want my lawyer," I said.

"Would you . . ." Chief Clark glanced around the men and women he'd been meeting with, the mass of papers and maps on the boardroom table before him. "Would you all excuse me for just a minute?"

Chief Clark marched past me, bumping Gamble on the shoulder. The two cops looked at each other. We followed Clark down another hall into a smaller boardroom, this one crammed with chairs stacked against one wall.

"What the fuck is this?" Clark snapped at Frisp.

"We . . ." He looked at Gamble for support. "You asked us to bring you Ted Conkaffey. You said, 'Get Conkaffey. Bring him in.'"

"Yes, I said, 'Bring him in!' Not '*Bring him in.*'" Chief Clark squeezed his brow, making the skin above his eyebrows pucker. "I literally meant bring him here, to this place. Not arrest him and march him in handcuffs past a hundred officers. Holy fuck. Did any press see him?"

The cowboys looked at each other, then at the chief. Then all three men looked at me.

"I want my lawyer," I said.

I was uncuffed. I sat in the small boardroom and listened as Chief Clark roared at the two officers on the other side of the door. I winced as he slammed the wall between us with his palm to emphasize his words.

"Did you *honestly believe* that if I thought Conkaffey was a person of interest I'd have sent two fuck-knuckles in a squad car to pick him up?"

"Well, I mean—" Frisp said.

"You didn't even have an arrest warrant!"

"We thought . . ." Gamble struggled with his words. "You know. With his history and all. We just assumed . . ."

I rapped my fingers on the boardroom table and fantasized about poking my head out the door and requesting a coffee. When Chief Clark came back into the room he had my phone, which he set on the table between us as he sat down, taking a moment to rub his face hard with both hands. His stubble made a rustling sound against his rough palms.

"There has been a terrible mistake," he began.

"You reckon?"

"All I can do is offer you my apologies. I didn't bring you here because I believed you were a person of interest in the case I'm dealing with."

"Well, that's just dandy." I smiled, taking my phone from the table between us. "Have a nice day, Chief." I stood and turned to leave the room.

"There's a boy missing," he said.

I paused, my hand on the polished chrome doorknob. The phone was vibrating as messages, no doubt from my lawyer, came through. I waited.

"He went missing from a room upstairs that had three other boys in it," the chief continued. "Last night, around midnight, we think. The boys were all sleeping. Their parents were downstairs in the restaurant. We're approaching seven hours, and there's no sign."

I let my hand fall from the door.

"Oh, I get it," I said. "Child goes missing. Those shithead officers assumed you'd pick up the local pedophiles, give them a shake, see what falls out."

"We've looked at you already." Clark sat back in his chair, folded his arms, shrugged.

"You had no legal cause to do that," I snapped. "I'm no longer a person of interest in the Bingley case. To you I should be just a regular, law-abiding citizen."

"Tough luck," he said. "I did it. Of course I did it."

I sighed.

"Someone at your address was using the internet to stream a movie until about eleven thirty p.m.," he said. "And someone used your phone at that location to play a game called Candy Crush until about eleven forty-five p.m. The phone was idle then until three a.m., when it was transported to a veterinarian's office. Your credit card was used there."

"Sick bird," I said.

"Sorry to hear it," Clark said, the sentiment totally devoid of warmth. "At the end of the day, the timeline doesn't fit. You didn't have enough time to get to the hotel to abduct the boy."

"Unless I had someone use the phone and internet at my place as an alibi," I said, for some reason.

"Did you?" He raised an eyebrow.

"No."

"Look, I'm satisfied it's not you," Clark said. "We don't have your car on CCTV in Cairns. We don't have you on the hotel cameras. And your former accusation, however unproven, involved a teenage girl. I'm sure you know most pedophiles tend to stick to a certain type."

I felt my back teeth lock together.

"You haven't been my concern," Clark continued. "Crimson Lake is where bad people come to disappear. I've got every kind of scumbag you could imagine on my beat. There are runaway rapists, drug dealers, wife killers, and retired hit men in my jurisdiction. The place is a fucking jungle. A quiet accused pedophile who lives on the edge of the lake fifty k's from the nearest kid doesn't interest me."

"Then why am I here?"

"The boy's mother has requested you."

I pulled out the chair I had just been sitting in and sat down. We both knew I wasn't going anywhere yet. "Seven hours. She's calling in backup already?"

Clark shook his head, weary.

"Why does she want me? Are you going to allow it?" I asked.

"I don't know why she wants you. She didn't tell me. It could be all the press you got over the last case. Maybe she's one of your . . . fans." He looked me up and down, his lip curled. He meant the league of supporters I'd accrued over the time since my arrest, a group assembled around a podcast that professed my innocence.

"If you agree to take on the case," Clark continued, "I'll allow it on the proviso that you report anything and everything of interest you uncover to me. You'll be the closest person to her in the investigation, and you're not police. She may let something slip to you that she doesn't want us to know."

I put my elbows on the table and held my head. I needed sleep. Coffee. A minute's reprieve from the screaming fight-or-flight panic still thumping through my brain that hadn't quieted since my ride in the squad car. A thought pushed through the chaos, that today was the day my daughter was arriving from Sydney. If I took the job I'd be trying to find a missing child while I was supposed to be spending time with my own. The selfishness of the thought didn't escape me. My phone was still going mad in my hand. I slipped it into my pocket.

"Why are you in charge of this case?" I asked Clark. "You're Crimson Lake. This is Cairns jurisdiction."

"Robert Griswald, the Cairns chief, was in Sydney on holiday when the call came through. I was the first ranking officer to respond, so I've bought it."

"So I'd be working alongside your team?"

"Every team in the region is on this," Clark said. "And we've got specialists in Sydney on standby. They'll get approval to head here at the twelve-hour mark."

"Aren't we getting ahead of ourselves?" I asked. "It's seven hours. The kid could have gone for a walk."

"He's not on CCTV leaving the hotel from any of its four entrances."

"He could still be here. Hiding in a cupboard somewhere."

"We've done a top-to-bottom search of the hotel. We're about to do a second one."

There was a different feeling creeping up my insides now, like cold fingers trailing along my ribs. Chief Clark and I sat in thought for a few minutes. Questions kept coming, but I knew there was no point in asking them now. I needed to take a breather, get my head straight. Sort out the avalanche of actions I would have kicked off between Sean, Amanda, and Val. Figure out how I was going to take this case with my daughter in my care.

I stood again, and Clark remained seated.

"There's one more thing you need to know," he said.

"What's that?"

"I'm approving you to assist on this case," Clark said, clasping his hands firmly on the table. "But I don't want Amanda Pharrell anywhere near it."

I should have known this was coming. During our last case, Amanda and I had been tasked with discovering who killed two young bartenders in a roadside hovel east of the lake. We'd worked alongside the police, and Amanda had taken the lead, as I'd been tied up down in Sydney fighting a new accusation against my name. Amanda had indeed discovered who murdered the bartenders, but a newly appointed detective in Crimson Lake had been killed. It made sense that Damien Clark blamed Amanda for Detective Inspector Pip Sweeney's death. They'd been working together, like partners, and Amanda was just as hated for her own dark past as I was, having served eight years for the murder of her classmate Lauren Freeman. I found myself shaking my head immediately, hardly giving the issue any thought.

"No deal. We're a team. Amanda and I work together."

"Not on this case you don't." Clark's eyes were hard, fixed on mine. "She's not to have a hand in it.

I don't want to hear her name spoken. I don't want to see that woman within a fucking kilometer of this hotel."

The door burst open beside me so hard it slammed against the stacks of chairs along the wall, almost toppling them over. As though summoned by the chief's words, Amanda strode triumphantly into the room and thrust her arms in the air.

"Never fear! Crack a beer! Let the people cheer, for *Amanda is here*!" she bellowed.

There's something deeply wrong with Amanda Pharrell.

Whatever it is, it defies logic. It's a slippery, indefinable thing that arms her with an eternal supply of social confidence, while at the same time preventing her from doing anything except horrifying, disturbing, or annoying people everywhere she goes. She has apparently no emotional range, no gut-deep reservoir of guilt or anger at her bloody past, and yet she wears the consequences of that same past on her skin in neck-to-toe tattoos. If she is scarred at all by her past, the only outward evidence of it is the jagged pink scars like lightning strikes that crack and crease her tattoos, the results of a crocodile mauling that almost took her life. When she was young, Amanda killed her teenage classmate by accident, stabbing wildly in the dark at the first thing she fell upon, trying to defend herself from a rapist. Amanda suffers a physical twitch from the incident, cannot travel in cars because of it, spends her life as the town pariah because of it, and yet claims it means nothing. She has militant rules for those around her, and none for herself, and those are just the beginnings of her problems. Having spent a year observing Amanda's deep-seated quirks, I was only mildly surprised to see her there in the doorway, materialized out of thin air, in a gold-sequined minidress and six-inch stiletto heels painted with red flames.

Clark, however, was more surprised. His face stiffened and flushed with color. He rose unsteadily from the table and without a word slipped by us and disappeared down the hall.

Amanda turned to me.

"What's the drama, bwana?" She punched me in the ribs.

"There are many dramas. How would you like my monstrous morning presented?"

"I'm thinking . . ." She tapped her chin thoughtfully. "Reverse chronological order."

"All right," I said. "You just burst in on Chief Clark as he was demanding you have nothing to do with our new case. We have a new case. A boy is missing. I was arrested this morning, accidentally, by a couple of douchebags who assumed that I must have taken him. I have a sick goose. Lillian is supposed to be visiting today."

Amanda stared at me, bug-eyed.

"None of the aforementioned events involved me drinking coffee," I said.

"Who's the boy? How old is he? Where was he

when—" Amanda began, but I pointed a finger in her face.

"Nope. My turn," I said. "How did you get here so fast and what on earth are you wearing?"

"This?" She did a little shimmy. The gold sequins hanging off the dress were as big as ten-cent coins, her movements sending them twisting and glittering. "I wore it last night. I was already here. I came to see a Kenny Rogers tribute band and stayed in the Sea Breeze, around the corner."

"You like Kenny Rogers?"

"No." She picked a loose thread from the shoulder of the dress. "So I guess you don't need the cavalry then?"

I looked at my phone. There were seventeen missed calls from Sean, three from Val, and none from Amanda.

"I'm going to sort out the mess I've made." I held up the phone. "You're going to go change into something more appropriate. I think I was accidentally marched into a briefing with the bigwigs when I arrived here. That means there will be an all-staff briefing soon. I'll meet you out the front and we'll go in together."

"What's appropriate for a missing kid case?"

"Smart casual," I said. "Discreet, Amanda. Clark's serious. He doesn't want you anywhere near this. The mum has hired us. And he'll have a go at you if you get in his face."

"He's going to have to take a number and get in line on that one." Amanda flapped a hand dismissively.

"There must be a hundred cops out there. Who's going to notice me?"

Amanda walked into the palm-lined valet parking area of the hotel half an hour later wearing denim cut-off hot pants and a shirt that read *Queenslanders like it hot and steamy*. The sunglasses she pushed up into her streaked black-and-orange hair when she saw me were studded with dozens of tiny diamantes. A couple of press in the growing crowd beyond the roadblock outside the hotel recognized her and started snapping. She lifted an arm and waved, like a hung-over rock star.

Most of the guests I'd seen being processed as they left the hotel were now gone, and the police presence in the foyer was minimal. I handed Amanda the cof-fee I'd bought for her when I got my own, and we followed a couple of patrol cops toward one of the larger boardrooms. Before we could squeeze into the already overcrowded room, two cops glanced back at me, angry dogs assessing us from the corners of their eyes.

"Got the prime suspect here already, you ask my opinion," one of them said. The other snorted.

Chief Clark was holding court at the front of the roomful of officers, shuffling papers behind a lectern while two non-uniforms talked at him. There were more angry glances thrown toward Amanda and me, but she didn't seem to notice them. She was looking out at the gathering appreciatively, as though judging the turnout at a wedding. There were two spare seats in the last row of chairs, but as I looked over at them the nearest officers straightened, jaws set, almost daring me to sit down.

We stood at the back as the gathering quieted, and Chief Clark told us the story.

The boy was Richard Henry Farrow. Richie to his family. He was eight years old, tall and thin for his age, and had two very large front teeth. A photo of the boy flashed onto the screen before us, the sunny and slightly sad victim picture I'd seen a thousand times, a moment captured in the tragically unreachable past. The picture had been taken at a local crocodile farm the previous day, just hours before the boy went missing. On his arm the boy nervously balanced a white cockatoo in what looked like the petting-zoo section of the park. His mother, Sara Mairee Farrow, had taken the picture on her phone.

The boy and his mother were part of a group that had come up from Melbourne and had been staying in the hotel for two days. Each family had only one boy, a quirk that had brought them together, Sara standing out as the single parent while three sets of others wrangled a boy of their own on the trip. On the first day, the three couples, their three boys, Richie, and his mother had set out for a day of sightseeing. They'd left the hotel and been bused to the marina to take a cruise of the Great Barrier Reef. They'd had lunch on the boat, returned to the hotel in the afternoon, and the families had split up to nap, shower, watch TV, and relax in their rooms. In the evening, the parents had taken the kids across to the Esplanade out the front of the hotel and, while the boys had messed around in the fountains and aquatic park, the seven adults had drunk wine and watched the sun set. That night, the four boys had been left unsupervised in one of the hotel rooms. They'd dragged blankets onto the floor, opened packets of chips and cans of Coke, and waited for the three pizzas that had been ordered for them to arrive. Sara Farrow had been the last parent to be with the boys before they were left to watch a selection of movies downloaded for them on a laptop. She'd paid the pizza guy, told the boys to behave themselves, and reminded them that all the parents would be in the restaurant on the ground floor. Although a mobile phone had been left with the boys, they'd also been told that if any trouble arose all they had to do was dial seven on the hotel-room phone and ask for one of the parents.

The boys were warned that if they left the room, there would be dire consequences. They had no key to get back in, so would have no choice but to go down to the restaurant and ask their parents for one. If they turned up at the restaurant because they'd broken the rules and gone roaming around the hotel causing mischief, they'd better be prepared for trouble.

Everything went swimmingly. All seven parents had dinner at the Clattering Clam, a short walk out the grand front doors of the hotel and around a corner past a Sunglass Hut store. Every hour, on the hour, one of the parents went up to the room and checked on the boys.

The first time the boys were checked on, two of them were watching a movie on the laptop, and two were jumping from one bed to another.

The second time they were checked on, all four were watching the movie.

The third time they were checked on, they were all huddled together in a blanket-and-cushion fort, giggling behind their hands.

The fourth time they were checked on, all the boys were asleep.

At dinner downstairs, the parents reveled in the absence of their children. All day the boys had run around, climbed on things, wrestled one another, and made wet, loud fart noises—a new talent they'd discovered as a group and hoped to hone. They'd touched buttons they'd been told not to touch, picked noses they'd been told not to pick, hung headfirst over railings on the side of the cruise boat, beyond which certain death lingered. The parents consumed a bottle of wine each. They were warned twice by restaurant staff that they were making too much noise and unsettling guests nearby. They stayed until closing, went upstairs, and the three families whose boys did not belong in the room retrieved their sleeping children.

With such an arrangement having proved successful, the second night was planned the same way.

During the day the four families had separated. Sara Farrow had taken Richie to the crocodile farm, stopped with him for ice cream on the way back to the hotel, and lay down on the double bed with him for a nap around five o'clock. She'd been sunburned, and Richie had been too, unaccustomed to the sneaky Cairns weather and its ability to roast you through the stifling humidity. The two had overslept.

At seven, she'd dressed and escorted Richie next

door to the room where the other boys were. The three couples had already gone down to the restaurant, and the boys were twenty minutes into a movie. She'd dropped Richie off and taken the elevator down to dinner.

Sara had told the other parents she was so dehydrated, so sunburned, so hungover from the previous day's festivities that she wouldn't be drinking that evening. She'd volunteered to do the hourly checks, and had conducted four, just like the night before.

Each time she checked, Sara found the boys engaged in the same kind of behavior as the previous evening. The first time, they were having a competition to see how many marshmallows they could stuff into their mouths, the movie playing, unwatched, behind them. The second time, they were watching the movie. The third time, they were lying on the floor, whispering and plotting and snorting with laughter.

The last time Sara checked, three boys were asleep.

And Richie was gone.

There was nothing to suggest the boys had left the room. The man in room 607, Martin Askin, had arrived from Los Angeles on business and told police he went to bed, exhausted and jetlagged, around 5:30 p.m. He'd heard the boys in the room throughout the night playing and romping around. The windows of the room did not open. While there was a small manhole above the kitchenette, searches of the ventilation system had proved fruitless, and the boys would have had a lot of difficulty accessing the manhole without a ladder. While there was an adjoining door to the next room that staff had unlocked for the families, the situation was the same there. The room next door was the Farrow room.

If indeed the boys had left the room, which they said they hadn't, they would not have been able to leave the hotel through any other room, as all the windows were secure. They would not have been able to access the service areas of the hotel, as these doors were accessed only by swipe cards belonging to staff, and any of the dozens of members of staff working in offices, drinking coffee in the break room, or changing in and out of their uniforms behind the scenes of the hotel would immediately have noticed the boys and known they were out of bounds. The boys were not picked up on CCTV traversing the hotel's foyer, nor did they appear on any of the cameras covering all four sides of the building and the parking lot.

The only explanation for Richie's disappearance that was offered came from the other boys he'd spent the night with, and their account of what had happened simply did not make sense. One minute Richie had been with them, and then he'd disappeared.

The briefing came to a noisy finish, with scraping chairs, talking, teams getting together to head out on their assignments. When Amanda and I returned to the foyer there was a group of handlers leading a pack of three search dogs into the elevator, the animals already snuffling at everything within reach of their leads. A couple of cops shoved past us, murmured something about Amanda being a killer.

Amanda slurped the last of her coffee with an exaggerated sigh of satisfaction and looked around for a bin, but they'd all been confiscated to be emptied in search of evidence. She put the cup in the base of a potted palm tree.

"Well, all the boys left the room," she said.

"How do you figure that?"

"I don't know." She shrugged. "But four eight-year-old boys don't stay in a room quietly all night long without their parents while there's a huge labyrinth of adventure just beyond the door. Seven o'clock until midnight—that's how long they were left unattended both nights. Five hours. They're kids, so time is double."

"Time is double?"

"Yes, time and gravity are double for kids," she said. I let it go. "So that's ten hours each night. Even I'd have gone nuts. I'm telling you, they got out of the room."

"They say they didn't," I reminded her.

"They're lying."

"How'd they get back in?"

"Well, they didn't prop the doors open," Amanda mused. "Those key card doors send an alarm to the security office if they're left open too long. It's possible the door was faulty."

"Or one boy stayed behind to let the others back into the room while three went out adventuring. Or two stayed behind and two went out. Maybe they took turns."

"*Pfft.*" Amanda rolled her eyes. "You ever seen eight-year-old boys try to take turns?"

"However they arranged it," I said, "they had plenty of time to get it right."

Chief Clark exited the hallway near us in the company of three plainclothes officers.

"You better scram," I told her. "I'll go get our instructions from the big boss and meet you on the—"

"Forget that," she scoffed. "I'm not creeping around this hotel like a leper trying to avoid him. Hey, Clarky!"

Amanda marched off toward the group of detectives like a madman striding toward a cliff edge. I caught up to her as the three men stopped short at the sight of the pint-sized, tattooed pixie fluttering into their midst.

"Clarky, mate." Amanda grinned. "We need to meet our client and get the lowdown. Can we have a run sheet?"

She was asking for the sheet that detailed the parents' contact numbers, their addresses, heights, weights, ethnicities, marital statuses—all the basics officers could then avoid asking the distraught parents themselves. The run sheet would have all the info on the kids, the most detailed data being about Richie himself. There would be a draft timeline of the events leading to the disappearance and the contact details of all the staff in command. Amanda put her hand out and the officers with Clark made their excuses and left as a distinctly red color crept up the chief's neck like mercury in a thermometer.

"I told your offsider," Clark seethed, "that I didn't want to see your fucking face during this investigation. The mother requested Conkaffey, not you."

"Well, that's just too bad, Clarkles, because we're

a two-for-one deal." Amanda slapped my chest, somehow knowing without looking at me that I was standing behind her. "I know you're upset about Pip, but—"

"I'm not *upset* about Detective Sweeney." Clark managed to keep his voice under control to get the words out. "I've mourned the bright, brilliant, dedicated officer you recklessly endangered by leaping into a lethal situation with your head in the clouds, the way you do everywhere you go. My concern now is that you're going to put another of my officers in jeopardy, or prevent one of them from finding the missing child with your mindless, selfish . . . *twittery*!"

Clark spat the last word after grasping around for it, running out of breath, his face the color of an overripe peach. Amanda's eyes slid to me, full of humor, and I gave her the darkest look I could. She took a resigned breath.

"Clark, I'm not leaving." She threw her hands up. "And you're not arresting me, either. You've already falsely arrested one guy this morning." She slapped me again. "And the press would only need to catch a whiff of that for you to have a lawsuit on your hands. Ted has proven how skilled he is at the old litigation-ruination situation. You don't want me to try my hand at it too. Now give me the run sheet."

The chief slid a sheet from his paperwork and handed it to me. He didn't look at Amanda as he walked away. I felt numb and guilty, like a kid leaving the principal's office after a good roasting.

"Can you maybe leave my pending legal situation

out of further discussions we have with people in this hotel?" I asked. "Everyone hates us enough."

A few months ago I had agreed to do an interview with the country's leading current affairs program, and instead of helping me clear my name the producers had hit me with a second, unfounded accusation that was retracted at the last minute. I was suing, and my detractors were not impressed.

"Ted." Amanda turned to me. "The next man who tells me what to do around here is going to get his nads kicked so hard he's going to taste them at the back of his throat." She tapped me gently on the shoulder with her index finger. "Don't let that be you."

We found Sara Farrow standing by the windows inside one of the first-floor suites, her hands clasped around the back of her neck. The room had been given to Sara that morning while her original room was searched, fingerprinted, and photographed. She was exactly as I'd seen her pictured in the happy snaps from the day before: round-cheeked and sandy-haired, the curls she'd passed on to her missing son pulled up on the top of her head. She had indeed been badly sunburned yesterday, hit worst on the chest and the back of her hands, where people forget to apply sunscreen. She turned toward us and smiled at me like she'd been waiting a long time and felt relief at my appearance.

The truth was I didn't want to be sat in a room where Richie Farrow clearly wasn't, interviewing his mother, standing still while the rest of the world searched for the boy. There was a painful hunger in my chest to search the hotel myself, to go room to room looking under beds and in cupboards, calling his name. I wanted to walk or drive the streets, go shop to shop and hotel to hotel until I found him. He must surely be nearby. But I couldn't follow that instinct. Other people were doing it, or had done it already, and the investigation needed planning and patience rather than instinct and bravado right now.

I noticed immediately that Sara Farrow hadn't been crying. In fact, she'd applied mascara that morning and it was still in place, and her clothes looked fresh.

"Ms. Farrow, I'm so sorry that Richie is missing," I said after the initial introductions. "I'm sure he's going to turn up and that he's going to be fine. He seems like a clever little guy."

"He is clever," she said, sitting on the end of the bed, wringing her hands. "He's funny, too. I've never laughed as hard as I have the past couple of days hanging out with him. His father and I are in talks about custody at the moment. He spent the first weeks of the school holidays with him in Melbourne."

Amanda had wandered into the little kitchenette of the hotel suite and pried open the minibar fridge. She was rustling through the snacks, clattering tiny liquor bottles together, but I knew she was listening. Her eyebrows had jumped at the mention of a custody battle.

"I'm really glad you're here," Sara said as I sat down in an armchair near her. "I know all about you. I'm a big fan of the podcast. I know you're innocent, Ted."

Innocent Ted was a globally successful podcast about my case, run by a journalist I'd met just after my release from prison. The podcast had presented evidence of my innocence, and had a following of millions. It was still weird to hear someone talk about being a "fan" of the story of the worst years of my life.

"I know I'm going to be accused of this," Sara said.

Amanda straightened abruptly, almost hitting her head on the kitchenette counter. She had a mouth full of Snickers, the half-eaten bar in her hand.

"Well *that* was a weird thing to say!" she laughed.

"That . . ." I struggled, looking out the windows at the day beyond. "That actually was rather a weird thing to say, Ms. Farrow. Why do you feel like you're going to be accused of your son's disappearance?"

"Because I was the last one to see him. My ex-husband and I are fighting over him. He's gone. He's *gone*." She leaned forward, fixed her eyes on mine. "I must have been questioned by twenty different police officers this morning, and every time a new one comes to speak to me they get more and more cranky."

"There's nothing to suggest your son has met with foul play," I said. "They're still conducting searches of the hotel. Richie could be hiding somewhere. He could be stuck in . . . in a forgotten room, or . . ."

"This is not him." Sara shook her head, clasped her hands on her neck again like she was trying to wring tension from the muscles. "He doesn't do this. He's a sensible kid. Something's happened, and I know that you know what it's like to have everyone turning and looking at you for answers, Ted."

I let her words linger in the air for some time,

hoping, perhaps, for help from Amanda. But I've always known Amanda to be happy to let people dig their own graves with their words, my partner totally immune to the discomfort of long silences. I glanced at the air conditioner, knowing it was probably not operating with the door to the hall open.

"There's something else," Sara said. She drew a long breath. "This isn't the first time I've had dealings with the police about my kids."

She told me her story. Eleven years earlier, Sara and her husband, Henry, had become the parents of a little girl, Anya, born three years before Richie. Their marriage had been thriving, and they'd just purchased their first home in Meredith, a featureless redbrick place with a bare-dirt yard west of Melbourne. Four months after the baby was born, tragedy struck. Sara had gone to check on the infant after she hadn't woken as usual in the early hours, and found the child turned on her side, blue in the face, lifeless. When paramedics arrived the parents were absolutely beside themselves, Sara hugging herself and rocking on the back porch, Henry pacing and weeping in the front yard.

"It looked like sudden infant death syndrome," she said. "But the medical examiner found pillow fibers in Anya's lungs."

A hot, heavy urge to leave the room had been gradually pressing on my body since Sara had begun speaking. The door was open, uniformed and plainclothes officers walking by now and then, talking about ventilation ducts and utility rooms. I went to the door and took a few breaths, but the air was no fresher there.

"Did the police charge you with anything?" I asked.

"No." Sara sighed. "But they questioned us. I mean they really leaned hard, and it wasn't just them doing it. Our friends and families . . . People look at you differently. Or maybe they don't and you just think they do. I don't know."

Sara lifted her eyes to me.

"That's why I wanted you," she said. "You understand what it's like. And if the police come after me, that's fine. I get it. But while they're wasting time, I need someone out there looking for my child. You can tell me what the police are doing, if they're taking this seriously or not. You can keep me informed if there are any leads."

I pulled at the collar of my shirt. The discomfort infecting my being was coming from Sara, from the logical, cold way she was detailing her reasons for calling me in. I glanced at Amanda, and she gave a little bow and put her hand out like an usher showing the way to a theater seat. *After you,* she was saying. We were both thinking the same thing, but she was letting me lead. I closed the door to the room.

"Sara," I said. "I want you to listen to me very carefully."

"Okay." She straightened, a kid on the first day of class.

"You are going to fall under suspicion of whatever has occurred here because you're doing everything you can to make that happen."

She looked at Amanda, who was picking at the seal of a piccolo bottle of champagne. Amanda nodded her agreement, made a rueful click sound with her teeth.

"You're not crying enough," I told Sara. "You're thinking five steps ahead of the investigation, and you're not telling the police everything. You're covering your arse. It's going to be the little things that undo you. You've had enough presence of mind in the nine hours since your child had been missing to apply makeup and change your clothes. You've put your watch on your wrist. Do you have an appointment you need to get to?"

Sara glanced down at her watch, guiltily began undoing the band.

"I think you should tell the police about Anya," I said. "Right now. Before they find out themselves."

"But it's not relevant," she protested, looking to Amanda for help. "It's not—"

"Full disclosure," I said. "It'll . . . help."

As I spoke, my words faltered. Full disclosure hadn't helped me at all in my case. The police had dug deep into my life, and I'd hidden nothing. Full disclosure, an all-access pass to my intimate self, had left me burning under the gaze of the public as my porn DVDs were examined in the courtroom. They hadn't been at all relevant. I decided to stop pressuring Sara about her past.

"I'm not trying to be cruel," I offered.

"He's not a cruel guy," Amanda confirmed, popping her champagne. "He has geese."

"Just think about telling the police about Anya. And while you're doing that, focus now on how you're presenting yourself. You brought me in because I know what it's like to be falsely accused," I said. "Well, I know from experience that those twenty cops you spoke to this morning have all been analyzing your behavior. And, quite frankly, you're not distressed enough."

"You think I'm not distressed?" Sara's eyebrows knitted. She looked at the horizon through the window for a long time, a rich blue streak beyond the crowded promenade. "I'm numb. I can barely feel my body. I'm . . . I'm doing everything I can think of!"

"I mean you're not classically distressed," I said. "You're not exhibiting behavior people associate with distress. You should be hysterical. People expect you to be hysterical. *I* expected you to be hysterical."

Sara nodded, looking at her hands. What I was saying hurt. I understood that. But the truth was that she was giving off all the signs of someone who didn't care that her son was missing. I didn't want the police to go after Sara because of her behavior. If they wrongly developed tunnel vision on her, and Richie had indeed been kidnapped, it might make finding his abductor impossible. It was the same thing that had happened in my case. While I'd been locked up, Claire's attacker had been out there, free to reoffend, free perhaps to do what he had tried to do to Claire, and take a young life.

When I had been arrested, the analysis of my behavior had begun. I had, initially, been hysterical. I'd been locked up in my own police station and given no information about why I'd fallen under suspicion and what I could do to counteract the evidence against me. I'd not been allowed to call my wife, to be the one to break it to Kelly that our lives had now changed forever. Twelve hours in, I had succeeded in getting the attention of an officer passing by the inter-rogation room I was in and I had asked him to bring me something to eat.

The officer had walked off, disgusted.

I was innocent. Terrified, confused, barely able to keep my wits about me. But I was also hungry. The classic notion is that food is the last thing on a person's mind in their darkest hour, but it wasn't my darkest hour. It was my *twelfth* darkest hour, and counting. The "he asked for food" story had popped up a few times over the course of my incarceration, trial, and release. People wanted to know—had I really asked for food after my accusation? How could I eat at a time like that? Was I that fucking callous?

"You said in your initial interviews that you dropped him at the room with the other boys and everything seemed fine. That was room . . ." I shuffled the pages of the run sheet. "Room 608."

"The Sampsons' room." Sara nodded. "Same as the night before. The boys were sitting on the floor in front of the laptop, playing a marshmallow game. I told them not to be so gross. They were laughing and coughing up the marshmallows. Richie jumped right in. He didn't even say goodbye. I suppose he thought he didn't need to."

Sara put her face in her hands and sat there, un-moving, her nails gripping the curls at her hairline. I wanted to press further, to hear for myself the answers to the standard questions asked in a kidnap situation. Had Richie said anything weird that day, or the two other times she saw him that night? Had Sara seen anyone odd hanging around the room, the hall, the restaurant? Had she received any phone calls or messages that might suggest someone was going to take Richie? From her ex-husband, perhaps? But I felt like I had already pushed Sara Farrow too hard by telling her she was digging her own grave with her behavior.

Amanda and I made our excuses, and left the missing child's mother alone in her room.

The man with the keys needed to get back there. Really make sure there was nothing he could do to fix things. Every cell in his body knew that there wasn't, that the catalyst for his collapse had happened and was over and there'd be no going back now. Still, he had to try. If the boy couldn't be saved, perhaps *he* could. All his life, he'd let circumstances dictate his actions. All those years blowing like a leaf in the wind, following whatever voices invited him, from one town to the next. Highway by highway and truck stop by truck stop, he'd been a slave to fate. The winding, effortless path had taken him to some terrible places, darkness seeming to pull him ever onward.

Once, he'd awakened at dawn in a crack house outside Perth to find himself the only person there still alive. A bad batch at a party he'd slept through completely, men and women flopped on couches and mattresses on the floor like they'd fallen from the sky.

He'd taken his backpack and left them there, calling the police from a payphone on the highway. He'd wondered for years if he'd checked every pulse. Every room.

He'd got tangled up with some standover men in Sydney and had stood in the corner of a caravan, his fist in his mouth, while his men clipped the toes off a gambler with a pair of pruning shears.

He'd spent his life tumbling from one pit to the next, never building a foundation, never believing he deserved one.

But things had changed.

He didn't know how completely until now. He was looking at the cracks. He couldn't lose it all now. Please, God, he thought, don't let it happen again. Don't let me lose it all again.

He stood outside the White Caps Hotel staff meeting, playing with the keys on his belt, watching the circus parade of worried-looking workers exit the conference room. There were animals of every species here: chefs in their checkered trousers and sauce-splattered hats, housekeeping staff in their black dresses, highly groomed receptionists in their red blazers, all of their faces mournful, worried. He met eyes with as many of them as he could as they passed, wanting them to remember him standing there. Yes, he had attended the meeting, blended in with everyone else. Like the rest of the hotel staff, he didn't know anything. He was just as hopeful as they were that the boy would be found safe.

He went to the elevators now, pulling his cap low, and tugged his swipe card from the tether on his belt.

He entered the elevator, two officers in patrol uniform getting in with him, both of them on their phones. The elevator only went up one floor before the doors opened. The two cops got out, and one blocked the door before it could close.

"Whoa," the cop said. "Where are you going, maintenance man?"

"Oh, I . . ." The man with the keys tried to swallow, coughed instead. "I've got to do my rounds. I was just—"

"Nope." The cop shook his head. "All hotel staff are to be processed through the lobby, and then you're out of here. The building is in lockdown until further notice. Police and approved persons only. We don't know where's a crime scene and where's not."

The cop got back into the lift with him. The maintenance man played with his belt, his mind racing, and squeezed the ragged edges of the keys so hard they dug into his fingertips.

"Don't suppose you saw the boy, did you?" the officer asked suddenly as the doors opened again on the foyer. The maintenance man thought about saying something then. He could feel the words rising up through his chest, spiky at their edges, cutting, the way they had when he'd called the police about the crack house full of bodies. The words stung behind his lips the way they had when he'd walked out on his father the last time, when he'd walked into the hotel for the first time, holding his résumé against his chest so they wouldn't see his hands were shaking.

He turned in the doorway, looked the cop in the eyes, and drew a breath.

Then a dog barked. Search dogs at the automatic doors to the foyer, being led in by a team of officers in navy blue.

The maintenance man gripped at his throat, stopping the words before they could fall from his lips.

He shook his head and walked quickly away.

I got a cab home at 11 a.m., my mind turning over completely from worries about Richie Farrow to my own child. My ex-wife, her boyfriend, and Lillian were due to arrive at my house at midday. Kelly and Jett were both personal trainers, and together they'd left the gyms where they worked and started their own company, training clients for marathons and body-sculpting competitions. A week-long exercise retreat for their customers in the Tropical North was the perfect opportunity for Lillian and me to have a practice run at being together, alone, for the first time since my incarceration. At least, that had been the plan.

I picked my fingernails on the way home, the anxiety creeping up again as I thought about how I was going to explain to Kelly that I now could not take a week off work to spend every minute with my child. There was also guilt, that though I burned to see my daughter, a part of me wanted to turn around and rush back to the search for Richie, to forget about Lillian and go after a boy I didn't know while the hours he was missing ticked slowly by. One concern fed into another, and in time I was staring blankly at the walls of corn-yellow cane narrowing into eternity before me, trying to decide where I would bury Peeper if she died. When the cab pulled in to my driveway and I saw a familiar car parked on the grass, the anxiety melted away.

Dr. Val Gratteur was standing on my back porch, a lit cigarette hanging from her lip, her withered arms folded across her narrow chest. Celine spotted me from her bed on the end of the porch and came running, barking in a high pitch with sheer relief at seeing me, I supposed, after I was abducted right before her eyes by strange-smelling men.

Val saluted with her cigarette as my animals gathered around me, the geese waddling to my sides and pecking at my pockets, looking for grain pellets.

I'd explained the false alarm to Val on the phone, but she sat on the porch steps beside me anyway and listened as I explained again, trying to make sense of it all, bouncing ideas off her about Richie Farrow's disappearance. She didn't ask me the inevitable question about who would care for Lillian while I was working on the case, as I'd hoped she would. I sat jogging my knees nervously, watching the water, a smoke trail on the distant shore probably signaling the campsite of some fishermen stopped for lunch. I'd just taken the deep, resigned breath I needed to broach the topic when she put her hand on my knee.

"I watch your geese and your dog. Why wouldn't I watch your kid?" she asked.

"Oh." I sighed. "Thank you, Val."

I wanted to say something meaningful, something that might hint at how grateful I was to have this woman in my life. There was no way I could explain it in its entirety, and so trying to say any of it seemed impossible. The truth was, Val was my only option as a babysitter for my dogs, my geese, my child. I had no other friend within a thousand miles, besides Amanda.

"When is she supposed to arrive, the little pickle?"

I glanced at my watch. "Any minute now."

"Maybe I'll take a walk," Val said.

"No, stay. Please. You should meet Kelly and her meathead boyfriend."

"I dunno." She stood, pushing herself up with a hand on her knobbly knee. "I get the feeling the handover will be tense enough."

I didn't know what that meant. I had been hoping the handover wouldn't be tense at all, but I didn't argue. Val left me, and I wandered the house nervously, straightening the chairs at the dining room table and peering in at Lillian's room.

I was immensely proud of Lillian's room, partly because it had been so difficult to assemble. Being who I am, I can't wander around department stores in the children's section, browsing the pink model bedrooms with their fluffy pillows and polka-dotted coverlets, trying to decide between fairy and mermaid themes. I can't buy toys or children's clothes without the threat of being verbally abused, intimidated, or outright chased out of stores, so everything had to be purchased online. I'd asked Kelly a limited number of questions, not wanting to sound like I didn't know what I was doing, or that I didn't know the size of my own kid's shoes, when of course I didn't. I'd picked up in conversations with Kelly that Lillian was out of a cot and into a "big-girl bed," a half-size bed that was low to the ground so she could get up and go to the bathroom when she needed to, so I'd purchased one of those and probably more pillows than was required.

As I stood in the doorway, looking at the room, it seemed like a little girl's paradise to me. I'd added touches that probably weren't "necessary" for the short amount of time I'd have her, but that I thought she'd probably enjoy. I'd found a thick shag-pile rug in fuchsia that really gave the room warmth, and I'd added a little bookcase and a pile of books I guessed she'd like. The paint I'd chosen for the room was a soft purple, and I'd hung a butterfly wind chime over the window that chimed in the breeze.

My confidence plummeted when a car pulled into the driveway, and I looked out the screen door to see Jett behind the wheel, squinting at the boarded-up windows at the front of my house. Celine nosed my fingers, having snuck in from the porch while I was distractedly rearranging and perfecting things around the place. She can open the door by scratching at the dented bottom of the frame if the catch isn't closed properly. I led her back outside, fixed my hair in the hall mirror, and fluffed the front of my shirt where the midday heat had stuck the fabric to my chest with sweat.

They were out of the car when I opened the door, Lillian bigger than I remembered her and Jett and Kelly smaller. My ex-wife had taken to her fitness passion with concerning enthusiasm since our breakup—concerning at least to me, who knew nothing about women's body mass and fat percentages. Her cheekbones were sharp and high in a way I'd never seen them, and she and Jett wore a matching caramel-brown tan that made them look like they'd lived their whole lives on the baking sands of the Gold Coast.

But I only had eyes for my daughter. I jogged down the porch steps and swept her up into my arms, noticing immediately that she was heavier against me, even though it had been only two months since we'd last seen each other.

"Boo!" I squeezed her against me. "I've been waiting for you! My beautiful Boo is here!"

I lifted her into the air, arms outstretched, and the little face looking down at me was exhilarated but wary, like a kid sitting impatiently while the roller-coaster car clicks up the incline. She looked at Kelly for confirmation and then gripped my hair as she usually did, wrapping her legs around my chest.

"Hello, Daddy!" She giggled as I covered her in kisses.

My daughter vaguely knows who I am. That sounds terrible, but it's a grand improvement from the days after my incarceration when she not only didn't recognize me but was actively terrified at my appearance. While in the early days Kelly had trained her to recognize me with an old photograph at home in Sydney, pointing and smiling and saying "Daddy" at regular intervals, Lillian and I saw each other at supervised and then unsupervised visits in a range of public places full of distractions for very short periods of time. Sometimes I was bearded, sunburned, wearing glasses as a disguise. Sometimes I was tired and depressed, and sometimes so wild with longing to see her I had to restrain myself from squeezing the breath out of her little body. She always warmed up to me gradually, that collection of memories fusing in her mind into a fractured familiarity. It hurt, but at the time it was all that I had of Lillian, and stressful or anxious meetings were so much better than nothing.

"I've got so many exciting things to show you," I told Lillian, sweeping her shiny black curls off her forehead. "We're going to have so much fun while you're here."

Kelly and Jett, the two sculptures in bronze, were hovering nearby, examining the burn marks on the low brick wall from vigilantes blowing up my letterbox. I went over, Lillian on my hip, and put an arm out, in case Kelly wanted to hug me. Sometimes she did and sometimes she didn't. She gave me a halfhearted pat on the shoulder and I shook Jett's hand.

"How was the trip?"

"Long," Kelly said. "And hot. The air-conditioning in the car is useless. I don't know how you stand this humidity."

"It's good for you." I joggled Lillian up and down against my side. "You fitness people are all about sweating out toxins, aren't you?" Jett gave a snort that might have been laughter or derision.

I took them into the house and set Lillian down, swelled with pride as she walked into the bedroom I'd made for her and looked around.

"This is your room, Boo-love," I told her. I took her to the bookshelf and showed her a handful of the colorful titles I'd ordered, books I'd remembered from my childhood. Clifford the Big Red Dog and Dr. Seuss. The urge to squeeze her and kiss her was biting at me, a longing held for too many days, to smell my own child's scent, her soapy skin and milky hair. I lifted a curl off her shoulder and extended it, let it spring back. My curls. "Look how big you are. You're a real girl, Lilly."

"Who this room?" she asked, lifting a fluffy pink bunny rabbit from the shelf.

"It's yours, baby. You're going to stay here with me."

"She's not going to get it," Jett said from the doorway. I could hear Kelly wandering around my kitchen, assessing my ability to care for myself and our daughter. "She's going to have an epic meltdown when we leave."

"We'll deal with it," I said, rising to my full height, a good foot taller than my wife's new partner. "It's the first stay. I'm sure it'll take some adjustment. She'll be fine."

Jett gave another little unconvinced snort, leaned in the doorway, looking at the purple walls. Lillian ran by him and down the hall, and I wanted to follow, but didn't want to push past my adversary.

"You've done an . . . *interesting* job on the room."

Jett took a moment to appreciate the fuchsia rug. "You ever hear the phase 'gender stereotyping'?"

"You ever hear the phrase 'Go fuck yourself'?" I asked.

"Ted!" Kelly called. Her tone was sharp. I pushed past Jett and jogged toward the kitchen. Celine was at the screen door to the porch, thumping the boards with her tail. She and Lillian had locked eyes, and my daughter was approaching the dog at a crouch, like she might run at any minute.

"Ohhh." Lillian gave an exaggerated sigh of excitement. "Puppy!"

Kelly turned on me. "You didn't tell me you have a dog."

"I have a dog," I said.

"You . . . We . . ." Kelly's face was so tight I could see the muscles working in her temples. "We haven't discussed this!"

"What do you want to know?"

"What do I want to *know*?" Kelly looked at Jett for help. "Is it aggressive? How long have you had it? Is it safe with children?"

"I've had Celine for a few months," I said, shrugging. "She's not aggressive. Although I heard her growl for the first time this morning. It was pretty badass, actually."

"What was she growling at?"

"Just a couple of morons who stopped by for a visit."

"Ted." Kelly worked her throat with her fingers as though trying to force herself to swallow. "Lillian is at the prime age for being badly injured in a dog attack.

She's not experienced with dogs. She doesn't know the warning signs."

I looked at my daughter. She was pressing her fingers against the screen and giggling as Celine tried to lick them through the mesh. I looked at Jett, but he was frowning at the wine bottles on my windowsill, probably calculating their calorie content.

"I think she's going to be fine, Kelly."

"What breed is it?"

"She's a northern pointy-eared lard-arse."

"Jesus, Ted."

"Settle down, Kelly." I could hear my own tone changing. This was not the tensionless handover I'd hoped for. "Come outside and meet her."

I opened the door and Celine rushed at Lillian, licking her face and whimpering with excitement. Kelly and Jett watched the display but seemed no happier with the whole dog situation. I picked Lillian up and walked down the steps into the yard, the feel of her arms around my neck making my heart ache.

"I want to show you something, Boo."

"What is it?"

"What do you see down there, in the shade?"

"Ohhhh." She gave that full-chest gasp again. "Ducks!"

"Not ducks, geese."

"Cheese?"

"Geese, baby." I kissed her head.

"Cheese?"

"Okay, ducks will do."

I set her down near the birds, who were resting like round, gray stones with their feet tucked beneath them. Celine bounded between the birds and Lillian, eager to facilitate an introduction but instead disturbing the flock and making them rise and waddle away. Lillian looked to Kelly, her grin spread wide, her humorless mother approaching me with her arms folded.

"Ducks, Mummy!"

"Yes, I see them. Leave them alone, honey. They'll probably bite you too." Kelly smiled tightly. She stood beside me for a while, watching our daughter chasing the geese around, Celine keeping up until she was out of breath. In time Lillian and Celine settled in the dappled shade of the palms lining my property, Lillian trying to catch Celine's foamy tongue jiggling between her jaws as she panted.

"Don't worry about the dog," I told Kelly. "I won't leave them alone together. And if there's a hint of anything, I'll have Celine go and stay with a . . . friend."

My throat tightened as I remembered Richie Farrow and the case in Cairns. Kelly's face had softened a little, but I could see the familiar hurt there, the weariness at yet another challenge set down by our broken marriage, our ruined family. It was times like this when I looked at Kelly and saw the woman I had fallen in love with, hiding, faintly showing through her new tanned and terrific exterior. She didn't deserve to have to navigate access to my child with me. She didn't deserve to have to share her baby between homes, to be apart from her, to worry about her safety. All these new pains stemmed from one man's actions years earlier, on a roadside, with a teenage girl. Twisting, poisonous vines stretching out from a planted seed. The man who had done this to us was dead, and yet we were still dealing with the fallout. I took a deep breath and prepared for the next stage of Kelly's anger.

"We have to talk," I said. "I can't be here during the day with Lill."

"What?" Kelly's eyes grew wide. Jett was circling the goose coop, picking at the paintwork. As I explained the situation to Kelly, he pretended to be consumed with interest in the structure, but he smiled as Kelly descended into a swearing fury.

"Who the fuck is this woman?" Kelly howled.

"I've told you about her. She's my friend. The medical examiner."

"That morgue woman?" Kelly let her hands flop by her sides. "You're leaving our child in the care of a *morgue woman?*"

"I don't like to discriminate between morgue women and gym women, Kelly."

"Would you do me a favor, Ted?" she said. "Would you make some friends who don't have anything to do with dead bodies? No one who *creates* dead bodies, and no one who *plays around* with dead bodies."

"I'm not sure those are the exact job descriptions of either of the women you're referring to."

"This is bullshit, Ted." Kelly sighed. "I can't believe you're laying all this on me today. What else don't I know?"

"Nothing. I have a dog, and Lillian will have to be babysat during the day."

"I can't take Lillian to the retreat with me!" Sweat

was rolling down Kelly's neck. "I'll be working! Jett and I will both be working!"

"That's why I arranged a babysitter."

"This is absolute *bullshit*!"

"Well, I'm sorry, Kelly!" I snapped, finally pushed over the edge. "Let me just call the guy who kidnapped the kid in Cairns and ask him to put the boy back where he found him. Just one sec." I whipped my phone out of my back pocket and held it to my ear. "Excuse me? Yes, hello. Is this the child abductor? Hi. Ted Conkaffey here."

"You are such an arsehole." Kelly's eyes were narrowed and black like a snake's.

"This kid is missing, Kelly. He's gone. Minute by minute, he's slipping away. Our child is safe. I have to prioritize the unsafe one."

Kelly and I turned away from each other. Lillian was watching us from the shade, her hands buried in Celine's fur, her bottom lip fat and trembling. Our anger dissolved.

We went to her together. Kelly picked her up, and though putting my arms around my family was no longer my privilege, I stood as close to them as I could, listening to them breathe, wanting them with every muscle in my body.

"When I go, it's going to be bad," Kelly said quietly, over the top of Lillian's head. "Just . . . hang in there, I guess."

"We'll get through it," I assured her. "It'll be fine."

It wasn't fine. I watched my child out of the corner of my eye as Kelly briefed me on how many phone calls and texts and photos she wanted, aware that Lilly indeed wasn't "getting it." Kelly and Jett said their goodbyes and Lillian accepted them, happy and wide-eyed, coming along to the car with them anyway, convinced the goodbyes were some sort of game and that they were all leaving together.

When the car doors shut without her, Lillian burst into tears.

It was all very curious to Amanda, maybe a little bit exciting, but she had learned long ago not to let on about that. The kinds of things that excited Amanda were those that made normal people frustrated—puzzles and unexplained occurrences, actions without apparent motive. Whenever reality dipped into the impossible, Amanda felt like she was wandering in that narrow realm between the ordinary and the absurd where she belonged, where she had, even just for a moment, the upper hand.

So she kept quiet as she moved from floor to floor of the hotel, surveying the giant puzzle constructed around her, trying to decide how many possibilities there were for the boy's whereabouts, if indeed he was still inside the building. She went to the first possibility, the starting point, and leaned her head into the doorway blocked by crime scene tape. This was where it had begun, the mystery that had so completely hooked her. Amanda Pharrell and the Unexplained Absence of Richie Farrow.

The room was different from the one she'd visited that morning to meet with Sara Farrow. The theme was the same—dark wood veneer with chrome finishings and bleach-white walls, the framed artwork a local artist's photographic tour of Cairns. Impossibly perfect gray stones placed along deserted beaches, impenetrable forests reaching like fortress walls into the spotless sky, the inevitable disgruntled-looking cassowary, and playful clownfish swirling above the reef. Amanda saw disturbed sheets through the doorway to the bedrooms, and pizza boxes stacked on the white marble countertop. A photographer was taking far too much time to consider his angles on the pizza boxes evidence shot, perhaps intimidated by the collection on the walls. Amanda surveyed the fingerprint expert's work on the doorframe until he became annoyed by her presence.

This room was 608, the Sampson family's room, used as a base camp by the boys on both nights. She checked the things the briefing had told her. No, there was no balcony. Yes, the adjoining door was unlocked. The windows weren't just shut tight but were designed without hinges or latches—just glass panels in the walls. She looked at the manhole to the ventilation duct. It was big enough for a boy to crawl into, but it did not appear that the screws on the front of the duct had been disturbed. Still, officers with dogs were going floor by floor searching the shafts, the obedient dogs crawling fearlessly into the dark on long leads.

It was unlikely, Amanda decided, that Richie was

still in the room somewhere. And she made much the same assessment of the Farrow family room and the Cho family room, located in 609 and 610. The Erretts' room, 611, was a little down the hall and around a corner, and it was neater than the others but just as empty of clues.

All of the Farrow family's belongings had been confiscated by police for assessment. They would be tested for blood and other bodily fluids, and their electronic devices had been sent to a specialist to be analyzed for any hidden clues to the boy's whereabouts. Samples of Richie's DNA would be taken on the chance that his body was found somewhere, unrecognizable due to trauma or decay. The data sheet had vague pictures of what Richie had been wearing when he went missing—dark blue-and-red shorts, a white Billabong brand T-shirt. An Iron Man figurine his father had bought him was missing and was presumably wherever Richie was. Amanda examined the picture of the metallic, red-uniformed toy with the lift-off gold mask and the goateed Robert Downey Jr. likeness molded in shiny plastic underneath.

It was possible that Richie was somewhere in the hotel still, undetected by humans or by the search dogs. The dogs would be overwhelmed by residual traces of the hundreds of people who came and went through the hotel every day and, of course, by the food that traveled in and out of every hallway and room. The scents of pork and beef, Amanda knew, were very attractive to cadaver dogs, and there were several items on the Clattering Clam's menu that featured them. The Clattering Clam was the hotel's room service provider, so the dogs, accustomed to working out in the wild, would be up against it to single out Richie's scent in close quarters, mixed in among the millions of other interesting scents available to them.

When Amanda stopped by the second-floor business center being used by a crew of surveillance experts to survey the hundreds of CCTV tapes collected from the hotel, she found that a briefing by the White Caps security manager was under way. She felt like a kid showing up late to class, trying to avoid the attention of the teacher. She took a chair by the door, her little notepad at hand, and ignored the stares of several police officers who noticed her entrance. Black-and-white footage was playing on screens all around the room, with some officers watching the recordings as they listened to a burly man in a black suit. A small plastic name badge on his lapel read simply *Reed*.

"There's no CCTV covering the halls leading to the rooms, or the elevators," Reed was saying. "The hotel decided to spend big on quality, rather than quantity, and so we've got the trouble hotspots covered with HD cameras, but not much else. There's coverage in the parking lot to deal with theft from vehicles, which has happened a couple of times in the past, because the parking lot is easily accessible from the street. The foyer, business center, and conference rooms are covered, as well as the hallways to those rooms, because visible cameras in those areas make corporate clients feel safe. That's also where you get laptops and phones going missing or visitors messing with the printer. There are cameras in the service elevator, because we've had difficulty with housekeeping staff getting sticky-fingered with guests' belongings. There are cameras on all four sides of the building's exterior to spot vandalism, or disturbances on the hotel grounds."

"What about the restaurant?" someone asked.

Reed leaned against the edge of the table and sighed. "Yes, the restaurant and the bar attached are covered for liability reasons. Guests getting too drunk, underage drinkers, that sort of thing." Reed took a handkerchief and wiped sweat from the top of his bald head. The suit was probably company policy, but with the ventilation shafts and air-conditioning system shut down for investigation, he was burning up.

"We've got footage of the parents having dinner," Reed said. "Nothing unusual there. They got a bit rowdy both nights, but it was all jovial. We've got their waiters' activities both on the floor and behind the bar. The registers are all covered to discourage theft by the staff."

Everyone waited while Reed gathered himself. He was not used to being the presenter. He sat in a chair to the side of a computer, so everyone could see the screen behind him.

"We don't have a lot of footage of the families," the security manager said. "We have them all coming home yesterday, parking in the lot, and then we have the parents coming down to dinner. That's about it." He showed some snippets of the Sampson, Errett, and Cho families parking in the two-story parking lot. Everyone watched as Sara Farrow pulled her car into the lot and parked close to the elevators.

"So." Amanda raised a hand, drawing the attention

of the gathering. "With the halls and the elevators unsurveilled, the boys could have left room 608 and had access to eight floors, with twenty rooms on each floor, all night long."

There was a silence while Reed the security manager considered this. As he opened his mouth to speak, a detective with a bristly black mustache sitting by the printer broke in. His name badge read *Ng*.

"The boys didn't leave the room, Pharrell. They were checked on every hour and found where they were supposed to be. They had no key to get back in if they went out, and no one saw them running around the halls. Don't waste our time with questions if you haven't caught up to what's going on in the investigation."

"They said they stayed in the room," someone added.

"They lied," Amanda said.

"The guy in room 607 said he heard them playing in the room all night long," Ng said.

"Maybe he heard them on the hour or close to the hour." Amanda shrugged. "When they came back to the room to be present for their parents' checks before going out again."

"My understanding is that the boys didn't have a key to get back into the room," Reed broke in. "Now, we've checked the mechanism on the door. It's not faulty. They couldn't have jammed or propped it open. The only way they could have got back into the room is if someone let them in. That means one or more of them staying behind."

"They didn't stay behind," Amanda said. "There's

no way four eight-year-old boys would peacefully negotiate some of their party sacrificing their time in the room while the others got to go out and play. I mean, how would they ration it? One stays in the room twiddling his thumbs for ten minutes while the other three play, and they organize a rotating roster? Forget it. Only one of the boys had a watch. How would they divide the time? Girls of that age could have found a workaround, I'm sure. But boys? No way. They're basically animals. I'm betting they all left the room together."

"How?" Ng snapped, throwing up his hands. "What, they stole one of the restaurant worker's key cards? No, wait. They convinced different members of housekeeping to let them back in every hour without telling their parents."

"How many keys were issued to each couple?" Amanda asked. "Did the families all check in at the same time?"

An officer nearby drew up footage of the foyer and typed some commands into the laptop before him. There, at the long, high counter, were the seven adults and four boys that comprised the Farrow, Sampson, Cho, and Errett families, their bags scattered all around them, a circus rolling into town.

"It was one key for each adult," Reed said. "We've confirmed that with the receptionist on duty."

"Is that the standard?" Amanda asked.

"What do you mean?"

"Did they ask Sara Farrow if she wanted a second key, or did they just give it to her?" Amanda folded her arms.

"The standard is one key per adult guest." Reed's gaze wandered the floor at his feet. "I think."

"Isn't that a bit awkward?" Amanda said. "Asking a guest on their own if they want one key or two? What if they want to go out on the town and pick someone up? Slip them the key across the bar, give them a wink." She gave a wink for good measure. "I stayed at the Sea Breeze last night. They gave me two keys without asking."

"And did you invite anyone back?" a female detective nearby asked. There were snickers all around Amanda.

"Sara Farrow was the only single parent traveling with three other couples," Amanda continued. "If it was me behind reception, I'd probably just have given her two keys, like the other parents. I'd have assumed her husband was off somewhere in the bathroom or parking the car. It doesn't cost anything to assign two keys to a room. The receptionist in that footage is busy. Flustered. Look." Amanda pointed. Everyone looked. The slim woman wearing a blazer at the counter was alone, serving all four families at once, dashing between two computer screens. There was another couple at the corner of the video, waiting, looking at their watches. Amanda continued. "If the receptionist gave Sara Farrow two keys, instead of one, the boys could have gone through room 608 and into the Farrow room, 609, and used the additional key to get in and out through that door."

"The receptionist said she only gave Ms. Farrow one key," the detective at the printer said. Ng shook his head at Amanda, infuriated.

"You're going to rely on her memory, are you? You're going to conduct this entire investigation assuming everyone is telling the truth?" Amanda snorted. "Are you new to this job?"

Ng stood. The officer in the seat beside him put a hand out, a barrier.

"I reckon the boys were running around the halls and elevators," Amanda said, unconcerned. "The abductor, if there was one, didn't go to the room and pick Richie up. They met him outside, in the halls."

"We can check the system," Reed breathed, keeping an eye on the detective staring Amanda down. "See if the receptionist is mistaken."

"Assume they got out of the room," Ng said, his voice icy. "That just widens the cordon from the room to the hallways. The boys didn't get into the service elevator. No one saw them in the staff areas. They didn't go to the foyer or the parking lot. No cars left the hotel between the time Richie was last seen in room 608 and when he was discovered missing. No bins were picked up. No guests wheeled bags out without them being searched. I mean"—Ng shrugged angrily, looked to his colleagues incredulously— "what's your genius solution to that?"

"Oh, there are heaps of possibilities." Amanda waved dismissively at Ng. "I can name at least three off the top of my head."

"Please do," Reed said, genuinely fascinated.

"Meat mixer." Amanda held a finger up. "Garbage compactor. Industrial incinerator. Have we checked if the hotel has these things? What about a disguise? Are there any kids at all on the footage? Someone could have walked the boy out drugged and dressed as a girl. How long was it before all the occupied rooms were searched? Say the boy weighed thirty kilos. I know butchers who could carve up a sheep that size, pack and vacuum-seal it in half an hour. All you'd need is a bathtub and a good chef's knife. The sniffer dogs wouldn't smell a vacuum-sealed bag of meat slipped into the lining of a suitcase or taped to someone's leg."

A female officer beside Reed was holding her hand against her mouth.

"Of course." Amanda tapped her chin with her finger in thought. "Who would do that? What would be the point? And all those options suggest so much premeditation. Why make things so hard for yourself by choosing a kid in such a public space, giving yourself so little time to enjoy the experience of chopping him to pieces?"

"Someone tell her to stop," the female officer moaned.

"Jeez, this is a great puzzle, isn't it?" Amanda said. "It'll be such an adventure trying to solve it."

"An adventure?" Ng's mouth fell open. A couple of the officers around Amanda shook their heads, returning to their screens. Amanda took her notebook and folded it closed. Ng was working a muscle in his temple with his fingertips as she left the business center. She had caused enough trouble there.

I've seen kids cry before. I've seen them genuinely upset after having fallen over in the park, knees grazed, tears rolling down chubby cheeks. I'm also no stranger to the sight of a weary parent in the confectionery aisle, their child red-faced and wailing on the scuff-marked floor.

But Lillian's reaction to Kelly and Jett leaving was nothing short of biblical. It was fire and brimstone. Swirling, storm-like rage and openmouthed shock and betrayal.

"I want my mummy," she growled, hardly getting the sentence out between body-shaking sobs. "I . . . want . . ."

I stood on the lawn and simply marveled at my screaming child for a little while, glancing up and down the isolated dirt road with the knowledge that she could probably be heard for kilometers. My small, rosy-cheeked girl stood at the edge of the road and stared after the long-disappeared car, seeming to gather herself for a few seconds before she turned and spotted me. Yes, not only had she been abandoned by her Judas mother in the middle of nowhere, but she'd been left with *me*. Her mouth fell open, and she howled helplessly at the sky.

There was no consoling her. I took her into the kitchen, knelt by her, squeezed her body to mine and whispered placations and promises. She had worked herself into such a frenzy that her entire body was fever-pink and hot to the touch, spittle dripping from her mouth. At the screen door, Celine watched on, whimpering in solidarity with my inability to defuse Lillian's horror.

The front door opened and closed, though I hardly heard it, my eardrums pulsing with my daughter's screams.

Val walked into the kitchen, picked Lillian up, and sat her on the kitchen table with the care of someone setting down a sack of potatoes. She went to the counter beside the sink, extracted two slices of bread from the loaf sitting there, and opened the fridge, taking a pre-cut slice of cheese from a packet. She put the cheese between the bread and handed it to Lillian. My child took the sandwich gingerly, her whole body racked with throaty sobs.

"Now listen," Val said. Lillian's sobs fell in volume immediately, then transformed into gasping, sucking sounds, which she further stifled with the corner of the sandwich. Val put her hands on her hips.

"Your mummy's going to be back in a few days," Val said.

"I want . . ." Lillian said, her mouth full of saturated bread and cheese, her eyes going to me, the monster in the corner she surely would not be left unsupervised with again. "I . . . want . . ."

"Your mummy," Val said, slower and firmer this time, "is coming right back. Just a few sleeps. In the meantime, you're going to stay here and you're going to have a fabulous time with your dad. You'll have lots of fun together. You, him, and that sweet little doggo out there."

She pointed, and Lillian and I looked. Celine stamped her feet and whimpered when all eyes fell on her, desperate to demonstrate her enthusiasm.

"Look at that pup," Val said. "Look how sad she is at you, with all this crying and carrying on."

Lillian considered the dog at the door, snuffling and munching her sandwich. She looked at me, then Val, taking tiny bites, rubbing her running nose on the back of her hand.

"Ducks?" she asked.

"The ducks too, of course."

My child seemed to come to some decision about the situation, slid forward, and let Val lift her down from the table. Celine turned in a triumphant circle as the little girl pushed through the screen door, barely managing to keep her cheese sandwich out of the dog's reach.

Val looked at me. I pressed my lips as tight as I could.

"Don't you start," she said, pointing a gnarled finger in my face. "It'll be a knuckle sandwich for you."

We went to the windows and looked out. Lillian

was heading for the geese, who were already rising in anticipation of being chased. Lillian tore her bread into pieces and Celine tried to muscle in to the huddle of snapping beaks and flapping wings to get the morsels the girl tossed.

"How did you do that?" I asked.

"The hidden skills of a morgue woman," Val smirked.

"Oh god. You were listening in?"

"No. But you'd be surprised how sound travels across the water." She patted my shoulder. "I have a boy. He's forty-seven now. A doctor in South Africa."

"You never told me."

"Well, we don't get on so great." She straightened her shirt, brushed breadcrumbs off her palms. "It's been a long time since I was a parent, but some rules don't change. You lose control—shove something in their mouth and tell 'em who's boss. And speaking of . . ." She pointed to the bread on the counter. "Make yourself something and get out of here. You've got a job to do."

Chief Clark called me on the drive back to Cairns, almost distracting me from the hazard ahead: a four-foot-long goanna marching slowly across the heat-hazed asphalt. In my rush to get back to the search for Richie I didn't see it, and swerved as I answered the phone through the Bluetooth, watching in the rear-view mirror as the enormous lizard disappeared, apparently unperturbed by the near miss.

"What has she done now?" I asked.

"She's wandered out into the property behind the hotel and found a bunch of workers putting the final touches on a ten-by-ten concrete slab. She's helpfully pointed out that the ground beneath the slab needs to be available for a search, because it's possible the Farrow boy was buried there during the time period he went missing." I thought I could hear Clark's jaw clicking as he talked. "She's out there lecturing them about the expense and reliability of ground-penetrating radar, and I'm here getting my ear chewed off by the construction boss."

"We should probably have all construction near the hotel halted," I said.

"That's not helpful, Conkaffey."

"Sorry."

"I'm sending you video of the interviews with the three couples, and the boys," he said. "I'm also sending you a list of local suspects that are being checked out, and a temporary login for the database. There's one guy on the list I've assigned especially to you, because he has a history with police. He might hold important details back. If you're going to go out on a job, go online and make your intentions known so we can avoid double-ups."

"Aye-aye, Captain."

"Did you talk to the mother?"

"We did."

"I assume you're not blind, and you're getting the same vibes we're all getting," he said.

"There may be a reason for that. Has she, uh . . . spoken to you about her past?"

"What past?" Clark said. "I'm yet to receive the full report on Sara and Henry from the officers doing background checks. Is there something I should know?"

I drew a long breath. "Sara Farrow has been questioned about the safety of her children before." I told Clark the story Sara had told me about Anya, the first child she had lost.

"Were charges brought?" Clark asked. His voice was smaller than it had been when I answered the call.

"No," I said. "I've looked into it. Sara and Henry were officially questioned but the investigation was cursory. There were pillow fibers found in the child's lungs, and they aroused suspicion. Babies suffocate on pillows, yes, but the fibers matched a pillow that was found in the corner of the room, not in the crib. Police decided in the end that Sara might have flung the pillow out of the crib when she found the baby unconscious and simply not remembered that she had. It was possible the child had accidentally been put to bed with a pillow and suffocated on it. There was no circumstantial evidence to support a wrongful death investigation. Sara and Henry had a happy marriage, and she displayed no signs of postnatal depression. The child hadn't suffered any other injuries and had never been reported to child services."

"Jesus," Clark said. "Why did she have a pillow in the crib in the first place? Everybody knows you're not supposed to put anything in bed with a baby. You can be charged with child endangerment just for that, even if it was an accident."

"Show me the prosecutor who's going to charge a

grieving parent with that," I said. "And the forensic expert willing to sign off that the pillow was ever in the bed, even if the kid's lungs did show fibers. If it were me, I'd say the baby was rolling around on the pillow before she was put to bed."

"Hmm," Clark said. "You still have to ask, did Sara Farrow put the pillow in the bed? And if so, why?"

"You've got me. But we'll never know, and in any case, it doesn't prove anything," I said. I thought there was probably a host of reasons why Sara might have put the pillow in the bed. People do stupid things. In my time as a drug squad cop I'd seen shockingly neglectful and apparently perfect parenting from millionaires addicted to heroin and lifelong junkies living in squalor.

Clark was quiet. I listened to the sound of people bustling through the hotel in the background of the call, a phone ringing somewhere.

"Sara was rattled by the questioning," I continued. "Police dragged her and Henry into the station and put them in separate interrogation rooms. Had them in there for hours. Then, when Richie was born, child services turned up to check on the family every few months. Just dropping by to say friendly hellos, you know, with their eagle eyes roaming about the place." I thought briefly of Jett examining my child's bedroom, licking his teeth, judging.

"It would have been in Sara's best interests to tell us all this up front." Clark sighed.

"You would have dug it up eventually, I guess," I said. "She's scared. I know the feeling."

Clark gave the new information some thought, but

like most cops, he didn't share those thoughts unnecessarily. He would go back and requestion Sara now, I knew, cornering her on film with the fact that she had deliberately withheld a key piece of information from police. If Sara was smart, she would say nothing and hire a lawyer. That would look bad for her. But it all looked bad for her. If she wasn't used to it, she would be soon enough.

"It's fifteen hours," Clark said. I glanced at the clock under the dash. We were past the halfway mark. Specialists would now be arriving from Sydney—abduction and land search experts, forensic profilers, and special crimes analysts. The clock was ticking. If Richie wasn't found in the first twenty-four hours after disappearing, the search would turn from a hunt for a boy to a hunt for a body.

I found Amanda on the steps of the hotel, watching the press mob that had been pushed to the other side of the street. Under a sprawling poinciana tree, a reporter in a white sundress was trying to find an angle that would give her a shot of the hotel in the background and not leave her hair blowing in the hot breeze across her face. It would storm that evening, as it did almost every night in the wet months. The humidity would rise to maddening levels just before sunset, and the black clouds gathering over the distant blue hills would descend on the cane fields.

I went and stood beside my partner, still fighting that reflex to dive into the hotel or out into the streets and go running around trying to find Richie myself. Nearby, a small gathering of uniforms was getting instructions about doorknocks they were about to conduct around the neighboring businesses.

"Did you know concrete and cement aren't the same thing?" Amanda asked.

"I did not," I said.

"Our whole backyard was concrete when I was growing up," she said. "My mother was allergic to grass."

"I don't know a lot about your mother." I turned toward her. Behind the black lenses of her sparkly sunglasses, her eyes were a mystery.

"Not much to know." She shrugged. "She wasn't very interesting. Wasted the first half of her life in a cult. One of those end-of-the-world UFO cults. Then she had me. Then I killed someone and she disappeared."

"And where is she now?"

"Dunno." Amanda tilted her head to face the sky. "One of the outer galaxies, I guess."

"Yeah, you're right," I said. "A real snoozefest."

"How's your sprog?"

"Oh, Jesus," I laughed. "I'm never ready for that word."

"I know, right?" She grinned. "I love saying it. It sounds both mechanical and somehow amphibian. Sprog. *Sprog*."

"You can stop saying it now."

"But how is she?"

"Devastated," I said. "She's been dumped unceremoniously in my care and she hardly knows me. I hardly know her. I can't wait to get back there and spend some time with her, actually *get* to know her. I'm full of questions. I wonder if she's playing with the toys I got her right now. Maybe she doesn't like them. Maybe they're too gender stereotyped. Am I supposed to read her a bedtime story? What time does she even go to bed?"

"Ask the megabitch."

"I'm not asking Kelly stuff like that." I waved her off. "She'll think I'm an idiot. It'll be on the internet somewhere."

"You're going to ask Google how to raise your child?"

"Well, you're certainly not helping."

"You're right." She gagged, her head poking forward like a cat trying to cough up a furball. "Children. Bleurgh."

The knot of officers nearby was dismissed, their arms full of sheets bearing Richie's photo and information. A couple of them came and stood near us, hovering intentionally without going so far as to speak. I turned, expecting another snide remark, but found a pretty officer with shiny chocolate-colored hair looking directly at Amanda. She had all the hallmarks of a new recruit just recently let loose on the streets—the spit-polished name badge and squeaking gun belt, the leather not yet worn in. But she was old for a new recruit, early thirties, holding the papers against her chest like a university student with a folder of assignments.

"You probably don't remember me," she said to Amanda by way of greeting. The name badge said

Fischer. Amanda took her sunglasses off and examined the cop and her offsider, a skinny ginger guy with big teeth.

"I'm Joanna Fischer," the officer said. "I was Pip Sweeney's old partner at Holloways Beach."

I took a step up and across, bracing to defend Amanda from some verbal or physical assault. Joanna was playing it cool, but the fingers on the edge of the paper stack she was holding were picking at the sheets anxiously. This was a routine she had practiced. Amanda seemed barely aware of the danger.

"Oh yeah." Amanda yawned.

"She was my first partner, Pip," Fischer explained to the red-haired doofus, her nails wandering over the pages as though on guitar strings. "When Pip got the promotion to detective at Crimson Lake, I put in my transfer to join her. We were going to run the station together one day, we said. She was my best friend."

"I've got to tell you, this conversation is fascinating me," Amanda said.

"I was there the night she died," Fischer said.

"All right, that's enough. We don't have time for this," I said. Pip Sweeney had died trying to defend Amanda from a pair of killers she had stumbled upon in the course of our last major investigation. While Amanda had attempted to fight the two men off, Pip had intervened without waiting for backup and been shot dead. "Move along, both of you."

"Nah, nah." Amanda brushed my arm. "Let her finish."

Cops were gathering within earshot, members of the

doorknock crew and a couple of old detectives having a smoke.

"I was there," Fischer said, the false friendliness she'd used to start the conversation dropped like a stage curtain. "I went to her body on the lawn behind the house and I . . . Seeing my friend like that. Someone so strong. So brave . . ."

I knew the story of Pip Sweeney's death, though I hadn't been there. Pip had died in Amanda's arms, and I had heard that Amanda had told officers responding to the scene that before Pip died, the two had kissed. I didn't know why they'd kissed, or why Amanda had told anyone that, or if there had been some romantic relationship between Pip and Amanda. Amanda's love life was a mystery to me, as were most aspects of her being.

"Oh yes." Amanda glanced at me, a smile of comic deliciousness playing on her lips. "It must have been a devastating scene. I can imagine you clutching her limp body in your arms, shaking your bloody fist at the heavens. *Sweeney! Noooo!*"

"Amanda," I warned.

"See, Amanda told the first officers on the scene that Pip was dead," Fischer explained to her offsider, and the dozen or so officers pretending not to listen. "But I was right behind the first crew to go in. I rushed around the side of the house and found my former partner. It's like I could sense where she was. She was still alive. I heard her take her last breath."

The people around us were loving this, including, it seemed, Amanda. I wanted to take her arm, to lead her away, but there's no touching Amanda. It's one of her rules.

"Her last breath." Amanda elbowed me in the ribs. "It's like something out of Shakespeare. But what could she have said with her last breath? Oh, tell us, Fischer."

"She said I was a good friend." Fischer jutted her chin defiantly. "And she was sorry she was leaving me. I tried to tell her how much I loved and respected her, but . . ." Joanna paused for a moment, her fist pushed tight against her mouth.

"This is such a great story." Amanda's eyes grew wide with intrigue, then looked almost sad. "It would be so much better still if it were even half true."

People were gathering around us now, all pretense abandoned.

"Of course it's true," Fischer snarled. "Pip's face. Her words. I still hear her sometimes in the middle of the night, telling me she's sorry. Trying to breathe. I can feel her body in my arms."

"Nope." Amanda shook her head. "No you can't."

"We should go," the ginger-haired cop said, perhaps sensing somehow that the tide was turning. Joanna was struggling to form words through her outrage.

"It's a great tale, Fischer." Amanda clasped her chin in one hand, her elbow cupped in the other, the mock Sherlock Holmes about to drop an inquisitive bombshell. "The dialogue's a bit hammy, maybe. But there's a bigger problem. See, I do actually recognize you."

Everyone looked at Fischer. She remained unfazed, her shapely eyebrows arched.

"You didn't let me respond when you walked over here. You said, 'You probably don't remember me.' Trouble is, I *do*. I remember you perfectly from that terrible night."

Fischer squinted, wary.

"The night Sweeney died, I was smacked around pretty badly." Amanda turned to me. "Two lugheads had caught me, and Sweens McBeans was trying to come to my rescue before they pounded me into a fine paste. I ended up with seventeen stitches in my noggin. Right here. Have I shown you these?"

Amanda felt the ridges in her skull, looking up at me. I didn't answer.

"Anyway, Pip was already dead. Sheet over her. Kaput. They zipped her up in a body bag and put her in the ambulance. They tried to chuck me in one too, but I wouldn't go. I don't do vehicles. I said I'd ride my bike there. I argued with the medic for a few minutes and she finally gave up and treated my worst wounds there with me sitting on the edge of the ambulance cabin. While she was seeing to my cracked melon, I was listening to the two ambos in the front seat, chatting, when one of them mentions an interesting quirk of fate to his partner, who's just come on the shift. Turns out, he remarks, that Sweeney is the *second* police casualty of the evening. Can you imagine that? Two cops in hospital in one night!"

Fischer was shrinking slightly beside her partner. She shuffled the pages in her hands, trying to recover a couple that were slipping at the bottom.

"So I get to the hospital," Amanda continued. "They've taken Sweens off to the morgue. They take me into the emergency room. I'm looking around everywhere for this second police casualty, because I'm curious. I like coincidences. I think they're magic. But I don't see anyone in uniform."

Fischer said nothing.

"The only way I knew the woman in the bed across from me with the cast on her foot was a cop was when the nurse called her *Officer* Fischer."

"We're going." Fischer looked at her partner, but he didn't move. No one did.

"You drove yourself to the hospital on your day off, because you were washing your car and you left the handbrake off and it rolled over your foot." Amanda looked around the faces gathered near her to make sure everyone was enjoying this moment as much as she was. "The ambos couldn't believe it. You drove all the way there with a broken foot. *Well,* you told them. *I'm pretty tough. I'm a cop, after all.*"

An older detective behind me burst into a wet snigger, which turned quickly into a cackling laugh. No one else was laughing. Amanda had dropped her Sherlock Holmes routine and now grinned excitedly at Fischer, waiting for a response. But Fischer simply turned and walked away, trailing a few cops behind her. Amanda's shoulders fell. She put her hands on her hips, the prize fighter in the ring watching her opponent climb over the ropes after the first blow.

"Fischer!" she called. "I'm not done. I want to know more about Sweeney's last breath! Fischer, get back here!"

The gathering around us disbanded. Amanda slumped, disappointed, but her pep returned when she looked at me and saw my hand held out discretely by my thigh.

"Nailed it," I said.

Amanda flipped her sunglasses down and gave me a half-strength low-five like it was no big deal.

There were interview transcripts to gather, evidence records to check, another all-points briefing in the boardroom that was led this time by a senior detective I didn't recognize. The major new development in the case had been pioneered by a detective named Ng, who had begun to wonder whether Sara Farrow had been issued two keys by the busy receptionist who had checked her in. There had been an adjoining door between the Sampson and Farrow rooms, which would have given the boys access to a second door to the hall. After meeting with the receptionist and looking up the key issue log, it turned out that Sara had indeed been given two keys. Sara didn't recall ever seeing the second key, but in all the stress of Richie's disappearance, she admitted it was possible she had been given a second key and simply left it on a tabletop in the room for Richie to take without her noticing. Because of Ng's clever thinking, it was established that the boys could have been going in and out of the room adjoining 608, Sara and Richie Farrow's room, during the night, using Sara's second key to get back in. The guests and staff who had been in the hotel were being reinterviewed, the focus now on whether any of them saw the boys in the halls or elevators, and how on earth Richie could have left the building, if indeed he did. Everyone clapped for Detective Ng except Amanda, who was busy examining her fingernails.

I found Clark by the hotel doors, handing out the evening run sheet while he talked on a phone sandwiched between his ear and shoulder. When he'd finished his call I stood with him, cops walking between us, grabbing papers on the run.

"What's next?" I asked him. "If you give me some locations, Amanda and I will pick one of the canvasses and join in."

I knew that all over Cairns and the surrounds there would be officers knocking on doors, showing Richie's picture and interviewing residents. In the fields and swamps there would be State Emergency Service volunteers assisting with the land search, looking for clues in line-by-line formations. I couldn't go home and not participate, not when I knew Richie's clock was still ticking. Clark seemed to sense my hunger.

"You're not going to like this"—he held a hand up, placating—"but I don't want either of you in the line-by-lines."

"What?"

"I can't have my officers distracted by the two of you during the physical searches. You know the effect you both have on a group of police officers. Everybody gets upset. Everybody stares. I want my teams scouring for the tiniest sign of the kid, and you—and particularly Amanda—will disrupt that."

"That's bullshit, Clark. Let me join and Amanda can go home."

"Conkaffey, I want you to rest up. This might be a sprint, but it might be a marathon. I don't want to—"

"Clark—"

"—to burn everybody out on day one." Clark raised his voice. "You've got your assignments. Go home."

I drove home begrudgingly at five o'clock, slowing along the bridges where roadblocks were searching cars, while men in orange uniforms poked and prodded the muddy riverbanks. A speedboat cut laps through the water with a rifleman keeping an eye for crocs, whipping the reeds along the banks with brown foam. I knew that the council croc hunters who dispatched nuisance animals throughout the region would be bracing for a catch that seemed a little too heavy over the next few days, no one wanting to find Richie in the belly of a beast. Val and her colleagues were probably doing the same—waiting with dread for the phone call that said a child's body was being brought in for an autopsy.

I found Lillian and Val on the porch, sitting together and watching the sheet lightning over the mountains on the other side of the lake. Squishbird, one of my more tame geese, was sitting at Lillian's side, enjoying gentle strokes down her feathered neck and the firm, flat feathers of her wings. I stood at the edge of the porch for a while and watched the scene, which could have been shared between a grandmother and grandchild. When they turned and discovered my presence, I saw that Lillian's hair was prickled with sweat.

"You hot, Boo-love?" I asked when she came into my arms.

"She's a Sydney girl all right." Val glanced at the

mountains, plucking at her cotton shirt. "We need this weather to break and give us some relief."

I peeled off Lillian's dress and shoes and lifted her down from the porch, ducking under the house where I kept a hose and multi-stream sprinkler. Lillian grinned as she recognized my purpose and went to the middle of the yard, giggling and dancing around before I'd even got the water running. I sat with Val and watched her prancing in her underwear, the geese rising and waddling excitedly into the spray with her, their wings flapping. Even Celine, who doesn't like a bath at the best of times, followed Lillian around, snapping her jaws at the water when it rotated toward her.

Squishbird stayed with Val and me. I patted the bird, a heavy sense of dread in the pit of my stomach over the missing member of their party, Peeper. I had not heard anything from Dr. Laney Bass throughout the day, but had never lost the worry over the bird from the moment I dropped her off that morning.

"Long day, huh?" Val said.

"We didn't find the kid." I rubbed my eyes. "We're running out of time. The mother's acting weird. The father arrives tomorrow morning."

"Tomorrow *morning*?" Val looked at me. "If it was my kid I'd be here now. He could have been here on a plane in a few hours!"

"He told investigators he had to get a few things organized."

"What things?"

"I don't know. You never know with these sorts of things. People go into denial. Get paralyzed by fear. I don't know what the relationship between him and the kid is. I'll interview him tomorrow and meet with Sara again, and then I've got a list of people of interest to go see."

We watched the lightning. The storm was so far off, no sound of thunder reached us.

"It's going to absolutely smash down tonight," Val said, pulling a packet of cigarettes from the pocket of her shirt. "I hope that boy isn't out there somewhere in it."

We watched my daughter laughing and twirling in the sprinkler spray, queen of a menagerie of wet animals, her arms thrust out and a head of dripping hair hung back with glee. I took no comfort in knowing there was one child in the world that was safe and happy.

Amanda wasn't welcome at the bikie camp in the swamps. The men who frequented the spot made that very clear from the first time she arrived, seemingly without any purpose, climbing cheerfully from the airboat she had parked on the small, gray strip of beach. She'd visited before with Ted Conkaffey, looking for leads on a missing author, and that was fair enough. But then she started coming and just hanging around. The first time, the bearded, pot-bellied, graying ex-gangsters had shouted and sworn at her until she left. She'd been back a few days later, standing at the edge of the gathering around a fire pit, laughing along to one of their drunken stories.

Their boss, Llewellyn Bruce, had taken her aside once, let her follow him into the forest where they kept their garbage disposal unit. The tall, tattooed, bald-headed thug and the small, tattooed, twitchy investigator had stood and watched the occasional bubble rising from the stinking creek, the only indicators of the three-seater-couch-sized crocodile hidden just below the surface. No one wanted Amanda there, Bruce said. Her constant blathering was annoying, and she wasn't even interesting to look at, having a teenage boy's body and the scrappy hair of an un-washed dog. No tits, an arse like two eggs in a hanky. He had nothing against her, but she needed to rack off. The woman seemed to be listening, nodding oc-casionally while she poked at crabholes in the clay with a stick.

She hadn't, in fact, been listening. She kept coming. Over time the hurtful shouting and snarling when Amanda appeared settled to a low simmer, rising to comedic peaks only now and then. Amanda was like herpes, someone exclaimed one day. Every time you think she's gone for good, there she is again.

The bikies had almost forgotten all about her when one day, as a few of them were lined up pissing in the creek, she suddenly perked up, her voice foreign and arresting, like birdsong on a construction site.

"What's that?" she'd asked, pointing into the creek.

The men had looked. The creek was lower than usual, and out of its surface poked one sludge-covered handlebar they all recognized. The standard practice was to ignore Amanda's questions, hoping sustained silence might one day drive her off. But, for some rea-son, someone had answered her.

"It's a German World War Two bike," Rocko said.

"A BMW R75?" Amanda had asked. The men glanced at each other. "What's it doing in there?"

The bike had gone into the creek with its owner, a

prison snitch dispatched to the reptilian garbage disposal about a year earlier.

"I want it" was all she'd said.

She'd hopped off the rock she had been sitting on and waded into the water.

There was no hesitation. No consensus made. The men who hated Amanda, who told her so daily, ran into the water after her, shouting and waving their arms. Someone, Poundy maybe, sprinted back to the camp, yelling for help. The men had grabbed Amanda just as she reached the bike, their faces twisted with terror, looking out all the time for the giant beast they knew was in the water somewhere with them. It had taken three of them to peel the wet, struggling woman from the bike. She'd got it maybe a couple of centimeters up, the edge of the cracked side mirror showing briefly above the muddy surface before they carried her out of the creek.

In the end, there was no convincing her that the bike was irretrievable. That a sludge-covered, submerged heap of scrap metal was not worth risking their lives for. Every time they let Amanda go, she headed back into the creek.

They'd winched the mud- and reed-covered bike out of the water, six men hauling it up with ropes thrown over a tree limb while a team of four others distracted the croc well down the creek with raw chicken parts thrown into the shallows. The bike had maintained its shape, but the exposed mechanical innards were twisted with reeds and roots, and the tires were heavy with water.

The first day, she'd simply sat in the dirt by the

ruined bike and looked at it, like a kid on Christmas morning sitting under the tree and marveling at the brightly wrapped presents. She'd turned up the next day with a small flamingo-pink toolbox, from which she extracted a folding knife. She'd begun cutting away the roots and reeds from the bike, piling them methodically at her side. The men had watched from the corners of their eyes, surly and muttering over the rims of their beer bottles. The bike wouldn't go, even if she cleaned it up. She'd get down into the depths of the engine and find the gears rusted and the oil tank full of clay. The whole electrical system would have to be replaced, and that's if she ever got the thing apart. The men had started betting on when the tattooed woman would give up her ridiculous mission.

The days passed, and Amanda carried on and on, her bare, colorful shoulders working in the sun. After a few weeks, the men started to notice the shape of the bike changing. She'd dragged a plastic tub from behind one of the sheds, and was slowly filling it with removed parts. Sometimes they looked over and found her sitting in the shadows beyond the fireplace, scraping rust from some part or another with a wire brush.

She got stuck when she couldn't separate the fuel tank from the body of the bike. And then suddenly, without explanation, she'd done it. Accusations worked their way around the camp. Someone had helped Amanda with the bike. An unspoken line had been breached, and everyone wanted to know who had aligned themselves with the camp interloper. The culprit didn't identify himself. Amanda had nothing to say about it.

Someone helped Amanda separate the unsal-vageable parts of the bike from those that could be repaired. Somehow she knew she needed new spark plugs, and that the muffler needed to be patched. Now and then a man would go over to Amanda, backing discreetly away from the gathering as though to take a stroll along the shore. They would point to parts of the bike with their boot or murmur things out of the side of their mouth to her as she worked, their eyes locked on the distant horizon and face half-hidden behind their beer bottle. But no one admitted to helping Amanda. To do so would have been treason.

Only Amanda herself knew exactly who had helped, and how much. She'd listened silently to Chooko's whispered recommendations about electrics and or-dering the right tires for the bike, and she'd caught Poundy fixing a strut she'd put on backward while all the other men were down at the creek. It had been Rocko who'd taken her out into the depths of the rain-forest early one morning while most of the crew were sleeping, patiently teaching her how to kick off on an old, muddy dirt bike.

Richie Farrow had been missing twenty-one hours when Amanda arrived at the camp that night. She hefted her backpack onto her shoulder, her thoughts full of dark wonderings about the boy, and followed the sound of men's laughter up from the beach toward the camp. The fire was burning high, Jimbo feeding wood into the battered washing machine barrel while bright embers swirled around his weathered face. She nodded at him as she went to the table, where the men were gathered around Llewellyn Bruce. The boss was leaning back in his plastic lawn chair, his huge boots on the table. He blew a smoke ring and rubbed his round belly when he saw Amanda.

"Oh, Jesus," he complained. "The bitch is back."

"You again!" Kidneys wailed. "What are you doing here? I thought I told you to go fuck yourself."

Amanda had been about to launch into her request when she noticed that her bike, which usually sat on its blocks at the back of the half-erected shed the men lounged in, had disappeared.

"Where's my bike?" she asked.

"We threw it back in the creek." Bruce pointed with his beer bottle toward the tree line. "I ordered a whole-camp cleanup. I've tripped over that hunk of junk too many times. Nearly took my toenail off, it did."

"You didn't throw it in the creek." Amanda put her hands on her hips, rolled her eyes. "You're a pack of arseholes, but you're not that bad."

"Serious. We did."

"God's honest truth. I hurled it in myself."

"We took it apart first," Grimsy laughed. "Just to be pricks."

Amanda huffed and went down to the creek.

The bike was standing off to the side of the bare earth patch where the men usually stood to piss, leaning against a tree. Amanda didn't recognize the machine at first, impossibly higher and somehow stronger-looking now that it had tires. The men had not only added the tires she'd ordered, but they'd fully assembled the parts she hadn't got to yet, wired the electrics, and replaced the cracked side mirrors. She ran her hands over the newly polished chrome parts, her shaking fingers rising up over the glossy black crocodile-hide seat. She almost couldn't look at the fuel tank, which had been airbrushed with a scaly design. The gloss finish squeaked as she traced the immaculate reptilian scales, the searing white-and-yellow lettering that seemed to glow from the side of the metal.

"*Swamp Monster,*" she read, her voice a quivering whisper.

When she rolled the bike up the path toward the camp, leading a pack of excited dogs, the men at the table hardly looked at her. Rocko was telling his story about finding his ex-wife in their bed with another man, his hands gripped around the bottom of an imaginary two-by-four.

"I can't believe you did this," Amanda said. The men glanced at her, practiced boredom, then at the bike in her hands.

"The fuck are you talking about? We didn't do that."

"I've never seen that bike in me life."

She swung a leg over it and started the bike, revving the engine and grinning as the sound of it echoed around the trees.

"Sounds like shit." Llewellyn Bruce locked eyes with Amanda as she revved the bike, a silent understanding passing between the two. She took the battered helmet someone tossed to her, the smile never leaving her face as she pulled it on.

I didn't end up needing to dive into the depths of the internet for precious nuggets of parental wisdom on getting my child to sleep. We ate the spaghetti Bolognese Val had left in the fridge for us, and then we spent the evening in her room. I lay on the rug with a pillow under my head and watched as she pulled out three drawers of neatly folded clothes and proceeded to try every single item on, twisting and dancing in the mirror, singing songs I didn't recognize, hurling the clothes in a pile when she was done with them. She came over occasionally to show me patterns or bows on the garments like I hadn't seen them before, and each time I nodded and joined in her enthusiastic exclamations. She kept thrusting her arms up and asking "Whaddaya think?," which sounded like something she'd picked up from an American cartoon, and now and then she judged her own image as the prettiest or bestest "in all the town."

In time she went to the bed wearing a tutu and sequined top and started going through the books, making stacks around herself, and before I'd got back from fixing myself a drink she was asleep. It was 7 p.m.

Kelly texted later that night, wanting her first phone call with Lillian, but I texted back a picture of our sleeping child. When she didn't answer, I called.

"Can I ask you a question?"

"Go ahead," she said. I could hear lorikeets in the background of her call, a glassy tinkling in the falling night.

"I'm looking at Lill's bag," I whispered, walking from the girl's darkened bedroom with the bag in my hand. "It says Lillian Hill."

Kelly sighed. "I meant to talk to you about that. But it was so chaotic there, and with Jett hanging around, I didn't want to embarrass you." She took a deep breath, paused like an actor trying to remember her lines. "I want to change Lillian's name back to my maiden name."

I stopped in the hallway. I'd known this was coming when I saw the name on the tiny backpack. But it still hit me like a hand around my throat, arresting my words.

"It's safer for her," Kelly said. "Conkaffey is a very unusual name."

"We picked Lillian because it went with Conkaffey," I said, knowing it was useless. "Lillian doesn't go with Hill. The kids will call her Lillian Hillian."

"That's . . . not a major concern for me, Ted, I've got to be honest."

"Do me a favor, will you?" I said. "Leave her middle name as Emma, for my mother. Don't change it to Gillian or anything."

"Now you're just being juvenile."

"I know I am."

"I'll send you the paperwork," Kelly said, and hung up, a style of disconnection she'd performed many times with me. I went into the kitchen and poured myself another drink.

The storm turned out to be a fizzer, hitting north of us, hardly making a dent in the heat. I found I couldn't relax knowing Lillian was in the house, her safety and happiness solely my responsibility. I kept waking from light dozes, gasping at a creak of the floorboards or whisper of wind from outside, convinced she was in the room with me. When I went to check on her, I only found her sleeping in the exact position I'd left her in, the books packed away and her ballerina getup replaced with light pajamas. Then I began to wonder why she wasn't tossing and turning at least a little and began paying hourly visits, squinting in the dark to make sure she was still breathing. I thought, as I tiptoed through the dark, about Sara Farrow finding Anya lifeless and cold, about her reaching for Richie's blanket in the hotel room and finding it empty.

The late hours were a good time to download the videos of the interviews with the Sampson, Cho, and Errett families. I sat up in bed and clicked the files open on my computer, finding the first video I downloaded to be a combined interview with all three boys. Jaxon Cho's spiky black hair was still mussed from sleep, and Tommy Sampson was rosy-cheeked and hiccupping from barely suppressed tears. Luca Errett, a lean and slightly bobble-headed kid, had his arms folded and was staring straight into the camera as the officer gave the date, time, and precautions necessary for the recording. The boys had been allowed to give the interview without their parents, and the recording being made was number six in a series related to the case. I guessed the other interviews in the sequence were interviews with Sara Farrow and the parents.

OFFICER CREIBORN: Okay, boys. So, you know we've just been discussing how important it is to tell the truth when you're talking to the police, no matter what. Doesn't matter what your mum or your dad or anyone else told you to say—when you talk to the police you tell the truth, don't you?

SAMPSON: Yep.

CHO: We're not lying.

OFFICER CREIBORN: Well, that's great. Good kids. You see, we just want to know—

CHO: If you lie to the police they put you in jail.

OFFICER CREIBORN: Not necessarily. But in this case—

ERRETT: They *can* put you in jail, but, if they want.

OFFICER CREIBORN: We just need to know absolutely everything that happened from the moment Mrs. Farrow brought Richie into the hotel room, until the moment you guys were woken up by all the parents last night. How did you spend the evening? Did you play games?

SAMPSON: We just watched movies. We didn't do anything bad. My mum said that they were going to come and check on us all the time, so we just watched movies like they said.

ERRETT: That's not all. We played Chubby Bunny. We played fart bombs. We made a fort. We did heaps of things.

CHO: We didn't make a fort. That was the night before last night.

ERRETT: No it wasn't.

CHO: Yeah.

ERRETT: I think I would remember better than you. I'm two months older than you.

SAMPSON: Is Richie dead?

OFFICER CREIBORN: No, no, no, there's nothing to suggest that at all.

ERRETT: My dad said he could be dead.

OFFICER CREIBORN: When did your dad say that?

ERRETT: I don't know. Ages ago. Before the police came. He told my mum. He has secrets.

OFFICER CREIBORN: What do you mean he has secrets? What kind of secrets?

ERRETT: I don't know. They're secrets!

OFFICER CREIBORN: Then how do you know he has them?

CHO: I know a secret!

ERRETT: He was talking to me, not you.

SAMPSON: Is Richie really dead? Really? How did he die?

OFFICER CREIBORN: Tommy, mate, there's no need to cry.

SAMPSON: I want to go home!

OFFICER CREIBORN: Boys, it's very important that we focus right now. We've got to be brave, stay on track, and think hard. Did anyone come to the room and knock on the door while you were alone? Did anyone other than your mums and dads visit the room during the night?

CHO: Yeah. Someone did.

OFFICER CREIBORN: Who was that, mate?

CHO: The pizza man came.

ERRETT: He's not talking about the pizza man. He's talking about a killer or a murderer or a stranger.

CHO: I saw a show about a murderer once on the TV. My mum didn't know I was watching it. It was a bit scary. When the murderer came on the TV screen I just hid my eyes like this.

I didn't envy Officer Creiborn in his battle against the boys' distracted, fragmented observations. I watched the group and solo interviews, some from right after Richie went missing, some that had been added as recently as that afternoon. I started to get a sense of each of the boys. Cho was the dreamer, often looking around the room as he spoke, as though there was an audience of a hundred crowded before him and he had to make sure he addressed everyone. He became fixated on the idea of the stranger, wanted to get everything he knew about "Stranger Danger" out in the interview, no matter how unrelated it was to the case. I saw in him a hidden excitement, and I could understand that—nothing like this had ever happened in the boys' lives, and they probably felt special sitting in interviews with police, having their words recorded, the opportunity to solve a real-life crime in their very hands. The reality of Richie's disappearance hadn't hit them, and perhaps wouldn't for years to come.

The boy with perhaps the best conception of the

gravity of the situation was Tommy Sampson, who cried through his entire solo interview and almost half of the group one. A look of pure devastation crossed his features when Officer Creiborn presented him with the notion that he and his friends had in fact left the room against their parents' orders, not long after Detective Ng's discovery of the second key to the Farrow room. He broke down and confessed with all the sorrow and remorse I'd seen in the expressions of accidental killers, his parents appearing from behind the camera and holding him to their chests. Though Officer Creiborn assured Tommy he wasn't in trouble for leaving the room, that they just wanted to know what had happened on the boys' adventures around the hotel, Tommy was too distressed to continue with the interview.

It was Luca Errett who really intrigued me. I saw immediately that he was making some attempts to judge what information he should and shouldn't let on to Officer Creiborn in his solo interview, sometimes coming back with a question to avoid answering the one Creiborn had presented him with. He sat on the edge of a bed in front of the camera with his arms folded, now and then glancing into the lens. It was clear his parents were there, behind the camera, and from the voices at the beginning of the tape it sounded like his father was sitting on the right side of the screen. Luca kept looking off to that side as though to get approval before he answered. I picked up the photograph of John Errett from the run sheet. He shared his son's close-cropped hair and slightly oversized head, staring right down the camera like he was having his mug shot taken.

OFFICER CREIBORN: Whose idea was it to go wandering around the hotel?

ERRETT: Someone, probably. One of us. I don't know. It wasn't me.

OFFICER CREIBORN: Was it Richie's idea, perhaps? You boys used Richie's mum's key to get back in after you'd gone wandering around.

ERRETT: Yeah, we found the key in their room in the little paper folder.

OFFICER CREIBORN: That was on the first night.

ERRETT: No, last night.

OFFICER CREIBORN: Well, it had to be on the first night, though. Because you went wandering around the hotel on both nights, didn't you?

ERRETT: I meant the first night. Yeah.

OFFICER CREIBORN: And what did you do while you were outside the room?

ERRETT: Did anyone see us walking around?

OFFICER CREIBORN: We can talk about that later. I want to know what you guys did.

ERRETT: Well, we had lots of fun actually. We played knock-and-run. We played with the eleva-

tors. We had races. Played some Bullrush. Heaps of
stuff. We didn't break anything and we didn't steal
anything, but. So we should probably only get in a
little bit of trouble, like no video games or no going
to our friends' houses or something.

OFFICER CREIBORN: And how is it that every time
your parents came and checked on you, you guys
were all in the room?

ERRETT: Tommy has a watch, so we just went back
up to the room and snuck back in when it was almost an o'clock time.

OFFICER CREIBORN: Did you see anyone in the
halls or in the elevator when you went around?

ERRETT: Yeah, but when we saw someone we just
would hide. There were heaps of places to hide.

OFFICER CREIBORN: When did you notice that
Richie was missing?

ERRETT: Um. It was maybe . . . I don't know.

OFFICER CREIBORN: Was he there when you all
went back to the room to sleep?

ERRETT: We didn't go back to sleep, we went back
to build a fort 'cause we got bored.

OFFICER CREIBORN: Did you build a fort on both
nights?

ERRETT: No—Yes.

OFFICER CREIBORN: Because it says here in our notes that you built a fort on the first night.

ERRETT: We were in the fort when all the mums and dads came in and started yelling and some of them were crying.

OFFICER CREIBORN: That's . . . maybe. That's not what we have here, but maybe. It's very important not to get the two nights mixed up, because they're very similar.

ERRETT: All the mums were crying.

OFFICER CREIBORN: Pretty scary, huh?

ERRETT: They kept asking us, "Where's Richie? Where's Richie?" but I didn't know. I couldn't remember. I said he wasn't there. Maybe he went somewhere else.

OFFICER CREIBORN: He went somewhere else?

ERRETT: Like maybe he was still sleeping or something.

Watching the videos of the boys was frustrating. It felt almost as though they had the answers, but were unable to find the words to convey what they knew.

I browsed through the other files Chief Clark had made available to me, watching CCTV of the Sampson, Cho, and Errett parents at dinner with Sara at the Clattering Clam. The women and men switched seats midway through the night, the women leaning in conspiratorially at the end of the table, the men leaning out, lounging in their chairs.

I scrolled through the tape, watching the restaurant workers clear the tables one by one and put up the chairs. They vacuumed, shut and locked the windows, and turned out the lights.

With the lights out, the lamplit street at the side of the hotel became more visible. I kept rolling, the palm trees twitching in the sea breeze, and stopped at the sight of a man going by on a bicycle. The time stamp read 4:14 a.m. I tracked the footage of the man back and forth a couple of times, watching him glide along. He was wearing worker's coveralls, and a big set of keys gleamed on his belt.

I was distracted from the video by the sound of bare feet on the floorboards. The sun had risen while I worked and Lillian was standing in the doorway, wiping her eyes and clutching at the shorts of her pink-and-orange pajamas.

"Where's Mummy?" she asked.

"Mummy's gone away for a little while, remember?" I asked. "She'll be back in a couple of days."

Lillian's bottom lip grew heavy and trembled.

At that moment I got a text on my phone and opened it. Saved by the bell.

"Come on, let's get dressed," I told her. "I've got something cool to show you."

* * *

Celine had the typical dog reaction as we walked into Dr. Bass's clinic, the smell of the building causing her to shrivel at my side, her tail between her legs. Lillian perked up at the same scent, sensing new and exciting creatures nearby.

"Oh, the zoo!" She pointed at the bags of feed stacked against the wall, the pictures of happy horses and guinea pigs.

"Almost," I told her. Something flickered in Laney Bass's face as I led my daughter inside, her smile faltering for less than a second.

"I didn't know you . . ." She gestured to Lillian, seemed to try to brush the comment away as soon as it was out of her mouth. "Never mind, I—"

"She's visiting," I said, lifting Lillian onto my hip. "She lives down south with her mother. Look, Lillian, this is Laney. Her name sounds a bit like yours."

The two greeted each other, Lillian's eyes going straight where mine did, to Laney's shiny gold hair braided loosely down the side of her head. She was wearing a lab coat that caught the girl's attention, Lillian reaching out and fingering the stiff lapel.

"Come and see," Laney said excitedly, rubbing her hands together. "I think you'll be quite pleased."

She led us through the surgery into a room lined with cages. Peeper was sitting on a folded white towel, her beak nestled in her chest, one eye watching us approach.

"Well, hello," I told the bird. "Feeling much better, are we?"

"A little," Laney answered as I crouched and patted Peeper through the wire. "She's eating again, which is always a good sign. Her blood work's better. I can't give her back to you just yet, but I'm really liking the signs. If they get through the first night, I always start to have hope."

Lillian pressed her nose against the bars of Peeper's cage and tried to squeeze her whole hand through the gap to pat her, grunting with effort.

"I want to pat duck!"

"Actually"—Laney looked at me, her eyes full of mischief—"I've got something totally awesome you could pat, maybe. If your dad lets you. Stay here."

She dashed away. There was a strange, unfamiliar happiness surging in my veins, relief perhaps that Peeper was doing better, but maybe something more. Laney had not, it seemed, discovered my identity, and I considered that if I was lucky enough she might never do so. If I played my cards carefully, Laney might even end up being a friend. The simple pleasure of adding a new person into my life, someone unstained by my past, made me feel warm.

I saw what Laney was carrying before Lillian did. An infant crocodile no longer than my hand, its narrow snout taped shut and yellow eyes bulging. Laney raised her eyebrows, and I nodded, and she tapped Lillian on the shoulder, distracting her from the bird just beyond her reach.

Laney and I crouched together to best witness Lillian's reaction, our shoulders touching.

"Look, Lill," I whispered.

"A tiny baby croc!" Laney grinned.

"Ohhh." Lillian's eyes grew wide. She filled her lungs with air. "Tiny cock!"

Laney and I looked at each other. We burst into laughter, the vet almost forgetting the reptile in her hand, wiping tears from her eyes with the back of her wrist. Lillian watched us, bewildered. The vet put a hand on my chest. I couldn't breathe.

On the highway heading for Cairns, still smirking to myself now and then over Lillian's choice of words and Laney's reaction, a motorcycle rider wearing pink Converse shoes cut me off and slowed until she was only a car space in front of me, the tinted shield on the helmet flipped down, hiding her face. The biker waved backward at me and then pointed forward, full arm extended, like a general leading a battle charge. As she sped off, I shook my head, too tangled in thoughts of my daughter to make any kind of connection.

I found Amanda in the back parking lot of the Cairns police station, ruffling her helmet hair, her battered leather jacket zipped up to the tattooed flowers on her neck.

"What is *that*?" I asked. She leaned on the bike like she'd owned it for a decade, grinning, then seemed to decide the position was too casual to demonstrate her pride in the machine. She draped herself over it like a *Playboy* model.

"It's the Swamp Monster, of course."

"This thing is bloody awesome." I ran my hand

over the crocodile-leather seat, gripped the handles. "Where did you get— Oh, no."

"Oh yes," Amanda laughed.

"I've warned you about hanging out with those bikies, Amanda."

"Yeah, but you've already got a daughter, chum." She shrugged. "She's three, and she's not me."

I was about to launch into my usual complaints about criminal gangs and then grimaced, reminding myself of Kelly. My ex-wife had told me to get some friends who had nothing to do with dead bodies, and here I was about to request that Amanda clean up her own pool of friends. I simply patted the machine appreciatively.

"So you've got a girlfriend now, have you?" she said.

"What?!" I laughed. "What are you talking about?"

"Whoa, you *do* have a girlfriend!" Amanda stumbled back as though slapped. "Who is she? Oh Christ, she doesn't know who you are, does she?"

"This is . . ." I struggled for words. "You just say things sometimes, Amanda, and you assume they're true."

"Oh, it's true," she said. "That's your courtroom shirt. I've seen you wearing it on the news."

I stroked the shirt self-consciously. "So?"

"So it's the nicest shirt you own. What are you doing wearing the nicest shirt you own, with no occasion to wear it, regardless of the terrible memories it must bring up for you? You must have pulled it out of the wardrobe this morning and judged how good it would make you look versus the attached memories. The girl won out. You wore the shirt."

"It's just a nice shirt!"

"And you were driving along the highway smiling to yourself like an idiot when I passed you."

I sighed.

"Then I present you with the accusation of a girl-friend and you just about lose your lid. And not in a good way, either. I know your face. There's excitement there but also sheer terror."

"That's enough looking at my face." I held a hand up. "I don't need to be psychoanalyzed every time I step out of the house."

"The girlfriend." Amanda waggled a finger. "Is that why you were trying to call me last night? To spill the beans on the brand-new squeeze?"

"I wasn't calling you."

"Huh. Really? Someone called me a bunch of times from a private number, and then when I'd pick up there would be no one there."

"Probably the lunatic asylum, asking where you went," I said.

"Probably *you* butt-dialing me while you were makin' out with your girlfriend." She squinted at the sky. "That, or a ghost."

"Both equally likely explanations."

"I swear I heard someone knock on my door at about three a.m., too," she said. "Not even a knock so much as a thump. No one there again."

"Definitely a ghost."

"The ghost of Richie Farrow?"

"Oh, Christ." I paused with her before the automatic doors of the police station. "No mention of that in here, okay?"

"What?" she said. "His ghost's been talking to people all across the nation. I had five emails from psychics waiting for me when I got home last night. One of them was in Fremantle. They say Richie's crossed over to the other side and he's trying to let us know where he is. He's near water, apparently. That's the general consensus."

"I wonder why the kooks email you and not me," I said.

Henry Farrow was sitting at the table in the interrogation room with his head in his hands when Amanda and I found him. We had to wander the building looking for him, as no one seemed willing to give us directions. Amanda slid into the seat across from him and lumped her arms onto the table like a kid sitting down to a school lunch.

Richie's father was the picture of sleepless grief. He smelled of sweat and his handshake was brief and bone-cracking.

"Can Richie swim?" Amanda asked, before I'd even settled in my seat. Henry Farrow frowned, and I kicked my partner under the table.

"What?" Amanda kicked me back.

"Yes, he can." Henry looked at me. "Why are you asking?"

"We're not," I sighed. "Mr. Farrow, we'd like to start by saying we're so sorry this is happening and we're doing the best we can to find your boy."

"Yeah, that." Amanda waved at me. "All that stuff."

"Sara called me and told me she'd hired you,"

Henry said, pushing back his greasy hair. "I think it's a good idea. You know what happened with our daughter?"

"We do."

"Maybe you can tell us things the police can't," Henry said. "All the officers have been very kind and considerate but no one's telling me about any leads or sightings or anything. They say they've got to keep quiet about anything they get in case they alert a suspect."

I nodded, feeling helpless. I was well-versed in why the police were keeping Henry and his ex-wife in the dark, and that's because they probably hadn't been ruled out as suspects yet. Henry would have been placed under surveillance as soon as he arrived in Cairns, and Sara would have had a couple of officers watching her closely from the moment she raised the alarm about her son's disappearance. The Farrows' phones, hotel rooms, and cars would be bugged, the vehicles fitted with GPS to see where the distraught parents went when police allowed them downtime.

"I can be vague," I offered. "The police will be checking in on all known sex offenders in the area, taking DNA samples, and doing searches of their properties. Amanda and I are attending to one of those after this. They'll also be reinterviewing all staff who were in the hotel on the night of Richie's disappearance, and any of the guests with criminal records."

"But have any of those things panned out?" Henry fixed me with his desperate eyes. "Is there anyone on the table?"

"I just can't say, Mr. Farrow."

He put his head in his hands. I could see the muscles of his jaw flexing. When he looked at me again, his eyes were wet.

"You look tired," I said, trying to ease into the questioning. "Was your trip up all right?"

"Fine."

"Took you a while to get here. Why did you drive rather than flying?"

"I can't fly." Henry rubbed his eyes. "It's just something I can't do. I've never been able to handle it. And I had to organize my life. Borrow a mate's car. Call work. Call my relatives. Pack my bags. The news reporters started calling me right away, heaps of them. People I didn't even know. Everything was just a mess, I couldn't think straight." He inhaled and exhaled deeply, his shoulders slumped.

"What do you think happened?" he asked. "It's a pedophile, isn't it?" He sobbed a couple of times.

"We don't know."

"It has to be, doesn't it?" Henry grabbed his head.

"Not necessarily. There's still hope." My heart felt heavy at the uselessness of my words, their feeble sound as they hit the air. "Anything could have happened. We just don't know until we know."

"Jesus, I can't do this," Henry cried. "I can't do this. I need a drink."

I looked at Amanda. She nodded vigorously and left the room.

I went to the chair beside Mr. Farrow and put an arm around his shoulders while he cried, and tried to tell him the things he needed to hear. That all hope was not lost. That we would get through this together.

That he was not on his own. But in truth I'd never laid eyes upon a man so utterly alone in his life. His grief was untouchable, an electric pulse under the surface of his skin.

"Why don't you tell me a bit about Richie?" I said.

Richie was a comedian. As an only child he spent much of his time at Sara's or Henry's houses alone, so would explode into comic or acrobatic routines in social settings like a bored circus monkey kept in a trailer for weeks and then finally released on stage. He was wiry, thin but all muscle, so when he walked on his hands around the rim of Henry's backyard trampoline his father would see the veins and sinew in his arms straining. Richie could walk upside down and hold a conversation at the same time, his face reddening and sandy hair cascading down while his father walked along beside him, trying to get gossip on the boy's mother.

Yes, the relationship wasn't great. The breakup was fairly recent, and Sara and Henry had both been mourning the loud, boisterous child when he spent time with the other, resentful of the silence and cold, empty rooms he left behind. Richie was exciting to be around, not simply for his performances but for the drama he constantly created. He "accidentally" bought hundreds of dollars' worth of upgrades on the home gaming system, logging into the online account and purchasing the game packages without realizing they weren't free. He got in trouble at school for scaling the side of the toilet block to retrieve a ball that had gone onto the roof, standing up there like a victorious pirate raining treasure on the children from above, missing balls and hats and Frisbees falling. He stuck his head through a wrought-iron railing in a shopping center and had to be smeared in grease and washing detergent to be freed. Being around Richie was thrilling and unpredictable, like being the sidekick of a bumbling superhero.

It had been difficult to decide who would be the one to back away from the friendship group. Henry and Sara had been together when Richie met the Sampson, Cho, and Errett boys at Scouts—the group brought together by all being one-child families with rambunctious sons. The families had huddled at the coffee and biscuits station, commiserating about how impossible it was to raise boys, to keep them occupied without siblings in their age range. While the parents talked, the boys sat in a circle in the dusty hall, tying ropes and trying to lasso each other as a Scout Leader tried desperately to retain their attention. Henry got on particularly well with Michael Cho, who was also a quiet and reserved sort of guy. The two men couldn't fathom where their kids' confidence came from. They both hated to be the focus of anyone's attention.

His lack of confidence had perhaps been why Henry decided to take a back seat, to let their friends side with Sara after the divorce. She had said she wanted them—had arguments as to why she needed their Scouts friends more than he did, because he had friends of his own from his job in construction. Henry hadn't wanted to fight, didn't have Sara's whip-quick comebacks. He still picked Richie up from Scouts if the boy was coming to stay with him, but he only waved to his former friends from the car.

He was fighting for custody now, though. That was something he wasn't going to back down over. Sara had assumed primary custody but agreed to share their child, and in the beginning Henry had welcomed the boy into his new house almost every weekend. It was hard in the beginning. Henry couldn't cry in front of the boy, because it made Richie cry in sympathy. But the very sight of him barreling down the driveway toward his mother's car after two days made Henry lose it every time. He got used to the distance, phone calls instead of hugs, and photos, lots of photos. Then, after a while, Sara began to require Richie at home on certain weekends for acting classes she had enrolled him in. And then the boy was sick, or off at a friend's place, or at camp. Fortnightly visits turned into monthly visits. Then one day Richie came to visit and looked significantly older than he had the last time his father had seen him. Henry realized four months had slipped by since he had seen his child. Enough was enough. Henry wanted minimum custody times stipulated by the courts.

I listened intently to Henry Farrow's tales about his wife, thinking about Sara sitting on the bed at the White Caps Hotel, her makeup done and her watch on her wrist. Perhaps I was judging her too harshly. She'd had a difficult life, the loss of Anya and her separation from Henry, and now Richie's disappearance, weighing on her. Maybe keeping her appearance and her composure together was all she could manage. Maybe, under the surface, turmoil was swirling.

"So you aren't going for full custody of Richie?" I asked when Henry was done.

"No, no." Henry sniffed, wiping tears that had been shed as he talked. "I could never take Richie away from his mum. Not completely. And she's better at it than I am."

"At what?"

"At raising a boy," he said. He took his phone and began tapping at the screen. "You've got to be tough. Consistent. You've got to refuse to give them what they want sometimes—what you *want* to give them— just because it's better for them. Sometimes I'm so happy to see Richie I let him run wild, eat whatever he wants, go nuts. I just don't have the discipline. Look."

He showed me a video on the phone. Richie had set up an obstacle course in a small living room, with pillows and chairs and objects scattered about on the floor. He was leaping from one object to another, try- ing to avoid touching the floor, giggling and flailing his arms madly to avoid losing his balance. His face was almost maniacal with joy and excitement. Hyperac- tive, a kid going wild. In his hand he clutched a fistful of red licorice strips.

"Dad! Dad! Look! Double backflip, ten thousand points!"

The boy on the screen tried to backflip off the couch, landed awkwardly, and rolled into a pile of pillows.

"He goes bonkers on those red things." Henry dragged the phone toward himself and watched the video like he was alone, his chin in his hands.

"It can be hard being the bad cop in the relationship," I said.

"I know," Henry said. "I shouldn't be the good cop as much as I am. Sara gets all the tough jobs."

"Does it ever bring her down?"

"I wouldn't be able to tell." Henry shook his head. "She's usually pretty sour when I'm around at the best of times."

"What about after Anya's birth?" I asked. "Did anyone ever ask if she'd had postnatal depression, before or after Anya died?"

"Sure, they asked us. But Sara was all the things she was supposed to be. They say you glow when you have a baby. You know? You glow while you're pregnant and you glow afterwards. You're happy and warm and filled with love. That's exactly how it was. At least from what I saw."

"Everything she was supposed to be," I repeated to myself.

Sara Farrow had acted exactly as was expected of her when she'd had her first child, and now, when her second was missing, she was not toeing the line of the grieving mother. She was flat, emotionless, cold. What did that mean? Had Sara been acting then—or now? Or was I, and perhaps Henry too, totally misinterpreting what I was seeing?

"Jesus Christ, where is my kid? Where *is* he?" Henry wiped his nose on the back of his hairy arm. "I can almost convince myself now that he's just with his mother. But it's different. When I try to think of where he is I just feel a hole in the pit of my guts. Like, when you try to step on a step and it isn't there. You know?"

"I know," I told him, patting his warm back.

Silently, I felt a wave of gratitude that I didn't, in fact, know.

Amanda made a couple of phone calls to contacts in Melbourne as she walked to the bottle shop. The breeze had picked up—warm and damp from the swamps rather than a cool breeze off the ocean, bringing with it the smell of decay and primordial life. Tourists sat fanning themselves on benches in the shade along the Esplanade, and in the huge poinciana trees flying foxes writhed, unfolding and rearranging their bat wings constantly in the shade.

She stood in the air-conditioned bottle shop for some time, staring at the shelves of Scotch. Eventually the bored shop attendant came and stood by her.

"Stuck?" he asked. "What's the occasion?"

"Well, that's just it." Amanda threw her hands up. "We don't actually know."

The attendant, a young man with lazy, stoned eyes, gave a quarter-frown and looked at the scars on Amanda's arms.

"If I took a stab at it," Amanda said, "I'd probably say death. I mean, that's the most likely scenario. We're thirty-four hours in. But, you never know. The occasion might end up being a celebration. These things can turn on a dime."

The attendant stared at her. Amanda stared back.

"Death," she said finally. "That's where I'd put my money."

The attendant rubbed his eyes and looked at the bottles.

"Well, you don't want to go cheap for a death," he said, reaching up toward a higher shelf.

On the way back to the police station, box of Scotch in hand, Amanda noticed a man in gray coveralls with the sleeves rolled up to the elbow standing and smoking at the gate to the back entrance of the police station. His ponytail of dark brown wavy hair was tucked against the back of his neck, tendrils of hair stuck to his skin with sweat. He plucked at a small goatee as though some of the hairs were tangled. Amanda stood beside him, waving at the security camera to be let in.

"You're one of the investigators," the man said.

Amanda turned and saw that on the chest of his coveralls, the crest of the White Caps Hotel had been embroidered. She looked at the battered, sagging belt at his hips, covered in keys and tools, and guessed maintenance.

"That's me," she said, still waving at the camera.

"Are you, like, a detective?" the man asked.

"Private," Amanda replied.

"Oh." The man nodded a little too hard, dropping his eyes to his feet. Amanda could see that the camera above the entrance was on. There was undoubtedly someone at the front desk of the police station watching her standing there like a cat meowing to be let in from the rain, their finger hovering above the button, fucking with her. It was something she would do, given the chance.

"Are there any leads in the investigation?" the maintenance man asked.

Amanda stared at him, tried to get a read on his face. But it took her a long time to get to know faces, and this one was by turns distracted, downcast, or squinting at the horizon. She shuffled the Scotch bottle under her arm.

"Oh, there are some. There are always some. Good ones and bad ones. Sometimes there are too many. Can you imagine that? You've got to pick through them, pry them apart. Why, have you got any?"

"No, no." The man lifted his belt. "I was just wondering if there were any suspects. Anyone you were focusing on."

"Could be there are no suspects at all." Amanda shrugged. "Maybe it was just an accident, and no one's to blame. Who knows?"

"I was shocked when I heard," the man said, fixing his eyes on Amanda. "It's very sad. Very scary. I was really hungover that morning, too. I was pretty sick. Some people might have seen me being sick, you know, and they thought I was sick over the . . . um. You know, the situation."

Amanda nodded.

"I really love my job at the hotel," the man said. He

seemed to be struggling to find his words. "I don't just love it. I *need* it."

"Uh-huh."

"That probably sounds . . . anyway. I'm just saying. When stuff like this happens . . ."

Amanda started waving at the camera again, more frantically this time.

"Anyway, I've gotta go." The man walked off.

Amanda let a chest full of air leave her as the gate finally clicked and started to roll back.

Amanda set the box on the table and plonked herself into the seat across from Henry and me, fanning her face with a brochure about domestic violence she must have snagged from the waiting area.

"Jesus Christ." I swiped the bottle and looked at the gold embossed label. "I think Mr. Farrow was thinking more about taking the edge off, Amanda. How much was this?"

"I'll take anything." Henry reached for the box.

"You can't go cheap on a death, Ted." Amanda rolled her eyes. I felt my whole body stiffen.

"What does that mean?" Henry asked.

"Nothing." I kicked Amanda under the table as she opened her mouth to answer. "It's an old Cairns saying."

Amanda and I watched as Henry poured a nip into his empty coffee cup with trembling hands. Some of the liquor splashed on the table.

"So did you tell him about the life insurance policy?" Amanda asked.

Henry set the bottle down too hard. I didn't know what Amanda was on about, but I tried to warn her with my eyes, since the kicking didn't seem to be working.

"What are you talking about, Amanda?" I asked gently.

"I have a mate who works in insurance fraud down in Melbourne," Amanda said. "Another private detective. He investigates claims. You know, bricklayers who have thrown their back out one week and the next week they're lugging bags of gravel on their shoulder for a cash job. This one case, he had a woman claim she'd strained a ligament in her leg, wanted six months' worth of lost wages. Bank manager. Pretty hefty claim. Next thing you know, my guy's following her into the parking lot of an ice-skating rink, and—"

"Amanda."

"Anyway, less than a month ago you took out a life insurance policy on Richie." Amanda locked eyes with Henry as she fiddled with a corner of the Scotch box. "Did you not?"

Henry paused, then nodded slowly, gripping his cup with both hands. I watched, battling the sensation that I was losing my handle on the situation, as Henry poured himself another nip.

"Why did you call an insurance investigator?" I put my hands out, trying to keep up.

"The guy's getting divorced." Amanda gestured to Henry like it all made perfect sense. "He's had to break ties with Sara and reset his entire life. New bank accounts. New mortgage arrangements. That also means updating his insurance policies. I wanted to see if he kept both Richie and Sara on his policy. It's not a half-bad plan: bump the kid off, wait a month or so and then bump the wife off. Write a suicide note in her name expressing regret for killing the kid—bingo-bango, collect the payouts for both. Two birds, one stone."

"Oh, Jesus." I hid my head in my hands.

"You did take Sara off your policy," Amanda said to Henry. "But it turns out Richie was only on the former policy for accidental death and suicide. Now he's on it for wrongful death—including homicide or negligence occasioning death. He's been upgraded!"

I gripped my hair with both hands. Henry let air ease through his lips, his eyes locked on his hands.

"Did you not think"—Amanda poked her head forward, trying to meet Henry's eyes—"that mentioning the insurance upgrade to someone before this very second might have been kind of, maybe, just a little bit, I don't know . . . *incredibly important*?"

"I didn't mention it because I knew . . ." Henry's lip trembled. He drank the Scotch in one. "I knew it would cause trouble. It didn't mean anything when I took the policy on. I called up the insurance company to separate my policy from Sara's, and they just mentioned that I could keep Richie on my policy and upgrade his cover really easily. Cheaply. They had some kind of deal going."

"A *deal*?" I asked. I felt nauseated.

"A special sale. You know these insurance companies," Henry pleaded. "They sell you whatever they can. They said I could cover the wrongful death of a dependent for only a small amount extra per month. The woman was really pushy on the phone."

"How much is the payout?" I asked quietly.

"A million schmackos." Amanda jigged her eyebrows up and down.

"But the policy only pays for a dependent," Henry sighed. "Sara currently has full custody."

"So why'd you get the policy?" Amanda asked.

"I don't know." Henry put his cup down and folded his arms on the tabletop, hid his face in them. His shoulders heaved with sobs. "I don't know."

We drove south. I watched Amanda, on her new bike, disappearing into the distance or weaving in and out of traffic, her lean body angled forward and her gloved fingers dancing on the handlebars to music she was playing under the helmet. Now and then I would pass her standing at a highway lookout, surveying the landscape, her hands on her hips and her boots spread apart like a superhero looking out over the city under her watch. Once I passed her sitting sideways on the bike outside a petrol station, eating a pie out of a tinfoil tray, her chin jutting forward and eyes sliding sideways as I went by waving.

Of the five known sex offenders living in a fifty-kilometer radius of the White Caps Hotel on the night of Richie's disappearance, none were spotted on CCTV in or around the hotel. None of their cars were captured on traffic cameras in the area, and none of their credit or debit cards showed transactions at any of the bars or restaurants nearby. As they had done with me, the police had tracked the phones of these men and discovered their whereabouts in the critical time period, and then widened the search for offenders outside the fifty-kilometer exclusion zone.

A name turned up. Todd DeCasper. His car's license plate was picked up on a traffic camera on Reservoir Road, a major arterial into Cairns. The time logged was 5:21 p.m.

Todd DeCasper had already been interviewed by the police, and had, by all accounts, been cooperative. But it's surprising what a person will remember sometimes when they tell their story to a different party a second time—and perhaps what they'll change or leave out.

Chief Clark had asked us to speak to Todd DeCasper because he thought the man might be distrustful of police, and would perhaps be a little more receptive to someone in my situation. I believed he was right.

Mr. DeCasper, as his students called him, had been a Year 6 teacher at a public school in Zeerich, in the mountains behind Cardwell, a couple of hours south of Cairns. He was an artistic kind of guy, which his pupils appreciated—he encouraged them to see, feel, and experience the things they learned, rather than leaning heavily on reading and writing skills. When they studied ancient Egypt, he arranged a mock archaeological dig for them in the school playground, burying clay artifacts in the sand. When they learned about pirates, he dressed as a bedraggled sea captain and led the students in an invasion of another classroom. He was well-liked by staff—ever the cheerful

volunteer at the fundraising barbecue, and the orga-
nizer of enormous, colorful cards signed by all staff
to celebrate pregnancies, retirements, or promotions
across his cohort.

Later, when interviewed for the newspapers, Todd
DeCasper's colleagues would acknowledge that they
had at times witnessed a darker side to him, but how
much of this was invented or embellished to suit the
narrative of his public disgrace, it was hard to say.
There were stories about him drinking too much at the
teachers' Christmas party, becoming belligerent and
sleazy, and apologizing profusely the next day with
a series of remorseful visits to specific classrooms at
lunchtime. They talked about him having apparently
no romantic life to speak of, shying away from blind
dates the other staff tried to organize and flat-out
shrugging off the flirtations of a visiting teacher who
took an interest in him. When I heard these stories, I
was skeptical. A rash of the same types of tales had
come out after my arrest, of me fighting with my
neighbors over parking spaces and making physical
threats, of me meeting with drug dealers on suburban
street corners and getting into cars with unsavory
types.

In truth, it was Todd DeCasper himself who had
raised the alarm about his secret life. He had walked
into the Zeerich police station on a Saturday morning and asked to speak to a supervising officer about
reporting a serious crime. He'd been edgy, evasive,
wanting to speak in "hypotheticals" and refusing to
be recorded. He'd wanted promises of protection,
and the police had told him he'd been watching too

many movies. They'd told him to spit it out, and, in a brightly illuminated back room, over a Styrofoam cup of coffee, he finally did.

Todd DeCasper was attracted to children. He'd known this for some time, probably ten years. He'd realized, when he finally moved out of the university classroom where he'd obtained his education degree and into the active school classroom, that he felt more than just a creative, protective, nurturing interest in children. There was something more. Something bad.

He went online for diagnosis, hoping to find treatment options, sitting sweaty and short of breath as he clicked through every link, not wanting to stumble onto anything that might get him into trouble. He found psychologists, expensive ones, who were mostly out of state. He wrote down their phone numbers but never called them. Todd inched his way toward the less visible websites. He found a chat room. Then he found a man living not an hour's drive away who wanted to listen to his story.

Their first meeting was awkward. Neither Todd nor his new friend, Barry, could say the word, and turning the conversation too swiftly toward the point of their connection made both of them fall back into soulless small talk. Though they hadn't actually made any great leaps in supporting or understanding each other, just sitting with Barry in a roadside bar, knowing someone else out there had his same problem, gave Todd reassurance.

For a year, Todd and Barry met at the same bar, at the same table, and over beers they spoke about their urges. Todd found that Barry was the more confident one, that he got carried away and would sometimes fantasize openly. Sometimes Todd didn't stop him. Todd told Barry he was terrified of offending. That the opportunity to do so was rife. He asked Barry if he should leave his job as a teacher, whether the sacrifice was worth it to protect the children that he put at risk simply by being in the same room as them. Barry didn't have any solid advice. He just wanted to talk about himself.

One day Barry came to the bar shivering and wired. Todd wondered, initially, if he was on something. They made small talk, and when that ran out, Todd asked Barry what was wrong with him. Barry came out with it, almost without hesitation. He'd offended against a coworker's kid.

Todd stayed up all night, lying in his bed, staring at the ceiling, too cold without blankets and too hot with them on. The next morning, he'd walked into the police station. After his statement was given, and all the personal details he had on Barry filled out neatly on an official statement, Todd was read his rights by his interviewing officer and placed under arrest.

He was smaller than I'd imagined. But I suppose I'd been unfair in assuming that someone at the center of such a colossal storm had to be of a certain height and weight. Todd DeCasper was waiting for us on the steps at the front of his house, hidden from view from the street by a lemon tree, a cigarette trailing smoke from one hand, a leaf twirling idly in the fingers of the other. He was a battered, windswept midforties. The property was shaded and cool, a Spanish-style stone place nestled in the mountains, the neighboring houses barely visible through the surrounding foliage. I'd learned from reading Todd's file that the place had belonged to his deceased mother, and was in her name, which wasn't DeCasper. A good hideout, but one that wouldn't last forever. As I pulled into the driveway, I could already see a man across the street raking leaves who was taking an interest, probably on the lookout since he'd noticed police cars here yesterday.

Todd's downfall had come after mine, so the public hadn't been as interested in the story. I'd read the news about his arrest in the papers in the prison common room, the article followed by an opinion piece by a current affairs commentator wondering if there was an epidemic of child sex offenders in the public service. Todd had only been incarcerated at the watch house for a couple of weeks, arrested under the suspicion of acts against children, but not brought up to the court on charges. Police had delayed charges until they had something tangible to prove that Todd had offended, telling the court in his absence that he was a self-professed danger to children. Todd, apparently wanting to do whatever he could to please the police, didn't apply for bail. Though Todd's life was turned upside down in pursuit of some proof he had acted on his urges, he was never formally charged. This didn't stop his story from reaching the national news while he was locked up. He had "outed" himself to the entire country without ever having been charged with anything.

But, as I knew intimately, a man didn't need to be

convicted of a crime for the whole world to hate him for doing it.

Six months had passed since Todd's arrest on the day I walked up his driveway. He had the short, messy beard of a man on the edge, the heaviness and darkness of the hairs a stark contrast to his pale skin. He was lean and dressed in baggy clothes that smelled of mothballs when I shook his hand, the garments probably packed away and lovingly stored by his mother when he went into custody.

"I thought you said you had a partner," he said, looking around me down the street.

"She'll be here any minute," I said. "Let me warn you now—she has absolutely no tact. She's likely to be insensitive toward you."

"I don't expect sensitivity," Todd murmured, his cigarette burning into a long cylinder of ash. "Not under the current circumstances. You've got a boy missing. There's no time for tact."

I took out my phone, pretended to hold it to the light to read an email and took a picture of DeCasper for my records. Todd's agreeable attitude was strangely annoying. He offered me a cigarette, and I shook my head, the politest refusal I could manage.

Amanda rolled up and parked her bike on the pebbled driveway, shaking her hair out of the helmet. She grinned at Todd like they were old friends.

"What's up, Teach?" she asked.

The house was full of dust. It lay in a fine sheet over everything, coating a glass ashtray on the table beside the couch and the lids of the transparent plastic tubs stacked against the wall. The stasis of Todd's life, the days without the morning commute, ringing bells, coffee in the staff room, lines of kids walking from the classroom to the football field, the field to the hall. The only thing that moved was the pendulum in an old grandfather clock. I stood and looked at the tubs, a dozen or so of them, filled with colorful stacks of paper and swathes of cheap fabric. Marker labels on the sides of the tubs. *Ancient Rome—Years 5–6. Antarctica—Year 4.* There were folders of tattered papers, rolls of stickers in gold and fluorescent colors. Amanda popped a box open without asking and peeled a sticker that read *You're a star!* off a roll, sticking it to the breast of her T-shirt.

"I'm a star," she mouthed to me behind Todd's back, jabbing a thumb proudly in her chest.

"I don't know what I'll do with all the teaching resources I still have," Todd said, sinking into a well-worn groove in an ancient brown couch on the other side of the coffee table. "I haven't had time to sort them."

"You haven't had time?" Amanda raised her eyebrows. "In six months?"

"Oh, you know." Todd sighed. "The motivation, I mean. I've been passing the time as I can. Watching a lot of television. Reading. I'd hate to see them go to waste, though. They'll be of some value to someone. You don't get much of a budget in the public system. The costumes are handmade. My mother did the pirate one."

"Mr. DeCasper," I said, taking a seat on the couch opposite, "I understand the police have already been out here and spoken to you. Is that right?"

"Todd's fine. Yes, they came yesterday. They had me sign a statement. Walked around the yard a bit. They didn't tell me much about the case itself, but I've read some stuff about it in the papers." He glanced over his shoulder at Amanda, who was snooping through the photographs on the mantelpiece. "Can I get you guys a cup of coffee? You're welcome to take a seat."

"She's fidgety," I said. "She likes to wander."

"It's a terrible thing," he said. "Disappeared right out of the hotel, they think? And nothing on the cameras? It's so scary. I imagine the police will be doing the rounds of all the people of interest in the area. They came to your place, did they?"

I felt a spark of pain, like a needle poked into the back of my skull. "No. They had no reason to come to my place."

"Of course, of course!" Todd held a hand out. "I didn't mean it like that. I just—"

"I'm not a pedophile. I've never admitted to being a pedophile. And there's never been any evidence to suggest that I—"

"I just meant—"

"Never mind." I inhaled slowly. "Mr. DeCasper, I believe you were in the vicinity of the White Caps Hotel at the time of Richie Farrow's disappearance. That's bad news."

"It really is," he sighed. He watched Amanda as she neared the television set, a three-foot-wide, ancient wood-veneer job. I'd had a television like that in my room when I was a kid. It had been heavy, unmovable, the remote only responding to every third or fourth push of the buttons. Amanda bent and ran a hand over the curved gray screen, making a *tink-tink-tink* sound as she knocked on the glass.

"Are you sure you wouldn't like to sit down?" Todd asked.

"I'm fine," she said, smiling and walking around the back of the couch I was sitting on.

"You know," he said, looking at his hands in his lap. "I realize that I shouldn't feel sorry for myself. But I do feel a little sorry for myself sometimes. I did the right thing, at least to my way of thinking. I knew I had a problem, a big problem, and I tried to tackle it. I've never committed a crime against a child. I've never committed a crime at all, actually. And when I came to realize that my friend, someone I trusted very deeply, had done something awful, something criminal—well, I went right to the police, didn't I?"

I said nothing. Amanda picked up an orange china cat from a table by the end of the couch, examined it, and set it back down.

"They couldn't charge me with anything," De-Casper continued. "Talking to someone in a pub about your . . . your predilections . . . that's not a crime. I've never looked at child pornography or exchanged it with anyone, and believe me, the police tried everything they could to disprove that. They interviewed all my students, present and past, and they talked to all my colleagues and my family members. They even went to Tasmania and spoke to my young cousins. I haven't seen those kids in years."

"Todd," I said.

"I feel like I did the right thing."

"It *was* the right thing," I said carefully. "Reporting your friend."

"You're a star, Mr. DeCasper!" Amanda gave him a thumbs-up.

"He's in jail now," Todd said. He looked at the curtains, the shadows of leaves playing on the lace. "Where I was. Same cell block and everything."

"Why were you in Cairns last Friday night, Todd?" I asked. He didn't answer immediately, was fixated on the window like he was watching something across the street. Amanda had moved back to the television, turned and rested her butt against the huge machine.

"I deliver oxygen tanks," Todd said suddenly, as though he'd had to fish around for the information in his disorganized mind. "That's what I do now. I'm lucky to have a job. I don't have any direct contact with the company. I've never met the bosses. I get an email in the morning with the addresses, and I load up the tanks and drive them out. They're mostly emphysema patients, but sometimes it's hospitals with bulk or emergency orders. You'd think it would have convinced me to give up smoking." He gave a short, halfhearted laugh. "I've actually started smoking cigars. You've got to have some vices, haven't you?"

Amanda flattened her sticker against her breast. Todd watched her, his look still slightly glazed, distant.

"Friday afternoon I had a delivery in Redlynch," he said. "I was there around four o'clock. Then I stopped in Cairns for dinner and a couple of drinks. I guess time got away from me. I was home about eleven."

"Did you approach the White Caps Hotel at any

time?" I asked. "Even to walk past? Did you park in the adjacent parking lot or go into the lobby?"

"No," he said.

"And you didn't see any boys in the street during your time in town? Did you speak to any children? Were any children in or around your car that night?"

"No," he said again, a detached, awkward smile painted on his lips. "No, I didn't go near any children."

"You came into Cairns via Reservoir Road?" I said.

"Yes."

"But you didn't drive home that way."

"No."

"It would have made sense to take Reservoir Road, route 91, or the Bruce Highway south. But you didn't take either of those."

"I sometimes drive places a stupid way," Todd laughed. "My sense of direction is terrible."

"Terrible or not, your sense of direction leaves us unable to determine what time your car left Cairns," I said.

"Yes." Todd pursed his lips. "It does."

A silence descended over us. Todd watched Amanda, and I watched him, trying to regather myself. As much as I hated to hear Todd try to relate to me, Damien Clark had sent Amanda and me because he thought I might be able to connect with Todd in a way the police could not. That perhaps I could offer him a safe place to speak his thoughts, and from there I might be able to derive leads. I caught Amanda's eye and jutted my chin toward the kitchen. She wandered in there, her arms folded, and I heard her open a door to the backyard.

"I guess this is my life now," Todd said, even before I could attempt to pick up the conversation. "A kid goes missing and they come poking around. I suppose I'll have to get used to dealing with police. I was so nervous when I walked into the station the first time. They're not a bad bunch, though, not really. A bit gruff."

"I'm sure it's nothing personal," I said.

"It never goes away, does it?" he asked. "I mean, it's been, what, two years for you?"

"About that," I said.

"Can I ask you—" He leaned forward, his hands clasped between his knees. "Were you able to, uh . . . Are there people in your life? I mean, I know you've got your partner . . ."

"I have friends," I said. "They're few, and they were difficult to acquire. I had to get used to my own company, but prison helped with that. I lost my wife. My child. Not completely. They're still in my life but it's carefully managed."

"You don't notice how much you use the phone until something like this happens," Todd said, still smiling oddly. "I never realized it before, but I was constantly texting people. Calling people. Going out to dinners and drinks and things. I used to talk to my brother every couple of days. It's so quiet now that I sometimes go a week without looking at my phone or emails. Maybe that's why I stayed so long in Cairns. Sometimes I like to be out around people. To hear other voices. Everyone just . . . flees. They flee right out of your life like rats jumping off a sinking ship."

I thought about Laney Bass. There was no doubt in

my mind that she was going to discover who I was, whether I told her or someone else did. I had the sudden impulse to take out my phone, text her, tell her I was going to come and get the bird. I would flee from her before she fled from me.

Amanda came into the room, holding an ax by her side.

At first it didn't register in my mind. She held it casually, like a kid with a stick, tapping the butt against her calf. She swung the tool up and let its weight fall into her other hand, testing its balance, turning the thing by the handle with her wrist like a sword fighter.

"Check out this big boy." She grinned.

Todd turned and caught sight of her, then leapt off the couch, his mouth falling open.

"What are you do—" he began.

His words were cut off by the thunderous crunch of the ax into the top of the television set. Amanda had swung the ax up and over her head in a perfect arc, her thin, colorful arms straining under the momentum, the blade splitting through the front left corner of the wooden box and embedding itself in the machinery of the set. The glass screen crashed out of the box in a shower of shards. The small wooden legs at the front of the set gave way and the television collapsed like a fat man on his knees.

"Holy shit!" I shouted. Before I could voice more of my surprise, Amanda had lifted and swung the ax again, cutting through the back half of the set, spilling the box and its contents on the floor.

I could barely hear Amanda's voice over my panting, over Todd's gasps and moans of surprise and horror. My partner was cheerfully shifting chunks of glass and machinery away from the wreckage of the television set, exposing the tight rolls of fabric that had been stacked carefully all around the inside of the television's wooden casing.

"It's like a Christmas bonbon," she was saying, crouching and picking wires and splinters of wood away from the little fabric bundles. "Crack it open and *BOOM!* An explosion of treasures."

"What is all that?" I asked, initially addressing Amanda, then turning to Todd, who stood not far from me, watching my partner with his mouth open and his hands by his sides like a sleepwalker. "Mr. De-Casper? What are all those things?"

He didn't answer. Amanda took one of the little rolls and unwrapped the elastic band that secured the fabric. She tossed the band away and flipped the fabric roll open with a flourish, like a waiter opening a napkin to lay across a patron's lap.

She held up the item. It was a pair of colorful boys' shorts.

I had Amanda keep an eye on Todd DeCasper while I went to the car to get evidence bags. When I left the house he was sitting on the couch with his hands on his knees, palms down, fingers straight, like a child waiting for a school photo. I told him what he likely already knew, that I'd have to secure the collection of clothes for evidence, call the police, and see what they wanted to do. They would come, re-search the house, requestion DeCasper about where the children's clothes had come from and why he had them. The former teacher didn't offer any explanation for the clothing items hidden in his television set. I stood and watched Amanda carefully picking the little rolls of fabric out of the remains of the TV unit for a little while, and then went outside. There must have been fifty rolls, some of which looked like T-shirts, others shorts or trousers.

I keep a full police-standard evidence kit in the boot of my car. Although I'm no longer a cop, crimes flutter around my investigative work for Amanda, and some of the items prove to be useful. Latex gloves and tweezers, fiber collection tape. I opened the boot and started rustling about, my jaw clicking with anger, the sound of Amanda's ax crashing through the television screen still shuddering in my brain.

When a text came through I paused and took it, looking for any distraction the world could offer me from my dark conclusions about Todd DeCasper.

It was from Kelly. *You didn't forget about the strawberries, did you?*

At first I thought the message must have been a mistake. I texted back.

Huh?

Lillian's strawberry allergy.

I stared at the message. The neighbor who had been raking leaves was on his nature strip, hosing flowers along the fence, watching me. I called my ex-wife.

"Lillian's *what*?" I asked as the line connected.

"I knew you'd forget," Kelly said. She gave a harsh

sigh. "Lillian's allergic to strawberries. Lucky I reminded you. You never remember these things."

I was lost for words. My mouth opened and shut but no sound came out.

"Kelly," I said eventually. "Never in my life have you ever, *ever* told me anything about Lillian having an allergy."

"I did tell you," Kelly said. "I told you months ago, when I saw you. I made sure you knew. I wouldn't let you look after our child without knowing."

"Oh no. No you didn't." I pointed, as though she could see me. "You did not. I would have remembered if you told me."

"You—"

"*I'm* not allergic to anything, and *you're* not allergic to anything, so the fact that our child is allergic to something would have stuck in my mind for two reasons—first, because I'm her father and I should know these things, and second because it's interesting!"

"I told you."

"You didn't tell me, Kelly, because you're ringing me right now completely out of the blue to tell me. You're not doing that because you suddenly realized *I'd* probably forgotten. You're doing that because you suddenly realized *you'd* forgotten."

"I don't know why you're yelling at me," Kelly said. "You're yelling at me and shoving evidence in my face like you're still a cop or something. You're not a cop, Ted."

"Is she allergic to anything else?" I asked. "What kind of allergy is it? Does she get a rash or does she have an EpiPen? Christ! Where's the EpiPen? Is it in her bag?"

"She's not allergic to anything else," Kelly huffed. "She gets a severe rash and a couple of times she's become hoarse but she hasn't been prescribed an EpiPen. The doctor thinks she'll grow out of it."

"Kelly, for fuck's sake!"

Kelly hung up on me. My hands were shaking so badly I could hardly get to Val's number in my phone. The sun was searing on the back of my neck. I walked to the shade of a nearby tree and stood chewing my lips until she answered.

"What's wrong?"

"Lillian's allergic to strawberries," I managed.

"Well, let's not throw her in the bin just yet."

"Have you given her any strawberries? Are there any strawberries in the house?"

"No, there's not," Val said. I could hear Lillian talking in the background, a child's run-on babbling. "You sound frantic. What's happening?"

"I didn't know she was allergic to strawberries. Kelly just told me. She said she told me months ago. I don't think that's right! I would have remembered!"

"Maybe she didn't tell you."

"Val," I breathed. "I could have given her strawberries. I could have killed my own child because I didn't know she had allergies. What if I'd given her a big bowlful and sent her to bed? How did I not know she had allergies? What kind of father doesn't know that?"

"Ted," Val said carefully, "you didn't give her any strawberries."

I leaned against the tree trunk and listened to the background noise of the call, Lillian's feet clattering through the house, the screen door slamming, and Celine barking.

"You didn't know," Val said. "And it doesn't matter whose fault it is that you didn't. But now you do. No harm has been done. So instead of turning into a puddle on the floor, you're going to gather yourself up, brush off your shoulders, fix your hair, and carry on."

I stood, wiping the sweat from my brow with the hem of my T-shirt.

"Is she allergic to anything else?"

"No," I said.

"Well, good-o then," Val said. "Nothing to worry about."

I sighed into the phone. I was about to express my thanks, but the sound of a gunshot cut off my words, the unmistakable *pop* noise coming from inside DeCasper's house.

I ducked behind the low front wall, looked across the street, where the neighbor was still watching me. He'd heard the sound, and now took my reaction to mean it was exactly what he thought it was. He dropped the hose and ran. I hung up on Val, ran in a crouch to the car, and got my gun from under the front seat.

Please, I thought, *don't let this be Amanda*. Even in my rising panic, I knew there was only a slim chance the gunshot had nothing to do with my partner. She had fired on DeCasper, or he had fired on her—the two equally likely scenarios flashing through my mind with sickening clarity.

"Amanda!" I called from behind the front wall, shoving the magazine into the gun. "Amanda!"

There was no sound from inside the house. I turned and jumped over the neighbor's front fence, landing awkwardly in loose bark chips, stumbling along the side of their property. There were two Rottweilers barking at a diamond-wire gate at the side of the house. I didn't have the time or the patience to avoid them. I needed to get to my partner. As I landed on the other side of the gate the dogs split and bolted for the back door, their aggression a display they weren't prepared to back up. I ran toward the back of the garden, hopped the side fence and landed near the back stairs to DeCasper's house.

"Amanda!" I called. My voice was high with hope. "Are you okay? I'm coming in!"

I heard her before I saw her, the rasping of a cigarette lighter barrel striking the flint as she pushed the screen door open with her free hand. She came out onto the little porch in front of me, waving the lighter over the end of a cigar.

"Don't bother," she said, the cigar gripped in her teeth. She exhaled smoke into the blazing day. "It's a crime scene now."

I pushed past my partner and went into the dusty little house. Glass from the smashed television set had reached further than I realized. It crunched under my boots in the short tiled hall off the living room.

DeCasper was lying on the kitchen floor, his head sprayed all over the turquoise-painted lower cupboards, a small black revolver lying in the corner of the kitchen near some fallen cornflakes. There was a blue towel slowly turning purple with blood, making a dam at the edge of the kitchen, where the tiles met the carpet.

I went back out to Amanda, who was now sitting on the back steps, her shoulders slumped, the cigar trailing blue smoke.

"What the fuck happened?"

"It's my fault," she sighed. "I thought he looked sad, I guess, but I didn't really know. He was just sitting there shaking, not saying anything, as you walked out the front. I tried to think of something consoling to say, but I had nothing. I said, 'You all right?' and he said, 'No,' and I said, 'I'm not surprised.'"

Amanda looked across the long, empty lawn. There were piles of dirt in the shade under the trees at the end of the property, lumps of damp wood. Someone might have been planning on putting in garden beds.

"He said, 'They'll have to come again, won't they? Ask more questions. Do another search. This doesn't look good.' And I said, 'You bet your arse it doesn't look good.'"

I sighed. She went on.

"He asked if he could have a drink of water. Said he felt sick. I said sure. What was I going to say? I ran this case for a woman in Holloways Beach a couple of years ago, before you started with me. Caught the guy cheating on his wife with his male business partner. He was so sick about the whole thing he yacked all over my shoes."

"Amanda."

"I was going to get DeCasper a water, but he got up and went into the kitchen. I went in too. I thought he was going to pull down a glass and fill it from the tap. Nope. He pulled down the gun instead and popped his own weasel. Didn't even say goodbye."

My hands were slick with sweat as I pulled out my phone.

"Probably didn't want to do it all again." Amanda puffed her cigar. "The questions. The arrest. The looks. It never ends. They'll be rocking up to his nursing home in forty years' time wanting to talk to him about every kid who goes missing from here to Brisbane."

"He must have been thinking about it already," I said. "He had the gun. He didn't even hesitate."

"Meh." Amanda blew a smoke ring and poked a finger through it.

I called emergency services. They put me on hold.

"How'd you know about the television set?" I asked, cupping the receiver.

"He said he spent a lot of time watching television." She shrugged. "Why say that? It clearly wasn't true. There was dust all over the remote control on the table beside the couch."

"There was dust all over everything," I said.

"Shouldn't have been, at least on the power button," she said. "The channel up and down and volume up and down buttons. And where's the digital converter? Plus, when I went over there and stood near the set the guy got ants in his pants. Dead giveaway. Oh, snap. See what I did there? Dead." She snorted to herself.

The operator came back on the line and I requested police and an ambulance. Amanda smoked her cigar. DeCasper's cigar.

"Did you put that towel at the edge of the kitchen?" I asked when the operator disconnected.

"You didn't see that carpet in there?" She turned and looked indignantly at me. "Are you blind? That's vintage shit, man. One hundred percent polyester short-shag with a relaxed twist, avocado green. Someone's going to cut that stuff into rugs and sell it to the hipsters for three hundred bucks a square meter."

There was a police car in the driveway. There shouldn't have been. I had only just disconnected the line to emergency services and walked along the side of the house with Amanda, a total of maybe three minutes. As we came into view of the two officers on the lawn, I felt something stir in Amanda, her stride stiffening.

The officers standing there were Joanna Fischer and her orange-haired goon. I was so surprised by their presence that I didn't even notice that Amanda's bike, which she'd parked at the top of the driveway, was lying on its side. She didn't gasp or cry out with horror. My partner simply walked to the bike, ignoring Fischer and her friend, and picked the machine up. A piece of steel and some shards of mirrored glass fell from the bike and clattered on the concrete. The side mirror was broken.

"What are you two doing here?" I asked Fischer. Her partner's name badge said *Smith*. He wouldn't meet my gaze.

"We got a call from dispatch," Fischer said, watching Amanda. "Suspected suicide. People just drop like flies around you, don't they, Amanda? You leave a trail of corpses everywhere you go."

"You didn't respond to a call from dispatch," I said. "You were three minutes away. We're two hours south of Cairns. You must have been following us."

Joanna Fischer shrugged, squinted at me as though seeing me for the first time. Her eyes had a frightening kind of blankness to them. Amanda's lack of emotion about the bike was also worrying me. It was as though only I had absorbed the gravity of the situation, Joanna's previous attack on my partner and her presence here, the machine broken without explanation, Smith's obvious guilt as he stood there like a dog with its tail between its legs.

"She pushed the bike over, didn't she?" I said to Smith. He played with the radio on his hip.

"The bike was on its side when we got here." Fischer smiled.

"I wasn't talking to you, Constable Fischer. I was talking to your offsider." My chest was prickling with rage.

"He's not going to tell you." Amanda gestured lazily at Smith. "His name's not even Smith."

Smith twitched. I tried to follow what that meant but the anger about Amanda's bike wouldn't leave me.

"I want to see the squad car's dash cam footage for the past five minutes. I believe a crime has occurred here. Vandalism of private property."

Fischer laughed, a sharp, birdlike sound. "You want *what*? Who the fuck do you think you are, Conkaffey? You're a citizen now. You can't go around giving orders to the police."

There was a pain behind my eyes, like a growing migraine, Kelly's words echoing out of Fischer's mouth. *You're not a cop anymore.* Amanda put a hand on my arm, the fingers lighter than they should have been, cold and calm.

"Get off the property, fuckheads." Fischer jutted her chin toward the roadside. "This is an official police crime scene. You're to wait at the roadside there until I call on you for a statement. Go on, git."

I stormed over to the roadside as the two officers went inside. Amanda wheeled her bike slowly, picking pieces of broken glass off the top of the fuel tank.

"You're not angry enough about this," I snarled at her. "That bitch knocked your fucking bike over."

"It's just a bike."

"It's not just a fucking bike!" I knew I was getting in her face, that she didn't deserve my tone or my furious breath fluttering the hair at her brow, but I couldn't help myself. "It's *your* bike. You're *my* partner. It's *our* bike."

"That doesn't make any sense."

"I know!" I growled. The pain behind my eyes was suddenly blinding. "I know it doesn't!"

Amanda watched me.

"Who is she?" I demanded. "I mean, what is her fucking problem? Chief Clark needs to get her off you. You can't have someone stalking you because of Pip's death. You didn't kill Sweeney, Amanda, and you didn't endanger her."

Amanda scratched her nose.

"I've got a bad feeling about this woman," I said. "She attacked you in front of the hotel, then she follows us here. You tell me if you run into her again."

"Ted, it's just The Life," Amanda said, looking off toward the highway south of us, where the sound of sirens was rising. I'd heard Amanda talk about The Life before: the inescapable adjustment to existence that comes with having been shamed in the public eye, with having been incarcerated, separated from the everyman and then thrust back alongside him, a fox among the hounds. Resigning oneself to The Life meant accepting that things would never be as they were before the downfall. It meant accepting, even anticipating, hatred from other human beings, perhaps forever. Amanda believed she would never escape her crime. She had killed, and because of what she had done, because of the reputation she had in Crimson Lake, everyone would blame her for Pip's death and for the peril that befell anyone who dared to be near her. She was a walking curse.

I hated to hear Amanda talk about The Life; always tried to change the subject or leave the conversation when she did. I didn't believe it was what either of us deserved.

It seemed to take forever to get home. Amanda and I sat like naughty children on the bonnet of my car while police and paramedics dealt with the crime scene. We were questioned by a pair of detectives from Zeerich, who were aware enough of our reputation to treat us with grumpy disdain. They berated Amanda about the towel she had placed in the kitchen, me about walking back into the crime scene after Amanda had told me what had happened. We submitted to photographs of our hands for defensive wounds, and I paced the roadside with my fingers crossed on both hands, silently praying that they wouldn't decide to bring us in for an official, recorded statement. The sun was low in the trees, and I was aware of the seconds ticking by that Val had to remain at my house with no idea when she would be relieved, and precious moments I could have spent with my child dripping slowly away.

I drove home like a madman, but still didn't catch

up to Amanda at any point. I looked for her at the roadside stops and petrol stations, but after zipping ahead of me on the turnoff to the highway she simply disappeared. I tried to play some Neil Diamond to calm my nerves, but almost as soon as I put the music on my phone rang, Sara Farrow's name appearing on the screen.

"I'm hearing some crazy stuff around here," she said. People were talking in the background, what sounded like a busy room. "We just did a press conference and I heard a couple of officers say there was a shooting down south?"

"A suicide," I said, wincing. "Amanda and I were questioning a suspect in Richie's disappearance, but there's nothing solid to suggest at this point that he's connected to our case."

"What do you mean, nothing 'solid'?" she asked. Sara Farrow was sharp, I thought. I'd had bosses across my time as a cop who would pick out singular words like that, hold them to your throat until you explained yourself. I told Sara about the boys' clothes in the television set.

"Can I get a look at the clothes?" she asked. "This is . . . I mean, why so many sets of clothes? Richie's not missing anything from his bag except the clothes he was wearing."

"I'll get you pictures of the clothes. Can you do me a favor?" I said. "If I send you a picture of Todd DeCasper, would you go back through all your photographs from the trip and see if you spot him anywhere?"

"No problem," she said. Again, I was struck by the

sharpness of her tone, the no-bullshit, work-to-be-done attitude of it. Maybe I had been wrong about Sara when I first met her. Maybe she wasn't cold, but a woman running hot, an engine constantly turning over on her mission to find her son. She had become the investigator, setting emotion aside, doing what she could to contribute and not worrying about what it looked like to those around her.

"I'm so glad you're here to give me updates on what the police are doing, Ted," she said. "People are very careful, the way they talk to me. It's like they think they'll say something and bring me crashing down. I need a man on the ground."

"You've got it," I said.

"It's going to storm again tonight," she said. I glanced in my rearview mirror at her words, and saw, almost on cue, a finger of lightning touching down on the black landscape. There was more ahead of me, flickers of sheet lightning above the mountains. I thought of a boy lost in the rain, of a body lying in the wet and decay of the marshlands, raindrops sliding down lifeless feet. I thought Sara was about to sign off with me, but instead she took a long breath that made the phone crackle.

"Look. There's something I need to tell you," she said. "I hit Richie."

"What?" I glanced at the phone, as though I could see Sara through it as the machine relayed the call. "When?"

I scrambled for my phone in the passenger seat, trying to keep my eyes on the road, hitting the record app while Sara gathered herself for her confession.

"When he was very small," she said. "We were having those monthly visits from child services, the ones they put in place after our first child died. Henry and I were fighting. We weren't getting any sleep. We had to keep the house immaculate because they showed up unannounced. Every time I turned around, Richie was bumping into things, leaving bruises on himself, or totally trashing things. He got into the kitchen and spread flour everywhere while I took a phone call one day. I had my back turned for two minutes. Imagine if they'd turned up then?"

"Was there ever a report made?" I asked.

"No," she said. "But I imagine Henry will tell you about it."

"We've spoken to Henry. He didn't say anything."

"When the news first came out, I asked him not to tell them about the time I smacked Richie, or about Anya."

"Why did you do that?"

"Because I was trying to protect myself, okay?" she said, her words strained with exhaustion. "This is why I need you. I need you to help me pick the right moment to bring this to the police. Yes, okay, I'm a bad person. In the hours after my kid went missing, I've thought about protecting myself a few times. But I bet you wish you had, after you were accused. Right?"

We were quiet for a while. I tapped the steering wheel.

"How hard did you hit him?"

"Does it really matter?" She gave a sad laugh, and a sniff, like she was crying. "Not hard. There was a little red welt under his eye. I just snapped. You're a parent. You must get it."

I thought about Lillian standing at the roadside, watching her mother and Jett drive away into the distance, that growly, squealy, breathless racket she had made. I hadn't felt rage at the sound of Lillian's crying in that moment, but I'd felt a deep, primal urgency to stop the noise at all costs, a tightness in my arms and chest like the muscles wanted to work of their own accord.

I told Sara Farrow I couldn't talk, that I'd hit traffic and needed to concentrate, but in truth as I hung up the road ahead of me was empty. I floored it toward home.

As I walked up the driveway, a shopping bag in each hand, two small silhouettes appeared in the gold-lit hall behind the screen door. I hadn't realized how heavy and stiff my face was until I felt the smile spread widely across it.

"It's Daddy!" Lillian bashed the screen door with both hands, Celine spinning in circles beside her, barking. "Daddy's home! Daddy's home! Daddy's home!"

I had to nudge the two of them away from the door to get inside. I dropped the bags and grabbed my child, crushing her against my chest. She smelled of dirt and candies.

"That's it!" I roared. "You're mine now. I've got you. I'm going to make you stay here with me and greet me at the door with kisses and hugs every day for the rest of my life."

"Oh no!" she squealed as I covered her neck and face with kisses. "Oh no! Oh no, Daddy, no!"

I put her down and she ran away, a child's furious, desperate love and sudden, shocking abandonment in favor of other entertainments. Val was in the kitchen picking up toys discarded on the floor, gathering them into a pile in her arms.

Lillian announced my entrance. "Nanna, Daddy's here!"

"Nanna?" I snorted.

"Old, female." She shrugged. "I guess that equals 'Nanna.' You find that boy today?"

"No." I put the bags on the counter, took the toys from her and hurled them indiscriminately into Lillian's room. "Amanda and I threw in together and got you a little gift for the morgue table."

In oblique terms I told her about DeCasper's demise while I crouched and patted Celine, Lillian running up and down the hall, doing excited laps of the house. Through the screen door to the backyard I could see the geese crossing the lawn in a loose formation, pecking and tugging at the grass, their bodies making long shadows on the grass in the light of the porch. I plugged my phone into a speaker on the window and put on some tunes. There was a message from Kelly on the screen.

I'm sorry. I lied. I did forget to tell you about the strawberries, and I tried to blame it on you. I'm a bad mother.

You're not a bad mother, I texted. *We'll work this all out. It's just going to take time.*

Val was putting away dishes that sat on the countertop. Lillian kept coming to me, desperate for me to see and approve of a seemingly endless collection of rocks, sticks, feathers, and other things she had collected from the garden that day. I was tired, worried about Richie Farrow, and couldn't offer much enthusiasm for her treasures. *Bad father*, I thought. I'd only had my child in my life mere hours, and I could barely scrape together intrigued sounds and expressions for the pitiful scraps of garden material Lillian had been forced to entertain herself with throughout the day. Val was on call, and preferred to stick around the house with the child in case she was needed suddenly at the morgue. Lillian couldn't have been having a good first visit with her father. I wasn't there physically, and when I was I wasn't there mentally.

I thought about Sara Farrow and the young Richie trashing her kitchen after a long, awful day. Had she been tired, mentally checked out, tense with guilt like I was, when she struck the child? Even as I thought about her, Lillian started begging Val for a chocolate from the fridge and I winced at the sharp whine in her voice.

Like a million parents before me, I dragged Lillian toward me, feeling somehow that she might have sensed my dark thoughts.

"You're a good kid," I told her, kissing her soft brow.

"No, no, no," she laughed, pushing me away.

The Clattering Clam had been officially closed since Richie Farrow went missing, but unofficially it was open to approved investigative staff. Amanda hadn't yet walked through the restaurant, but she found it amusingly gaudy. The cartoon clam of the restaurant's namesake was everywhere: happily directing patrons to wait to be seated by a chipped, battered waiter's station in the entryway, announcing the specials on a board above the bar, its buggy eyes brimming with glee. Throughout the sprawling room filled with empty tables and stacked chairs, the ceiling and pillars had been adorned with nautical artifacts—blue and green glass buoys strung with twisting white rope, and fishing nets hung with colorful plastic fish. Amanda took a seat at the polished mahogany bar and fingered a napkin holder shaped like a walrus while she waited for someone to notice her.

The potential someones in the restaurant to notice

her were only two. Chief Clark sat on a stool three down from hers, a glass of some neat yellow liquid at his fingertips, papers spread across the bar two meters either side of him. There was a young female bartender texting near the windows. Amanda got her attention and ordered a Scotch, watching a wriggling vein pulse in Clark's temple.

He turned to Amanda, and his face darkened. She watched as he stood and started gathering his papers.

"You know who walks off in a melodramatic huff every time they run into someone they don't like?" she asked.

Clark was stuffing papers into folders. "Who?" he grunted.

"Teenage girls." Amanda sipped her drink. "Are you a teenage girl, Clarky?"

Chief Clark looked at himself in the mirror behind the bar, sighed again, and slipped back onto his stool. He emptied his drink and pointed to it to request another. Amanda dared to move one stool closer, strumming her fingers on her glass casually, like someone approaching a prospective love interest, not wanting to signal her intentions too obviously.

"I've been thinking," Amanda said.

"Here we go." Clark rolled his eyes.

"I have a theory that you really do like me," she said. "Secretly."

Clark smoothed back his blond flattop, almost stroking himself with consolation.

"I mean, what's not to like?" Amanda continued. "I'm a crack investigator responsible for putting two of your jurisdiction's major cases back in black, both of which had international interest. I work privately, so my invaluable assistance on those cases didn't even have to come out of your very tight budget, and best of all, I complement my services with a cheerful attitude and world-class comic relief."

"I don't like you," Clark said. "I don't like your 'crack' investigative style, either. One of my officers was killed on your last case. You're reckless, annoying, and obtuse."

"Obtuse?" Amanda laughed. "A footloose obtuse goose, ready to produce . . . ready to deduce!"

"That's putting it very kindly."

"You want to like me, Clark," Amanda persisted. "But you need a reason for Pip's death. Someone to blame. Pip Sweeney was your protégé. You took a risk giving her a promotion she maybe wasn't ready for, and you felt proud when she started proving herself. Maybe you felt a sense of fatherly pride. But then, suddenly, she's gone. She walks into the middle of a fray without backup. Why? No reason. She knew to call for backup. She knew what she was doing was dangerous. Still, she's gone. You can't blame her. You can't blame the victim."

Amanda waited for a response from Clark. There was none.

"I think you'd like to believe that I'm death herself," Amanda said. "Someone told me today that I leave a trail of corpses everywhere I go. It's not a bad idea. If I'm death, or a trouble magnet, or whatever you want to call me, then you just stay away from me and it won't happen again. The people you love will be safe. Hate me from afar. It's easy. Everyone else does it."

Amanda leaned over, looking at the side of the man's head.

"I'm not death, Clarky," she said. "I'm just a super-intelligent ex-con who likes to solve mysteries."

"Are you finished?" Clark asked, looking at her out of the corner of his eye. The vein in his head had sunk back into place and stopped throbbing. "Because I'm trying to take the edge off here, and listening to you is like having razor blades pushed into my ear canals."

"Even if you didn't suffer an aching, unrequited desire to like me, you need me," Amanda continued. "You need my unparalleled powers of crime solving."

"You sound like you think you're Batman or something."

"Well, I have just as much mystique, but my exceptional powers of observation are better than his," Amanda said. "You can have all the expensive tech in the world but that doesn't make you a genius. You've gotta be born with that shit."

"Your exceptional powers of observation?" Clark drew a long breath and let it out slow.

"Yeah." Amanda smiled. "Like, uh . . ."

She looked around her, at the bartender and the people she could see through the doors to the street. As she was watching, Detective Ng and another officer walked in and took a booth by the windows.

"Like I bet you didn't spot that Detective Ng is on the take," Amanda said.

"*What?*" Clark snapped.

"Yeah, look." Amanda slid closer to the chief, jutting her chin at the two officers by the window.

"Detective Ng over there, he heads up your drug investigations, right?"

"And?" Clark sighed.

"The toe of his left shoe is glued," Amanda said. "Look closely. You can see the brown glue stains. Two-part epoxy. Tough stuff."

"So what?"

"So look at the watch."

"What about it?" Clark squinted. Ng felt himself being studied, and Amanda and Clark turned on their chairs to face the bar.

"That's a TAG Heuer Carrera Calibre watch in gray phantom titanium," Amanda said. "He's got it with the black titanium carbide-coated folding safety clasp."

Clark glanced at his own plastic sports watch, shrugged angrily. "Again, so what?"

"What's a guy who glues his shoes doing with an eight-thousand-dollar watch? Sounds like someone without a lot of money who splashed out suddenly for something obscenely expensive, something so expensive it's not in keeping with the rest of his life. Sudden big purchases come from sudden big money."

"It could be a fake." Clark tugged his shirt uncomfortably down from his throat. "It could be any kind of watch. What do you know? You're not a jeweler."

"No, but I'm a private investigator," Amanda said. "A good part of my job is spent trying to track down priceless heirlooms and obscenely expensive jewelry ripped off from rich houses in Holloways Beach that the robbery squad is too busy to chase up. I can spot a Tiffany engagement ring from a mile away. That watch stands out like dog's balls."

Clark wrung his fingers, shrugged. "It could be a gift. He could have got a loan."

"All right, well, you go check the evidence room records and tell me whether he got a loan or not." Amanda sniffed, nonchalant.

"You're a good investigator," Clark said. "I never said you weren't."

"So why don't you just give me one more chance?" Amanda said. "That's easy enough, isn't it? People who give second chances are good people. Sure, this is maybe more like my one hundred and twelfth chance. But it'll be my last one. What do you think?"

Clark said nothing. Amanda slapped the bar top.

"It's settled then," she said. "Now, while we're basking in the warm, loving glow of our newly formed truce: I'm having a problem with one of your officers. We need to talk about it."

I'm walking through Cairns at night. The streets are lit but impossibly empty, bars on the main street flashing soundless football games across deserted tables, half-drunk beers going stale in the wind. It's so hot that condensation is gathering on the glass of the traffic lights, directing no one. As I reach the front steps of the White Caps Hotel, the automatic doors open and Richie Farrow walks out.

He looks at me, turns, and walks toward the water. I follow him across the street, through the little water park where the fountains are spraying the tiles and the air is strangely empty of children's squeals. He keeps looking over his shoulder at me, smiling that overexcited, hyperactive smile I'd seen in the video his father took of the boy leaping from couch to couch. The face is wrong. Maniacal, in contrast with his slow-moving limbs. There's lightning out over the ocean. I know that Richie's heading for the dark horizon slicing through the bone-yellow sky beneath the clouds, and I want to tell him to stop. That people are looking for him. He waits for me to catch up, and puts a hand on my arm.

The real sensation of a hand on my arm dragged me out of the nightmare, and I sat up with a gasp. Lillian was shocked by the noise and stepped back, a tiny silhouette against the boarded-up windows. There was no telling what time it was. The air smelled of rain, and as I came into full consciousness I heard it hammering on the roof like gravel being poured on the tin.

"Daddy." She gave a hitching sob. "I'm scared."

Thunder cracked outside, giving the little shadow in the night another jolt. She had come all the way from her bedroom to mine, through the pitch-black house in her bare feet, the crashing outside punctuating the sheets of rain and the barking of the frogs. I swept back the sheet and patted the mattress beside me.

"Climb up here, little mouse," I told her.

Her weight wasn't enough to dent the mattress. She had to put a foot onto the frame and haul herself up with both hands. I held her to me and felt her trembling as blue lightning stuttered through the cracks around the boarded-up windows, her impossibly soft curls brushing against my lips.

"Don't you know I'd never let anything hurt you?" I asked. She didn't answer, just lay against the pillow by my side as the sobs receded. I thought how selfish it was that I felt so good having her with me. My tiny child needing me, and me being there, for once.

We both lifted our heads at the sound of scratching. I heard the screen door slap closed, Celine having sensed somehow that a barrier had been crossed. Her nails trip-trapping on the wooden floors, and then a pause before her weight landing on the end of the mattress made the bedframe shake.

"Uh-oh," I told Lillian. "Celine's here."

"Uh-oh," she whispered.

Celine did a couple of exploratory circles, then crashed into a heap, giving the bed another shake. Lillian and I put our heads down.

I listened to my child's sniffles as they turned to even, sleeping breaths, trying to remember a time I'd been so content.

Midnight. Amanda curled on the couch before the television set on the ground floor of her office-apartment, three cats making a warm pile on top of her bare feet, another wedged into the gap between her back and the couch. It always amazed Amanda how physically tiring a case could be. Some cases weighed so heavily on her brain she felt almost as though her hair follicles were bruised, her eyes feeling like they were protruding from her skull. It seemed a million miles, the distance from the couch to the stairs, the stairs to her bed. The light flickered against her closed eyelids.

A thump at the front door.

The cats did nothing, of course. But Amanda rose and stared at the closed door, waiting for the thump to come again as it had the evening before. There was thunder in the distance. She got up and walked to the door, taking the enormous Smith & Wesson Model 29 she kept on a hook behind the hatstand as she reached for the doorknob.

Another thump. Despite herself, Amanda squealed in fright, which really annoyed her, because she was not a squealer at the best of times. She growled and flung open the door on the empty night.

No one.

Across the empty street, lightning flickered between the buildings, illuminating a dark shape. Amanda walked there, her tough bare feet immune to the rocky asphalt at the edges of the road.

"Fischer, you arsehole," she called as she approached. "Is that you?"

The shape was only a stack of boxes draped with a burlap sack. Amanda tapped her gun against her side. She turned back toward her house in time to see the front door slam closed. As she watched, the light in the building clicked off.

Amanda walked back across the street, raising the gun as she went and firing through the front door.

The shot blasted a hole in the wood the size of an apple. Amanda looked through it, seeing only blackness, hearing only the mewling of frightened cats. She opened the door and flicked on the lights.

No one.

Amanda went to the back door of the house, a trail of curious felines following, the more cautious of her brood having scattered and crawled under various bits of furniture. Amanda found the back door open. She looked out into the rain, only noticing the photograph pinned to the inside of the door as she tried to pull it closed.

It was a picture of Pip Sweeney. Both her eyes had been poked through with a pin.

He watched the press conference twice. The first time it came on he was so restless, so pained, that he barely heard the words of the mother and father as they sat at the long conference room table. He wandered his little caravan, going to the tiny bedroom and standing over the bed, wanting to collapse into it, the voices of the parents reaching him in the dark but hardly breaking through his raging thoughts.

All the channels were punctuated by reports about the boy. His face flashed on the screen over and over, golden-skinned and stretched taut with a nervous smile.

For so long, the man with the keys had asked the world for nothing. He'd met a lot of people in his travels who expected things, who believed the world owed them something. He'd camped on corners in the Sydney CBD with men twice his age, sleeping in piles of blankets with warm, mixed-breed dogs, listening while his temporary friends talked of the government school teachers who hadn't understood them, the child services officers who had ignored their pleas, the Centrelink workers who had cut off their payments and demanded answers they couldn't give on forms they couldn't read. The man with the keys hoped for food and warmth, but didn't spit and swear at the businessmen and women who went by without filling his cup with change, and didn't throw bottles at the police officers who moved him on. He didn't call his father and ask for money, hadn't had the man's number in years.

Living the rough life had been a kind of aching freedom for him. The first time he'd taken off, he'd been standing outside the school gates with a friend. Instead of going in, they'd walked off. Soon he was nicking off for another day of wandering, less than a week after the first time. Over the years he would nick off from jobs, from apartments when the rent got too much to pay. He walked out of a kitchen once where he'd been cooking eggs and bacon for elderly couples in a huge, apricot-painted breakfast room. He heard the eggs popping and sizzling on the grill as he closed the door behind himself and bolted.

He'd fled from loving relationships, criminal partnerships, financial agreements. Once he gathered together ten thousand dollars from a drug-running job and rented an apartment. Filled it with furniture. Bought a DVD player, brand new, and a big flat-screen set. He was gone a week later with nothing but a backpack.

Cairns had been different. It wasn't so much that

he'd built his nest here. The first twig had been added when a new mate doing a deal for some coke in the bush behind the bus station had asked him if he wouldn't mind staying in his caravan for a couple of weeks, keeping an eye on the place. The same mate had got him a cheap van across the park, view of the water and everything. The people in the caravan park had given him things—twigs for his nest in the form of an old television set and the occasional container of leftovers from a big cook-up. Before he knew it, the nest was sizable, with a strong base to it, the sides climbing upwards on their own. Someone had mentioned a maintenance job going at the local flashy hotel—they knew he was good with his hands because they'd seen him pottering around his caravan, putting together pot plant stands and patching the broken window on the bathroom.

He'd never wanted a nest. But now he had one. And then a little boy had come along out of nowhere, threatening to blow all his lovingly placed twigs right out of the tree. The man reached out to the coffee table before his recliner, the boy's parents still on the screen. He picked up the Iron Man action figure and worked its stiff plastic arms.

Amanda woke up proud of herself.

All her life she'd followed her instincts when trouble showed its face in her little world. Sometimes that was exactly what was needed, and sometimes it made things worse. In school, it had often been the latter. One of her earliest memories was of a small boy flicking paint at her off the end of a heavy brush at the crafts tables, her hair and neck and dress becoming speckled with red like a cartoon girl with chicken pox. She'd let the teacher wipe her clean while she decided what to do about the boy who'd attacked her, and then she'd gone over to him in the yard and grabbed him from behind and shoved him to the ground. She'd pulled down her pants, sat on him, and peed. Though Amanda remembered being very satisfied with her response, it had apparently been the wrong one. The boy had run into the staff room, his clothes soaked, screaming like he'd been bitten. Amanda had been sent home.

Amanda rolled out of her bed with a smile that morning, knowing that her response to Joanna Fischer was the right one.

She'd approached Chief Clark, Fischer's superior officer, and plainly and calmly explained that she was being targeted. She hadn't reacted violently when she'd discovered her bike tipped over, though every cell in her body had been telling her to pluck Fischer's eyes out with her bare hands. Clark had not spoken to Fischer right away—last night's fun and games proved that. And, sure, perhaps she shouldn't have fired on Fischer through her door. That wasn't good. She'd lost her temper. She didn't like being startled and made to squeal. But she hadn't hit Joanna, so Amanda decided to ignore that little slipup.

Her restraint was something to be commended.

Amanda would get the bike fixed, avoid Fischer as much as she could, and let Clark handle it. A totally normal-person response. The man had seemed willing to assist, after all—though it was possible he'd been so agreeable because he just wanted Amanda to go away.

She stretched, and the cats that slept on her bed rose and stretched too, spreading their paws on the Batman coverlet and yawning. She led a parade of four of them down the stairs to the office and kitchen, unplugging her phone from the little side table on the way. There were sixty-one missed calls from a private number. Fischer. Amanda rolled her eyes.

As she went into the kitchen to make her coffee, her remaining seven cats rose up from their various sleeping spots all over the lower floor, the entire collection assembling for breakfast at her bare feet. She watched them, meowing and rubbing against her calves, while the kettle boiled, Six looking like she wanted to leap up onto the counter as she usually did, her eyes fixed on the steam rising over the sink.

A gentle knocking at the door shattered Amanda's morning reverie. Through the bullet hole in the wood Amanda could see a woman looking unsettled, trying to discern what had caused the hole. Amanda led her parade of felines there and pulled it open, her black silk negligee, printed with gold Batman symbols, fluttering in the warm morning breeze.

The visitor was a sour-faced, elderly woman in gray trousers and a cotton top. She was holding a clipboard, a pen poised over the information there as the door swung open.

"Amanda Pharrell?" she asked, eyeing Amanda's negligee and bare legs.

"Good guess," Amanda said. "What's the scoop, Professor McGonagall?"

"I'm from Cairns Regional Council," the woman said. "The animal protection department."

I was expecting Amanda when the knock at the door came. Lillian was outside, sitting among the geese, picking pieces of grass and feeding them by hand while one of the geese tore impotently at the hem of her skirt. I'd slept well, despite waking once to find her lying diagonally across the bed with her feet under my chin, and once to find Celine nestled between us, snoring deeply. The little family I'd started when I fled to Cairns was growing, and though there was a low alarm sounding in the back of my mind that I could lose everything again at any time, I felt happy. I thought about the previous evening as I did the dishes, Val sitting barefoot on the porch step, Lillian dancing in the sunset.

Through the screen door, I spied the police cruiser over the red-haired officer's shoulder before I really took notice of him. Smith looked at the car guiltily, fiddling with the front of his tactical belt as I walked down the hall.

"You've got twenty seconds to get off my property," I said.

"It's just me," he said. "I'm alone."

"I don't care if you're alone or you've got the Queen of England and her royal guard waiting for a private meeting with me. I'm not here. Go away."

"It's about Amanda," he said. He straightened to his full height as I reached the entryway, glancing warily at my hand resting on the wooden door as though he expected the door to be slammed in his face. He was silent while I decided what I was going to do, his front teeth resting on his bottom lip like they couldn't all fit in his mouth at the same time, a patient rabbit waiting to be eaten or set free.

I opened the screen door and showed him in, sat at my kitchen table, and didn't invite him to join me. He took his cap off, and I saw for the first time that his head was shaved almost to the white scalp on the sides, only a fine dusting of orange hair remaining. On the top of his head a cap of curls remained, thick ringlets as round as my finger. I tried not to stare.

"Amanda said your name isn't Smith." I looked at his name badge. "What was she on about?"

"Oh." He looked at the badge himself, breathed in and out heavily. "It's a bit of a long story." His tone was flat, unrattled.

"I've got time," I assured him.

"My name is Supevich," he said. "Lawrence Supevich. On my first day at my previous station in Redlynch, our captain struggled over the pronunciation of the name and it came out in front of the entire station staff as Superfish."

I quickly stifled a smile, bit my tongue.

"The name Superfish was quite amusing to my colleagues," Superfish said. "Very amusing, in fact. I was new to the station, and not long out of the academy. As I'm sure you're aware, it's traditional to pull pranks and make fun of the new guy. The youngest crew member. The pranks were fish-themed. The other officers would fill my locker or my desk drawer with fish."

I covered my mouth with my hand but a couple of laughs escaped. I cleared my throat, trying to match Superfish's seriousness.

"There is a kind of connection between fish and crime," Superfish mused. "People say, *There's something fishy about this. Something smells fishy. Red herrings.* You know. It makes for good comedy."

"I see," I managed.

"I don't mind a prank or two but my partner was

older than me, a sergeant at the station. He would sometimes find his desk drawers full of fish and it became very wearing for him."

"I, uh." I cleared my throat again. "I can imagine."

"So when I transferred to Holloways Beach my captain and I agreed that Smith would be easier to take as a professional name."

"I see," I said. "Supevich—what is that? Russian? I didn't know there were ginger Russians."

"I have a complicated ethnic heritage," Superfish said.

"Okay." I tried to get my mind firmly off the fish in the desk drawers before I totally lost it. "So tell me what you want."

"I think Amanda is in danger," he said. "Real, physical danger from my partner, Joanna."

"You mean Joanna has made threats?" I asked.

"Not exactly." Superfish shifted uncomfortably. "It's just that I know how close Joanna was with Pip Sweeney. They were partners before Joanna and I were assigned together. I would see them at the station talking and whispering. They went everywhere together. There were rumors around the station that they were in a romantic relationship."

I remembered that Amanda had allegedly told a crowd of officers at the site of Sweeney's death that she was a "good kisser."

"Did those rumors hold any water?"

"I don't think so," Superfish said. "I don't believe they ever actually got together. Joanna talks too fantastically about their relationship for it to be true."

"What do you mean?" I asked.

"It's like the confrontation on the hotel steps," Superfish said. "The story of finding Pip dying. The things she said. Her last breath. It was too perfect to be true. Joanna talks endlessly about Pip. She admired her neatness, her thoroughness, her triumphs on the job. I sit in the patrol car with her sometimes for hours listening to tales about Pip leaping over fences, chasing down criminals. Following incredible hunches and solving cases on instinct alone. She sounds almost—"

"Like a superhero."

Superfish nodded. "I think Joanna admired Pip greatly. Too much, in fact. And I think, whatever their relationship was, Joanna has overestimated that, too."

I knew from my mother's death when I was a teenager that grief could put a magnifying glass over memories. Sometimes I thought of her, and I knew that what I was seeing was too intense, too perfect to be real. She had become an angel for me. Endlessly giving, endlessly patient and beautiful. Her image was at once brought into super focus and distorted.

"As I see it," Superfish continued, "we have two big problems. Joanna has a casual relationship with the truth. And she loved Pip very much, whether they were in a relationship or not. I think she's grieving and angry, and her proclivity for fantasy is making Amanda into . . ." He shrugged.

"Into what?"

"Into someone who needs to be punished," Superfish said. "By the only person who loved Pip enough to do it."

I sat at the kitchen table, thinking about Superfish's

words as they slowed to a thoughtful stop. He'd noticed Lillian approaching the house from the yard, and inevitably she rushed up the porch and burst through the screen door, sliding to a comical stop when she caught sight of Superfish.

"Oh!" she gasped, pointing at his face like an accuser in court. "The police!"

"That's right." He smiled, saluting. "At your service."

Lillian giggled and crawled up into my lap, blushing and hiding her face in my chest. I squeezed her and joggled her on my legs while I appreciated a man I now knew I had deeply misunderstood. I gestured to the chair opposite me, and Superfish came out of the corner of the kitchen and took it, putting his cap on the tabletop before me.

"What do you think she's going to do?" I asked him. "Why do you think Amanda is in danger?"

"Joanna has talked a lot about Amanda since Pip's death," Superfish said. "She has become obsessive. The talking has slowly become more and more hateful, and in the past couple of weeks Joanna has driven us past Amanda's house just to look. I discovered her at work looking up Amanda's phone number, googling her, reading news articles and documents from her murder trial. Once we followed Amanda as she rode her bicycle, and I had to quite sternly insist that Joanna stop. Then came the confrontation at the hotel. That really surprised me. And then she knocked Amanda's motorbike over."

"Yes," I said, my jaw feeling tight. "And you did nothing."

"I was shocked," he said. "It just happened. It was the first physical aggression I had seen."

"You could have said you were appalled on either occasion."

"Sometimes it takes me a while to decide what I am going to say." Superfish sighed. "I am not good in a verbal fight, when people are speaking very quickly. I don't have a great deal of . . . confidence, I suppose. My quiet nature almost excluded me from entry into the force."

"Huh," I said, looking him over. Lillian slid off my lap and ran away.

"I was always taught that the fool speaks and the wise man listens," Superfish said.

"It's a useful way of thinking," I agreed.

"I was appalled on both occasions, though. I hope you know that."

I nodded. Lillian came out of her bedroom in her tutu and a glittery top.

"Whaddaya think?" She put her hands out to Superfish, palms up.

"Oh wow." He clapped his hand loudly to his forehead. "That's just about the most beautiful outfit I've ever seen in my life."

Lillian looked to me to see if I'd heard, snickered devilishly, and ran back to her room. Superfish's face had softened when my daughter presented herself to him, and now it hardened again, like a switch had been flipped.

"I don't dislike Joanna." Superfish fiddled with the strap of his police-issue ball cap. "I came to be her partner after Pip, and I've been on the force for less time. Joanna showed me the ropes. But I cannot let her fixation with Amanda go on any longer."

"What does Joanna want from Amanda exactly?" I asked. "Does she just want to harass her until she cracks and does something violent? Is she hoping she'll lose her license, or does she want to drive her out of town?"

"To be honest, Mr. Conkaffey," Superfish said, "I hope those things are all she wants."

Amanda arrived right after Superfish left. I was standing in the yard holding a hose on the geese, who stood bristling and preening under the cold spray, their big wings beating the water up against their softly feathered sides.

Lillian came running to my side.

"A fairy!" she cried, panting and pointing. I turned and saw Amanda walking toward me in black sequined shorts and a torn cotton singlet that left her flat midriff exposed. There was a saxophone near her navel blowing purple music notes.

"Wow, Lill," I said. "You're having visits from all sorts of characters today."

"Have you had that sprog's eyes checked?" Amanda said by way of greeting. "She called me a fairy."

"I can see it." I appreciated my partner. Her hair, which she never brushed or styled, stuck up off the top of her head in a spiky wave.

"You're nuts," she said. "The two of you. Fairies sprinkle glitter and float around in pink bubbles farting wishes out their arses. I've fought off crocodiles and rapists with my bare hands."

"In other news," I said, "I found out Smith's real name. How did you know it wasn't Smith? Have you heard his story?" I could already feel a grin creeping into the corners of my mouth.

"I haven't heard any story," Amanda said. "I saw his signature in the crime scene logbook at the hotel. Too long to be Smith. What is it really?"

I told her and she just about fell on the ground laughing, hugging herself and moaning with hilarity. Lillian squealed with delight, watching on, wanting to be part of the joke.

"Oh, Superfish," Amanda cried. "That is literally the best name I have ever heard. Why do I have to have such a boring name?"

"I feel bad," I said. "We shouldn't make fun."

"I'm not making fun." Amanda wiped tears from her eyes. "I'm dead jealous."

Lillian was crouching by Amanda's leg, trying to get a better look at the flowers on her calf. She reached out and touched the smooth, colorful skin with her little finger and Amanda jumped like she'd been stung.

"Get it away from me, Ted," Amanda warned.

"Look, Lill." I picked up my daughter and showed her the tattoos on Amanda's neck and shoulders. "A kitty. A fire engine. Treasure chest. What else can you see?"

"I'm not a picture book." Amanda slapped at me. "Take your disease-spewing human larva out of my face. I hate being sick. If she makes me sick I'll kill you."

"I can't believe this." I let Lillian run away to play with Celine. "You don't like kids? You're so child-spirited yourself. I would have thought you'd be right at home among them."

"Nope." Amanda brushed off her shoulders like Lillian's presence had somehow covered her in dust. "They're stupid. They're needy. They have zero immune systems. They go around everywhere spreading filth and mucus. I haven't been sick in six years. I'm probably already infected. Oh, and on top of being festering virus-bags, they also have strange fleshy little hands that are always cold and damp. Look at those hands. Urgh."

"What's got into you this morning?"

She was noticeably twitching. Amanda's twitch is something I've become accustomed to, something I rarely notice. But when she's agitated the gentle ticking in the muscles of her neck and shoulders and jaw becomes exaggerated. I heard her back teeth click together as her jaw snapped unexpectedly shut.

"The council took nine of my cats this morning," she said.

"What?!"

"Someone reported me," she said, watching a boat carve up the water. "In Far North Queensland, you're allowed to have two cats. Any more and you've got to apply for a cattery license."

"So they just came and took them? Can you get them back?"

"The license can take months to come through, so if you breach the rules they confiscate the offending animals and put them up for adoption," she said. "If you can get the license before they get adopted, you can have them back. But they won't hold them especially for you. They're cracking down on excess animals after that woman died in Kuranda with two hundred cats in her house, and they ate her face."

"This is bullshit!"

"I kept your cat-wife, Six. And I kept Eight. Eight's my mate. He's great, first-rate." I watched my partner, her halfhearted rhyme fizzling under the weight of her thoughts. My anger softened into sadness.

"Amanda, I—"

"They're just cats," she said. "Don't get your ball sack in a twist."

"This is Joanna Fischer. She's done this."

"It's handled."

"What do you mean 'it's handled'?" I asked.

"I mean, it's being handled."

I felt the breath leave me, a collapsing of my chest, like a weight had fallen on me. My fists were balled so tightly the knuckles cracked.

"Amanda," I said. "Don't do anything stupid."

She shrugged. "I tried to handle it the normal-person way. I spoke to Clark. But that was before. Things have changed now. Those are my cats."

"But you just said 'They're just cats.'"

"Yes," she said. "*My* cats."

"What have you done?" I asked. "Did you speak to the bikies?"

She didn't answer.

"I'm warning you," I said. "I know guys like these from my time on the squad. They love a revenge mission. If you turn them loose on a cop you'll start a war."

"I tried," she said again, looking at my eyes. Her tone was casual, but there was nothing casual about her glance. The wheels were turning inside her head, and dark things were on the horizon of her mind. I knew that look. My body felt heavy with dread.

Lillian waved to Amanda as she walked back up the yard toward the driveway.

"Bye-bye, fairy!" the child called.

Amanda waved. "Smell you later, sproglet."

There was a journalist in the parking lot of the White Caps Hotel. I didn't notice him until I parked my car beside Amanda's motorcycle and got out. He must have been hiding in the shadows by the dumpsters. I jumped as he put a hand on my shoulder.

"Ted Conkaffey!" he said. "I thought that was you."

I turned and was blinded by a camera flash. The petite man with side-parted blond hair grinned as he checked out the picture on his phone screen.

"I do not give you permission to use that picture," I said.

"Hasn't stopped me before, has it?" he said.

"What's your name, mate? I want to get it right for my lawyer."

"Parrett." He smiled. "With two *R*s, an *E* and two *T*s. Stan."

"How did you get in here? This building is a crime scene."

"Same way you did, through security on the boom gate. All right, no, I tell a lie—I climbed the retaining wall to the second floor," he said.

"So we'll have CCTV of you entering an active crime scene without permission," I said. "Perhaps I'll just go grab that tape now then, shall I? See if the chief wants to press charges?"

"Go ahead," Parrett said. "It's nothing I haven't beaten in court before. Weird world we're living in, huh? People like me have to climb through windows, people like you walk around freely wherever they want."

He held his phone up to my face, the microphone near my mouth.

"So what are you doing here? Are you part of the investigation now? Is it true you were questioned on the day Richie disappeared? Are you a person of interest?"

I tried to walk toward the elevators, but he blocked me.

"I have no comment, moron," I said.

"How's life? How's the lawsuit going?"

I faked a step to the left and slipped past him on the right, hitting the elevator button a dozen times in rapid succession.

"What are the leads on Richie Farrow?" he asked, walking to my side. "Are the police concerned about the mother's extramarital affair?"

"Huh?" I turned, sized him up. "What affair?"

"Oh, you don't know?" He grinned proudly. "Maybe it's only me with my finger on the pulse."

"Sara Farrow is having an affair?" I asked. "Who told you that?"

"Let's go get a coffee." He stepped back. "You like a whiskey, don't you? Come have a drink with me. We'll share tips."

The elevator opened and I got in, rapidly punching the "Close Door" button.

Chief Clark was standing by the reception desk when I exited the elevator, flipping through the pages of a thick manila folder. He handed me the new run sheet wordlessly and I stood there reading it, neither of us seeming to have much energy for conversation. The foyer was still filled with cops using the building as a base camp, Amanda regaling a group of skeptical officers by the conference-room doors with a tale that seemed to require plenty of hand gestures and expressions of horror.

"Has your team heard anything about Sara Farrow carrying on an affair?" I asked.

"No." He looked up at me. "Where'd you pick that up?"

I explained my encounter with the journalist. He sighed at the papers in his hands.

"How is it an affair? She's separated," he said.

"Maybe it comes from earlier. Maybe it's been going on a while."

"Just a journalist on a fishing trip, if you ask me," he said. "We've been through Sara's phone records. No sign of any of that."

"Mmm."

"We've just hit ten thousand tips on the information hotline," Clark said, rubbing his stubbled jaw. "We're getting a call every seven minutes, on average. The usual stuff. Sightings. Theories. Clairvoyant bullshit. A few confessions and ransom demands. One caller claiming he is Richie and he's run away to Alice Springs."

"Have you slept at all?" I asked.

"Of course not," he said. "I mightn't have a choice soon, though. I feel like I'm going nuts. I keep having the maintenance guy take me on walk-throughs. I must have looked at the elevator shafts ten times. We've opened up all the old garbage chutes and dumbwaiters from when the place was built. I just can't understand how they got him out. Every single exit was covered by a camera. The trash hadn't been collected, but we've sent officers to the dump anyway."

He rubbed his eyes. Sometimes it's like this. The lead officers just need to say it out loud, hear it, bounce ideas off anyone who will listen.

"They have these big barrels of cereal in the kitchen for the continental breakfast buffet," he said. "Waist-high drums of cornflakes, muesli, Coco Pops. I had them empty them all out. I've looked in every washing machine and dryer in the industrial laundry. I've had officers poke holes in every mattress."

"You're doing everything you can," I said.

"Everyone's pissed at me," he replied, as though he hadn't heard me. "None of the hotel staff are working. They'll all miss their paychecks this week."

We stood watching Amanda as she mimed some kind of explosion. The officers all looked at one another incredulously.

"Has Amanda—"

"She has," Clark said, putting his hand up. "I've spoken to the officer involved and put a stop to it.

There shouldn't be any more trouble. I understand there's a tradition of picking on Amanda Pharrell in this region that I'll never stamp out, but my officers should know where the line is. And, frankly, their priorities should be elsewhere at the present time."

"Thanks," I said.

He made a couple of attempts to begin what he said next, struggling to find the words, deciding on them and then changing his mind.

"She's not so bad," he said finally. It seemed to be a huge leap for him, something he said and then puzzled over as it lingered in the air between us. He looked at me as though to gauge my reaction, perhaps to see whether or not I agreed. I smiled.

Amanda and I had been tasked with reinterviewing Jaxon Cho that morning, in light of new information his parents had told Chief Clark the boy wanted to share. The police were spread thin, and my partner and I were to determine if there was anything of merit in the new statement. I walked with Amanda through the hotel and into the offices beyond the foyer, finding the Cho family in the small room I'd been escorted to in cuffs the day Richie disappeared. Jaxon Cho was trying to climb the stack of folded chairs against the wall, and his mother, Clarina, was shouting him down. Michael Cho was slumped in his chair, flipping through his mobile phone, and I could see in the reflection of his glasses that he was playing some colorful puzzle game.

Jaxon Cho took in the sight of Amanda with a long, low gasp as my partner and I introduced ourselves to his parents.

"Whoa!" the boy scoffed, pointing at her tattoos. "You are . . . You are cool!"

"This kid knows the score." Amanda nudged me.

"How many tattoos do you have?" Jaxon marveled at Amanda. "I know! You have one thousand!"

"I like to think of it as one big one," Amanda said.

"Are they all over?" the boy asked, his lips twitching with a hidden smile. "Are they on your . . . butt?"

"Jaxon!" Clarina snapped. "Good god. My apologies, Ms. Pharrell. Little boys are frequently *very disrespectful*." She glared at the child.

"Mate." I put my arms on the table, trying to draw Jaxon's eyes from Amanda's body. "Your mum and dad told the police that you had something you'd like to tell us. Amanda and I, we're not the police. But we're friends with the police. So you can tell us everything you know."

"Well"—Jaxon's eyes grew wide with excitement— "I know who stole Richie."

"Someone stole him?" Amanda asked.

"Yeah." Jaxon nodded vigorously. "I didn't remember when I woke up and the police were coming and all the mums and dads were crying. And then I just forgot about it. But now I remembered and I said, 'Oh, I remember now!' and I told my mum."

"Okay, great." I shifted uncomfortably, glancing sideways at Jaxon's parents, who were watching their son with deep frowns. "Why don't you tell us what happened?"

The night had been a fun one. The boys had walked all over the hotel, going up to the roof of the building via a set of dark stairs and watching the stars for a while, making wishes. They'd run laps of the rooftop, whooping and yelling, and had seen a silver object shaped like a dinner plate sailing through the clouds above the mountains. There had been flashing green lights rotating around the dinner plate–shaped object, which floated low over the top of the mountains before zooming away without warning. The boys had considered reporting the sighting to their parents, but had decided not to. They'd returned to the room to jump on the beds, and Jaxon had done a double somersault in the air off the end of one of the mattresses, landing perfectly on the floor by the wall with his arms up above his head like an Olympic gymnast. All the boys had cheered and agreed that Jaxon was the best guy in the whole world.

The boys had decided to try to find some paper to draw on, perhaps to fashion some kind of medal for Jaxon's achievements. They had been searching the hotel suite's small kitchenette when there had come a knock at the door. Richie had answered it, and a man had come into the room, quickly checking the hall to see if anyone had noticed him before shutting and locking the door behind him. Although the man had been wearing a black-and-white ghost mask with fangs, Jaxon recognized him as the pizza delivery man who had delivered the boys' dinner earlier in the evening. He was still wearing his red-and-black uniform with matching cap, a clue to his identity only Jaxon himself seemed to notice. The man had grabbed Richie from among the terrified boys and picked him up off the floor by his shirtfront. Jaxon had taken a big knife from the kitchenette and tried to threaten the masked intruder, but the intruder, while still holding Richie against the wall, had grabbed the knife by the blade and flung it across the room. The intruder had informed the boys that he was taking Richie away forever, and instructed them all to pretend they were asleep and not tell any of the parents that they had seen him or that he had taken Richie. Carrying Richie under his arm like a surfboard, the intruder had fled from the suite's bedroom window into the night.

Amanda held her emotions in check until the very last second of Jaxon's tale. She glanced at me, her eyes glistening with tears, and then burst into hacking laughter, slapping the tabletop with both hands as she struggled to breathe. Jaxon didn't know how to respond. He seemed delighted that he had amused Amanda, but was painfully aware that no one else was laughing.

"That story is the greatest thing that I have ever heard," Amanda moaned, wiping her eyes. She held out her hand and Jaxon, grinning, gave her a high five.

"Your kid is fucking awesome," Amanda told the Cho parents. "What a little champ." Jaxon's parents looked tired.

"Mr. Cho," I said. "Your son's version of events is—"

"We know." Michael Cho held up a hand. "Believe me. This new version of the abduction is even more extravagant than the one we heard this morning. The UFO is a new addition. Next time he tells it, there'll probably be a sasquatch."

"What's a sasquatch?" Jaxon asked. Amanda lifted her arm and showed him a tattoo of a sasquatch walking through a field of sunflowers just below her left armpit. The boy smiled.

"There must be something at the core of the story that's true," Clarina reasoned, her eyes now and then flicking to Amanda, who was trying unsuccessfully to suppress her snickers. "Our son witnessed some kind of violence. Threats. A man came into the room. Jaxon has mentioned this pizza delivery man a few times over the past couple of days."

"We'll take the story into consideration," I said. "But the video evidence we have shows the pizza man delivering the food and then leaving, and we don't have any vision of him returning. He's alibied all night long by his delivery route."

Jaxon and Amanda were both leaning over the table, almost nose to nose, conspiring. I caught some words about UFOs before we made our excuses and left.

"That was brilliant." Amanda was still giggling to herself as we walked down the hall toward the foyer. "Kids are terrible, but that one at least has something going for him. I guess we can totally discount the kids as witnesses now."

"I wouldn't be so sure," I said. "Maybe there is some truth in there. During my trial, my lawyer dug deep into the research around children's memories to try to see if we could make an argument around Claire Bingley identifying me as her abductor."

"Oh yeah?" Amanda took a seat on a plush leather sofa in the foyer. I sat beside her. "So what did you find out?"

"It's messy," I explained. "There's a lot of debate.

Basically, a kid's powers of observation and memory are less reliable than an adult's. They can only fit a certain amount of information into their heads at any given time, so if the boys were fixated on the movie they might have totally missed someone coming into the room and quietly taking Richie away. Kids have been shown to magnify events or invent them completely, and the younger they are, the more likely they are to do that. They're enormously egocentric, so they're not walking around remembering conversations or events that happened that don't relate to them."

"So Jaxon's fight with the pizza man was probably just a magnified version of some interaction between them," Amanda mused. "The pizza guy said something mean and Jaxon's blown it up in his memory into a whole physical confrontation."

"Or Jaxon's just had the idea that someone abducted Richie suggested to him enough times, and now he's recounting it," I said. "Think about it—all the kids have been hearing for days is *Someone took Richie. Someone took Richie. Someone took Richie.* They're also being told they *must* have seen something. They're being led to believe that they have the answers, and they want to please the adults around them."

When my alleged victim, Claire Bingley, was questioned over her abduction and rape, she had been shown a set of photographs that included my picture. Simply by presenting the photo set, the police had suggested to Claire that one of the men they were showing her was the perpetrator. She had seen me that afternoon. She wanted to help the police. In her young, frightened mind, she was led to believe that I had been the one to hurt her.

"Claire Bingley was thirteen and she misremembered events because of her suggestibility," I said. "These boys are seven and eight."

"It might be just as important to know what happened on the first night the boys were running around the hotel as the second night," Amanda said. "They might have seen or heard something relevant. Someone hanging around. Someone approaching them. Or perhaps they've seen something like that on the second night and they believe it was on the first. How are they supposed to tell the difference between two identical nights if their memories are so whacked out that they're adding details of things that never happened?"

"I'll watch more of the interview tapes tonight, go back and see what they said in their initial interviews," I said. "With every hour that passes we get further and further from what happened. If they know the truth, it's being twisted by everyone's desperate desire to know it and the boys' desire to help."

We had been assigned a booth at the back of the Clattering Clam as a workspace. We set up our laptops there, spreading papers over the polished wood tabletops and pushing aside the sticky, laminated menus advertising chip-basket sizes and kid-friendly meals. Amanda walked behind the empty bar after a while and made herself a cappuccino without seeking anyone's permission or asking me if I wanted one. She sat slurping it across from me, running one finger down a printed list of sex offenders in the Cairns region and their various known depravities. I watched the video of the Clattering Clam dinner with the seven parents on the night of Richie's disappearance, rolling my cursor backwards and forwards through time, making the people at the table writhe and wriggle on the screen.

My eyes were drawn to Sara, who sat at the corner of the table beside the rough-edged John Errett and his wife. I played a few clips of her, following her eyes across the table to Michael Cho and Ivan Sampson. She watched them as they talked, her chin resting on her fist, her face seeming placid in the grainy footage. I tried to zoom in on her, to get some sense of her emotions as she sat there at the table, but the screen just filled with white and gray pixels.

"Have you heard anything about Sara Farrow having an affair?" I asked Amanda.

"No, but she seems like the type," she said.

"What makes you say that?"

"She's a good liar," Amanda said. "A practiced liar by omission. They're one of the more dangerous types of liar."

I trust Amanda's intuitions. They're not always terribly consistent, sure. At times she seems to know exactly what a person is thinking, literally the words that are about to come out of their mouth, and yet at other times she can be completely unaware of her effect on people. I have seen her slowly rile a man into a steaming frenzy, only to be shocked when he finally explodes, and then turn around and sense my deeply hidden feelings as though she's reading my mind.

For all her genius, Amanda has these theories. They come from nowhere, and once they're established they're as rigid as morals. I knew her theory about liars would have been something she made up, a sudden law of the universe she had decided upon based only on her unreliable observations. I decided to hear it anyway.

"There are different types of liar?" I asked.

"You betcha." She scraped the foam from the top of her cappuccino and spooned it into her mouth. "Some people give you bullshit—planned liars. And some people give you nothing—unplanned liars. The former kind just replaces one truth with another. Like cutting a chapter out of a book and putting a different one in its place. You've got to craft the new chapter ahead of time and splice it in, hope that the book doesn't read weird."

"Okay," I said.

"But people who tend to lie by omission are deliberately riskier. They leave gaps in the narrative and don't plan how they're going to fill them, because they might not have to. They leave the chapters missing and just hope to Christ the reader doesn't pick up the book and feel it's a bit thin. When the missing chapters are discovered, they not only have to fill them in on the fly, but they have to account convincingly for why they left them out in the first place. One lie suddenly becomes two."

"Uh-huh." I appreciated her theory. "You're referring to Sara Farrow not telling the police about her baby's death."

"Specifically, I was referring to her hitting Richie."

She sprawled her elbows on the table and slid her phone beneath her face, tapping distractedly at the screen. "I've listened to the phone call you sent me. It's very good."

She played the clip.

We were having those monthly visits from child services, the ones they put in place after our first child died. Henry and I were fighting. We weren't getting any sleep. We had to keep the house immaculate because they showed up unannounced. Every time I turned around, Richie was bumping into things, leaving bruises on himself, or totally trashing things. He got into the kitchen and spread flour everywhere while I took a phone call one day. I had my back turned for two minutes. Imagine if they'd turned up then?

"She tries hard to account for what she did," Amanda said. "Not telling you about the incident. She talks about the monthly visits from child services. Fights with Henry. Lack of sleep. The stresses of keeping the house clean and the kid getting into everything like an uncontrollable little monster."

"Mmm," I said.

"She's setting you up to feel bad for her," Amanda said. "She doesn't fail to mention the death of her first kid, just in case you'd forgotten. And then she tries to relate to you."

I just snapped. You're a parent. You must get it.

"I did relate to her," I said. "I understood completely."

"Because kids are disgusting and horrible?" Amanda smirked.

"You didn't seem to mind Jaxon Cho."

"That kid is a hilarious adult man trapped in a kid's body."

"I related to Sara Farrow because it's not easy being a parent."

"Whatever," Amanda said. "Point is, she foresaw that you were going to discover the gap she'd left in her narrative, so she went back and arranged a very attractive, very relatable new chapter to fill its place."

"I don't know." I played with the video before me. "Henry Farrow failed to mention his million-dollar life insurance policy on the kid."

"And what was his excuse for that?"

"He didn't offer one," I said.

"Mmm-hmm." Amanda went back to her papers. "He has no new chapters. He left a hole, and he admits it. You can't conflate the two. Sara is far more deceptive than Henry. But you want to defend her because you feel sorry for her. You know what it's like to be suspect number one."

I looked at Sara Farrow on the screen before me. Amanda was right, of course. Since I'd set eyes on the slightly plump, exhausted-looking mother sitting helplessly in the hotel suite she had been given, I'd been recalling my time under suspicion. I had intimate knowledge of everything Sara was experiencing right now. The sideways glances, the whispers, the awkward silences. Sara must have known it was only a matter of time before the papers dredged up the child services records on Anya Farrow's death. Before they sat her ex-husband, her neighbors, Richie's teacher down and asked them what kind of mother she had been.

Her nights, like mine, would be filled with nightmares, hellish reimaginings of *This Is Your Life*.

My phone rang. It was Chief Clark.

"They think they've found a burial site at the De-Casper place," he said.

I wandered with the phone to my ear, watching the journalists camped across from the hotel through the restaurant's front windows, wincing as a few turned and took photographs of me. It was bad news. Clark explained that after the paramedics and crime scene techs had finished their work on the DeCasper house, the property had been sealed off and guarded overnight. Early that morning, a member of the dog squad had taken a trained search-and-rescue animal from the Zeerich region out to the DeCasper house, where it had shown interest in an area of disturbed earth near the back fence, within view of the house. The disturbed earth might have been related to the unfinished planter boxes, officers thought, maybe blood and bone fertilizer mixed in with the soil that confused the dog. They sealed off the section of yard and set up a crime scene tent around the area. The crew of three dogs that had searched the hotel for any signs of Richie on the morning he disappeared were loaded up into vans and driven south. This move was an important one, as journalists lurking in the cafés, restaurants, and bars around the White Caps Hotel had been keeping an eye on the movement of the dog squad vans. Where the hounds went, there was sure to be a body, so the vans were trailed by cars full of reporters down the highway toward Zeerich.

The Cairns dogs backed up the Zeerich dog's indication that something about the area at the back of DeCasper's yard was of interest to investigators. One of the dogs was a specially trained cadaver dog, so this led investigators to believe it was less likely he was confused by any organic fertilizer. While the reporters settled in to DeCasper's street, doing door-knocks of his neighbors and calling in their findings, officers bagged a shovel, gloves, and any garden tools they could find in the storage shed in the corner of the yard and conducted a new search of the house. The decision was made to wait for a ground-penetrating radar unit to be flown up from Brisbane.

"I know the parents are anxious," Clark sighed. "But I don't want to fuck this up. If DeCasper wasn't working alone, there could be biological or fiber evidence on that body or in the soil. The Zeerich chief wanted to go in with a fucking excavator. Every news channel in the country is watching."

"So what's your gut feeling?" I asked. "Is it him?"

"He was in the area on the night of the abduction," Clark sighed. "He's a known offender."

"No, he's not," I reminded him.

"Well, he's a known 'wannabe offender,'" Clark snapped. "Do we need to be so politically correct?"

I bit my tongue.

"I sure as shit hope the clothes in the television set aren't linked to the grave. Or Richie. I hope it's not a grave at all," Clark said. "Christ, don't let it be a grave."

"At the very least, the search should keep the press off the hotel," I said.

"That's why I called," he said. "That may not be exactly what we want. If there's a body out there, they *are* going to need an excavator eventually, and a trained dig team, and a couple of forensics vans. The commissioner will want to be there on the ground if it looks like we've likely found the boy, and I'm sure the parents will want to go. It's going to be a fucking circus."

He drew a deep breath.

"Look," Clark said. "I know you don't want your face on any more front pages. But there will be a certain number of journos hanging around who have been assigned to follow you and Amanda."

"Yes, I told you I ran into one this morning," I said. "He was delightful."

"It would be very useful for me if you could stay at the hotel today," Clark said. "Keep as many as you can off the Zeerich site."

"I can do that," I said. By now I had wandered through into the hotel's foyer, to a small side entrance used by the valets. The ground was peppered with cigarette butts. I felt the presence of someone beside me and assumed it was Amanda.

"It might not be a grave," I told Clark. "Keep your hopes up."

Clark made a bitter sound. I hung up and turned to speak to my partner, but there was a man standing there dressed in gray coveralls, the underarms of the heavy garment stained with sweat. Maintenance guy. A ponytail of chocolate-colored hair rested on his shoulder. The man was small beside me, but most people are. I imagined he was apt at squeezing through vents to retrieve dead rats and at climbing ladders to change chandelier lightbulbs. I remembered him in the CCTV vision, riding his bike to the hotel at 4 a.m. on the night of Richie's disappearance.

"You must be our long-suffering maintenance man," I said, putting my hand out. His palm was sweaty when we shook, his grip too tight. He kept his head low as he introduced himself in a voice so small I had to ask him to repeat it.

"Dylan Hogan." He forced a smile, drew on his cigarette hard, as though sucking up courage.

"Ted Collins."

"Were you just saying . . ." He pointed to the phone in my hand. "Uh, I didn't mean to eavesdrop."

"They're conducting a search for the boy south of here," I said. "I can't say more than that."

"Did they say there was a body, or . . . ?"

I put my hands out, shrugged, unable to divulge anything to him about what I knew of the crime. I remembered doing the same shrug, pulling the same face, for gawkers at the edge of crime scenes when I was a drug squad cop. Dylan the maintenance man stubbed out his cigarette and followed me inside again, a step behind and to my left, wanting to come along and hear any more tidbits that I dropped but not wanting to seem like he was fishing for them. I gave him a nod as I turned back toward the restaurant, a creeping feeling making me glance over my shoulder to see if he was still following even as I reached Amanda and our cluttered table. Amanda was scooping the undissolved sugar out of her coffee cup and sucking it off her index finger as she read her papers.

"Have you met the maintenance man yet?" I asked.

"Yeah, he asked me some questions outside the cop shop yesterday," Amanda said. "Looky-loo. Wanted to know how the case was going. Could be one of the journos is paying him to be curious."

"Maybe. I just ran into him at the smoker's door," I said. "He wanted to know if they'd found a body," I said. She didn't look up. I thought about Clark's request that Amanda and I stay grounded to the hotel for the day.

"Want to take a tour with me?" I asked her.

Amanda, being Amanda, was delighted to take a tour of the White Caps Hotel's "bowels," as she kept calling them. One of her more annoying eccentricities is a penchant for randomly spouting historical or scientific trivia, so she listened carefully as Dylan Hogan explained the background of the hotel, taking us through a service door behind reception and into a long, featureless labyrinth of hallways, our voices echoing off the high ceiling.

The building had originally been christened The Grand Hotel, the pet project of a retiring engineer who had come into the region to buy up surplus army equipment, building materials, and textiles left over from the Second World War. Douglas Aaronson had fallen in love with the gray pebble and white powder sand beaches of Cairns, and decided to build the hotel and live out his days in its penthouse suite overlooking the ocean. As is the experience of many people who buy businesses in which to retire, the venture was a devastating one. Aaronson overspent on the lavish, eighty-room hotel and found it difficult to recoup the cost, with Cairns tourism still growing. He underestimated the amount of work that would personally be required of him, and ended up putting in a hundred hours a week running the place, dealing with the growing pains of undertrained staff and a populace not accustomed to the hotel's lavish look and pricey room charge.

Aaronson recruited his entire family to keep the beast he had created alive, but in 1948, just two years after The Grand's opening, Aaronson died of a heart attack in the hotel bar and his embittered children sold the hotel to try to claw back some of their inheritance. The building stood empty for almost a decade before it was bought and re-christened the White Caps.

Dylan explained that the hotel still had many of its original finishings, as the Queensland Heritage Council forbade the new owners from ripping out a lot of the useless but historically significant equipment. There was a boiler room under the staff change rooms that didn't operate, the fifty-square-foot space packed with rusty, ancient equipment that did little more than collect dust. Amanda and I poked our heads into the darkened space and looked around, but it was clear to me that the room had been searched extensively. There were dog footprints in the dust on the floor, and the familiar print of police-issue boots.

Dylan showed us an old dumbwaiter chute off the

empty kitchen, allowing Amanda to pull the rickety wooden box down from where it had settled only feet above the iron doors accessing it. The dumbwaiter access points on every floor, he told us, had been used by the room service staff in the old days to move trays of food up and down the building, and ingredients up and down from the kitchen's storage room one floor below. Dylan handed me a torch from his utility belt when I requested it, and I sent the box up and looked into the empty cavity beneath it. When Amanda pulled the box down, I stuck my head into the space and looked up at the seemingly endless rising chute.

Amanda skipped ahead of us, pulling open doors and rummaging through cupboards indiscriminately, while I strolled, keeping a close eye on Dylan. It was clear to me that he was a shy and socially awkward fellow, but as I watched, his body gave up its secrets one at a time. I noticed a couple of scarred slash marks on the flesh of his right forearm, a clumsy suicide attempt or the result of a knife fight, I guessed. The skin of his first two knuckles on both hands was scarred, and a kind of nervous tic had him scratching the inner rim of his ears now and then so hard that he almost drew blood with nails that were slightly too long. The keys on his belt had been split into one big clump and a smaller one, the little set featuring a plastic tag that read *Van 6A, Big Lots*. Caravan park.

As Dylan took us through the fuse room, the security office, the staff change rooms, and the storage rooms under the parking lot, I noticed his nervous tic beginning to extend down into his feet. Whenever we stopped walking, he scraped the toe of one steel-capped boot into the concrete, making a grinding sound, his eyes invariably avoiding ours.

It took two hours to see the entire hotel.

"That's about it," he said eventually, opening his hands like a man showing a dog he's out of treats. We were standing outside his tiny office beside the pool gates, the filter system humming loudly nearby as an aquatic cleaner chugged along the bottom of the pool. "Uh, I think I've taken you through everything you need to see."

I glanced at Amanda, wondering if she'd picked up on the oddity of Hogan's expression—that he'd taken us through everything we "needed" to see and not everything that there was. She was peering through the window into his office, and Hogan, receiving no confirmation from us that he was released, took the door handle in a grip so tight his knuckles were white.

"What about the elevator shafts?" Amanda asked.

Hogan's shoulders lifted by an inch as his muscles tightened. He opened the door to the office and stepped in defiantly, the space only big enough for Amanda and me to hang our heads in the doorway.

"Oh, you can see those if you want," he said, shuffling papers on the desk and a huge, tattered diary. "But the police have been through them a million times. That's the first place they checked. Thought the kid might have fallen down underneath the carriage or something."

"Let's look anyway," Amanda said. "I've always wanted to see inside an elevator shaft. Haven't you?" She poked me in the ribs.

Hogan scratched his ear and looked at me, and in his eyes I saw a strange desperation that a casual observer might have mistaken for fatigue.

"Let's go," I said.

The maintenance man nodded resignedly, jangled the keys on his belt, and led us back around the pool toward the foyer doors.

"There's something odd here," I murmured to Amanda as we followed Hogan to the elevators. She nodded, smiling pleasantly at the small man as we stepped into the carriage together. We rode the elevator down to the basement floor of the hotel in silence, the inside of Hogan's left ear now smeared with a fine sheen of blood.

"Tell us about the elevators," I said as the numbers counted down. Hogan looked at the stainless-steel walls around us like he was unfamiliar with the space. He stood for a few seconds transfixed on framed posters advertising happy hour at the Clam and the Kenny Rogers tribute concert Amanda had attended.

"I don't, uh . . ." Dylan shrugged. "What can I say?"

"You had so much to say about everything else in the hotel," Amanda said. "Surely you have some interesting facts about the elevators."

"Oh, well." Dylan nodded vigorously at the challenge. "It's just, I don't service them or repair them. We bring in a company to do that. I don't even clean out the bottom of the shaft. I have a key that switches them on and off, and sends them up and down, that's it."

"They look pretty modern," I said, running my hand

over the polished chrome railing beside us. "When were they installed?"

"The hotel always had elevators," Dylan said.

We arrived in the basement, a long, empty space filled with the hotel's spare supplies, stacks of beer kegs, laundry tubs, floor polishers, and loading trolleys. Amanda and I watched while Dylan opened a panel at the side of the elevator with a key and sent the elevator back up one floor with a switch.

"Whoa." Amanda grinned, watching the machinery in the cavity spin and clunk into place. "Check this out."

The space was smaller than I had imagined, accommodating the elevator carriage between two huge, black, oily shafts that guided the box up and down the chute. There was not much space for anything else, gears and rails nestled on either side of the elevator. The floor of the elevator shaft was blackened and scuff-marked concrete, as was the back wall. Amanda didn't hesitate. She stepped down into the two-foot-deep space and stood staring up in wonder at the bottom of the elevator.

"Amanda, would you please get out of there?" I sighed. "If that thing falls down it'll crush you like a bug."

"Crushed by an elevator," she said. "Wouldn't *that* be a memorable way to die."

"The carriage can't really fall," Dylan said, distracted by his fingernails. "The old types used to be just a box on a cable fed through a giant pulley, with a counterweight attached. This one's hydraulic. There's no cable. Those three shafts there, the two at the sides and one at the back, they send the carriage up and down. If one of the shafts fails, the box is still held up by the two others."

"So this elevator is new, then?" I said. "Did the original one have a counterweight?"

"Mmm-hmm." Dylan cleared his throat. I leaned into the shaft as far as I dared and looked up at the perfectly square bottom of the elevator. The shaft smelled of engine oil.

"So many great movie scenes play out in elevator shafts." Amanda put her foot up on a ridge in the side of the shaft and attempted to hoist herself onto the wall, humming the *Mission: Impossible* theme. "Man down, Ethan. Man down," she said gravely. I reached in and pulled her out.

"All right," I told Dylan. Relief flooded into his face, until I said, "Show us the other two elevator bottoms. The service elevator and the backup one in the foyer. Then we'll go to the roof and look down at the carriages from above."

He swallowed and seemed to want to offer something in protest. Instead, he stood with his arms hanging by his sides as Amanda climbed out of the shaft.

There was nothing to see of the bottoms of the other elevators. Amanda climbed into each one and stood, cheerfully defying death, looking up at them from underneath. We rode the elevators to the roof, and

Dylan played with the radio on his belt, switching the signal dial on and off. I didn't expect that we would find anything when we looked down at the elevators from above. I decided that the maintenance man's discomfort must have been coming from the sheer proximity of Amanda and me, the minutes ticking by in our presence while we edged around discovering whatever it was he didn't want us to discover.

"So how long have you had this gig?" I asked conversationally as we rode the elevator to the roof.

"Oh, a couple of years." He smiled stiffly.

"Pretty sweet, seems like," Amanda chimed in. "You just rock around on your own all day fixing stuff up as you see fit?"

"That's . . ." He shrugged. "That's about the gist of it."

"You haven't got any assistants?" I asked.

"No."

"You set your own hours?"

"Oh no," he said. "I have a roster. I have to be available if anything stuffs up. If there's nothing to do, I just do paperwork."

"So on the morning of the boy's disappearance," I said, edging closer, "you rode to the hotel on your bike. You live nearby?"

Dylan's shoulders twitched again, and Amanda cocked her head at him, her clockwork mind collecting observations.

"I don't have a driver's license," Dylan offered. "I always ride to work. It's not far."

"The Big Lots caravan park?"

"Yeah."

"You've lived in the caravan park for the whole time you've worked here?"

"I'm single." He ground his boot into the floor of the elevator. "I don't need much space."

"Where were you before that?"

"Here and there." He glanced at me. It was the first time I'd seen a flash of anger in him, a little prickle of frustration he was trying to keep buried deep. I guessed he'd been homeless, a junkie maybe. His sleeves were rolled to just below the crook of his elbow. There might have been track marks or tattoos he was hiding.

"Four in the morning is a pretty brutal start," I said. "Why do they put you on so early?"

"I wasn't rostered on for four," he said. "I was rostered on at seven. I came in early because I had a backlog of stuff to do, thought I could get it all knocked over in a day, you know? Get back on track."

"You told me you were deadly hungover," Amanda said. "To the point of being sick."

This was new information to me. We both watched Dylan for a response.

"I was hungover," he said, offering a small, tight grin. "It took a while to come on. I guess riding the bike, you know, getting the air in my face. I was pretty rusty by seven."

We arrived at the eighth floor. Dylan led us through another service door, up a short flight of stairs, and onto a rooftop. The sun was blazing as the afternoon set in, baking the dusty concrete. I went to the edge of the roof and looked out over the ocean, making my way between huge stacks of air-conditioner units as big as cars. Hot air thrummed out of the machines, searing against my skin. The edge of the roof was waist high, splattered with seagull shit and feathers.

There were children's footprints in the dust and dirt near the rooftop, no distinct shoe prints, just small smears. I knew they had likely already been photographed by the police units, but I took my phone out and snapped them anyway. There was no telling how old they were, and a thousand explanations might have accounted for them. Any staff member with access might have led their children up to the rooftop to look at the view.

I walked back to where Amanda and Dylan were standing over a wide, rectangular section of concrete, upraised from the surface of the roof by a meter or more. There was a heavy iron door over the top of the elevator shaft, sectioned into lift-out panels. Alongside the iron door there was a strip of rusty steel mesh bolted to the top of the concrete. The mesh was rusted completely through in parts, holes big enough for a person to put their fist into. I squinted through the mesh but couldn't see anything, my eyesight ruined by the blazing sunlight.

"One of the boys recounted being on the rooftop to us this morning," I told Dylan, folding my arms. "Is there any way they could have had access to this place?"

"No way," Dylan scoffed. "I told the police that on

day one. No one is allowed up here. Certainly not guests. I mean, I've let some of the staff up here now and then. New Year's Eve, some of us come up here to watch the fireworks. But no, those two doors were locked." He pointed back toward the stairs.

I looked at Amanda to see if she was convinced, but she was squinting in the light reflecting from the second elevator bank, the mesh shining, newly replaced.

"Can you bring the other elevators up to the top floor?" I asked Dylan. "I'd like to see the top of each carriage."

Dylan nodded and walked away in the direction of the doors. Amanda and I stood watching the cloudless horizon.

"I feel like we're right on the edge of it," I said. "A part of me wants to just throw him into an interrogation room and sweat him for eight hours, see what he's hiding."

"Could be he's just nervous around cops," she said. "He's a bit of a rough old tomcat. See the fight scars? The caravan key?"

"Yeah."

"Let's do a background check," she said.

"You think he had something to do with this?"

She stood with her hands in the pockets of her shorts, searching her feelings. "He told me he needed this job," Amanda said eventually. "He didn't just want it. He *needed* it."

Dylan returned, opening the iron doors on the top of all three elevator shafts. Amanda and I leaned over and looked into the dusty blackness. There were no shoe prints or traces of a body on the top of any of the elevators. The grime and grit lay undisturbed but for the dripping of oil from the hydraulic shafts.

Leena Ainsbury was run off her feet, but that wasn't an unusual occurrence. The Happy Scratch Cat Refuge in Yorkeys Knob tended to attract volunteers who were more interested in cuddling and playing with the center's kitten population than the kind willing to use a little elbow grease.

The bell above the door rang just as Ainsbury was finishing off the paperwork on that morning's surrenders—a van-load of felines rescued from a suspected hoarding situation. She looked up over the rim of her glasses as a pair of heavy boots with clanking steel buckles traversed her spotless floor, leaving dirt prints on the tiles. The man who approached the counter was heavyset, deeply sun-weathered, his bald head shining in the light of the overhead fluorescents. He didn't smile, and neither did she. On his wrinkled neck she could make out the shape of an ancient tattoo, a red-back spider.

"I'm here to adopt some cats," the man said.

Ainsbury took her glasses completely off, squinting at what she thought was gold teeth flashing beneath his untrimmed mustache.

"You . . ." She glanced at a stack of forms on the counter, suddenly forgetting completely what they were even for. "I'm sorry. You're here to . . . ?"

"To get some cats," the man said. He took a crumpled slip of paper from the inside of his leather jacket, unfolded it, and glanced at the writing there. "I want two."

"Well, two is the legal maximum, yes," Ainsbury stammered.

"One of them," the man continued, "has got to be orange, with white feet and green eyes. I want the other one to be black, yellow eyes, with a small white patch on its chest."

"Well, sir." Ainsbury shook her head, bewildered. "I can't guarantee that any of our animals will match your *specific* description."

"Oh, I think they will." The man gave a menacing smile, and Ainsbury confirmed her sighting of the gold teeth. She picked up an adoption form, feeling oddly faint.

The bell above the door jingled again as she set the paper before the man.

"Would you mind if I asked you to . . ." Ainsbury spied the second man. He was almost a carbon copy of the first, muddy-booted and windswept, though his boxy skull was covered in black hair that didn't seem to thin before becoming his heavy brows and beard. As he reached the counter, he drew a piece of paper from his jacket, his words halting as he struggled to read the writing.

"I am here to . . . adopt . . . two cats," the man read. "One of them is . . . gray with yellow eyes. One of them is . . ." He paused, squinted at the paper. The bald man, filling out his form with his pen clutched in his fist like a knife, stopped his writing and leaned over.

"Tortoiseshell," the bald man read.

"Tortoiseshell," the hairy man said, smiling.

Ainsbury fanned her face with her hand. She looked at the big, clumsy lettering the first man was scrawling on the adoption form. In the first name section of the page, he had written "Kidnees." He had left the surname box blank.

Ainsbury took up the receiver of the phone beside her, thinking it might be best to get both men filling out the forms and then call the refuge director for advice. Before she could make a decision, the bell above the door rang once more, and three more men walked in, their heavy boots clunking on the tiles.

Lillian took Kelly on a virtual tour of the house, holding my phone in both of her small, chubby hands, walking from room to room and babbling out descriptions as though she and her mother hadn't been here together just days earlier. I lay on the back couch and listened to the sounds of the phone call rising and fading as Lillian did a circuit of the place. Celine was stretched on the boards beside the couch, groaning now and then as I scratched her rump with my foot. The mountains across the lake were being stroked with gray fingers of rain, bringing us an early twilight.

I might have spent the evening delving into the fantasies that plucked at my brain of Lillian living here permanently, some miracle allowing us to spend every evening like this, the child bashing at the screen door every time I returned home, the air filled constantly with her pattering footsteps on the floor. But I was hungry for news about Richie Farrow and disturbed by our meeting with the White Caps Hotel's maintenance man. I had watched and rewatched the hotel's CCTV footage of Dylan Hogan leaving work at 6 p.m. the evening before Richie's disappearance and returning at four in the morning. I didn't see how it was possible that he had orchestrated Richie's vanishing, when no camera showed him entering the building between those times. Richie would have had to go missing on his own between eleven and midnight, with Dylan finding him and taking the boy from the building after he arrived back at the hotel after 4 a.m. By that time the hotel had been completely locked down, and every guest suitcase and vehicle had been checked before it was released.

Still, I couldn't keep my mind away from the man. I searched the photographs Sara had sent me for any sign of Dylan Hogan and didn't see him. I tortured myself by slowly going through the pictures of the four boys jumping and splashing in the aquatic park on the waterfront, their joy-filled faces and gangly, growing bodies caught in twisting, leaping poses. Richie was captured in all the awkward tourist shots—standing by the Welcome to Cairns sign on the Esplanade, buried in the sand up to his neck, licking melted ice cream off the end of a waffle cone.

I decided to request that Clark allow me and Amanda to tail Dylan Hogan, or, if not, that he put a couple of officers on the maintenance man to monitor his behavior. Lillian came strolling toward me, bored with her video meeting with her mother, and handed me the phone, running away to chase the geese.

"Look at you," Kelly said as I held the phone above

my head. "Pegged out on the couch, soaking up the afternoon. Some things never change. You got a good book?"

"No, but our daughter makes for entertainment enough." I turned the camera on Lillian and her pursuit of the birds.

"She was going on and on about things she did with 'Nanna,'" Kelly said.

"Well, 'morgue woman' is a bit of a mouthful for such a little girl."

"Lillian has a nanna already, Ted."

"Yes, she has one," I said. "And since my mother is no longer with us, that gives me one free 'nanna' title to assign to someone."

"I guess."

"How's yoga camp?" I said. "You fix your chakra yet?"

As Kelly tried to explain the many misunderstandings I had about chakra, and how it might actually help my life, I opened a couple of messages that had been delivered while Lillian had possession of the phone. There were two of them, both from Laney Bass.

I've got a sick cow I need to visit on a farm near your address, and Peeper's fine to come home. Shall I bring her over?

I checked the time on the message. It must have come through just as I handed the phone to Lillian. The second message, coming twenty minutes after the first, made me shoot up on the couch.

I'll chuck her in the van and see if you're around.

"Oh fuck!"

"What?" Kelly asked.

"Nothing." I stood, and Celine stood with me, jumping up from the ground with alarm. "Someone's coming over, that's all."

"Someone who?"

"No one."

"A woman." Kelly rolled her eyes. "'No one' means a woman. You know, you don't have to keep this shit from me anymore. We're not together. We're allowed to talk about it. Who is she?"

"It's no one, really, Kelly. My vet, that's all. I've got stuff I have to do. Kelly, I've got to go."

"Jeez." She smirked. "She must be some important vet."

I hung up on Kelly without taking the bait and shouted to Lillian. She came running up the yard as fast as she could, infected by excited panic without understanding at all what had spurred it.

"Lill, you've got to help me!"

"Oh, help!" she cried.

"Laney Bass is coming over!"

"Mamey Bass!"

"She'll be here any minute!"

Lillian screamed, her hands up and fingers spread wide. I grabbed the child and ran to the bathroom, stripping her off and starting the shower. I grabbed my belt and then paused.

Before my arrest, when Lillian was just a tiny infant, I had showered with her plenty of times. Kelly and I, both sleep deprived and busy, had sometimes taken the baby under the warm water to save time in setting up the bath. I'd loved holding her against my chest under the stream, kissing her wet head. Showering with my child had seemed completely natural, but now as I looked down at my daughter waiting for the water to warm up, I held my belt buckle and wondered what might happen to my life if Lillian told Kelly or Jett or anyone at all that she had seen me naked. That we had been naked together. It hit me that we had been in my bed together, too. I hadn't even thought about it. She was my little girl. It had seemed the right thing to do.

With a sense of guilt and dread where there had once been joy and comfort, I stripped off and hurriedly washed us both under the warm water, deciding I didn't have the time or the patience for a moral debate with myself. Lillian was covered in a day's childhood adventures: dirt under her nails as black as coal, and leaves and twigs in her hair; around her mouth, Vegemite, crumbs, more dirt, a smudge of green ink that had also somehow ended up in her ears and down her legs. I scrubbed us both, hustled her into her bedroom and left her to dress herself while I threw on a nice shirt and clean jeans. When I came back to her she was sitting naked on the rug, singing a song about owls and blowing kisses at herself in the mirror. The doorbell rang as I was dragging a shirt onto her damp arms. I gathered all the toys from the floor in one mad swoop and heaved them into the cupboard, taking mine and Lillian's discarded clothes from the hallway floor and chucking them into my bedroom.

I was breathing hard when I tore open the door. Laney stumbled back.

"Whoa!" she laughed. "Slow down, cowboy."

"Sorry." I smiled, pushing my damp hair away from my forehead. "We were just playing chasings. Come in. Let me get that."

I took the animal carrier from the porch beside her and followed her into my house, the big bird inside the container shifting as I lifted it. Laney tried to greet Lillian at the door of her bedroom, but the child dissolved into embarrassed giggles and hid.

"What's with the boarded-up windows at the front?" she asked as we walked down the hall.

"Oh, um. Termites. I've got termites in the frames. I'm having them replaced."

I led Laney out the screen door to the porch, where Celine mobbed us, snuffling and licking the vet's hands.

"This is nice." She nodded appreciatively, looking out across the yard, at the glassy lake beyond the wire. "A quiet slice of paradise, all of your very own."

"It's not a bad spot," I told her. "If you don't mind the racket the crocs make at night."

I led her down into the yard, pausing at the steps while she pulled off her sandals to avoid them getting muddy. I wanted desperately to look at the pale yellow dress she was wearing, her loosely braided hair falling out of its weave behind her out-turned ears, but I was afraid of being caught admiring her. Something at the back of my mind was insisting she wasn't dressed to treat a sick cow, but it seemed dangerous to hope she had dressed up to come to see me. I told myself she probably had a dinner date or something after she dropped Peeper off with me, even as she stood beside me in the wet grass in my yard and breathed in the cool, earthy air coming off the water.

We talked about the geese and the little house I'd fixed up for them, Laney gathering the folds of her dress and tucking them between her thighs so she could crouch among the birds and feed them grain from her hand without getting the hem wet. I brought the carrier down to the group and let Peeper out, and Laney and I smiled while Peeper settled in with the others, the birds seeming to welcome her back by gathering into a kind of huddle, rubbing their chests against each other, battering excited wings.

"You did this," I told Laney, gesturing to the geese. "I can't tell you how grateful I am. I know they're just birds, but—"

"Don't be silly," she said. "They're not *just* anything. My whole life is all about animals. I understand how important they can be, especially when you're on your own."

I nodded along with her comment, even as I felt my stomach plunging at her observation that I was on my own. She'd probably noticed the distinct lack of flair to my decorating, the total absence of the warmth and character Kelly had somehow brought to our home back in Sydney. I'd tried, over the time I'd been in Crimson Lake, to make my house look lived in, but my tastes were simple and the ever-present threat of losing everything again probably stopped me bringing home treasures, books, pieces of art. While I'd tried to kit out Lillian's room like any other girl's, there was no denying it lacked the authenticity of a room a child usually lived in. There weren't enough toys or books yet. There weren't stains on the carpet and half-scrubbed-off doodles in pencil on the walls.

With my confidence shattered, I figured I had nothing to lose.

"Can I get you a drink?" I asked. "Being on my own, I don't often have an excuse to open the good wine."

"Oh." Laney feigned surprise. "Sure. Why not? One won't hurt."

When I met Kelly, I was a newbie patrol officer responding to a house party that had got out of control. A handful of teenage girls had decided to have a boozy sleepover and pool party while the parents were away, and the next thing they knew, half the local high school soccer team had got wind of it and was outside, loitering suggestively while the girls peered out the windows. Word spread, and when the police got there concerned neighbors were standing in their front gardens and the street was packed with teens revving their cars and hollering. Someone had chucked an Otto bin through the front window of the house in question, and the girl who lived there was hyperventilating and crying in the driveway. I'd spotted Kelly sitting on a fence across the street from the epicenter of the party, smoking a cigarette. She had a woven plastic choker necklace around her throat and black lipstick on. I told her to go home. She told me to fuck off. I knew then that I liked her, that some deep, primal thing in me had selected her and she was going to haunt me forever if I didn't get her name.

I knew as soon as I sat down with Laney Bass on my porch that I liked her, that she'd stained me already with a desire I'd never remove. All at once I realized how lonely I had been without this burning, hungry longing for someone, the absence of an object for my affection. I wanted to touch her. I wanted to talk to her. It was impossible to try to maintain any semblance of coolness or mystique. Without really knowing how badly I'd wanted to talk, all those months alone in the house, I was now barely able to keep quiet, and I hung on her every word.

I brought out a chair from the dining room set and gave Laney the couch to herself, Lillian recovering from her embarrassment in time and climbing up there beside the vet.

Laney was from Harrogate, and though she tried to edge around her story, not wanting to be "one of those people" who talks incessantly about their ex, she told me that the reason she'd moved to Crimson Lake six months earlier was because she had a broken heart. She and her ex-fiancé had gone to university together, then opened a practice together and treated the pampered poodles and Persians of her hometown. He'd asked her to marry him after four years, and she'd said yes, and they'd been in the throes of picking invitations and trying to decide on a color scheme when she'd found a pair of women's sunglasses in his car that weren't her own. She'd shrugged off the find, until she found a single sock in the household laundry that wasn't hers, either. She'd done some snooping around before she revealed to him what she knew.

Laney tried to downplay the seriousness of what she'd confessed to me with a very British shrug of her shoulders and swish of her hair when it was all out there in the open.

"What can you do? Move to the other side of the planet, I guess!"

"It was very daring," I said. "You must have picked Crimson Lake by throwing a dart at a map."

"Close enough." She smiled. "It was more that I did a Google search of veterinary practices around Cairns and found an empty patch. I've certainly had a lot of business since I've been here. People bring their pet cats in because they've been bitten by wild snakes. They bring their pet snakes in because they've been scratched by wild cats."

She sipped her wine. Nearby, a frog started barking, making the nightly rain forecast.

We both noticed at the same time that Lillian had snuggled down onto the couch cushion beside Laney. The child was falling asleep, rousing herself only to put her head on the woman's thigh.

"Don't go to sleep there, little Boo." I reached over and tickled my daughter's feet. "You haven't even had dinner yet."

"She's okay." Laney stroked the girl's head, lifting her curls from her neck and smoothing them across the back of her head. "Probably this heat is wearing her out. It sure did take some getting used to, I can tell you."

"I think she misses her mother," I said. "This will be their longest time apart since she was born."

"You said Kelly was nearby?" Laney asked.

"Yoga camp," I said. "That's what I'm calling it,

anyway. I think they do a bunch of things. Wellness and nutrition and . . . whatever. They're up in the mountains."

"Why did you come here?" she asked. "You decided to leave the police for private investigation—what—so you could make your own rules, or . . . ?"

I took a deep breath. It was my turn to talk about why I was "on my own," why I had chosen to come here, to the frayed green edge of society where only wild things felt at home. Step by step, inch by inch, I waded into a hot bath of lies by omission, as Amanda would call them, telling Laney things had simply fallen apart between Kelly and me, that I'd given up my job as a police officer due to conflict with my colleagues. Neither of those things were technically untrue, and yet, as she sipped her wine and took in my words, dread crushed deeper and deeper within me, making it hard, in time, to even get out full sentences. I knew what I was doing was wrong, even as I did it. Laney had just finished telling me how difficult she found it to trust anyone, how she'd questioned every single relationship she had after her breakup, even those she held with family members. She was a woman trying to step away from the fire, and here I was trying to lure her back into the flames while my sleeping daughter lay dreaming between us.

When campfires began to glow across the lake, and only the light from the kitchen windows fell on us, I noticed a mosquito on Lillian's leg and stood.

"I better get the mouse something to eat or she'll be up at midnight," I said.

Laney followed me into the kitchen, taking our

wineglasses and rinsing them in the sink as I fished around in the fridge for something for Lillian. Closing my eyes for a second was all it took to make the fantasy real. Laney and I putting Lillian to bed. The two of us staying up all night chatting on the porch, cuddling, looking at the water and listening to the call of the crocodiles.

I walked Laney to her van, watching her out of the corner of my eye, her lips trying to hide and then surrendering to a tiny smile.

"I really like this place," she said, finally, as we stood outside the driver's-side door.

"You're welcome here any time," I replied.

I don't honestly know who kissed who. One second I was trying to untangle myself from my doubts about saying Laney was welcome at my house any time, what that really meant, how she'd interpret it. The next second her arms were around my neck and her lips were on mine. I kissed her hard, desperately, aware even as I did that the seconds were draining away and that so long had stretched since the last time I had kissed someone, and there would probably be an equal stretch until the next time. Stupidly, I broke off the kiss and just hugged her, burying my face in her neck, feeling her hair against my cheek. It was probably a weird thing to do, but then as we kissed again she grabbed my butt with both hands and dragged me to her, the two of us pressed up against the side of the van like teenagers.

There wasn't much to say when we drew apart. I glanced toward the house, not wanting to let Lillian fall too deep into sleep before I had a chance to say good night to her properly. Laney had her hands in my back pockets.

"Look at us." She grinned. "Pashing in the dark."

"Pashing?" I laughed. She giggled against me.

"Isn't that what you Aussies say?"

"Maybe a million years ago."

"Frenching?"

"Snogging," I said. She laughed hard. "Isn't that what you Brits say?"

We looked at each other in the gold light from the house, smiling like idiots.

"I gotta go." She trailed a hand down my arm and opened the car door. I waved as she drove off, my face burning, tingles of excitement and terror rushing up my arms and into my chest.

Joanna Fischer knew who she wanted to be.

She wanted to be Pip Sweeney.

She'd wanted it from the moment she was first introduced to her partner at the Holloways Beach police department, the beautiful blond patrollie striding forward and pumping Joanna's hand hard. Strong, confident shake. Good eye contact. Immaculate uniform.

At the academy, an old chief super had told Joanna the best thing she could do in the job was find a role model and stick to them, someone who had been around for a long time and had their head on straight. Pip had only graduated six months before Joanna, but she knew she'd found her role model just from the incredible self-loathing she felt around the other woman. Joanna was messy. Undisciplined. Always late and always on the back foot.

Pip always had a sassy return to change room

banter from their male colleagues, always knew what was going to be covered in the morning briefing, what the job lists were, what the upcoming shift change would be before anyone else. She was a machine, sitting upright in her seat on surveillance detail for hours on end, her eyes trained on the house they'd been tasked with watching, her back rigid as a plank as Joanna sagged and dozed in the passenger seat.

She was perfect. While Joanna fumbled awkwardly around the families of car crash victims, Pip soothed them with soft, warm, gentle reassurances. Her handwriting on the crime scene reports was like calligraphy. No matter what Joanna did to try to emulate Pip, she could never quite get there. A curl worked itself loose from her wire-tight bun. Her ink smudged, and she stammered when reporting to their superiors. When Pip was called up to take an open detective's spot in Crimson Lake—a ridiculously early promotion, something that would have left Joanna in nervous tatters—Pip had accepted the news with a curt nod and sincere thanks. While the two women celebrated that night over wine and expensive cheese, Joanna had curled on the other end of the couch and listened to her friend talk about her excitement over her new posting. She'd been in awe.

Joanna not only admired Pip, she loved her. Her life was lived in privilege, watching Pip in action, listening to her thoughts, laughing with her in the dark of a bar or her neat, stylish house on the lake. Sometimes Joanna thought she would give anything just to be Pip for a day. To have people look at her the way they did Pip. To have her power, her intelligence, her understanding. It was like Joanna walked everywhere with fogged glasses, and it was only Pip who could really see.

When Pip died, all Joanna heard was talk about Amanda Pharrell.

Pip had been trying to save Amanda.

Her death had been witnessed by Amanda.

Her last words were spoken to Amanda.

Amanda, Amanda, Amanda.

Joanna could feel her own memories of her partner twisting and warping as thoughts of Amanda penetrated them. She would iron her uniform and think of Pip's hands working a cloth and ink-black polish as she sat in the change room working on her boots, and then she'd remember Amanda in her stupid slogan shirts and glittering sunglasses wandering around the hotel like it was her personal mansion. None of her colleagues wanted to visit Pip's grave. To talk about her. To honor her. It was all too depressing. Cops liked to be angry. They wanted to talk about Amanda, the walking curse, the murderer. They hated her. They didn't understand her. They were afraid of her. All that talking, watching, whispering, it was a fascination that made Joanna boil inside.

If people wanted to talk about Amanda so badly, Joanna was going to give them something to say.

Joanna got out of her car and stretched, the muscles in her left shoulder gathered into a tight bundle beneath her shoulder blade. Her day had been spent guarding operations at the DeCasper house, manning the outer cordon and facing off with journalists and neighbors who wanted to know what was going on. She'd stood in the sun for hours with her hand on her heavy belt, a glorified security guard, listening to the news reporters give their strange, hollow assessments of what little information had been released to the public, the camera operators taking atmospheric shots of the front of the DeCasper house from a range of angles. Joanna learned more from listening to the news reports than she had from her own command. The little boys' clothes found in DeCasper's house had apparently been sourced from the lost and found basket at his school. She learned that DeCasper's brother's house had been searched, and that Richie Farrow's father had made a statement saying how furious he was that DeCasper had taken "the easy way out" before giving police the truth.

Joanna tried to roll all the awful details she had learned out of her shoulders as she headed toward her house, cracking her neck as she walked up the front steps. She needed a bath, a glass of wine, and an early night. She didn't take notice of the motorcycles parked at the end of the street, visible as silhouettes in the cones of light from the streetlamps.

The first indicator to Joanna that something was wrong came when her key didn't meet any friction as she turned it in the lock, the door already unsecured. Her mind wasn't fast enough, didn't warn her to pause before stepping into the darkness of the living room. She walked in and the door closed behind her, pushed shut by a strange hand in the blackness.

Joanna reached for the light switch, but another hand was already there, flicking it on.

There were two men standing beside her on either side of the doorway. Though her heart seemed to slam against the inside of her ribs, Joanna didn't move, and neither did they. They were thickly built, graying, tattoo-covered men simply standing there in her living room, watching her as she came to terms with the situation.

On the coffee table before the television set, a display had been arranged. Joanna didn't recognize the half-empty Jack Daniel's bottle on the edge of the table, or the thick white package of powder split open at the center, trailing dust onto the polished surface. There were three lines racked on a mirror she recognized as having been taken from her bathroom, a set of micro scales dusted with powder and handfuls of tiny plastic baggies tossed on the coffee table and the floor nearby. In the kitchen, to her left, it looked like someone had staged a small party. There were used glasses, empty ice trays, a couple of pizza boxes stacked on top of the recycling bin.

Joanna's favorite armchair in the corner of the living room had been turned around on its rotating base to face the corner. As she watched in bewilderment, the armchair turned and Amanda Pharrell appeared, sitting with one leg folded over the other, a tortoise-shell cat resting in her lap. She had all the theatrical pomp and flair of the Bond villain she was obviously imitating, save for her delighted countenance, which cracked with an impossibly wide smile as the chair came to a stop.

"Welcome, Constable Fischer," Amanda said, barely managing to get the words out before she broke into laughter. "We've been expecting you."

She stroked the cat menacingly.

Joanna had to force the words out through her rising fury.

"What . . . the . . . *fuck* . . . is . . ."

"Allow me to explain my ingenious plan." Amanda gave a flourish of her hand. "You've just arrived inside your secret life. Yes, Constable Joanna Fischer: cocaine addict and maybe dealer. Drunk, slob, and receiver of stolen goods."

"Stolen goods?" Joanna stepped cautiously out from between the thugs at the door.

"They're not immediately obvious," Amanda said. "They've been artfully placed. In the bedroom cupboard, beneath a pile of folded blankets, you'll find two brand-new MacBook laptops and a couple of iPhones. Beside the washing machine in the laundry, there's a flat-screen TV. They were ripped off from an electronics store in Brisbane three weeks ago."

Joanna worked a muscle in her temple with her fingers, wincing as splinters of rage seemed to push up from behind her eyes.

"More troubling," Amanda continued, "are a couple of handguns that went missing from the Crimson Lake police department's armory at the end of last year. I'm not going to tell you where they're hidden. You'll have to find them yourself. There are also two more bricks of coke like this one hanging around in here somewhere, and I'm afraid they've got your prints on them."

"How could they *possibly* have my prints on them?" Joanna snarled.

"Come on, a gifted magician like myself never reveals her secrets." Amanda smiled, coy. "Point is, all of this looks very bad for you. You're lucky it's just me, Jimbo, and Rocko here, otherwise you might be in some very hot water. We won't tell anyone. But you can imagine the consequences if this happens again. You're at work. Maybe you're two hours' drive away, like you were today. The station receives a panicked call from a neighbor saying they heard a gunshot inside your house. The boss sends a unit here to see if you're okay. They bust in and find this."

Joanna folded her arms, the back of her tongue awash with blood from chewing the inside of her cheek, trying to contain the anger.

Amanda got out of her chair, flipped the cat, and held it like a babe in her arms. She approached, and Joanna felt her eye twitching as she tried to maintain a rigid expression.

"Imagine if some of this stuff turned up somewhere else in your life, Joanna," Amanda said. "What if you opened your locker down at the station one morning and you found a kilo of heroin? A bloody knife? Some pictures? What if you reached into the pocket of your jacket one day and found a key to a lockbox registered under your name?"

"You stupid little bitch," Joanna whispered.

"If you so much as *breathe* in my direction again," Amanda said gently, "I will take everything from you. I will leave you crying on the floor of some filthy prison shower block while women I knew when I was locked up redesign your face with their shoes."

The two women watched each other. The cat between them mewled and pawed at Amanda's chin, and the small, tattooed investigator broke away first, joggling the animal like an infant as she headed for the door.

Joanna went into the bathroom when they were gone and took a folded towel from the rack beside the mirror. She sat on the edge of the tub in the searing white light, pressed her face into the towel's soft folds, and screamed. The rage soared out of her, hot and wet and loud, a muffled growl in her cupped hands, trapped by the fabric like smoke. She screamed until her throat was ragged and her temples were damp with sweat.

Give her what she deserves, she thought. *Make her go away.*

When Joanna was done she put down the towel and went to the mirror, took a few deep breaths to regain her composure. She balled a fist, looked at her reflection, and smiled.

Then she punched herself as hard as she could in the eye.

The call came in the dark hours of the morning. I answered it before I was fully awake, lost in the wilderness between dreams and consciousness.

"We've got a problem," Chief Clark said.

"What is it?"

"That maintenance man, Dylan Hogan," he said. "You two may have been onto something. I put a squad car on him last night, and what do you know—they follow him straight from work to Bunnings Warehouse. They figure he's just stocking up on things for the hotel, so they follow him home, but while they're sitting on him they call the store to see what he bought."

I sat up in bed.

"Very interesting collection of things on the receipt," Clark continued. "Rope, duct tape, plastic drop sheets, a hacksaw . . ."

"Oh fuck," I said.

Lillian appeared in the doorway, rubbing her eyes.

"Oh fuck!" she yawned. I frowned at her.

"All the items were bought with his personal credit card, not the hotel's card."

"They could still be supplies for the hotel," I said. "He could be expecting to be reimbursed."

"I'm not through," Clark said. "The surveillance officers called the whole situation in. When I heard the list of items purchased I was suspicious but wary. I didn't want to jump on this guy too fast and cause a media sensation, or uncover evidence that I wouldn't be able to use without a search warrant. I called up for the warrant, and I was waiting for it to be rushed through when the two officers call me and tell me they fucked up."

"Oh sh—" I watched Lillian climb up the side of the bed. "Sugarplums."

"They thought they heard a kid's voice from inside the caravan. Keep in mind, I told these stupid *fucks* to stay *inside the car* and watch the caravan door. That's all they had to do."

I held Lillian to my chest. Her pajamas were covered in dog hair. Celine stalked guiltily past the door toward the kitchen.

"The officers stormed the van, fought with Hogan, and he bolted."

"Of course they did," I said. "Of course he did."

"Get your arse down here. I want you to join the search." Clark sounded like he was about to end the call, but he came back on the line. "And don't bring Amanda."

"I thought you two were cool."

"Not after last night's delightful surprise," he said.

"What does that mean?" I asked, but he was gone. I looked at the time on the phone. It was 5 a.m. I looked at my child.

"Fuck," she said.

"You said it, Boo," I agreed.

Amanda doesn't usually rise until ten. I called her seven or eight times before realizing she had probably switched her phone off overnight to avoid being awakened by dozens of prank calls from Joanna. I drove to her place through the morning mist, my foot hovering over the brake pedal as the dark silhouettes of kangaroos emerged at the roadside, munching and watching me approach, their paws hanging at their chests. I realized, as Lillian babbled about the view from her window, that I had not taken her on a single outing since she'd been left in my care. I hadn't taken her for ice cream, a stroll through the rainforest, a wander across the cane fields. Now I was shrugging her off so that I could join the hunt for a possible abductor running for his life. I pulled up at Amanda's place burning with guilt.

She opened the door in her Batman negligee, cats surrounding her bare, tattooed feet.

"What is *that* doing here?" Amanda looked at Lillian.

"I thought you'd lost all your cats," I said. "How'd you get them back?"

Lillian bowed into the furry crowd and tried to scoop whichever she could out of the writhing, purring collection, her clumsy fingers slipping over whip-fast tails and flicking ears.

"Kitties!" she cried, helplessly grabbing and coming up empty. "Lots of kitties!"

"Do you have any idea what time it is? You want to interrogate me about my cats in the middle of the night?"

"You need to take Lillian."

"Take her where?"

"I'll call you from the car and explain," I said. "I've got to get on the road. Is that a bullet hole in your door? Never mind. I don't have time. Can you please just mind her until Val turns up at my place? She should be there by about nine."

I crouched and squeezed Lillian. She kissed me on the neck.

"You're going to hang out with the fairy for a while," I told her. "I'll see you later. I love you."

"Fairy." Lillian smiled up at Amanda.

"This isn't happening." Amanda looked down at my child in disgust. "This isn't happening, Ted. It's not coming in here! You made it, now you have to take responsibility for it. It goes where you go."

"She's not an 'it,' Amanda. She's a little girl. A clever, funny, affectionate child you'd really enjoy spending time with if you gave her a chance."

"I'll have to disinfect everything." Amanda held her hand to her nose and mouth. "Urgh. I'll just throw it out. How would you feel if I just put her in a cupboard for a while? I'll give her water and a bowl of cereal and just put her in a cupboard."

"I don't understand this thing you have with kids." I stopped by the car and threw my hands up. "You know, I watched her sleeping last night. It occurred to me that, of all the things I'd seen in my life, that was the most beautiful. Her, asleep in bed. Can you understand that?"

Amanda considered me, still holding her nose and mouth.

"I saw an owl swoop down and steal a golf ball right off the fairway once," she said. "Must have thought it was an egg."

"I'll call you." I got in the car. "Thank you for this."

"No, seriously." Amanda came out and banged on my car roof. There were tradies on the next corner setting up roadworks. They turned and stared. "This isn't funny anymore!"

"She's allergic to strawberries," I said, and rolled up my window.

Amanda stood stock-still in the middle of the road in my rearview mirror, her shoulders high and her jaw jutted out with fury.

I headed straight for the White Caps Hotel but was redirected by officers at the scene to the caravan park where Dylan Hogan lived, a slip of paper with the address pushed through my window carelessly before I had time to grab it. The Big Lots caravan park was only a short drive south of the hotel, down a long, empty, unmarked road on the edge of the marshlands before Admiralty Island.

I called Amanda. She seemed too stressed about what Lillian was doing—picking up the cats and squeezing them like teddies—to listen very carefully to my update about Hogan. She shouted down the phone at me for a full minute about leaving her with babysitting duty while I chased a viable lead. I barely managed to ask her about the "delightful surprise" Clark had mentioned, but she didn't know what he was talking about.

The street that led to the park had been blocked off by police. The car in front of me held a family that appeared to reside in the park who were furious at not being allowed onto the property. I hung an elbow out the window and looked at the sprawling swamps beside the road while a woman got out of the car ahead and argued with the cordon officer. Colorful bugs were skipping across the surface of the stagnant water, a gray heron wading slowly and deliberately through the shallows.

"Just let us in so we can get some sleep and change our fucking kid! We've been driving all night!" the woman wailed, gesturing wildly at the car. A toddler with a milk-white bare butt made an appearance through the back window, clambering over the seats.

As I pulled in to the gravel lot crowded with police and forensics vehicles, a text came through to my phone. I was sure it was going to be Amanda despairing about my daughter, but the name at the top of the screen sent zings of electricity through my chest.

Laney Bass had written, *Woke up thinking about that kiss.*

I wish I could say the same, I wrote. *Rattled out of bed this morning by case news. 5 am. Can you believe it!*

I stopped outside the car and hid my face in my

palm. I was too used to being married. Laney didn't want to hear that I hadn't thought about our kiss, or about my crappy morning and work stress. She was trying to flirt with me. I hadn't flirted in more than a decade.

You looked incredible last night, I quickly typed. *When can I see you again?*

"Girlfriend?" Superfish appeared beside me, his arms hanging by his sides, the orange curls on top of his head beaded with sweat. I had to snap myself out of my thoughts about Laney to focus completely on what he'd said.

"What?"

"Girlfriend." He pointed to the phone.

"How does everyone know I have a girlfriend?"

"You looked stressed." He shrugged. "Trying to think of what to type."

"This is what happens when all the people in your life are in law enforcement," I said. "You're a walking behavioral science exhibit. I don't have a girlfriend. It's my vet."

"You text your vet?"

"What do you want, Superfish?"

"We have a problem," he said.

"I need people to stop saying that to me today."

"Amanda Pharrell assaulted Joanna Fischer last night," he said.

I stared at him, trying to form words. He scratched at his pronounced collarbone through his shirt, staring at the ground. The dense freckles on his neck didn't seem to thin before reaching his chest.

"At least, that's the story she told me," Superfish

said. "Joanna. She's not allowing command to file an assault charge. She told the chief she tripped and smacked her face on the freezer door."

"Jesus." I held my head. "Jesus."

"She told me Amanda and two of her bikie mates came around her place last night and bashed her. She's probably hoping I'll spread that quietly around the crew, get them all riled up. She told me not to tell anyone. She's acting scared but she's being very suggestive. She's letting people believe the worst. This is going to turn into a war if we're not careful."

I tried to call Amanda, but she didn't answer. I sent a quick text detailing the situation, asking her if she was at Joanna's last night and whether or not she could alibi herself if anything came up. Superfish simply stood there, squinting into the distance like a lone ranger longing for the mountains.

"Can you get me into the caravan?" I asked him eventually.

"This way." He beckoned.

Officers were going door-to-door around the caravan park, interviewing whoever was willing to drag themselves out of bed and answer their knocks. There was a row of cabins on stilts down the hill at the end of the park, the sunlit water glistening like strips of silver between the small wooden dwellings. The rest of the park was crowded with narrow streets of single and annexed caravans, the base of each fenced in with lattice and surrounded by potted plants or piles of sun-bleached boating equipment.

Hogan's caravan was spectacularly decorated with plants on the outside. There were clumps of bright pink and orange bougainvillea hanging over the roof, cascading down either side of the door like an elaborate archway, the vines dipping into an army of potted flowers and ferns arranged along the front of the van. A terra-cotta turtle stood sentry in the pot nearest the first step, holding a wooden sign that read *Welcome!* I noticed a couple of marijuana plants nestled discreetly in the dense foliage at the side of the van, hidden in a tangle of almost identical-looking tomato plants.

Inside, the caravan was surprisingly tidy, a contrast to Hogan's cluttered little office at the hotel. The van was fitted out in a 1950s style, dark wood veneer with mustard-yellow curtains strung over the tiny rounded windows. The bed was made so tightly it hugged the mattress with a band of white, folded-back sheet. The faux marble kitchenette counter was almost empty. There were three recycled jam jars on the counter, holding tea, coffee, and sugar, and nothing else. I squeezed around the photographer taking shots of the tiny living room space at the opposite end to the bedroom. There was a single armchair, a narrow coffee table, and a television set. On the coffee table was a battered *Celeb Hype!* magazine with a label indicating that it had been loaned out from the caravan park's front office.

"Ex-con?" I asked.

"Very close." Superfish nodded, his hands in his pockets. "Long-term homeless."

Being a prisoner teaches you to have few possessions, to keep what you own neat and organized. If you own little, you have little to lose when guards smash your stuff up during shakedowns or pick through your valuables for things they can extort you with—the bunny toy your kid gave you when you went inside that you'll do anything to get back. If your cell is uncluttered you can tell immediately when something is missing, when your cellmate has traded something of yours, or another con has paid a visit during chow time.

It's the same for homeless people. Some fill shopping trolleys and old, battered prams with filthy clothes and worthless trinkets, while others prefer to carry only a single backpack so they can move quickly when they need to, when the other down-and-outs on the edge of the riverbank or under the highway overpass start whistling to warn you the cops are on their way to bust heads and chase bail-jumpers.

"Hogan has been transient since he was about eighteen," Superfish said. "In and out of shelters in Brisbane, Sydney, and Melbourne in that time, never a problem for the staff. Kept to himself, always neat. He has very few possessions here. Probably accustomed to traveling light, reluctant to put down roots."

"What's his major malfunction?" I asked.

"Just a misfit, according to his dad," Superfish said. "No head for school, no heart for sport. Preferred to hang around the wrong crowd his whole life. Chip on his shoulder about his mother walking out when he was a toddler. I would wager that the father didn't help matters. Sounds like a difficult man."

"What's Hogan's rap sheet like?"

"The kinds of things you see with long-term homeless," Superfish said. "Minor brawls with other transients over territory or jobs. Some thefts, loitering, public nuisance. He's been connected with drug-running operations in his time—almost went inside for being a runner after he was discovered guarding a stash house in the late nineties. He's never been charged orchestrating any of the drug activities. Always the bridesmaid, as the saying goes."

"Nothing sexually violent?"

"No, no sexual charges or convictions."

"This place doesn't smell like anything." I inhaled, watching as Superfish did the same. "How long has he been here?"

"He moved in a couple of weeks before he got the White Caps job," Superfish said. "His first long-term employment in over a decade. The neighbors say he's quiet as a mouse. Handy. He'll put your bins out for you if you forget to do it. They say he spends a lot of his time working. He works around the park or he works at the hotel. Sounds like someone who's afraid of losing his focus and going off the rails again."

"Is it possible he bolted because of something else?" I asked. "He's got dope plants around the side of the van."

"We found this in the bedroom," Superfish said. I followed him the five or six paces it took to traverse the living room and kitchen, and he pointed to the bedside table fixed to the curved wall. On the otherwise empty surface lay an Iron Man action figure. The photographer had set up a tiny yellow plastic label next to the doll marked with a black number three. The drawer was open, and as I stepped closer I could see there was a Bible, a packet of condoms, and some eye drops in the drawer, and nothing else. I looked around the room, wondering if Richie had been here, if this bare, characterless place was where the child had lost his life.

Children were disgusting. Of course that was true. But there was more to Amanda's discomfort with children than that, something she wouldn't have been able to explain to Ted even if she tried. She sat on the couch and watched helplessly as Lillian carefully selected books from the bottom shelves of her bookcase and stacked them on the carpet, making three neat piles without any apparent reason for their distinction, slamming each book onto its pile with both hands, making a satisfying slap sound. She talked to herself, wandering into songs she only seemed to know a couple of lines of, opening some of the books on the floor and fiddling through their pages. Her dark lashes, Ted's thoughtful, dark-blue eyes downcast, failing to take in the words before her. Amanda watched as the child abandoned her non-reading and flopped onto her backside, picking at something deep inside her nostril.

If other adults were a mystery to Amanda, children presented a universe of questions everyone else in her world seemed to ignore. Amanda felt anxious around them, having seen them burst into hysterics without any apparent provocation far too many times. She had spent her life trying to reconcile the connection between people's words, facial expressions, hidden and actual emotions, and how they translated to their intentions. With children there were no words, or few that made sense, and none of the emotions connected to the physical displays. They screamed with anger. Roared with joy. Fell asleep or cried in the midst of whirlwinds of activity like machines suddenly disconnected from power. All these hellish performances came from the freakish mutation of another person's face in miniature—Ted's face, his hair, the way he pulled in the corner of his mouth in thought replicated onto the likeness of a small girl.

Lillian seemed to finish her business with the books and came toward Amanda, almost stumbling over Two, who had been heading for a patch of sunlight on the end of the couch. Amanda crawled up the couch as the grabby-grabby hands came for her tattooed legs.

"Hello, Fairy!" Lillian beamed.

"Ehhh!" Amanda squeezed her eyes shut, braced for touching. The child wandered into the kitchen instead. Amanda followed, watching as Lillian pulled open a low cupboard and grabbed the handles of a large soup pot, grunting with effort as she tried to lift the pot down onto the floor.

"No, no, no." Amanda grabbed for the pot. "This is . . . What are you doing? What do you want? Are you hungry?"

Lillian set the pot on the tiles. She lifted off the lid and stuck her head into the iron cavity, yelled.

"I don't understand what's happening," Amanda said, sitting on the floor in front of the child. "What's the process here?"

Lillian dragged pots and pans out of the cupboard, arranging them on the floor. She lifted the lid from each, looked through the glass, set it clunking back into place. Amanda watched, baffled. Each lid was lifted, replaced, lifted again and set aside, the child taking a small saucepan lid and setting it in the middle of the large fry pan.

"Well, clearly that doesn't go there," Amanda said, watching the child's eyes. "I mean, you can see that. Right?"

The child took no notice of Amanda's directions to replace the saucepan lid where it belonged. She licked the lid in her hand, saliva running in a stream down the glass.

"Where's Daddy?" she asked suddenly, as though the thought had popped in her mind like a bubble.

"He's busy catching a kid-killer and leaving me completely out of it, sprog," Amanda said.

Lillian seemed to take the news hard. She looked toward the closed front door.

Amanda began to form an idea. She reached up and pulled open the drawer beside the sink, feeling around among the items there until she found what she wanted. She handed a wooden spoon to the child. Lillian tapped experimentally on a saucepan lid, making a hollow *ponk-ponk-ponk* sound.

The child broke into a grin. Amanda did, too.

I sat on the steps of an empty caravan not far from Hogan's and watched the hive of activity surrounding what had been his modest living quarters. The dog squad was there, leading their animals around and under the van, waiting for approval to take the dogs inside to see if they could scent Richie. To my right, through a tangle of rainforest at the edge of the creek that enclosed the park, I could see press vans adding themselves to the sizeable queue at the roadblock, drivers leaning out the window, pointing down the hill. The creek was lined with crocodile warning signs every twenty meters and bordered by a low chain-link fence. I wondered if a nuisance croc had once made an appearance in the park, attracted by the residents hosing off meaty barbecue grills near the banks and city dogs going wild and splashing in the water.

I checked the news sites, and Dylan Hogan had already made it up there. At their core, each article professed simply that police were seeking assistance from Hogan in the matter of the missing boy Richie Farrow, but a handful of sites ran a decidedly unflattering picture of Hogan from his addict days, more hollow-cheeked and ragged-looking than I knew him to be. His head was tilted back, the man eyeing the camera across a bonfire.

Violent homeless man wanted for questioning in Farrow abduction.

Dylan Hogan: New name in hunt for Richie's killer.

Manhunt: Police pursue vicious vagrant.

Superfish had dutifully joined Joanna Fischer outside the caravan park's reception building. I watched her as she listened to Superfish, her hands on her belt, her eyes flicking toward me now and then. Someone had done a good job on Joanna, that much was clear. Her right eye was surrounded by an ink-blue flower of bruising that faded to purple at the edges, the upper eyelid swollen and the whites of her eye bloodshot. There was also a pattern of lighter brown bruises on her left bicep, four distinct lines like someone had grabbed her too hard, and, though I couldn't be sure from this distance, I thought I could see a chunk of hair missing from the back of her head. I tried to call Amanda, but she texted that Val was there picking Lillian up and that she'd meet me at the hotel. There was also a message from Laney.

I've been thinking of checking out this cool bar in H/Beach, but I've had no one to go with.

A date. In public. In Holloways Beach. I was as well known in Holloways Beach as I was in Crimson Lake. In the beginning, when I'd first moved into the area, I'd been able to go there without being hassled by drunks and locals bored and looking for a fight. But a couple of times I'd run into trouble and had since stopped going. Nobody ever put up much of a fuss if I appeared at a bar once or twice, but nowhere wanted to be my local, to be known as a safe harbor for notorious pedophiles. Even as I knew I couldn't possibly do it, couldn't endanger Laney by appearing in public with her, I texted back anyway.

Sounds fun! Let me call you tonight and we'll work it out.

A shadow fell over me, and I stood, towering over Frisp and Gamble, the two idiots who had mistakenly arrested me at my house. Gamble's long, hairy arms were folded awkwardly, like two coat hangers interlocked.

"Where's that nasty little parasite you call an offsider?" Gamble asked.

"Excuse me?"

"Some of the boys want to have words with Amanda," Frisp said. "She assaulted a police officer. Either her or her mongrel, drug-dealer mates."

"Was she too ashamed to show her face?" Gamble asked. "Hiding at home, the filthy murderous bitch."

"I really hope you two give this gig up soon for something less mentally challenging." I shook my head. "You can't be all this country has to offer in investigative intelligence."

"We're smart enough not to count murderers as our friends," Frisp said. "Or rock spiders."

"But you're not smart enough to notice Joanna's bruise is on the right side of her face, and Amanda is right-handed," I said. "Joanna's right-handed, too. Why doesn't Joanna have any defensive bruises on her forearms? Why did she, a trained police officer, allow Amanda to walk up and clock her like that? Something about this doesn't make sense, boys. You've got to admit it."

They shook their heads, disgusted, but for some reason I pressed on.

"What's the bet we're not going to find a single scratch on Amanda? This wasn't a fight, and if it was, Joanna would have reported it and had the matter investigated. Instead she's playing for sympathy. If I had to guess, I'd say Joanna punched herself, and she's counting on you dickheads lapping up her bullshit and joining her crusade against my partner."

I gave Frisp and Gamble time to think it over, to look at Joanna and weigh my theory, but they didn't. The two of them edged me in, trying to back me into the caravan wall.

"Amanda assaulted one of ours, and she's dropped another in hot water. She's got Chief Clark up Detective Ng's arse with some bullshit about missing cash seized as evidence. She wants to fuck with us, she's going to get what's coming to her."

"Back off," I warned as they stepped closer.

"Tell Amanda that payback is coming," Gamble said.

"Is that a threat?" I asked.

"It's nothing." Frisp kicked Gamble's boot with his. They turned to go, but I stopped Gamble. He shrugged off my hand like it was red-hot.

"Don't do anything," I said. "I'm telling you, this

will get out of hand. And when it does, it's going to be very messy."

"Is *that* a threat?" Gamble lunged, shoved me in the chest.

I put my hands up. We had the attention of all the officers nearby, men leaving their conversations and starting to move toward us. I walked off as Frisp dragged his partner away.

I waited for Amanda in the bar at the Clattering Clam, having wandered in there to make myself a coffee. I wedged the phone between my ear and shoulder and called Sara, giving her an update on the Dylan Hogan lead. The café across the street from the side entrance of the hotel was so packed with journalists when I drove by that a waitress was standing on the corner crying from stress while another consoled her. A man was shouting at the manager, waving his receipt about. It was going to be another hot one, the bar full of fruit flies hovering and whizzing about over the dry beer taps. Someone had left a note on the counter for the manager, scrawled on the back of one of the restaurant's takeaway menus.

Simmo, when the fuck are we getting back to work? I need shifts!—Gavin

I heard shouting as I stirred sugar into my coffee— press on the steps trying to follow someone in and being stopped at the footpath by patrol officers. Instead of Amanda, Henry Farrow stormed into the bar. I smelled alcohol on him before he even rounded the counter, a sweet smell that mingled with the sweat coming off a thin, cheap shirt. The shirt had obviously been bought at a tourist shop nearby, the tag still hanging under the left armpit. He carried his phone with him, and slammed it on the counter in front of me.

"Seen this?" he said. I was too busy looking at him, trying to work out if he was still drunk. His blond stubble was a painful red around his neck, and his eyes were puffy. I took the phone and read the headline of *The Everyday Post*.

Missing boy's father parties hard in tourist paradise.

There were several photographs of Henry at the Rattle N Hum bar, a popular spot just off the Esplanade fitted out with heavy eucalyptus-log furniture and corrugated iron artworks. Big television screens lit green with the soccer game showered Henry in light as he shot rounds of pool in the crowded bar, laughed and hugged an unknown woman, held his hand up to the bartender, ordering two of something, his pale belly sagging out from under his shirt. I scrolled through the photos and handed the phone back.

"I want to hire you," Henry said. "I know you're working for Sara. But while you're doing that you can keep these fucking press bastards off my back. I don't want them within five hundred meters of me."

"Mr. Farrow, I'm not a bodyguard," I said. "Frankly, going to the bar last night was like throwing chips to seagulls. They'll be all over you now. I have no idea what you were thinking."

"I was tired." He held his hands out. "I was sad. I've spent the past couple of days sitting in a hotel room listening to child abduction experts and bloody forensics people and police captains talking about what they're going to do if they find my kid dead. They keep giving me statistics. There's a fifty percent chance he's still alive. Now there's a thirty percent chance. Sara won't speak to me."

"She won't?"

"She's completely cut me off. Won't tell me why. She probably thinks I've been ragging on her to the cops, but I haven't. I tell you what—I certainly could! I've got some stories about that woman, about her losing her temper and scaring our kid. She's a psycho. She throws things." He pointed out the door as though Sara was standing there. "She's thrown stuff at me over the years."

"Henry," I said.

"She should be on my side in this," Henry shouted. "I'm alone and I'm trying to help."

"I understand, but—" I tugged the tag off his shirt. The fabric crinkled against something on his bicep. I paused.

"I just wanted to blow off some steam last night, you know? Did you read the article? It says I danced with several women in the bar. That we laughed and flirted. That is absolute rubbish. That woman came up and hugged me and said she was sorry for what had happened, and—"

I stuck a finger under the sleeve of Henry's shirt and tried to lift the fabric. He flinched away from me.

"What is that?" I asked.

"What?"

"On your arm. Is that plastic wrap on your arm?"

"No."

"Yes it is," I said. "Is that a tattoo?"

"It's for Richie," he said. He lifted his sleeve. Through the plastic wrap and soothing cream I could barely make out a black-and-gray portrait of the missing child, his smiling face and big teeth. Beneath the portrait the words *Belle vie* had been inked in fine, curling cursive script.

I covered my face with my hands. Drew a deep breath, let it out hard.

"Where did you get that?"

"There's a place over on the north side." He waved.

"So you're telling me that in the past twenty-four hours you've dropped into a bar, shot some pool, hung out with some ladies you don't know, and got yourself some fresh ink?" I could feel my face flushing with color. "You got a memorial tattoo of your kid? You don't even know if he's dead!"

"It's not a memorial tattoo!"

"Does that script read *Beautiful life* in French or does it not, Mr. Farrow?" I asked.

"Well, it doesn't say beautiful death!" His eyes were blazing. "Who the fuck are you to judge me? My kid is missing. I'm traumatized! What am I supposed to do? No one is telling me what to do!"

I turned away from him, walked to the end of the bar, and sat down. I thought about how diligently I had listened to my lawyer, Sean, after my arrest, how comforting it had been to have someone simply tell me what to do. Get some sleep. Keep eating. Don't call anyone. Don't grant any interviews. Sign here. Transfer this amount. Henry Farrow was drowning, and everyone was standing on the riverbank watching him sink.

"I haven't just been hanging around in bars and getting inked," Henry reasoned, his voice fallen to a sad murmur. "I drove around the whole area yesterday, by myself, looking for any sign of him. I stopped along empty roadsides. I picked through discarded piles of clothes in ditches. I walked through the bush, trying to think of where you might dump a dead child. I was facing another night alone in the hotel room trying not to think about what that guy might have done to him. That maintenance guy. Or the one down south. If either of them is involved . . ."

I lifted my head. Henry stood scratching at the plastic wrap through his shirt.

"Henry, you're just going to have to hang in there," I told him. "And you're going to have to do that on your own. Those women in the bar last night were probably journalists or paid by journalists for that shot. Your tattoo artist will give an interview this morning, I guarantee it."

He didn't respond.

"I know you want to drive around looking for Richie but all you're doing is endangering lives. You're drunk. Go back to your hotel room. Lock yourself in. If you really do need to talk, just stick to your police liaison officer, and call me or Amanda if you need us. You can trust us, and the police, and that's about it."

I walked over and gave him my card. He stared down at it in his hand, his lips pursed and eyes wet. I heard the roar of the journalists again and saw

Amanda through the restaurant windows coming up the steps.

"Are you okay?" I asked Amanda as she strode into the hotel in ragged, paint-splattered chinos and a white singlet. She didn't appear bruised in any way, but most of her is covered in tattoos, so it was difficult to tell.

"Oh, I'm fine. I'm just fine." She shrugged stiffly, her jaw locked. "I've had to take a flamethrower to all my earthly possessions. I probably have the bubonic plague. But otherwise, I'm just peachy. Why?"

I explained the accusation made by Joanna Fischer. Amanda's eyes narrowed to glowing, menace-filled slits.

"Are you telling me," she said carefully, "that I'm going to get the rap for punching that stupid woman without even getting to enjoy doing it?"

"So you didn't do it?"

"No," Amanda said. "But I'm going to. I'm gonna smack that bitch so hard her grandkid will be born with my handprint on its face."

"Were you at her house with a couple of your bikie mates last night?"

"Of course."

"*Amanda.*"

"*Aman-duh,*" she imitated me. "You're the one who told me I wasn't angry enough about her pushing my bike over. I don't get angry, Ted. I just sear my visage deep into my enemy's brain with the flaming cattle brand of my devilish trickery. Then, in their nightmares, it's my name they hear whispered on the winds of darkness."

"Amanda—"

"No, it's more like *Amaaandaaaaaa*." She cupped her hands to her mouth and breathed the word.

I groaned. "Did you threaten her?"

"Of course."

"I don't want to hear any more of this." I walked through the back foyer doors and around the pool. "We've got to catch Dylan Hogan. We've got to find Richie Farrow. I don't want *any* bloody winds of darkness carrying *anything* about your feud with Joanna *anywhere* near me."

There was a crowd around Dylan Hogan's office, which had been set up as a crime scene. The equipment Hogan had bought at Bunnings Warehouse the evening before had been brought to the hotel to compare with anything that might already be in the hotel's stock. Like me, the officers Clark had assigned to the Hogan discovery wanted to be sure he hadn't bolted because of a different crime, hadn't somehow discovered Richie's Iron Man toy on his own and brought it home innocently. It was a long shot, and it was probably too late. Hogan's face would be on every news channel in the country. His family, friends, enemies—anyone who had anything to do with him as far back as his childhood—would be fielding calls from the press. He was, at that moment, Australia's most despised man, and I couldn't deny a small sense of relief that he had taken the title from me.

Hogan's equipment was laid out on a table in the shade, labeled and sealed in evidence bags. A uniformed officer was milling around the table guarding it as we approached.

Hogan had bought two rolls of silver duct tape,

clear plastic drop sheets that you might use while painting, a hacksaw, a small torch, and a whole lot of rope. I noticed Amanda's eyes went straight to the pile of rope at the back of the table, tightly coiled and sealed in one of the largest transparent evidence bags. I reached out and touched the label on the bag, trying to angle it down so that I could read it. The officer stopped simply glaring at us and finally piped up.

"Hands off the fucking evidence, Conkaffey."

"I'm not touching the evidence," I noted. "I'm touching the evidence bag." I smoothed out the label and read the details printed there. "Nylon rope, thirteen millimeters. Holy shit, there's one hundred meters of it."

"Why is there so much rope?" Amanda asked the officer. "What's he need that much rope for? The rope at least must be for the hotel."

"It doesn't match anything on site." The officer, a fat guy with glasses and sweat patches under his arms, looked me over with disgust. "It's obvious. He wanted it to tie the kid up."

"Why tie the kid up with this thick, slippery rope when you've got duct tape?" Amanda asked. "Too much duct tape, at that. One roll would do."

"You'd know, huh?" the officer sneered.

"Too much rope, too much duct tape," I mused.

"For a live kid at least," Amanda said.

I shifted the rope aside, having spotted something behind it. In another evidence bag there was a large iron hook, the kind one might attach to a boat or car for towing. I picked up the bag with the hook and examined it.

"Hey!"

"Calm your tits," Amanda told the officer. "He's not going to run off with it."

"What's the hook for?" I wondered. "Is he towing something?"

The officer snatched the bag from my hand.

"It's for hooking the kid to a cinder block and dumping him in the river," the officer said. "I don't fucking know. You don't need to touch this stuff to put together a theory."

"Why hook the kid to a cinder block?" I asked. "Why not just tie—"

"That's it." The officer beckoned to a couple of his mates standing at the door to Hogan's office. "You two are out of here."

"We've got approval from Clark to review the evidence," I said.

He was failing to get the attention of his friends, conflicted about leaving the evidence with us, doing an awkward shuffle between the table and a spot halfway across the pool area. I put him out of his misery and wandered away with Amanda. We stood in the painfully bright light reflecting from the pool.

"What's Hogan doing?" I asked.

"Climbing?" she said. "Nylon's good for towing and climbing. Doesn't stretch too much."

"Where would he be climbing?" I asked. "And without a harness or a winch?"

"You see either a harness or a winch at his caravan?"

"No." I shrugged. "But that doesn't mean they weren't there, I suppose."

We stood in silence for a long time, the sun roasting the back of my neck, a not wholly unpleasant feeling.

"All right, here it is. Another brilliant criminal prediction brought to you by Amanda Pharrell," Amanda said. "Hogan's taken Richie, killed him, and thrown his body down an embankment or a cliff somewhere. Realizes he's picked a bad spot, has to move it. He plans to retrieve it, cut it up, move it."

"It's not a bad theory," I said, watching her face, marveling at how emotionless it was. Only the streaks and shadows of the light bouncing off the rippling water moved against her eyes. She put out a hand.

"That's mine. Now you come up with one. Loser makes cake."

Amanda always bets cake, on cases, on the weather, on the outcome of football games. There's a standing agreement between us that whoever's responsible for solving each case we work together, the "winner" gets a cake made by the other, the "loser." I have demanded she make me complicated, elaborate cakes in an attempt to discourage her from arranging the bets so often, or talking about their outcomes in front of victims or police personnel, but she's persisted. I've found her drenched in sweat, surrounded by curious cats in her apartment, the kitchen a mess as she tries to temper white chocolate on a chilled marble slate. But I have also downloaded recipes for various candy-based no-bake slices to satisfy my obligations. I had no theory on Hogan's need for the rope and the hook he had bought, but I promised to mull over one.

"We better find this kid soon," Amanda sighed. "If he's been dumped anywhere around here he's going to be eaten. The crocs will get him in the swamps, and the dingoes will get him in the mountains."

The cops within earshot of us turned at Amanda's words, but before there could be any confrontation my partner walked off toward the foyer, smiling at the officers as she went.

Dylan Hogan had run east from his caravan in the upper section of the Big Lots caravan park, splashing through the creek with the croc warning signs and disappearing into the swamps where pursuit by sniffer dogs would be impossible. From there, we needed to guess where he'd gone.

I drove and considered Hogan's problem. If it had been me, I'd have made my way south through the marshlands, risking life and limb to try to make it to the Cairns Golf Club. From there, it was a straight shot west over the golf course, through the forests lining the fairways to the Bruce Highway, where it would be a mystery to police whether I'd hitchhiked north or south. I'd have gone wherever the traffic was heading, anything to get me out of the area before the roadblocks and cordons came down.

But Dylan Hogan was not me. He was tougher, leaner, and more practiced in running, a man who had lived a life shifting through the shadows on the edge of society, going days without food in the pursuit of shelter or days without shelter in the pursuit of food. It was possible he had gone east rather than west, into the kilometers of wilderness the locals called White

Rock, but which in reality was a sprawling green and brown tangle of impenetrable rainforest. If Hogan had managed to navigate the thick, stinking mud traps, collapsing sandbars, thickets of poisonous vines and croc-infested waterways here in the full darkness of the night, he might have made it out to Chinaman Creek, where there were any number of yabby-fishing boats and abandoned, barnacle-encrusted kayaks lifted up and carried away from the tourist parks. He might have taken one of these across the creek to Trinity Forest, a huge, featureless nature reserve manned only by rangers in four-wheel drives.

The question was where Hogan was going, and who would harbor him. I knew that there were dozens, if not hundreds, of abandoned little houses on the banks of the creeks and inlets twisting and winding away from the main vein of Chinaman Creek, dwellings that had taken one bad flood and not been worth the trouble to reconstruct. These places might have been a good option for Hogan to spend a night, but in the long term he'd need food, and the mosquitoes in those areas would drive him wild, the glass in the abandoned houses invariably having been punched out by bored local teens. There were dope growers nestled in the depths of the wilds, their crops made invisible from helicopters by the thick rainforest canopy, but you had to know where these camps were or stumbling upon them was near impossible, and there was always the threat that before getting anywhere near a camp you'd trip one of their homemade booby traps and they'd come and shoot you before you could explain yourself.

In the end, Amanda and I decided that if Hogan

hadn't hitched a ride from the Bruce Highway he would be holed up with the homeless of the Cairns region. They were his people. He knew their code, their practices, and among them he would be just one of many fugitives trying to start again, public enemies shying away from the light.

I followed Amanda along the winding dirt roads on the edge of the cane fields and marshlands, keeping up with her at times only by following her fresh tracks in the soft clay. It was clear almost immediately that the police were on the same mission we were—patrol vehicles popping up unexpectedly from around tight corners in the forest, officers giving me the stink eye as they navigated their car around mine on the narrow bends. I stopped at the first few camps and agreed to let Amanda go in ahead of me. With her tattoos, wild hair, and crazy stories, she seemed to get a curious if not appreciative gaze from the drunks and skittish men we found lounging on the banks of the rivers. I sat in the car and watched her gesticulating wildly at them in the midst of their little tent communities, unable to tell if she was describing our quarry or regaling them with tales from her extraordinary collection of half-true adventures. When the men nodded or shrugged or gazed off at the river at her words, she slipped them banknotes from a thick bundle she had folded into the pocket of her motorcycle jacket, and that seemed to get them talking.

She walked back to the car on the fifth or sixth stop and leaned in the window, squinting in the afternoon sunlight as she pushed her sparkly sunglasses up onto her brow.

"The fuzz is going through ahead of us and messing up people's camps," she said. "They're pushing guys around and kicking over their shit. It's not making for very conducive witnesses."

"You might end up spending your life savings just finding out the time of day." I glanced at her jacket pocket. "How much have you got there?"

"A bit." She gave me a dismissive wave. "It's fine. I'll claim it on tax. Work expenses."

I knew she wasn't serious, but the appearance of the money in Amanda's hands had sent shivers through me. A rumor had circulated after our last major case that Amanda had made off with millions of dollars belonging to an ancient corrupt police officer. There was no way to say if there was any truth to it. I knew how the Crimson Lake cops felt about Amanda, and most of the rumors had originated with them. The facts were that Amanda had busted a pair of men trying to find said missing millions, and no millions were found, and Amanda had at times demonstrated almost supernatural observational skills. Not much to go on. But Amanda had given me an unexpected pay raise mere days after the case ended, and here she was handing out twenties and fifties around the homeless camps of Cairns like a pint-sized Robin Hood touring Sherwood Forest.

The handout seemed to be generating goodwill. The homeless men and women were giving her tips about all kinds of local crimes, tidbits we could tuck away for use in future cases. But no one was willing to admit they had seen Dylan Hogan, and Amanda's pile of money was thinning.

We had arrived at a camp beneath an overpass off the Bruce Highway when my phone buzzed on the seat beside me. It was a message from Laney Bass.

Reminds me of you, the message said. There was a laughing face emoji and a link. I clicked the link and my phone took me to YouTube, where "Watching the Detectives" by Elvis Costello began to play. I laughed, then checked to see if Amanda could see me. She was adjusting something on her bike. I put the phone down and tried to think of songs about animals or veterinarians, feeling like a teenager writing secret love letters to my sweetheart at the back of maths class.

The dread and guilt about lying to Laney began to creep back in and I tried to shake it off, actually bristled in my seat. There was no need to ruin a good thing yet. It was possible, I told myself, that she would never find out. That we'd go on a date, have a great time, kiss and hold each other, laugh and roll around and make pancakes in the morning. It was possible that we'd go on like this for years, getting bored at work and sending each other funny texts. I remembered her patting Lillian's hair, the girl instinctively trusting her, and Laney naturally loving and caring for my child in return. Maybe it was a sign. The odds were a billion to one, sure. But if I never told Laney about my accusation, maybe it would never enter our lives.

I copied the YouTube link for "The Love Cats" by The Cure. Love was maybe a bit forward, but I thought it was worth the risk. I wrote *Got you in my head!* and attached the link, and had just hit send when I realized I had replied to the wrong number.

The phone started ringing. I squeezed my eyes shut and answered.

"Is there something you want to tell me, Conkaffey?" Chief Clark asked.

"No, Chief. There's certainly not."

"For the girlfriend, was it?" he asked. I got out of the car.

"No. Yes."

"Well. I was going to give you a call anyway. They've found a burn site at the DeCasper place," he said. "And they've found charred remains in the soil where the dig was conducted."

Amanda approached me, trying to analyze my facial expressions, my face flushing with embarrassment and then suddenly draining with dread.

"They think they've got bone chips. We don't know how old they are."

"Are they human?" I grimaced.

"We don't know. Dr. Valerie Gratteur is going to take a look at them. She's based in Cairns. She's very good."

More dread. If Val had agreed to look at the remains from the DeCasper dig, that meant she'd likely be taking Lillian with her to the morgue. My three-year-old daughter in a morgue with bones and a morgue woman. Kelly was going to kill me. I told Clark to keep us updated and filled Amanda in on the news.

"Could be anything." Amanda clicked her tongue, nonchalant. "A pig. A horse."

"Why would you burn and then bury a horse?"

"What else would you do with a dead horse?" she asked.

"I guess I've never had that problem," I conceded.

We walked toward the camp together.

The setup was much the same as the others we'd been visiting: a group of tents clustered at the bottom of the rocky slope beneath the bridge, their fabric tops spattered with pigeon droppings from a shelf above them. Some of the men here were passing through, but there were two more permanent-looking dwellings on the concrete verge before the river, fishing lines set up so that they could be tended to while a person slept beneath a sheet of corrugated iron propped up by slabs of plywood. A communal billycan was boiling over a rock-lined campfire, almost as though they'd put a pot on in anticipation of our arrival. Two men were lounging just out of range of the fire on blankets, one fanning himself with a scrap of cardboard, the other sleeping, his mouth open and sagging. By the water's edge, wearing only a black cotton dress that was pockmarked with moth holes, a woman was checking the fishing lines, pulling each up and testing the weight with her index finger to see if anything had stolen her bait.

"Hearty hobos! Tremendous tramps! Boisterous bums and feisty fringe-dwellers, lend me your ears!" Amanda announced as we arrived, thrusting out her arms. "I am Amanda Pharrell, scourge of Crimson Lake! I come for your assistance and I bring you offerings of shiny coins and ancient wisdom!"

She took out her stack of notes and "made it rain," as the saying goes, showering the sleeping hobo on the blanket with twenties. He didn't stir. The man fanning himself sat up and dug deep into his ear with his pinkie finger, as though clearing room for Amanda's words to get through.

"Whaddaya want?" He waved an arm at us. "Farg-off. We're allowed-a be here. It ain't council land."

"Clean your other ear out too, mate," Amanda said. "I'm not trying to move you on. I'm looking for this guy." She crouched before the fire and handed her phone to the man, the screen showing a picture of Hogan. I watched as she picked up a plastic coffee cup from a pile of debris near the fire. "Is this coffee? Don't mind if I do. Ted, you want a cup?"

"No thanks." I put my hands in my pockets, feeling strangely itchy and unwashed. The man on the blanket had noticed Amanda's twenties and was gathering them up, hardly glancing at the phone.

"Seen that guy around in the past twenty-four hours?" she asked.

"Nah, nah." The man glanced behind him to see if the woman at the water's edge had noticed the money. "I ain't seen anything like him."

"You hardly looked."

"I didn't look at all, mate." The man grinned at Amanda. "I've only got ten percent of me vision. I'm legally blind."

"That's interesting," I remarked. He hadn't had any trouble seeing the twenties littered all over his partner a few feet away. Amanda slurped her coffee loudly, smacking her lips and frowning into the cup.

"This coffee tastes weird. What's in this?"

"Hepatitis," the man laughed. He seemed to find his joke funnier and funnier as the seconds passed, eventually dissolving into giggles and rolling on his side.

The woman by the water had caught my attention. She'd finished checking the lines and glanced over at us before taking a pair of muddy black work boots from outside a tent and opening the zipper. She put the boots inside the tent and zipped it back up. I thought I saw something move against the taut fabric side of the dirty little dwelling.

"Have the cops come through here today?" Amanda asked, unfathomably still drinking the coffee.

"Oh, they came," the man said, fanning himself again. "I told 'em to fargoff just like I told youse. This here ain't council land. It belongs to me brother-in-law. Me dad's brother-in-law, I should say."

"Is it just the four of you here?" I asked.

"Yep," the man said. He folded one of the twenties in half and used the bent corner to scrape the dirt out of his toenails. The penny took a while to drop. "Three, I mean. Just the three of us."

"Right." I put a hand on the gun tucked into the back of my pants. Amanda put her coffee down. "Could I get you all out here so we can talk, please?"

"We're all here," the woman piped up, pushing her greasy hair back behind her ear. "This is all there—"

The man on the blanket grabbed the billycan off the fire with his bare hand and hurled it at me, the scalding water hitting my lower legs. I barely felt the burns. Amanda had sprung to her feet and bolted for the tent by the water's edge just as Hogan ripped down the zipper and emerged, almost losing his balance in the dusty earth as he turned and sprinted under the bridge. I drew my gun, shouted, but Amanda was doubling back toward me for her bike. I ran down the hill and under the bridge, Hogan by now a distant smear of color in the long grass.

"Stop!" I called, swinging the gun as I ran, every muscle springing awake in pain and protest at the sudden urgent movement. "Hogan, stop!"

I don't know how long we ran for. My body passed through its initial shock phase, the pain eased and I warmed into a steady rhythm, making gains on Hogan but too puffed to call out to him. My limbs remembered chases of days past, when I'd run through suburban or city streets in full tactical gear, climbing and leaping over fences, my heavy boots thumping the pavement. Amanda whizzed past me on the bike before I could hear its thick, puttering engine, almost knocking me off the path. Hogan heard the bike and ducked into the rainforest, blasting through a wall of vines and brush without stopping.

Amanda ditched the bike and we followed, panting, my partner having just enough breath to shout after our quarry.

"Hogan!" she yelled. "Stop, you stupid fuck!"

I lost sight of Hogan, followed Amanda, slammed into her as she lost sight of him, too. Around us the rainforest was alive with noise, birds in the canopy, wind through the undergrowth. Everything seemed to move. I couldn't catch my breath. Amanda had been whipped in the face by a low-hanging branch and her cheek was streaked with thin, bright blood.

"Motherfucker," she gasped, grabbing at a stitch in her side, her eyes darting around the forest. "Mo . . . ther . . . fu—"

She cut off her own words, seeming to spot him

in the distance. She ran, but the stitch was bringing her down. I pulled ahead. When I found Hogan he was standing at the edge of an embankment, his chest heaving beneath his filthy shirt, his arms lined with scratches the same as the one Amanda had across her cheek.

"Hands up." I lifted my gun. "On your knees."

Dylan Hogan was even more ragged on the run than he had been in his everyday life, the revelation of his crime seeming to have somehow stripped weight and strength from him, hollowing his cheeks, reddening the whites of his eyes. He looked over the embankment.

Amanda's gun appeared beside mine. "I will shoot you, Hogan," Amanda promised.

"It was an accident," the man said. His face crumpled momentarily as emotion overwhelmed him, his teeth showing between his lips. "I'm sorry. I'm so sorry. It was a bloody accident."

"We can talk about it later." I gestured with my gun. "Get on your knees now or Amanda will shoot. She's fucking crazy."

I felt Amanda glance at me. Hogan gripped his hair, spittle flying from between his teeth as he fought for breath, fought to hold back his tears.

"They won't believe me now," he said. "They won't believe I didn't mean it. I've ruined everything. I've ruined everything. Oh, Jesus. Oh, Jesus. I killed a fucking kid."

"Where's the body?" I asked, but Dylan didn't have a chance to answer. Amanda started walking forward. I didn't know if she was going to shoot Hogan, hit him with the gun, or try to make a grab for him without my assistance. I reached for her shoulder, and in the time it took to distract Amanda from her goal, Hogan threw himself off the embankment.

I heard him roll through the bush before I reached the point at which he'd disappeared. Amanda and I ran down the slope, crashing through the undergrowth, my feet somehow finding a place between the fallen branches and tangled vines. The sound of sirens rose like a wail from beyond the forest. I realized Amanda must have called the police when she ran back for her bike. At the same time, I saw the unmistakable pattern of blue and white checks whizz through the thinning rainforest up ahead.

The petrol station at the side of the road seemed to materialize out of nowhere. Amanda sprinted ahead of me down the muddy path, following Hogan toward the back door. I heard the crunch of brakes skidding on gravel out the front of the petrol station.

"He's unarmed! He's unarmed! Don't shoot!" I heard Amanda scream.

Two gunshots split the air.

Three seconds. Maybe less. That's all I needed to get ahold of the situation. I stepped inside the door of the petrol station and walked to the aisle where the drinks fridges lined the wall. And there I found Dylan Hogan on the floor, gripping two holes in his chest. Amanda was bowed over him, her hands covered in blood, desperately trying to gather the folds of Dylan's shirt and his own hands over the wounds, to somehow cover up and deny their existence and save the dying man's life.

I looked up and saw Joanna Fischer standing there,

both hands gripped around her black Glock 22, the smell of expired gunpowder still hanging thinly in the air. In three seconds I saw Dylan and Amanda and then Joanna, and I saw on Joanna's face the vicious intent in her eyes. The intent to fire again where the barrel of the gun was already pointed, right at Amanda's head.

Joanna's eyes flicked to me. Nothing else about her moved. She didn't even seem to be breathing. The decision was like a switch flipped. She took her finger off the trigger, and the intent drained from her features, sucked away instantly as footsteps sounded at the front of the shop.

"Oh no. Oh, man." Superfish assessed the scene and dropped his own aim, his gun slipping back into his holster with relief while his body slumped at the sight of Hogan. He turned and shouted toward the doorway, where more officers were sliding their cars into the lot. "Clear in here! Clear!"

When I looked back at Joanna, it was as though a different person stood there. Her eyes were already wet with tears. She holstered her gun with shaking hands.

"Oh god," she stammered. "I . . . I shot him. I shot him."

"Conkaffey." Superfish pointed at me. "Put your weapon away. Get Amanda's gun now, please."

I did as I was told, taking Amanda's weapon from the floor and ejecting the magazine. The small space around us was suddenly crowded with cops. Someone was taking my arm, shoving at me, barking. I was standing outside by the petrol pumps, feeling all the numb dread of a man facing the firing squad, suddenly unable to focus on anything but the ringing in my ears from the gunshots. The petrol station employees were gathering together at the pumps, wide-eyed and silent like frightened birds.

Joanna Fischer was crying into her hands. Chief Clark had appeared out of nowhere and was listening with his arms folded, Amanda and Joanna before him, the angry father assessing as one bullied child described a fray while the other waited for her turn.

"She shouted, 'He's armed! He's armed! Shoot!' So I shot him." Joanna was really putting on a show, her whole body shaking now. "I can't believe it."

"I did not say that," Amanda protested, watching Joanna's performance calmly. "I said the exact opposite."

"Why would you say he was armed when he wasn't?" Joanna howled at Amanda. "Oh god, I've killed a man. I've *killed* a man!"

I strode into the huddle, pushing Amanda aside.

"I can back up what Amanda said," I told Chief Clark, whose eyes were downcast, his fists clenching and unclenching. "So can the staff. Does the petrol station CCTV have audio? It'll be on the tape. I'm a witness. This is a setup. This is a *fucking* setup! Joanna shot Dylan Hogan and she'd have shot Amanda if I wasn't there."

Joanna gave a dramatic gasp of horror, grabbed at her throat and mouth like she was going to be sick. Clark was visibly trembling with rage.

"You're out." He pointed at me, at Amanda. "You're both out. Go home. That's it for you. That's all I'm willing to take."

"Amanda didn't—"

"Get out of here!" Clark roared so loudly and so hatefully that I stepped back, thinking he was going to swing at me. "Go now, before I knock your fucking face in!"

I stormed off toward the petrol pumps and kicked over a rubbish bin, picked up a squeegee and flung it at one of the pumps. I didn't know Amanda was behind me until I turned and almost shouted an obscenity in pure rage right into her face. I didn't get a sound out. Her bloody fist smashed into my left cheekbone with the full force of her body, a blow that pounded through my skull and seemed to leave in a red burst of energy at the back of my head.

She held up a finger as I tried to recover.

"Call me crazy again," she said, red rivulets of Dylan Hogan's blood running down her wrist. "I dare you, Ted."

I didn't say anything. I held my face, and we stood together in silence, watching as the ambulance arrived and Joanna was given oxygen while the paramedics worked on Hogan inside. I knew the maintenance man was dead when one of them came wandering out, talking on a mobile phone, his uniform splattered with blood.

Superfish looked over at me once or twice, but he stayed at his partner's side.

Lillian and Celine were doing their performance at the screen door when I arrived home, which might have brought a smile to my face were it not for the bruise throbbing and growing on my cheekbone. I snatched Lillian up from the ground as soon as I got inside the hall and held her, and the mere feel of her arms around my neck decreased the pain in my body by half.

"Daddy's had the worst day ever," I told her as she puzzled over my swollen, coloring cheek. "He's going to need constant cuddles for at least six or seven hours."

Val was in the kitchen reading a newspaper, half-moon glasses perched on the slope of her hooked nose.

"Worst day ever?" she said without looking up. "That must have been a real zinger. Weren't you falsely arrested for the second time not a week ago?" She finally looked up as I set Lillian down and went to the fridge to get ice packs. "Oh, wow."

"My partner punched me," I said. "A hobo threw boiling hepatitis coffee at me. The lead suspect in our case was gunned down, after admitting that he'd killed our victim. We have no idea where he's hidden the body, and we may never discover that now. I ran after him for bloody miles and some itchy plant has scratched my arm and I think I've twisted a muscle in my groin region."

"These nightly reports of your cheerful investigative jaunts around town are so alluring. They make me wish I'd been a private investigator in my younger years." She sighed dramatically. "Coulda shoulda woulda."

I slumped into the chair across from Val, and Celine stuck her nose under my hand for pats. The plant I'd brushed up against in the rainforest had spread a weird red rash down my left forearm. I held an ice pack to my eye and stroked the dog with my right hand, balancing another ice pack on the burn mark or twisted muscle near my groin that I hadn't yet examined. Val looked at me with amused pity.

"And how was your day, Nanna?" I asked.

"You know, the same old stuff." She let Lillian climb up into her lap. "I took one kid to the morgue to look at burned bone fragments possibly belonging to a different kid."

"Delightful," I said.

"She didn't see anything morbid. I had some nurses up in the children's ward watch her in their playroom while I worked."

"What was the verdict? Were they human remains?"

"I don't know yet," she sighed, curling one of Lillian's ringlets around her finger. "A good deal of what I did today was separating bone fragments from soil. The remains were burned for days, it looks like. I've had a look at the microscopic structure of the bones. The osteons are scattered and evenly spaced, which is consistent with human remains. But I don't have any other species osteons to compare it with. It's not my area of expertise. We'll need to bring in an anthropologist, do some chemical tests."

"I'm sorry, osteons?"

"Little bone pattern thingies."

"Right."

"Even if they are human, they're not the boy's. Is that what you're saying?" she asked.

I explained what had happened, the chase and Dylan Hogan's confession to me, the shooting in the petrol station. Lillian didn't seem to be listening. She talked over me, telling no one in particular a story that was impossible to follow.

"So the boy's dead." Val nodded when I was done, watching Lillian fiddling with a gold chain hanging around her neck. "I guess I'd held out a hope until now that he wasn't. I wonder what happened. I hope it was only an accident, like the man said."

I buried half my face in the soothing ice pack, and we both sat silently as my child sang a garbled, repeating song that seemed to be about beetles. In time I put a hand on the table, and Lillian reached over and slapped her little palm down into mine.

"There's only one thing for it, baby," I told the little girl. "It's time for the geese to have a party."

* * *

Amanda sat with her bare feet up on the plastic picnic table at the bikie camp, her toes wiggling against the gold light of the distant fire, impossibly small beside Llewellyn Bruce's boots. She could see her own reflection in one of the enormous polished buckles holding the leather tight around the old man's thick ankles. They were alone, the camp's three other occupants that night gathered on the water's edge, shadows moving between the palm trees. Deep in thought, she watched the flames and found herself huffing with frustration through her nose.

"If you're gonna sit there snorting and sniveling, I'm gonna move," Bruce said. She looked over at the big man lounging in the plastic chair beside her, his hairy, tattooed arms folded over his belly and a cap pulled down over his eyes.

"He doesn't trust me," Amanda said.

"Who?"

"Conkaffey."

"That's a shame," the old man sniffed. "He's about the only friend you got."

"How can he not trust me?" Amanda complained. "I've been right about everything. It was me who helped him solve his own case. It was me who discovered the thieves behind the Barking Frog. I'm always right."

"*I'm always right,*" Bruce muttered, on the edge of sleep. "Famous last words."

"He doesn't want me hanging around here with you guys," Amanda said. "I don't get it."

"I don't know why he worries about us," Bruce

said. "Bad people are predictable. We'll always do the wrong thing. It's easier. It's faster. Cops and heroes—those are the ones you have to worry about. The temptation is always there to cross over, to cut corners, to break the rules. Good people are always treading water, trying not to drown. Bottom-dwellers like us have gills."

Amanda nodded, sighed again. "I wasn't going to shoot Hogan," she complained. Bruce grunted his assent, but she wouldn't let go. She sipped her beer. "I mean, I wasn't *planning* on shooting him, anyway. It might have ended up being a good idea. But I didn't get a chance to decide. I would only have put one in his kneecap or something."

"Mmm-hmm." Bruce scratched his belly.

"Point is, I know what I'm doing," Amanda said.

"*I'm always right,*" Bruce said. "*I know what I'm doing.* You sound desperate. You better curb that shit. People will think you're weak."

"I'm not." Amanda folded her arms. "I've got Joanna Fischer handled. I'm not crazy. She's crazy. She killed a guy. I've got no problem with that, but, honey, at least get yourself a good reason first. That man died today so she could mess with me, get me off the case. Now that kid's bones will rot away in the earth somewhere and we may never find them."

Bruce said nothing.

"The petrol station CCTV is going to show what I said." Amanda nibbled at her cuticles. "I spoke to the owner on the phone. The shop's security system had audio, and it would have been running. Nothing to worry about."

They watched as the men at the beach began walking toward the camp. There seemed to be too many shadows between the trees. Amanda felt a strange twisting in her stomach. She watched as the shapes in the dark divided, seemed to multiply. But before she could understand what she was seeing, the slide lock on a gun ratcheted back sickeningly close to her left ear. She and Bruce stood at the same time, causing the plastic table to scrape in the dirt. There were two short, stocky men standing at the edge of the shed, their standard-issue police semiautomatic pistols pointed at the pair.

The men were masked, but Amanda recognized a couple of them. Constable Frisp was one of the two that walked Bruce and Amanda out of the shed. She thought she saw Ng among the five men who were holding guns on Jimbo, Rocko, and Kidneys as they walked them up from the beach. In the light from the campfire, the bikers exchanged nervous glances.

There was no plan for this. No one had ever considered the possibility of a quiet, controlled ambush on their own turf on an otherwise ordinary evening, seven men strolling in while the bikies' guns were littered about the place, useless now, the closest one sitting on an upturned bucket surrounded by wary, growling dogs. It was embarrassing how easily they were overcome, herded toward the firelight like civilian hostages.

None of their rival gangs would ever have dared this. These men were walking into a bullpen with a cattle prod. What they couldn't know was that just their hostile arrival was something that wouldn't be forgiven, maybe for decades.

Bruce watched as one of them put his gun away and took a baton from his belt, flicking it open with a sharp, grinding sound.

"This is a bad idea, fellas." Bruce shook his head ruefully.

"You know what was a bad idea?" one of the masked men asked. "Beating on a woman. Beating on a cop. We can't go around letting people believe they can rough up our people and get away with it. You pieces of shit need to learn your place—it's here, in the wilds, with the croc shit and the leeches. You're about to learn what'll happen to you if you set foot in town again."

"Big words," Bruce said. "I heard them. I'm impressed. Now fuck off out of here. This is your last warning." He nodded toward the water. "Leave now, before you do something you'll deeply regret."

One of the men walked up and whipped the baton across the air, a full-strength swipe. The end of the baton caught Bruce in the jaw, spraying blood and shards of teeth. It was the signal for the others to start. Amanda watched in the firelight as her friends fell under the blows. She tried to throw herself into the fray, but she only managed a step before a man caught her arms and twisted them behind her back, shoving her into the ground. She watched, not daring to look away.

A surefire cure for what ails me is a bathroom party with the geese. That's the case most of the time, at least. I poured myself a glass of wine, ran some warm water in the bathtub, stripped Lillian off, and let her climb in. The geese were hardly fazed by her presence in the tub, splashing and squealing with excitement as they came waddling in. They eagerly splayed their wings from their breasts, beaks open and heads high, as four headed into the shower cubicle while two flapped up onto the rim of the bathtub and splashed down into the water with my child.

"Real-life rubber duckies," I told Lillian as she grabbed for the geese paddling and fluffing themselves on the surface of the water. "I bet you've never seen that, have you, Boo?"

I've been hosting bathroom parties since the geese were small and fluffy, turning the shower on and sitting on the lid of the toilet to watch them playing around and flapping in the spray. All it takes to indicate to the birds that a party is about to begin is to throw some Neil Diamond on and open the screen door. The birds come waddling up the yard in a fumbling parade, hopping up the stairs, honking and muttering with excitement. Though it has always raised my mood, I sat that night watching Lillian bathing with the birds and couldn't tune in to the usual feelings of warmth and comfort. I knew it was probably trauma over Dylan Hogan's death, the heavy guilt replaying those terrible moments in the petrol station in my mind. If only I'd run ahead of Amanda. If only I'd called out. If only I'd been smarter about our approach to the homeless camp, made sure I blocked the path under the bridge while Amanda manned the path from the road. I drank my wine and tried to focus on my beautiful child, on the second to last evening I had with her, on the task of being a good, attentive, undistracted father fully committed to making memories with my girl.

I only managed it for mere minutes. I was dialing Clark before I could stop myself.

"I don't want to hear from you," Clark barked down the phone. "I'm too busy battening down the hatches in preparation for the *total career annihilation* that's about to be unleashed upon me after the Hogan shooting."

I held the phone and waited, knowing that speaking, interrupting his rant, would be useless. I'd let him get it out of his system. Most of the first minute was just obscenities, sighs, the rueful silences of a man trying to find the words to express his dismay.

"This is a nightmare," he said eventually. "A true nightmare. I don't know what you're thinking, continuing to partner with that woman. She's a curse. She's death personified. And those are her words, not mine. The longer you hang around her, the more you'll lose, I'm telling you."

"If I may humbly interject," I said quietly. "It was one of *your* officers who killed Hogan, not Amanda. You know Fischer's claim about Amanda saying Hogan was armed is bullshit."

"I don't know what to believe anymore," Clark said.

"The petrol station owner told Amanda there is a tape with audio."

"Yeah, well, if there ever was a tape, there isn't one now," Clark said. "We didn't find one, and the witnesses were too stirred up to know what had happened."

"Uh-huh." I chewed my lip, the anger rising. "Typical. The responding officers would have heard Fischer's claims and gone right into the office and pocketed the tape. How else can you explain its absence? I wouldn't be surprised if they heavied the witnesses."

"Conkaffey." Clark's tone was dark, heavy. "I'm not having this discussion with you right now. Okay? We're not talking. You and your mental-case friend are going to stay out of my face for the foreseeable future, or I won't be held responsible for my actions."

"We are talking," I said. "Something's not right about Hogan. Yes, he said he killed the kid, but where's the body? How did he get it out of the hotel? How did he get into the hotel undetected between the end of his shift and midnight? He said it was an accident.

Why didn't the dogs pick up a crime scene either at the hotel or at the caravan park? I think we should be looking more closely at other people. Other scenarios. I want to reinterview Sara. I want to know if—"

I looked at the phone. Clark had hung up on me. I tapped my legs with my fingers and watched Lillian, telling myself I was off the Richie Farrow case, that his body would be found without me, in the swamps near Hogan's caravan park or in a car we didn't know he owned. I told myself that Hogan had admitted to the boy's death, and that I didn't need to think about it any longer, didn't need to follow the pressing urge to go and get my laptop and go through all the video files again, the CCTV and interviews, video of the hotel room.

Lillian was dripping water off her fingers onto the back of one of the geese when I found what I was looking for in the video files. I stood and took a towel from the rack beside the door.

"Want to go for a ride?" I asked my child, shrugging off the guilt that hung like a barbell across my shoulders.

Luca Errett was in the window when I pulled into the parking lot of the Sea Breeze Motel, ten minutes' drive north of the White Caps on the edge of a small park. Richie's little friend was leaning his elbows on the sill, hidden from the room behind him by thick block-out curtains, staring idly at the empty lot, the street and the ocean beyond. I opened a game on my phone and gave it to Lillian to play with. When I exited the car, I knew what had driven Luca to the very edge of the room, fixated on the world outside, separated from where he wanted to be by a thin pane of sea-salt-encrusted glass.

John Errett's voice was clear through the door, a deep pulsing snarl from somewhere inside the room. "They think a few nights in a dodgy hotel are going to make up for a week's lost wages," he barked. "Well, I'll bill the fuckers. I'll figure out what I've lost this week in commissions and I'll fucking bill them."

As I approached the door and knocked, Luca Errett followed me with his eyes, his head still resting on his hands. I waved through the glass but he didn't wave back. John Errett tore open the door wearing a pair of cotton boxer shorts, and I tried to decipher the tattoos on his narrow chest through the thick mat of black hair. I watched the emotions flick through his eyes as he tried to decide who I was. Anger first, assuming I was with the police. Then curiosity, as he recognized my face. Inevitable contempt when he identified me.

"It's eight o'clock at night." He tapped the heavy silver watch on his wrist. "*Eight o'clock*. If you pricks want to hassle me, it'll be business hours only."

"Apologies for the intrusion," I said. I glanced into the room, where Caroline Errett was sitting on the edge of a battered armchair, drinking a beer and staring at the floor, obviously carrying on their argument in her mind. "It's only you I'd like to speak to. We can leave your family be."

"What do you want?" Errett squinted, looking at

my car, where Lillian was visible through the wind-shield, kicking her legs in her car seat. "The police have everything they need from us. All we want to do is go home. I've got contracts that I have to—"

"Mr. Errett." I tried to warn him with my eyes. "I won't be long. I really think you ought to speak to me."

He held open the door but I stepped back. Those calculating eyes appreciated me.

"Let's go to my car," I said.

He shut the door behind himself and followed me to the vehicle. I took my laptop out of the front seat and walked around the back, set the computer on the boot, and opened the screen. John Errett stood in double-plugger thongs and his boxers, sweating de-spite the disappearance of the sun behind the pale blue strip of ocean beyond the parking lot.

"The police won't tell us when we can go home," he complained, looking in the back window at Lillian. "They call us at all hours. One of them turned up at five this morning asking questions. Five! I'm losing money. You got the guy today, didn't you? You and the other private dick. I don't understand why we're needed here. I'm finding out more about what's going on from the news on my phone than from the cops."

"I can't comment on how long you'll be here," I said, clicking through videos. "I'm off the case."

"What?" Errett looked at me. "Then why the fuck are you here? Why am I talking to you?"

"Watch this," I said. I played a video of the Erretts, Sampsons, and Chos at dinner with Sara Farrow on the night of Richie's disappearance, the seven adults sitting at the long table in the Clattering Clam. The night was still young. There were bottles of wine on the table. We watched Sara Farrow glance at the watch on her wrist before sliding her chair back from the table and leaving.

"She's going to check on the boys." Errett shrugged, his arms folded.

"What's that?" I pointed at the screen, at a small black rectangle on the table by Sara's water glass. Errett leaned in, cocked his head.

"Her phone," he said.

"Interesting." I nodded. I clicked the video closed and brought up another. Sara Farrow walking across the empty hotel foyer, waiting for the elevator. Errett and I watched silently as she pulled a phone out of her back pocket and began to type on it with her thumb.

"Anything you'd like to say?" I asked. Errett balked at me like I'd called him a dirty name.

"What?" he scoffed, showing blackened teeth at the back of his jaw. "No. She's got two phones. Okay. So what?"

I indicated the time at the bottom of the screen. The numbers read 8:56 p.m. I brought up the first video, pointed again to the numbers at the bottom of the screen.

"Watch this," I said again. Errett watched himself on the screen. The lean, pointy-faced man in the video reached for his back pocket, alerted, it seemed, by a vibration through the fabric. We both observed the figure on the screen reading the text.

"I don't know what you're telling me, man," Errett said.

"Yes, you do," I said.

"I don't have time for this." Errett held his hands up. "What the fuck do you want?"

"I want you to explain why Sara Farrow was covertly texting you on a phone she failed to tell police she owned." I gestured to the screen. "Look at yourself. Look at how you lean away from your wife so she can't glance over and read what's on your screen. Look at the time."

"Covertly . . . fucking . . . *what*?" Errett's indignation was a thin veil, his face almost comical in its squinting, twisted expression. He struggled to find the words, the words that would convince me, drive me back out into the night so that he could think, plan his next move. Denial was his first strategy. He'd soon turn to aggression. "Man, what the fuck *is* this?"

"You and Sara," I said. "You're having an affair."

"*What?*" Errett's face dropped, the sharp squint falling and blank, dangerous rage beginning to boil.

"You can deny it all you want," I said. "But it's on the video, plain as day. The police will seize Sara's second phone, if she hasn't dumped it already. Even if she does dump it, and you go ahead and dump yours, records of your messages will exist somewhere."

Errett stared at me. His son in the window had sensed the hostility between the two of us and was perked up, watching carefully.

"I got the first hint of your affair from a journalist," I said. "That journalist has probably got contacts in the phone companies. Are they going to print your private conversations with Sara in the *Telegraph* tomorrow?"

"They won't print nothing," Errett said quietly.

"Because what happened between Sara and me has got nothing to do with her kid going missing. If I was you, I'd keep this to yourself. How's it going to look, you going and telling everyone a grieving mother is a home-wrecker for no good reason at all? Breaking up families. They caught the guy who took Richie."

"Did they?" I asked. "Or do you know more about the situation than you're letting on? You've already covered for yourself and Sara by keeping rather important details from police. You hindered an official investigation to protect your arse."

"You piece of shit." He spat on the ground at my feet.

"Your son told the police you have secrets," I said. "Is this what he meant? Or is there more?"

"Don't things look bad enough for you already, huh?" He stepped closer to me, trying to back me into the car. "Mr. Kidlover creeping around town with a little girl in tow, trying to destroy people's lives? Whose child is that in there? Should I be calling the police on *you*?"

"That's my daughter," I snapped, the rage sudden, never far from the surface. "Don't try to turn this around on me."

"Dad!"

John Errett and I turned. Luca was standing on the couch, both hands on the window, his face a mixture of excitement and fear. I shut the laptop and went around to the driver's-side door of my car, getting in and locking the doors as John Errett remained, still as a stone, right outside Lillian's window.

On the way home, I watched Lillian in the rearview

mirror. It was late for her. She was dozing off, the highway lamps making her perfect skin glow gold, her slowly closing eyelashes set aflame. Outside the car, the world was blue and wet. It had been ninety-three hours since Richie Farrow had last been seen among the living. He was out there somewhere, lying in the stillness, waiting to be found before he became a part of the lush landscape, before he was grown over, as everything that lay down for long enough in this place was.

"Hey, Boo?" I said, jolting Lillian from her sleep. She wriggled in her seat.

"I love you," I told her. She looked out the window at the cobalt mountains, pointed at nothing.

"Hey, Daddy?" she said.

"Yes?"

"Hey, Daddy."

"Yes."

"Daaaaaadddyyyyyy . . ."

"Yes, little mouse?" I laughed.

"I love you," she said.

I was afraid of taking my daughter out in public. I faced the truth of it after eight or nine hours lying on my bed staring at the cracks of moonlight showing around the edges of my boarded-up bedroom windows, then half a day wandering the house aimlessly, refusing to shower or dress or commit to any plans.

The truth was I'd had plenty of opportunities to take Lillian out. I'd told myself I was too tired the nights I had returned after searching for Richie, and too battered and bruised emotionally and physically the night Dylan Hogan was shot. I told myself I preferred sitting in the kitchen with her in the morning, watching her drip milk all over the surface of the table while she clumsily spooned single pieces of cereal into her mouth, rather than taking her out for pancakes or treating her to McDonald's. She was a strong girl. I could tell that by the way she carried on, ready for the next adventure, when somewhere in her heart she must have been in pain from longing—for her mother, her home, something familiar. I recognized that longing in her eyes because I had felt it myself for many years.

The clock ticked away the day as I failed to strike up the courage to leave the house. I knew that new horrors lay ahead if I dared to be seen alone with Lillian in public. They would come, inevitably, as so many adjustments to my life after the accusation had, forcing me to adapt to different ways of being in the world. People were going to look at her and me and make comments loudly, so that I could hear, or conspiratorially, their eyes filled with hatred. They were going to take pictures of my child and me. Some hysterical old ladies would probably call the police. I could see myself sitting on an empty bench at a public playground and watching the other parents telling their kids to stay away from Lillian, assigning someone to keep an eye on me while they escorted their little ones to the toilet blocks. I could see Lillian's confusion, sudden terror, as angry men came and blasted me while we waited outside a cinema to see a kids' movie, wanting to know how Kelly could bear to leave our daughter with me.

I was a coward. I had contaminated Lillian's life with my curse, and I was in denial about it.

I tried to retreat into fantasies about Laney Bass as the sun heated the house, making the cicadas in the trees roar and the roof tick as the corrugated iron expanded. She'd had a busy day the day before, she'd said. But she had sent me a cute goodnight message telling me how much she looked forward to our upcoming date, probably suggesting she was getting anxious that I hadn't actually arranged it yet. I opened the message as I wallowed in inactivity on the back porch and read it over again. Laney had heard about the Dylan Hogan shooting on the news, and wanted to assure me that I didn't have to talk about it if I didn't want to.

I'm looking forward to learning more about you, she signed off.

I sat miserably and watched Lillian making mud pies by the sprinkler. There's only so much entertainment a kid can gain from a pool of dirt and water at the center of an otherwise featureless backyard, and soon Lillian came stomping up the yard toward me, throwing herself into a hug and dribbling mud down my clothes.

"Oh! Hello, Boo," I said as she nuzzled into my neck. "What are you doing?"

"What you doing?" she parroted. It was a good question. I glanced at my watch again, crushed with guilt.

I know what I should be doing, I thought. *I should be calling Sara Farrow. Confronting her about the affair. Watching more videos. Looking at the records for her secret phone.*

"Shall we play with the duckies?" I asked Lillian instead. "Take the dog for a walk? You want to order pizza and watch a movie?"

I heard the sound of gravel on the driveway. I went to the end of the porch and leaned out, spotted Laney Bass's van in the driveway, the woman opening her driver's-side door like she'd materialized out of my thoughts. I brushed the mud off my shirt and jeans, my heart already hammering with anticipation.

"Laney Bass is here, Boo," I told her with a dramatic gasp. "Should we hang out with her?"

"Mamey Bass is here!" Lillian cried.

I went through the house to the door and opened it, but it was clear from Laney's stride toward me that something was wrong. I shut the door, almost catching Lillian's fingers, trapping her inside. She looked up at me in confusion. I walked out and down the porch steps, my breath suddenly halting, some deep-seated instinct already playing through what was about to happen just seconds before it did.

Laney's eyes were wet. She shoved a newspaper at my chest. It was awkwardly folded, crumpled. I almost didn't need to look at the front page. I let it fall on the ground. I was all over the cover. The shot Stan Parrett had captured of me in the White Caps parking lot was center stage, my hand up and mouth downturned. Then there was a smaller picture of Amanda and me standing at the petrol station, watching as ambulance crews rushed in to deal with Hogan.

Alleged sex offender and convicted child killer team up to botch Farrow case.

I let Laney speak, but she was so distressed she couldn't get more than the word "What" out for a moment. Over and over she said it. She was shaking, her face peach-colored and glossy. There was a strange beauty to her red-nosed, vulnerable expression. Lillian was bashing on the screen door with both fists.

"Mamey Bass! Mamey Bass!"

"What . . . what . . ." Laney growled, finally breaking through the mindless anger. "What the *actual fuck* was your plan, Ted?"

"I didn't . . ." I shrugged, swallowing back sickness. "I didn't have one."

"You just weren't going to tell me? You just weren't going to mention it?"

I searched for words, but there were none.

"I had to find out from my *work experience* girl," Laney spat. "She's *fifteen*. Here I am gossiping about this interesting man I've met and I mentioned you lived alone down by the lake. She said, 'I know that guy. That's the guy my mum told me to stay away from. He was in the paper just this morning.'"

"I'm sorry," I said, maybe for the ten thousandth time in my life. "I'm innocent." Maybe the millionth. "I'm no longer a person of interest. The police have said—"

"I'm so embarrassed," Laney said, rubbing her nose on the back of her hand. She was hiccupping with tears. She glanced toward the doorway, where Lillian had fallen silent, aware somehow that there were very bad things going on between the adults and hoping, perhaps, to decipher what they were. I thought of Luca Errett at the window of the crummy hotel room the police had arranged for his family, his hands spread on the glass.

"Can you imagine what would have happened if we'd gone out?" Laney asked. "I'd be the laughingstock of the whole town."

I put my hands in my pockets and bowed my head, resigned to let her get it all out, to say all the things she needed to say, so she would regret nothing when she walked away from me forever in only a few seconds' time. But it seemed that a kind of disgust had overtaken her, maybe at my refusal to defend or explain myself, maybe at my lying to her when she'd told me her life had just been ruined by lies, maybe at what the newspapers were suggesting I was: a pedophile who had escaped justice.

When I looked up she was watching Lillian at the door, her eyes big and trembling with tears.

"Don't look at my daughter like that," I said.

Laney turned her gaze on me and her eyes were somehow instantly dry, and she walked off toward the driver's door.

I marched back to the house. Lillian didn't move aside as I walked in, and I had to brush her out of the way. She bashed on the door as Laney pulled out of the drive.

"Mamey Bass!"

"Lillian," I called as I walked down the hall, "stop bashing the door."

"Mamey Ba—"

"Lillian, stop bashing the door!" I roared. I spun on my heel in time to see my words shock the small girl's body like a punch to the guts. She dissolved into those howling, openmouthed tears. I jogged back to her and swept her into my arms.

"I'm sorry. I'm sorry. I'm sorry." I lifted her, tried to crush the memory of what I'd done out of her tiny frame. "Oh, Jesus, Lill. I'm so sorry, baby."

I held her in the kitchen until she stopped crying, kissing her warm head, making her empty promises that everything was all right.

When Lillian had calmed down enough, I set her on my hip and grabbed my keys from the kitchen table.

"Fuck this," I said. "We're out of here."

They turned Amanda away at the front of the hotel. The officers saw her marching toward the automatic doors in the afternoon heat haze, right through the middle of the shrine to Richie Farrow that had amassed on the concrete steps. Her passage over the colorful chalk messages written on the steps by local children, between piles of flowers and sagging teddy bears and candles that had burned all night, sent the journalists and gawkers standing reverently at the edge of the shrine tittering and sighing. The two patrol officers were guarding the doors, and Amanda was trying to walk between them when they snapped together, shoulder to shoulder, like armored knights before a cartoon castle.

"I want access to the roof," Amanda said, pushing her sunglasses up onto her head. "I'll be a few minutes. That's all."

"You look tired, Amanda," one of them said,

ignoring her words and smiling at her bloodshot eyes. "Interesting night, was it?"

It had indeed been an interesting night. It wasn't an easy task for paramedics from Cairns Hospital to get their helicopter safely grounded on the gray beach on the edge of the swamp, the tide rising almost all the way to the palm trees lining the camp. Even when they managed it, they arrived in the camp to find five badly beaten, elderly men who refused medical treatment, one of them coughing up blood as he spoke, another struggling to maintain consciousness. The paramedics and the helicopter pilot had looked around at the guns; beer bottles; wild, scraggly dogs; and hotted-up motorcycles and despaired. Among the gathering was Amanda Pharrell, the area's most notorious killer, looking decidedly regretful that she had called for their assistance in the first place.

Amanda gave up on the men at the door of the White Caps and walked around the back of the hotel, past the parking lot guard station, to the east wall. The lowest windows were five meters off the ground. If she was fast enough, she knew anyone watching the cameras on the east side of the hotel might miss her movements. She shrugged off the backpack she had been carrying and stood judging the distance from the nearest palm tree to the edge of the building, rolling her shoulders and cracking her knuckles.

"Don't do it," someone said. She turned and saw Superfish walking along the side of the building toward her, his long hands bunched inside his trouser pockets and his eyes on the ground. He stood by Amanda and looked up at the window and the palm tree.

"You'll break your neck," he said, returning his gaze to his shoes.

"I'll break *your* neck if you don't clear out." Amanda spat on her palms and rubbed them together. "I'm trying to find a body. Mind your own business."

"You think it's still here?" Superfish asked. "I'd like to know how you figure that. They conducted another search this morning, in case Hogan was purposefully leaving something out. Didn't find anything."

"Men don't look for things properly," Amanda said. "They're too goal focused."

"What does that mean?"

"It means find me a way inside, boost me up this palm tree, or rack the fuck off."

Superfish gave a resigned nod, and turned on his heel. Amanda followed, then waited by a back door to the hotel while he made sure the coast was clear.

In the elevator, she watched the bulges in his pockets, his oversized fingers wriggling restlessly, barely constrained by the space inside the fabric. She wondered how he ever kept anything in there, the hand reaching in to retrieve change or keys immediately taking up all the available space.

"You really are a weird-looking person, aren't you?" she said. "You're all orange and oddly proportioned."

"I don't disagree," he said. "But . . . you know." He rubbed his nose too hard, glanced at her. "Glass houses."

"Your partner is obsessed with me," Amanda said. She waited for a response, but none came. "She's been in my house. She had all my cats abducted by evil government cyborgs and she's turned the entire police force against me."

"Well, they weren't exactly big fans of yours in the first place." Superfish watched the numbers on the wall blinking to life and fading as they ascended.

"I didn't hit Joanna Fischer," Amanda said. "Trust me, if I was going to lay into her I'd have given her more than a black eye."

"Violence is never the answer," Superfish said.

They arrived on the eighth floor. Amanda and Superfish stood in the empty, carpeted hall.

"Last night, a bunch of cops came and bashed my friends," Amanda said. "Joanna Fischer is bringing as many people into this as she can."

"Have you told Conkaffey this?"

"Why would I tell him?"

"He's your partner." Superfish shrugged.

"I'm giving him the silent treatment. Three more hours. He called me crazy. Nobody calls me crazy, or a freak. I smacked him. But if I didn't like him so much I'd have slammed his nuts in a sandwich press," Amanda said. "Plus, he worries."

"Why are you telling me, then?" Superfish said. "You don't think I worry?"

"You *should* worry." Amanda poked him in his hard chest. "She's your partner. You better put a leash on that bitch before she gets bitten."

"I think that's what she wants," Superfish said. "Don't you?"

"Huh?"

"Some people like conflict," Superfish said. "A war between the bikies and the police might be exactly what she wants. All its casualties will be your fault, and you'll never get any police cooperation in this town again."

They walked up the small concrete staircase to the roof, Superfish swiping through the locked doors with a white plastic card. The afternoon heat hit them like a wall as they stepped out onto the dusty space. Amanda marched to the nearest elevator, the wide rectangular concrete structure that capped the shaft, and set her backpack on the ground. Superfish watched as she dragged out a pink toolbox and opened it, digging to the bottom for an enormous wrench. The sunlight was bouncing off the new, shiny iron panel that stretched along one side of the concrete structure, taking up approximately a third of the surface of the elevator roof.

"I'm waiting for you to ask me to explain my genius," Amanda said as she fitted the wrench to the bolts on top of the iron panel. "Surely you're not just going to stand there and wait for it to unfold."

"Oh." Superfish cleared his throat. "Well, yes. I just assumed it would become clear in time."

"It's far more exciting when I explain it."

"Please do."

"Well," Amanda sighed, working the bolts. "I woke up this morning thinking about Hogan. How could I not? He was all over the news. Those journalists have really done their digging, the happy little moles. There were lots of pictures of Hogan provided by friends he's had over the years: in different houses, at parties, here at the hotel. In every picture, I noticed the neatness. The organization. Sure, he was always dirty. He was pictured in homeless camps, crack houses, halfway houses. But his belongings and his clothes and his hair were always neat. Neatness, organization, it was Hogan's way of maintaining control. I kept thinking about those pictures all morning."

Amanda unscrewed the bolts from the edges of the panels, lining them up one after the other like soldiers on the top of the elevator shaft.

"Before Ted and I got banned from the case," Amanda said, "the Crimson Lake cops sent us photographs of the contents of Hogan's maintenance logbook, as we requested. I had a look. Same thing: very orderly. Hogan wrote down the tasks he wanted to complete each day, and listed job numbers and receipts for purchases and completion dates for all his work. He forecast everything into the diary. Every day he emptied the pool filter. Every two weeks he cleaned all the exterior hotel windows. Every month he set rat traps in the basements. Every three months he conducted a sweep of all the rooms for aesthetic damage."

Superfish helped her loosen a particularly difficult bolt, the muscles of his forearms visible as they flexed beneath his white skin.

"The day before Richie went missing," Amanda continued, "Hogan was supposed to replace a rusted iron panel on top of one of the elevators with a new one he had ordered a month earlier. I believe it was this panel he was replacing."

She rapped on the iron cover with her knuckles, making the metal sing.

"But we checked the elevator shafts," Superfish said.

"We must have checked them fifty times. From the bottom and the top."

"Wrong!" Amanda smiled as they lifted the panel onto the ground. "Dead wrong."

They leaned over and peered into the space beneath the panel. Superfish tried to stand back, but Amanda clamped a hand on the back of his neck.

"No," she said. "Look. Really look."

As his eyes adjusted, clearing the red and green sunspots that had clouded them, he saw what she meant for him to see. Beneath them stretched a seemingly eternal tunnel, emerging slowly into his vision. There was no elevator in the narrow, featureless shaft.

"What the fuck?" Superfish gripped the edge, looking down into the darkness. The shaft they peered down was as wide as the elevator shaft on one side, but not on the other. It was about a third of the size of the elevator. The police officer stared into the blackness, his mouth hanging open.

"You've seen the elevator shafts," Amanda said. "You've seen them a dozen times. But what you haven't seen is this—a secondary shaft at the back of each elevator. Don't feel like an idiot. I didn't see it, either. I stood underneath the elevator carriages and touched the walls of the shaft on all three sides."

"So what is this then?" Superfish asked. "What's this empty space at the back of the shaft for?"

"The counterweight." Amanda smiled. "The old elevators had a counterweight that would slide up as the elevator went down, and down as the elevator went up. But when the hotel put new elevators in, they didn't choose the big ole counterweight-style ones again. These ones work with hydraulics. Three poles on the interior walls of the shaft on which the elevator carriage slides up and down."

Superfish leaned over again and looked into the space.

"When they put the new elevator in, it was smaller than the old ones," Amanda said. "The shaft was too big. So they split it. They erected a wall behind the elevator carriage and fitted the hydraulic pole to it. This space back here?" She pointed into the darkness. "This became blank, empty space. They walled it off, and capped it at the top."

"Why didn't we see this?" Superfish asked.

"Because Hogan took the lid off all the elevators and showed you the shafts with the carriage in them, so you could see that Richie hadn't fallen in and landed on top of the carriage. But he didn't tell us about this second shaft, and he didn't open the lid that covered it. He just hoped that if he seemed to be cooperating fully, with the sun making it hard to see into the shaft clearly, no one would ask a question about the square shape of the elevator carriage and the rectangular shape of the concrete structures on top."

Superfish pinched the bridge of his nose, took a deep breath.

"We had an architect come and examine the whole hotel this morning," Superfish said.

"Yeah," Amanda agreed. "And he probably fell for the same trick you all did. Without knowing the elevators had been replaced, he had all the same information as you."

"Do you actually know he's down there?" Superfish said. "Or are you just guessing? Okay, you've identified an unsearched space in the hotel. But are you sure it means anything?"

Amanda sat on the ground and rummaged through her toolbox. She took out two elastic bands and then extracted her mobile phone from her pocket.

"Hogan said to Ted and me in the bush that there had been an accident," Amanda said. "He told me, two days ago, that he didn't only like this job—he *needed* it."

"Okay." Superfish watched her fitting the elastic bands tightly around either end of her mobile phone.

"He bought far too much rope to tie up a kid," Amanda said. "He bought a hook. There's no evidence that Richie Farrow was ever at Hogan's place of residence. What does that tell you?"

"Well, the Iron Man toy was there," Superfish said. "We've confirmed that it's Richie's."

"Right," Amanda said. "So imagine this. Meticulous, orderly, teetering on the tightrope above oblivion, the runner's life; Dylan Hogan goes to work one day and sees in his diary that he's got to replace a rusted iron panel from the top of one of the blank spaces behind the elevator shafts. He goes up to the roof, swipes open the door to the stairs and the door to the roof. He wedges them open, because he knows he's going to have to carry down a big rusty iron panel and he doesn't want to have to open both doors again while his hands are full."

Amanda pulled a roll of twine from her backpack and started unwinding handfuls of it. She looped the twine through the two elastic bands secured at the ends of her phone.

"Hogan carries the new panel up to the roof," she continued. "He sets it on the ground. He unbolts the old, rusty panel. Then he gets distracted. The manager calls him on his radio. There's some problem inside the hotel. Sink blocked, microwave won't work, I don't know. He goes back downstairs. Completely forgets about the panel."

Superfish was watching Amanda, his pale scalp roasting in the sun.

"He goes home that night. At four o'clock in the morning he bolts upright in bed. Fuck! The stairway door. The roof door. The secondary elevator shaft gaping open at the night sky. We know what Hogan was like. Organized. Disciplined. He's horrified. He immediately takes his bike and rides back to the hotel at top speed. The CCTV inside the Clattering Clam catches him going past. When he comes up to the roof he finds both doors still open and the panels on the ground where he left them. He finds a kid's toy on the roof, and—"

"And all the hotel staff in a panic over a missing kid," Superfish said. He was gripping his belly with one hand as though he felt sick. "Police on the way."

"He puts two and two together," Amanda said. "He fits the new panel and discards the old one. He doesn't know for sure that the child has fallen in the hole but it's the only thing that makes sense. He knows the kids were on the roof. He knows the hole was uncovered."

"He said he needed this job," Superfish said. "He told you that. It was probably the only thing keeping him grounded. Keeping him from wandering off again into the dark life."

"Uh-huh," Amanda said. "He feels sick about what's happened. Physically sick. He tells the people who see him that he's hungover. But really he's formulating his plan."

"Oh, Jesus," Superfish sighed.

"Hogan must have known Richie would be dead," Amanda said, climbing onto the concrete ledge above the shaft. "Eight stories. No, ten—the shafts go right down to the basement. No kid would survive that. And there was no point putting his hand up and saying it was his fault. He knew there was no saving Richie. So why not save himself, if he could? He told no one about the secondary shafts. He went out and bought supplies. A hundred meters of rope was enough to send a hook down, try to catch the body and bring it up. If he was careful, he might have figured he could get the body out of the hotel without anyone knowing what he'd done. Sure, he didn't feel great about it. But he would do what he needed to in order to survive. To maintain control."

Amanda beckoned for Superfish's phone. He gave it without understanding why she wanted it, simply watching her plan unfold as she spoke. Soon the screen of his phone showed a wobbling camera image, the same as the image displayed on Amanda's phone. She picked up her phone and turned on the torch at the back.

"The kids said they'd been on the roof," Superfish said. "But they didn't say Richie had fallen down a hole."

"The kids said they saw a fucking alien spaceship." Amanda rolled her eyes. "It's possible they just didn't know what happened to Richie. A bunch of them go to the edge of the building to look at the water. Richie climbs up on the concrete ledge. He falls, hardly making a sound. When they turn around, their friend is gone, and they can't ask anyone where he went because they're not even supposed to be out of the room. They probably assumed he ran off to play hide-and-seek, or went downstairs to the restaurant to see the parents."

Amanda hung her phone over the hole before her, letting it settle as it swung on the end of the twine. With the elastic bands acting as horizontal braces, and the twine between them making a knot at the front of the phone, the phone's camera and torch pointed straight downwards into the gaping shaft. She handed Superfish back his phone.

"This is all just guesswork so far," Superfish noted. Amanda looked at him, standing by the side of the shaft, one of those big hands in his tiny pocket again, straining the stitching. "It's good guesswork, no doubt. But you might be completely wrong."

"If I'm wrong, I'll make you a cake," Amanda said. "Your choice."

Superfish watched the feed on his phone as Amanda lowered her camera into the hole.

Maybe I'm morbid. More likely, I was still looking for excuses to work on Richie Farrow's case. Perhaps I just wanted to see the wild, curious look on my daughter's face when she interacted with animals, the innocent joy that made her grab at cats' tails and chase the geese around my yard. But I put Lillian in the car and drove her to Macalister's Crocodile Park near Kuranda National Park, an hour north along the coast road. It was the last place Richie Farrow had been seen alive. The last photographs of the boy had been taken here.

I was still unsettled about Sara Farrow's affair with John Errett, though I'd held off confronting her about it, reminding myself that Dylan Hogan had admitted to killing Richie. Still, I found myself replaying our conversations. The way she'd listened quietly as I'd updated her about leads, never crying, never despairing the way her husband did. My mind wandered around and around her, picking at the woman, trying to find that look, that offhand comment I'd missed.

I told myself she was just a mother, an ordinary woman who made mistakes, who had affairs, who told lies, who occasionally lost it at her kid.

I told myself not to pursue Sara Farrow even as I drove to the park to try to retrace her last movements with the boy.

I'd interacted with this crocodile park before, indirectly. The first case Amanda and I had worked on had involved a famous author living in Crimson Lake, who had been fed to one of the enormous beasts by his son. The animal had been caught and harvested by Macalister's crew, and Jake Scully's wedding ring had been recovered from the belly of the beast. I knew it was strange to want to go there, even as I packed some snacks into the car and buckled Lillian into her booster seat. I put her seat directly behind mine so she could see the coast as we drove, the rocky beaches and sheer cliffs.

In the bag marked Lillian Hill, I'd found a CD with some overly enthusiastic-looking men wearing skivvies on it, so I'd chucked that in the CD player as we set off. The music, if it could be called that, was terrible—comedic warbling overset with bouncing-spring sound effects and dogs barking. It was the usual fare for kids' songs: octopuses having adventures under the sea and anthropomorphic cars following winding roads, beeping at everything. It was easy to ignore the sounds coming from the radio, though, when I heard those coming from my child. She laughed and sang her way through every song, throwing up her hands and cheering at appropriate times, clapping and beeping an invisible horn. The sting of Laney Bass's appearance at my house that morning settled from a raw, searing wound into a deeper, more familiar kind of ache.

Macalister's Crocodile Park had designed the front of their property with Jurassic Park leanings, which I appreciated. Tall bamboo fencing hid the mysteries inside, and the parking lot was shaded by short palm trees that battered the windows of the car as we pulled in. African drumming music and recorded bird calls played at the ticket counter. Lillian caught on to the idea that we were attending a zoo when she turned a corner and spotted a large tank filled with wet greenery, beside a collection of photographs of the celebrities who had visited the park.

"The zoo!" she cried, with heartbreaking, unbridled joy.

"Yes, baby," I told her. "Finally, the zoo."

It wasn't a backyard full of rescued animals. A vet I only frequented because I was lonely. An isolated road near my house where no one would spot us together, and possibly traumatize my child forever. I had finally gathered myself together and taken Lillian to the zoo. I lifted her up so that she could see the turtles paddling idly around the lush, dimly lit tank, pushing aside reeds and aquatic ferns with their strange little flippers.

"Wait till you see what else there is," I told her, as we followed the path of a dead boy into the park.

Left from the ticketing booth was a large area filled with log picnic tables and festooned with bougainvillea. A group of tourists were posing with a koala against a printed backdrop of a jungle scene while a staff member wearing khakis took pictures. Lillian ran up to a large aviary filled with lorikeets, startling a small huddle of the rainbow birds that had been gathered around some pieces of apple pegged to the wire. I walked to the wooden rail that marked the boundary of the area and looked out over the park, alleyways of diamond wire separating huge ponds of stagnant, depthless brown water.

"'Allo," a voice said.

A huge white cockatoo was edging toward me on the wooden railing, taking sidesteps with its ridged gray claws, swaying back and forth as its beady black eye took in my form. Its pale yellow crest rose and fell—curious, alarmed, curious, alarmed, curious. I stood still as it walked up and clambered onto my forearm, taking a beakful of my shirt and pulling itself up the hairy surface. Lillian was at my side, her eyes huge and mouth open.

"'Allo," the bird said.

"'Allo!" Lillian imitated. I put my hand between the bird's beak and Lillian, in case it was a biter, and crouched down so she could stroke the thick white feathers.

"He's a good one, isn't he?"

"Good one, Daddy," she whispered. "'Allo? 'Allo!"

As I balanced the bird on my arm, I realized there were no other sulfur-crested cockatoos in the area. This was probably the bird that Richie had had his photograph taken with, one of the last pictures of him alive, the nervous shot of him smiling with his big teeth as the bird spread its wings.

"That's Roy." One of the keepers in khaki appeared by our side. I straightened and the bird flapped to her shoulder. "He's actually one of our oldest residents here at the park. He was twenty-one last week."

"Twenty-one," I said, looking at the cockatoo. "Jesus. That's a good run for a bird."

Roy had lived more than twice as long as Richie Farrow. The thought sprang into my mind before I could contain it. I winced, rubbing Lillian's head as she hugged my leg. Thoughts about Richie in this space were almost blinding. It had been a mistake to come here, kidding myself that it was Lillian I was trying to get close to, not the boy and answers about him. I was speaking even as I told myself to stop.

"Were you working here a week ago when Richie Farrow went missing?" I asked the girl with the bird, touching the rough, almost scaly claws of the animal as it danced on her shoulder. "The boy and his mother were here."

"I saw them," she said. She had a thin, hooked nose and large eyes, not unlike the bird using her as a perch. "Are you a cop? The cops have been out here already and spoken to everyone."

"Yeah, I know, I'm just . . ." I sighed helplessly, looking down at Lillian. "Re-covering well-trodden ground. Anything weird about the two of them?"

"Nothing I can really remember." She shrugged, sending the bird up and down. "The mother was getting really sunburned, that's all. She was already sunburned when they came back to the kiosk area for the wallaby feeding, and I pointed out the sunscreen dispenser to her. I don't know if she used it or not. I think I saw the boy use it. He wasn't sun-burned."

I felt a tingle of recognition, but was distracted by the tugging on the bottom of my shirt. Lillian was pointing out into the park, where a large crocodile was visible sliding into one of the ponds.

"Daddy, cocks!"

The girl in khaki choked back laughter.

I went to the sunscreen dispenser and slathered Lillian and myself all over, then led her back out into the park. I was still thinking about Richie Farrow and his mother as I bought a paper bag of grain pellets for Lillian to feed the eastern gray kangaroos that wandered the park freely, lounging in the shade of sprawling poinciana trees. Most of the crocodiles had retreated from the heat to the safety of their concrete pools, only the occasional muddy brown snout visible above the water in some cases, or the telltale trail of bubbles rising to the surface of the tea-colored water. We stopped by a wire fence, behind which one of the khaki-clad rangers was slapping the water with a long stick as a crowd watched. I lifted Lillian up onto my shoulders. She gathered handfuls of my hair and I held on to her legs against my chest.

I could see what was about to happen. The ranger had a skinned chicken carcass in one gloved hand. There were bubbles rising by the edge of the vast pond that was clustered with lily pads and aquatic flowers.

"What's in there, Lill?" I asked.

"Don't know."

"Look there." I pointed as the bubbles began to increase in size.

The ranger kept slapping the water as the tourists clicked away with their cameras. From the water there rose a single dome-shaped snout the size of an upturned cereal bowl, the thick ridges and bumps of a widening upper jaw coming slowly after. The thing was emerging from the water, taking slow, effortful strides, dragging its seemingly endless body out of the depths. Droplets sliding between scales, claws sinking in the mud.

Lillian squealed with delight, and the crowd around me bristled with excitement. The monster revealed. But as I watched the creature slipping out of the depths, mud dribbling down its sagging, scaly sides and soft, bulging neck, I felt the touch of something cold deep in my chest. This was the thing that haunted the tangled green world to which I'd fled, barking in the night beyond the reach of my property, smiling on painted *No Swimming* signs on the shore of every creek and river. The thing that had mauled and almost killed my partner once.

If Richie's body had been dumped in the Cairns region, the first thing that was going to come for him was one of these beasts. It would leave nothing behind of the child.

The ranger coaxed the thing completely out of the water while spouting facts about its species, dangling the chicken so that the enormous reptile lifted its heavy head, showing its strangely vulnerable, pale underbelly. A flash of teeth and a hollow sound like a knocking on an ancient door as the jaws snapped shut on the dropped bird.

The crowd applauded the performance and the park

ranger retreated from the enclosure. The tourists finished posing for selfies with the beast behind them. I realized I was alone, staring at the animal, Lillian jiggling on my shoulders impatiently, when the ranger put his hand on my arm.

"You all right, mate?"

"Fine." I wiped sweat from my brow. "Fine."

"Some people get a bit wobbly at the sight of them." He smiled, punching my arm. "I get it. I've seen what they can do. They look slow and heavy but I've seen this one here pull a man's arm right off. Ripped the thing clean out of the socket. Newbie keeper, didn't listen to my warnings. Keep your eye on the beast at all times, I told him. Don't turn away for any reason."

I stared at the ranger, who was smiling at the croc.

"When they want to be, they're quick as a flash," he said. "Take you under the water before you can make a sound."

I took Lillian down from my shoulders and led her away.

My phone rang as we were heading for the parking lot, the jungle sounds almost drowning out the noise from my pocket. I stopped Lillian in the ticketing area to take the call, showing her the turtle tank again.

"The results are in," Val said.

I took a deep breath, closed my eyes.

"Okay," I said. "Let me have it."

"It was a cow," she said.

"*What?*"

"At least one cow," Val said. I could hear her shuffling papers, the scrape of her metal chair on the morgue floor, a sound I'd heard a dozen times. "From the volume we have, it could be a couple of them."

I gripped my forehead, tried to understand.

"We're talking about the bone chips found at the burn site behind Todd DeCasper's place?" I said. "They were from a *cow*?"

"You got it. *Large domesticated ungulate* of the family Bovidae. *Bos taurus*, if you please."

"Who burns and buries a cow?"

Val snorted. "Oh, Ted. I'm well past trying to apply any logic to the behavior of human beings. The reason the analysis of these bone chips took so long was because my colleague was tied up trying to extract DNA from a burned body found in a motel swimming pool in Alice Springs. The victim had seventeen golf balls in his anal passage."

"That's . . ." I sighed. "No, on second thought, I don't have a word for that."

"Maybe he hit it with a car. Maybe he fancied himself a nose-to-tail backyard barbecuer. Anything's possible," Val mused. "Where are you?"

"At the croc farm, pretending I'm not still looking for Richie Farrow."

"Ted," Val sighed. "That case isn't yours anymore. Why don't you take the afternoon off, go see that girlfriend of yours or something?"

Lillian was wandering. I followed her out of the reception area to the parking lot, where she fondled the tropical flowers in the garden beds. I took her hand and started to lead her toward my car. She ran ahead of me as I made my excuses to Val and signed off, slipping the phone into the pocket of my pants.

When I looked ahead Lillian was standing with a woman by the door of my car. The two were holding hands.

I stopped walking and looked into the face of Sara Farrow.

I was struck first by the strange sense of confusion that comes with driving on autopilot and arriving at the wrong place, driving to work instead of home, the stunning realization that I was not meant to be here, that what was about to happen was not supposed to happen. Then came the inevitable, violent shunting of understanding into my brain, a suddenly deadening feeling. My limbs prickled with adrenaline. I couldn't move. I saw the small knife in Sara's left hand without really focusing on it, knowing that if I did, if I let myself be fully present in the moment, I'd lose control. My hands were in fists by my side. Even as I told myself to move them, they failed to respond.

"Are you armed?" Sara asked.

"No," I said.

She glanced in the direction of the park in the distance, beyond three or four rows of cars. I couldn't move my head. All I could see was my daughter.

"Where's Mummy?" Lillian asked, reminded perhaps of Kelly's absence by the feel of a woman's hand in hers.

"Let's get in the car," Sara said, looking back at me. She nodded toward the driver's side. "Slowly, calmly."

I did as I was told. I sat in the driver's seat as a woman who had killed her son strapped my daughter into the child's seat behind mine and slid into the seat next to her, the knife in her fist, flashing and twisting as she used her fingers to clip the buckles near my child's impossibly soft belly. Maternal instincts and killer instincts entwined. I reached down with one hand while Sara was working and pulled my phone out of my pocket, sliding it onto my thigh.

I had time for one message. Amanda. *SOS*. It was all I could think of.

"Give me your phone," Sara said.

I locked the screen and handed the phone back to her. She rolled down her window a crack and slipped the phone through the gap. I heard it clatter on the ground. She rolled her window up again. My hands were slick with sweat on the wheel as I followed her instructions and drove south out of the park.

Amanda began rolling the twine back up around the ball to lift the phone out of the concrete shaft. Superfish had watched as the camera showed the phone's path into the darkness, story by story, the concrete showing lines, ridges, and watermarks as Amanda let it descend. Amanda had felt the man beside her tense as she neared the end of her ball of twine.

She'd leaned in beside him to watch the screen as the outline of the bottom of the shaft emerged. There was an object there, but it was not a child. An old blanket or towel, steel-gray with age and covered in a thick layer of dust. A couple of neatly fallen leaves, probably sucked into the shaft on the breeze when Hogan left it open overnight. That was all.

Neither of them had spoken. They'd both been turned toward the concrete cap of the elevator shaft, the phone ascending slowly, only one story above the bottom, when a voice behind them they both knew made them look at each other.

"You're not supposed to be here," Joanna said.

They turned. She was alone, in uniform, one hand on her gun belt, squinting as the breeze off the ocean buffeted them, gathering dust from the rooftop in its path. The smarmy, confident Joanna was gone, and in her wake a blank-eyed, almost detached woman remained. Amanda noted the absence of what Joanna had been up until this time—a woman with a plan, a nemesis marking her next move as she watched Amanda's current one unfold. Amanda couldn't tell what lay behind the woman's features now. Something once deeply buried seemed to be crawling out of her.

"*You're* not supposed to be here," Amanda said. "You're on stress leave. You shot a guy."

"Amanda is here on my authority," Superfish said. "I'm supervising her while she pursues—"

"Shut up." Joanna turned her eyes on Superfish, nothing more, before letting them settle back on Amanda. "There's a trespasser at the crime scene, possibly destroying valuable evidence. I'll have to take her into custody."

In the shaft, Amanda's phone sounded a tone. A text message. She started rolling up the twine faster.

"Drop what you're holding and put your hands in the air," Joanna said.

"Joanna," Superfish said, his hand out. "If you draw your weapon I'll draw mine. You're not on duty, and we're not in a threatening situation here."

"We're not in a threatening situation?" Joanna examined her partner. "This woman is a violent, convicted murderer who less than twenty-four hours ago was responsible for the death of—"

"Of an innocent man," Amanda said, looking back, holding the twine in one hand, pointing at her accuser with another. "That's right, bitch. You've got as much blood on your hands as me. And there'll be more to come, don't you worry. You've started a war between the bikies and the cops. You lot handed their arses to them last night. When they retaliate, you'll wish you hadn't started this, I guarantee you."

"Amanda," Superfish said.

"I'm not responsible for Hogan's death," Amanda sneered at Joanna. "You *heard* me. You heard me say he was unarmed and you nailed him without thinking when you heard my voice."

"I didn't—"

"You probably didn't even look at who it was. You spotted me running toward the back of the petrol station as you pulled up in your car. You heard me calling out not to shoot. It could have been anyone. It could have been Ted."

"An innocent man . . . ?" Joanna's hand fluttered theatrically to her lip. "How do you know he was innocent? You . . . you made me kill . . ."

"Stop it." Superfish took a step toward his partner but she backed away. "Stop this, Joanna."

"You ruined my life." Joanna was sidestepping around Amanda, out of her partner's reach. "You took my best friend, and then you made me kill, just like you."

Her words fell away. Joanna drew the gun from her belt. Superfish snatched for his own, flicking the safety off as he raised the weapon and aimed at his partner.

The phone made another sound in the shaft. A reminder about the text message. Amanda held on to the twine, her face hard and her body still as she listened to Superfish trying to shout his partner down. She was prepared for an impact, if that was what was going to happen now. A bullet to the heart. Joanna was aiming there. Two shots, the way she'd been trained, the way she took down Hogan. The way Pip Sweeney had died. Amanda watched the bodies twisting, almost in slow motion, before her, Superfish reaching for Joanna, Joanna tightening her finger on the trigger of her weapon.

There were men in the doorway to the fire stairs. Officers. More guns pointing, sweeping over Amanda.

"Drop it! Drop it! Everybody drop it!"

Amanda let the twine go.

The emotions came in waves. The first was terror. Sheer, blinding terror that caused flashes of false realities to zing through my brain, as visceral as if they were occurring before me. Lillian's belly being slit open, spilling her insides. Her throat being slashed. I saw in an explosion of color every murder victim I'd walked in on during my drug squad career, men and women sprawled on beds, collapsed in corners, curled in the boots of cars, burned, or sunk into rivers. I held back sickness, tried to blink away the visions and keep the car on the road. A swell of hellish whispers rose, speaking my numbing, paralyzing guilt. They weren't fully formed thoughts but they meant something to me.

Her only trip out. Your responsibility. Your fault. The last time you'll see her. Kelly. Jett. Victim of your circumstances. Cursed man, spreading his curse down the bloodline, ruining her life before she's even had a chance. Taking her life. Taking her life.

I didn't know where we were going, but the terror became so hard and hot and painful that I had to take the car off the road. A steel hand had gripped my skull, seemed to want to shove my jaw out and my head down between my shoulders. I was shaking even as I gripped the wheel so tight the leather squeaked.

"What are you doing?" Sara asked. "I told you to drive."

"You have to know something," I said, watching my own blazing eyes in the rearview mirror, afraid that if I looked at either of them I wouldn't be able to maintain control. "If you hurt my child, that'll be it. I'll have lost everything. You're threatening the only thing I have left in the world, the only string that connects me to reality."

"So what?" Sara asked, but her voice was small.

"So you better plan what you're doing very carefully," I said. "Because if anything happens to her, I'll rip you to shreds with my bare hands."

There were other threats coming, sizzling and boiling through my brain, but I left them unspoken. They were dark, obscene, nonsensical things. A mind gripping at white-hot fury and trying to squeeze it into words. Sara shifted in her seat.

"Drive," she said. "Just drive. If you do what I say, your daughter will be fine."

I got back on the road, breathed through the rage with long, shuddering breaths that in time softened and slowed. I didn't know where we were going, but I could guess. She was taking me to where the boy was. Lillian kicked her legs in her seat, babbled a few things about what she saw out the window, asked where her mother was once or twice. Neither Sara nor I spoke. I watched my enemy in the mirror, scratching the flaking skin at the back of her neck, meeting my eyes steadily.

There was a gun under my seat. I remembered the weapon just as the thought also seemed to take form in Sara's mind. She hadn't prepared for this, had calmed when she remembered to get rid of my phone. But she'd seen me walking around the hotel with a gun tucked into the back of my jeans.

"Do you have a gun?"

"No," I said. "I was taking my child to the fucking zoo. Why would I have a gun on me?"

Sara judged my eyes in the mirror. Then she began fishing around the car. I leaned and reached under the seat as far as I could, trying not to make my actions known, but she spotted the movement. I felt her fingernails scratch against the back of my hand as she grabbed the weapon and fumbled for the magazine beside it.

"You stupid lying fuck," she snapped.

I said nothing, sweat rolling down my sides, making my shirt stick to my chest. I was speeding. There was no telling what she would do if we were pulled over, now that she had a gun and a knife. I forced myself to slow.

"You don't know how to use that thing," I said.

"It can't be that hard," she said. I heard her load the magazine into the gun. "There are only so many buttons."

Visions, flashes. An accidental discharge through the

back seat and into my spine. The car slamming into a tree. Lillian broken, a lifeless doll.

The tension in the car was almost a sound, a high ringing. I needed to bring it down, on both her end and mine. Lillian didn't seem to sense it. When I glanced at her she was drifting off, her head sagging against the side of her car seat.

"We need to talk," I said.

She smirked, humorless. "You sound like Henry."

"There's a way out of this," I said. "It might not look like it right now, but there is a way."

"The only way out of this is to get rid of you," she said. "John told me you'd been around to his hotel room. That you found out about us. I can't have the police continuing to look at me. They've got to believe the maintenance man did it. I need them to keep believing that."

"My partner knows about John," I lied. "If you kill me, she'll tell them anyway."

"She's my next stop, then," Sara said.

We watched each other in the rearview mirror until I couldn't look at her anymore. I locked my eyes on the road and asked the question I didn't want to ask.

"Is Richie . . ."

"He's dead," she said.

She talked, and I drove, the road before me disappearing, becoming the rooms she described: small, cold rooms untouched by the cheerfulness of fluffy, woolen toys that sagged on nursery room shelves and sat with glowing, unpushed musical buttons on the living room floor. The house she and Henry had owned at the beginning of their marriage had been like a black hole, she said. It ate light and color, sucked greedily at her limbs, so that within its walls she felt heavy and tired all the time. It was always cold. The food she took out of the oven seemed already cold by the time it got to the plate, and the baby was cold all the time, resisting the blankets and heating pads she swaddled her in, resisting the warmth of her body. She knew it wasn't the house itself, but something inside her that had failed to ignite, a pilot light that was switched off, had never been switched on. She'd been wandering around her whole life seeing the glow in other people's eyes, hearing them talk about it. She'd glow on her wedding day, and when she was pregnant, they said. The glow would drive out the cold.

She hadn't smothered Anya, their first baby. She'd gone into the room and found her blue like the walls, like the light that hung in the air, like the uniforms of the officers who attended. Though she hadn't killed the child with her hands, with a pillow, she knew she'd killed her just by not loving her. She'd failed to warm the infant with her breast, with the glow she and Henry were supposed to have created when they slipped gold rings onto each other's fingers. The baby had been frozen by the sheer fact of being unwanted.

The relief lasted a long time. It lingered quietly, guiltily through the sadness after Anya's passing, then it seemed to grow, blossom, create a strange warmth of its own. She had a secret from Henry, and that felt good. Perhaps by merely being a secret, the relief she felt that she was childless again rubbed against the sadness she presented to the world, and the rubbing created a glow. She began spending more time out of the house, bathing in the relief, bringing back a candle flame inside herself that kept her warm through the cold, cold nights beside Henry. When she was out she felt the thrumming of the world, the call of the horizon. She'd been told all her life to get married. Have children. She'd done both, but neither made her organs twist the way they did as she met the gaze of a strange man across the room in a café in a suburb that was not her own. As they walked up the stairs to his apartment together. As she arrived home in the morning smelling of his breath. She felt little tingles of it as she followed fantastical ideas, lying beside Henry in the bed. She could walk out any time. Blow their savings on a plane ticket. Change her name. Cut her hair. Drop the weight. New girl in town with eyes full of mystery.

The cry of a baby sent shivers up her spine. She would not make that mistake again.

And then Richie had come.

It was easier, the second time, to go through the motions. Other people came in and took over, not wanting a repeat of the first "incident." They moved, and Henry took on a job that kept him out of her way. His parents and her own took the baby, sometimes for days on end. She lay around and fantasized about her trip away, some truck driver on a lonely highway picking her up as she hailed a ride to nowhere. A slick-haired businessman asking her name across the aisle in first class as she flew to Paris. They were romance-novel fantasies, she knew. But even if they'd had some whiff of possibility to them, the baby and Henry and the mortgage and her parents and her out-of-date passport and her flabby belly and her thick ankles made all of it unreachable.

She moved slowly; heavy, drained. Walking through water, carrying bags of lead. When Richie was out of the house, he took half the gravity with him. Henry took the other half.

The absence of the child made her curious. She was surprised when he grew old enough to be genuinely amusing, challenging. She could see the changes in his body almost daily. He stopped needing her, stopped crying and squealing and started surviving on his own. He became the candle that warmed the house around her, a heat that occasionally distracted her from the fantasies. She started to admire the little flame, growing and growing, burning bright through the windows of the house when she arrived home. She could feel the heat of her love for the boy pulsing through the walls sometimes while he slept. She'd creep from the bed and stand over his sleeping form until her skin burned.

She separated from Henry. The boy was all she needed. She stopped messing around with anyone who held her eye for long enough, with Richie's third-grade teacher, with John Errett, with an old friend she'd known from high school. Sara had been ready to be the warmth that Richie needed, and for him to be that for her, and for the call of the night to be silenced. It was time to stop playing games. Thinking about faraway highways and expensive hotel rooms and rendezvous in flashy bars in trendy corners of the city. It was time to grow up. She was not childless. She had a child, and she loved him.

Then he'd turned against her.

Sara was staring out the window. She glanced at me in the rearview mirror, coming to herself. I didn't know how long we had been driving. The sun was red through the tops of the trees, something burning at the base of the mountains—a small spot bushfire being battled by local volunteers. The fields were featureless, scraped-back earth between rainforest and the wandering, endless reach of creek and mangroves. The wilds.

"You get married," Sara said. "You have kids. You fantasize about what you could have done instead, about what you're going to do when it's over. And then you realize it's never over. I was staring down the barrel of the next thirty years sitting across the table from Henry at weddings, Christmases, graduations. Sitting through Richie's inevitable teenage crisis caused by my leaving his father. His inevitable daddy issues. His own divorce."

Lillian stirred in her chair, turning away from a drool patch she'd made on one side. Sara reached over and swept a sweaty strand of hair from my child's head.

"Richie loved his father more than me," Sara said. "After everything I'd done. Everything I'd lost. He acted out after the separation, and I started threatening him that if he didn't behave himself I'd make him go live with his father. Well, that worked a few times, and then one day he said that was fine—he'd go live there. Can you believe that? His father was living in some shitty dive hotel. In the fridge at his place there was milk and cheese, and that's it. And Richie says he wants to go live there. I couldn't believe it."

I tried to think of things to say. That Richie was a child. That his father's new house was probably foreign and exciting to him. I remembered Lillian crying hysterically for her mother after she had dropped her at my place. The jealousy and hurt I had felt.

"Richie bit his fingernails down to stubs while he was with me," Sara said. "And he didn't do that at his dad's house. What does that tell you?"

"It tells me you were very sensitive to his relationship with his father, and you took it too seriously. It tells me you probably have postnatal depression," I said.

"Please." Sara rolled her eyes at me. "Richie was eight years old."

"Anya was a newborn," I said. "You had it then. That's maybe why—"

"I didn't kill Anya," Sara snapped. "She was a fucking baby." Her eyes in the rearview mirror were livid. Insulted. As though murdering a newborn baby was any worse than murdering a healthy eight-year-old boy.

"The fibers."

"It was exactly as the police said." Sara looked away from me in disgust. "She'd had the pillow in the cot with her. I don't know who put it there. Maybe it was me. I was tired, and I wasn't thinking. You do crazy things when you're tired. Put the phone in the fridge.

Park the car and walk into the house without turning the engine off. When I found Anya I must have thrown the pillow across the room. It's hard to remember. The shock hits you and you forget details like that."

I waited for some of her rage to cool, squeezing the steering wheel so hard it creaked.

"You must have been depressed after Anya died. You were depressed when Richie was born. That's why you handed him off to your parents. Henry's parents. I'm not an expert, Sara. But I think you're sick and you need help. You can get that help."

Sara gazed at the passing cane.

"There's still time," she said after a moment, so softly she might have been talking to herself. "There's still time to have the life I deserve."

She directed me to turn off the highway. I looked at a football field wedged between two farms, kids playing in the dappled light, parents pointing and directing as the kids wrestled and trudged in the grass.

We were soon on a dirt road heading into the rainforest, the little huddles of suburban houses we'd passed gone. I couldn't see the mountains anymore. I heard whispers of the ocean in the distance as we rose and fell over hills. There were only towering walls of green, fingers and arms of palms and vines embracing or kissing overhead against the pale purple sky. I wondered what she had told Richie as they drove here. The boy in the back seat, watching the last of his world sail by.

"Richie was never in the hotel the second night, was he?" I asked.

"No." Sara was watching my child sleep. "He never came back from the crocodile farm. He so loved crocodiles, I thought that might be a good way to end it. You probably saw them do the same show we did. Where they coax the thing out of the water."

I didn't answer. There was a lump in my throat.

"I worked it all out the day before," Sara said. "It was easier than I thought. They make the cameras around the hotel really obvious so you won't do the wrong thing, but then you kind of know where they are, so you can figure it out if you try. It was like a puzzle. I drove into the parking lot and parked so that the passenger-side doors were close to the elevators. When the police officers took me through the footage it was believable. I told them Richie was sitting in the back seat, so you couldn't see him from the overhead camera on the boom gates. And then I said he got out of the back and went straight to the elevators, so you couldn't see him over the top of the car. He was too short."

"The sunburn," I managed, swallowing, on the edge of sickness.

"I told the other parents that we both got fried," she said. "Made sure they really got a good look at me. I ran into the Sampsons outside our room and said Richie had already gone in and fallen asleep. We were dehydrated and sore. So they set the other boys up in the room and we said we'd come later, after I knew the parents would have gone downstairs."

"What did you tell the boys?" I asked.

She smirked. "I hardly told them anything." I watched her smile in the mirror, reflective, almost amused. "When I came in they were all lying on the floor watching a movie. I said Richie was going to come soon and they all mumbled and grunted. You know what boys are like. They're idiots. They can only pay attention to one thing at a time."

A mob of wallabies broke from the long grass beside the road and bounded across my path up ahead. Their flight felt like a warning. The rainforest was thinning, shrinking to sprawling mangroves.

"When I came back up the last time I made a huge fuss," Sara said. "Really screamed at the boys. I told them Richie was with them, that he'd been there all night, that they'd lost him. They said no, but I insisted. Yes, he'd been there. Yes, yes, yes. I could see them accepting it. I was so mad, I must surely be right. Once one kid starts believing, the others fall right into line. They had been dead asleep when I walked in, and now I was in hysterics." She glanced at me in the rearview mirror. "Just like you said. Hysterics."

I focused on the road.

"They were upset, confused. But I screamed at them for five minutes before anyone arrived. And then the other parents joined in, backing me up. Richie had been with them all night. Where was he now? They had to know."

I remembered Jaxon Cho's wandering eyes as he delved into his elaborate fantasies about the night the boys had spent together. Two of them arguing in the interview tapes about whether they'd built a fort on the first night or the second. The boys had confused the two evenings, been convinced by the parents that their friend had been with them when in fact he'd been absent. Their own parents and police officers in uniform with serious faces and guns and recording equipment had told the boys that Richie had been there. They were used to trusting the word of adults, and now frightened, frenzied adults were telling them something and they were all listening, believing, terrified.

Luca Errett had been the one to get the closest to the truth in the interviews. I had watched him and not understood the depth of his words.

All the mums were crying.

They kept asking us "Where's Richie? Where's Richie?" but I didn't know. I couldn't remember. I said he wasn't there. Maybe he went somewhere else.

Like maybe he was still sleeping or something.

"How long had you been planning this?" I asked. The questions kept coming. I knew I was distracting myself from my present danger by delving into Sara's plan, that I needed to focus, think of myself. Think of Lillian. But I had to know the truth.

"I've been thinking about it since he was born," Sara said. "But it was never real, just a kind of game. A fantasy. Lots of mothers think like that, but they just don't admit it."

I was silent. She rolled her eyes.

"Oh, come on," Sara said. "Don't be so naïve. It's the middle of the night and you're sore and heavy and he's been screaming for fourteen hours straight and you think *If I just gave his nose and mouth a little pinch.* You've driven for three hours with him in the car kicking your seat and complaining and farting and picking his nose and you finally get to some look-out in the mountains and he's standing by the edge, where you told him not to stand and you think—*If I just gave him a little push.* I know what it's like already. The aftermath. All the sympathy you get. All the help that suddenly comes."

Sara had lost herself. She realized what she was saying and her face hardened.

"But I was never going to actually *do* it. It was just . . . thinking. There's nothing wrong with thinking," she said. "But then it's every day. You're thinking about it every day. And the opportunities are suddenly everywhere. On this trip I was thinking about it a lot. Looking at the cameras. Talking to him at the park. Driving him into the mangroves. Maybe it was real and I just didn't want to believe that I would go through with it. He was right in front of me and I had the rock in my hand and I asked myself if I had covered everything. And I had. So I did it. I finally crossed the line."

"I don't understand why you hired me," I said. "Was I always part of the plan?"

"Not until I saw an advertisement for Conkaffey and Pharrell investigations in the newspaper on the first morning," Sara said. "They delivered it to my room. It's an odd name. I remembered your case. I thought you'd be a good safety buffer. You knew what it was like to be falsely accused. I thought you could probably give me the heads-up if anything real bad was coming my way from the police, and you'd be purely focused outwards on other leads. You might have found something. At least, that's what I thought." She locked eyes with me in the mirror. "I didn't expect you to turn on me. That wasn't your job."

The dirt road had thinned, had disappeared beneath grass and vines for a while and now was completely gone. I was rolling on a mix of clay and sand, knocking over fledgling plants and winding between trees. I slowed to walking pace. Sara looked out the windshield for the first time in a long time.

"Keep going."

"We're going to get bogged."

"It doesn't matter," she said.

We drove on sand, the fingerlike roots of mangroves poking up from the ground. When there was nowhere further to go, I stopped. We sat in silence for a long time, the car ticking. Sweat was creeping out of the hair at the back of my neck, dampening my collar.

I looked out at the lonely place where Richie had died. I didn't want to know how Sara Farrow had killed her son, but as I gazed upon the scene before me I saw that there were plenty of options at her disposal. Thick, twisted fallen branches and heavy clumps of moss-covered rock. The creeping tide rising, muddy, impenetrable water. And then, of course, we were now in the territory of the hellish, prehistoric creatures I had just seen captured and contained behind wire. As the thought came to me so did my awareness of the sounds outside the car, the swamps coming to life as they did every night. Birds giving their final song of the day, frogs and other amphibian things starting up their vigil chorus. And the crocodiles barking somewhere nearby on the banks.

"Think about this for a second," I said. My voice in the car seemed impossibly large, clumsy. "No one is going to believe I came out here and killed myself with my child in the car."

"Why not?" she asked. "Look at your life."

We stared at each other in the mirror. She was composed, calculated, her features carefully arranged, the way I'd seen her sitting on the end of the hotel bed when I first met her. Unemotional. There was no need to pretend now.

"Get out," she said.

"I don't believe you won't hurt Lillian," I said. "I don't believe you'll kill me and leave her unharmed. You've killed a child before."

"You don't have much choice, Ted," Sara said. "You can watch me do it now or you can tell yourself I won't do it after you're gone."

She flicked something on the gun, maybe the safety, maybe the magazine release, fumbling to make a sound with the weapon to warn me. I didn't move, took just a second to call her bluff. She raised the gun and fired right beside my ear, shattering the windshield.

Ringing. The distinct pulsation of my eardrum, like I'd been slammed with an open palm against the side of the head. I turned and saw Lillian snap awake, already screaming, her mouth and eyes huge. Sara Farrow was shouting at me to get out of the car. I could see her mouth forming the words but I could not hear them.

Sounds rushed back, muffled, numbed, starting with the clunk as I opened the car door and got out. Sara followed me a few paces onto the sand, a narrow bar in the water where we could get our footing, but only barely.

I turned and stood before Sara in the wilderness, listening to my child sobbing madly, calling for me. I tried to plan, looking around me, wondering if I sank to my knees whether I could grab a rock or a handful of sand and hurl it at her face, distract her. But I'd never get away with Lillian in my arms unless I disarmed her. The thoughts were crashing into one another in my brain, no conclusions, only impulses. And yet I couldn't move, couldn't get air into my lungs.

Then I spotted movement behind the car. The sliding, slithering movement of something creeping cautiously.

I was afraid to let my eyes settle on Amanda for too long as she moved toward the back of the car.

Amanda slid along the side of the vehicle and raised her gun, pointing it right at the back of Sara Farrow's head from five meters away.

Amanda and I locked eyes. I shook my head, just one twitch, my eyes wild as I moved them to Lillian, who was visible through the shattered windshield and just to Amanda's right through the back passenger door. I had no words, but I hoped my message seared through my eyes. If Amanda missed and Sara Farrow panicked, turned and sprayed gunshots wildly, as she was likely to do as an unpracticed gun user, she might hit Lillian. I felt tears on my face as I stared at my partner just beyond my abductor, willing her desperately to hear my silent thoughts.

Take her. Go.

"I'm sorry," Sara said to me. I was hardly listening, trying not to watch over her shoulder as Amanda popped open the door of the car as quietly as she could. "You seem like a nice guy, Ted. I wasn't lying when I said I had listened to your story and that I believed you."

"You can turn this around right now," I told Sara, watching but not watching Amanda unclipping Lillian from her seat. "You don't have to do this. Let's talk it through. Let me help you."

Amanda took the blubbering child into her arms and glanced back at me. I nodded, and she turned and sprinted away into the night.

Sara didn't seem to notice the sound of the child's cries receding. She raised the gun and pointed it at my chest.

Amanda couldn't get any breath into her lungs. She hadn't been able to in what seemed like hours, since she had begun to realize what was happening to Ted. She'd panted, gasped for air as she took her motorcycle to its mechanical limits down the highway, the rainforest becoming a green blur, the air in her helmet red-hot and burning in her mouth. She had breathed in short, heavy huffs as she sprinted through the forest and into the mangroves, stopping at what she hoped was a safe distance from where her quarry would be so that her motor wouldn't be heard. She couldn't breathe now as she kept running, the child slipping in her sweat-drenched arms as she fumbled her out of the mangroves, splashing and stumbling through water that looked like puddles but was knee deep. Gripping, sucking mud and bottomless sand. She'd lost the path the car had taken in her haste. Around her in the growing dark, things were barking and howling and croaking, the sounds only audible between the screams of the child.

Amanda stopped and held the girl out from her chest. She was wet all over, tears and snot and sweat. Amanda coughed, mosquitoes landing on them both, buzzing at her mouth and ears.

"Listen, sprog!" Amanda drew deep gasps, letting the words tumble out. "We're in croc country here. You! Need! To shut up! Shut! Up! Listen! You'll get us fucking eaten! With that noise!"

She gave the child a good shaking, but that only made things worse. Amanda wondered what Ted would do. With every cell in her body rebelling, her instincts screaming against her actions, she pulled the child to her again and squeezed it tight with her arms.

"I love you," Amanda said as she rocked the child, put her cheek against its hot head, bent and kissed it on the temple. "It's okay. It's okay. I'm here. I love you. I love you. I love you."

She patted the damp curls and kissed the child a dozen times. In a few moments it was quiet.

"Good work," Amanda said, hefting the child onto her chest and starting to jog on through the dark. "Good work, sprog."

She didn't stop, even as she heard the gunshots behind her.

I took a couple of steps toward Sara. The woman was on the edge, but she had fired the weapon already. She knew how to do it. She could do it again. Just like the killing of her own son, taking a life, my life, here in this place would be easier a second time. I could see her detaching from me, justifying it to herself, practicing what she would tell herself about the act later, far from here, when what she had done was only a memory. I was close to the gun, one hand out and reaching, and as she came back to the situation she raised it higher, aiming at my face, her teeth bared.

"Sara, listen," I began.

"I can't," she said, the gun shaking. "I can't. I'm sorry. I have to."

I had remembered the keys in my hand as Amanda opened the back door of the car to retrieve my child, some strange habitual instinct making me take the keys from the ignition as I exited. I'd wondered why I hadn't locked the car, why the door mechanism didn't seem to click when she lifted the handle. Absurd, logical, everyday thoughts, the kind that push through trauma's peaks of intensity, the brain trying to calm itself. I gripped the keys in my pocket and pushed the lock button on the car's remote control now twice in quick succession, and the car gave a short beep of protest right behind Sara.

It was enough to distract her just for an instant, her head twitching, wanting to look but too focused on me to fully let herself go. The gun swung slightly to the left and I slapped it away in the same direction, grabbing Sara's wrist as she dropped the weapon. But she was too wild, too full of the same adrenaline she'd needed to take my life, to be subdued easily. She collapsed, and I went with her, and as we hit the ground her hand was raking across my face and her knees were in my belly. I tried to force her into the sand, tried to turn her and wrap my arm across her face, my fingers fumbling at her hair. She bit down hard on my forearm and a howl rippled out of me.

Sara saw the animal before I did. It was only a movement in the corner of my vision, the hide and snout slicked with the same mud and sand that was everywhere, so that for a second as it rushed out of the water it seemed like the swamp itself had come to life. The croc ran at us, and we parted, screaming. Another strange, disconnected, rational thought pulsed through me, that the beast was my size, that its scaly shoulders were as broad as mine and its eyes were knowing and alert and thinking, calculating.

The croc paused for only a moment, its jaws open

and hissing before it turned and rushed again at Sara. I grabbed at the gun, getting a handful of metal and sand as Sara scrambled away into the water, slamming into a mangrove tree as she tried to flee, falling. The croc entered the water after her, disappeared as though it had turned back into the water itself, scales dissolving. The only indication of it was a V-shaped ripple on the surface as it advanced toward her.

"Shoot it!" she screamed. "Shoot it! Shoot it!"

I shot at the water before her twice. She stumbled again, hit a deep patch or was dragged down. I couldn't tell. She made no sound as her head disappeared beneath the surface.

The car was bogged. I ran through the falling dark, sinking sometimes to my waist in the water, dragging myself out by the roots of trees. The thought kept coming that I would never make it out, that something would take my calf in its jaws and drag me back and I would remain here with Sara and her son forever. The thought was followed closely by those same impossibly vivid pictures of Amanda and Lillian running, being cornered by groups of the creatures against merciless walls of trees. I almost didn't see the red and blue flashing lights until they were all around me. The ground was suddenly firm under my feet. Amanda was standing in the dark inside a circle of police cars with Lillian in her arms, both of them drenched and caked in mud, Superfish patting Lillian's back as she sobbed.

"Just give her to me," he said to Amanda.

"No way," Amanda was saying. "I'm covered in its

germified ooze now anyway. I'm holding on to it until he comes—"

I marched up and snatched my child from Amanda's arms. I couldn't help myself. She watched me in openmouthed horror as I dissolved into tears.

"I'm sorry," I told my child. "Lillian, I'm so sorry. I'm so sorry. I'm so sorry."

Amanda was watching me cry the way a person watches a stranger throw themselves from a bridge. I reached out with one arm and encircled Amanda's head and dragged her to me, held her with my baby against my chest.

"Oh no! No!" Amanda yelled, her face muffled in Lillian's body and mine. "Urgh! Urgh! Stop! No touching! Oh god! Stop!"

There were police officers around us, uniforms from Cairns and some others I didn't recognize, northerners responding to Amanda's call.

"Thank you, Amanda," I said. "Thank you."

I let my partner go and she gasped for air, wiped and flapped at her face and neck and chest with her hands like she was covered in swarming ants.

"Don't thank me," she said, her words so fast they almost ran into each other. "It was great. We had a great time. The sprog and me. Yep. Running through the swamp. Lots of adventure. Loved it. Please don't thank me again. No hugging. Nope. None of that."

She turned to look at Superfish for help.

"Don't *you* start crying!" she wailed at him. "Everybody stop crying!"

"I'm not crying." Superfish turned away.

The adrenaline comedown made things hard to follow. I held on to Lillian as Amanda and Superfish briefed the officers who came into our little huddle, each taking different pieces of information away. Clark arrived and I told him about Sara's murder of her child in the swamps and how I had seen her disappear into the water.

He said nothing to Amanda or Superfish, hardly looked at them. A helicopter rushed overhead and I walked away with Amanda to the edge of the gathering, sitting on a police car bonnet and hiding my face in my child's neck and hair.

Amanda was still wiping at her arms and hands, her hair sticking out at odd angles from behind her ears like she'd received an electric shock. She mumbled complaints I could hardly hear, pacing back and forth.

"Don't know why you didn't hug Superfish." She gave an angry wave in his direction. "He's the only reason I got to you."

"What are you talking about?" I asked.

"I never received your text," Amanda said. "Your SOS text. That bitch Joanna Fischer lost my phone for me."

She explained the confrontation on the rooftop at the White Caps Hotel, her nemesis walking in on her and Superfish trying to discover whether Richie Farrow's body was at the bottom of a hidden secondary elevator shaft. Joanna had pulled a gun on Amanda just as my text had come through to her phone, causing Amanda to drop the device into the shaft. A group of officers on their way to the roof, having heard a rumor that Amanda Pharrell had been spotted in the building, had inadvertently stopped Amanda from being shot.

Amanda had been placed under arrest for trespassing on a crime scene. Chief Clark had arrived on the rooftop to find his officers snarling and swearing at one another, Joanna Fischer in tears, and Amanda in cuffs kicking and screaming. The cops had wanted to take her to the Cairns police station in a car, and she'd been howling that if anyone put her in a car she would personally track that bastard down when she was released and bite all their fingers off one by one. Superfish, ever the calm and quiet voice cutting through the mayhem, had interjected at exactly the right time, volunteering to walk Amanda to the nearby Cairns police station. Clark had allowed Superfish to take her away from the fray in cuffs.

"I insisted on my phone call," Amanda said. "I was going to call you. Tell you that I'd been arrested. How funny is that? While I'm trying to tell you I've been arrested, you're trying to tell me you've been arrested. Or abducted! I think abducted would be more accurate." She turned, her tattooed skin purple and yellow and red in the flashing lights of the police cars. "Anyway, I made such a big deal about it that Superfish tried to call your phone as we walked to the police station. Some Japanese woman answered. She didn't speak great English but she mentioned the crocodile farm. It seemed like you'd lost your phone in the parking lot at the crocodile farm."

"Why didn't you just leave it at that?" I asked.

"It didn't seem right." She shrugged. "Why would you go there? I mean, you've got one day left to spend with your sprog and you go to *that* crocodile farm. I thought you were probably a bit dissatisfied with Hogan taking the rap for Richie's death, like I was. You went to the last place Richie and his mother were seen together, and then suddenly, *puff*! You've disappeared. Just like I always feared. Weird. No sign of you or your beard. It was like it was geared, engineered, you and the sprog had been commandeered."

Amanda had charged into the Cairns police station ahead of Superfish, with her hands still cuffed behind her back, and started shouting demands for someone to open her instant messaging account on their phone or a computer and read her last text. Superfish obliged, and they read the SOS message together. Amanda knew I hadn't been arrested. She thought about the crocodile farm. The last place Richie had been seen alive, in the company of his mother. Amanda had called for someone to track the GPS on Sara Farrow's phone and tell her the location, but the station commander was already berating Superfish for his ward's behavior. No one had complied with Amanda's GPS tracking request, so she kicked over a stand of brochures and knocked a laptop off a desk with her elbow, jumped up on a table and leapt from desk to desk as people tried to bring her down. Superfish had got her into a cell holding and quietly borrowed another officer's computer to find the location of Sara Farrow's phone, discovering that it was heading up the highway south from the crocodile farm.

"How did you get out of custody?" I asked.

"Superfish let me out." Amanda glanced around at a

huddle of officers taking a briefing from Chief Clark on a search of the mangroves. "He'll probably be fired for it. He let me out of the holding cell and out a back door at the station, gave me his phone so I could follow the signal. I told him to tell them I kicked him in the balls but I don't know. He doesn't seem like the lying type."

As though he'd heard his name called, Superfish approached us from the huddle of officers, looking grave. I checked on Lillian, letting her fall into the crook of my arm, and found she was asleep. In all the light and noise and chaos, she had simply blinked out of consciousness, all of it too much for her. I envied her, the dancing shadows of her eyelashes on her perfect cheeks.

"They're going to put some boats out, see if they can find Sara. Maybe some of Richie's remains," Superfish said. "The coast guard has offered to help."

"Are you people nuts?" Amanda threw her hands up. "That bitch will be half digested before you get the first engine started. You heard Ted. She's croc food. And that kid's corpse has been out there for five days. You'll have to net every beast in the area and put his bones back together like a jigsaw puzzle. It'll take months."

Amanda was making such a scene that the officers nearby were watching. Even in the red and blue lights of the patrol cars I could see Superfish was blushing.

"Probably worth it, though," he mumbled. "I'd appreciate your help. You have a good eye, and you know exactly where Sara disappeared from."

"You want *my* help?" Amanda snapped. "Look at

me. I'm covered in child filth and swamp filth. If I don't have the early stages of tuberculosis right now I've almost certainly got leeches. How am I going to search for anything like this? There are things crawling in my pants, Superfish. *There are things crawling in my pants!*"

My partner stared helplessly at the officer beside her, who seemed to have nothing to offer to counteract her complaints. I left them there in the chaos of the search, carrying my child to where more patrol cars were arriving in the hopes of catching a ride back home.

Amanda hadn't signed up for this. She sat at the bow of a small aluminum boat while Superfish steered, picking bits of dirt from behind her ears, only half looking at what the beam of the torch clasped under her arm showed of the riverbanks. Amanda had told herself after Pip Sweeney's death that she and Ted, and Conkaffey & Pharrell Investigations as a business, would not be working with the police again. They were far too annoying, with their sneering and sniggering, their neurotic crime scene preservation, and their kneejerk willingness to jump into boats and go zooming around searching for things that were clearly not there just so they could say they looked and no one would throw sticks at them later because they didn't. Too concerned with their own image, the police, Amanda thought. And their uniforms seemed uncomfortable and stuffy. The crotches were too high.

The decision had been made to send five search

boats out into the river, to send teams to place drag-nets up- and downstream three kilometers each way from where Sara Farrow had disappeared, and to put up two search-and-rescue choppers—one police, one coast guard. In the morning, when they found nothing, Amanda knew they'd bring in dogs. Amanda didn't envy the canines tasked with wading through the croc-infested waters looking for Sara's or Richie's remains, waiting to feel that inevitable brush of scaly skin against their furry hides. Crocs loved dogs. Their splashing and paddling was like music to their weird little waterproof ears.

They spied Joanna Fischer early in the search on the bow of another boat, Superfish and Amanda say-ing nothing, waiting patiently for some obscenity to be yelled across the water as the boats passed each other in the moonlit night. Nothing came, the woman watching emotionlessly as Amanda passed, the bruise under her eye like a dark smudge of mud. Superfish took them up the river and down a small, winding channel, the hull groaning as it sailed over rocks and roots. With his own torch he swept the banks, endless darkness populated by twisting, pale trees. There was the occasional panicked rustle overhead, something with luminescent eyes fleeing. The almost alien yipping of young crocs and frogs in the shadows. The channel narrowed so that on either side the banks were within arm's reach.

"Could I ask you to keep your torch on the ground?" Superfish said, letting the engine idle as they sailed along.

"I don't know, *could* you?" Amanda spat.

"You're pointing it at the tops of the trees. Perhaps you should actually hold it in your hand."

"What do you want to see?" Amanda aimed the torch at the banks. "Look. Crabholes. Thousands of crabholes." She reached out, quick as lightning, and snatched up a white crab that had been sprinting sideways away from her torch. "Crabs, too. You want to see them? Here. Look real close."

Superfish didn't flinch as Amanda threw the crab at him. He caught it just in front of his face and placed it gently in the water.

"I think I'll take a look along the banks." Superfish cut the engine and let the boat shunt into a sandy bank. "It's dry enough up there. You can stay in the boat if you're scared of the crocs."

Amanda gave an exaggerated groan and slid out of the boat, barely resisting the urge to remind Superfish she had bested a fifteen-foot croc not a year earlier. Superfish took his own torch and stood on the firm sand, looking out into the dark.

"Sara?" he called.

"She can't hear you," Amanda said. "At present she's the consistency of a beef casserole. Soon she'll be steak tartar and then she'll be liver pâté."

"I'll look this way." Superfish pointed. "You follow the bank up that way. Scream if you need help."

They split, Amanda shining the torch before her, crowds of tiny panicked crabs rushing into their bubbling holes in the sand, pincers flailing. She had only walked a hundred meters or so when she heard the sound for the first time.

A soft moan.

She almost laughed at herself, her pessimism at finding Sara Farrow or her son out here in the dark falling off her shoulders like a cloak. Amanda was never wrong, and yet here she was, ears pricked, waiting for the sound to come again. If she found Sara Farrow right now, Amanda was going to laugh her arse off. What were the chances?

"Help." A weak voice.

"Oi!" Amanda called. "Speak up. Where are you?"

"Help. Help."

Amanda followed the noise, sweeping the torch to look for crocs as she traversed a patch of deep sand, then a ridge of high, firm land covered in grass. The voice never seemed to get any closer. How was that possible? Was Sara walking away from her in the mangroves? Maybe she was disoriented. Trailing a munched-on leg hanging from her body by a thread. Amanda walked on, looking for a single footprint and a drag mark, maybe trails of blood. But there was nothing. Only the little crustacean citizens and their mass hysteria.

"Help."

"Stay where you are, idiot!" Amanda said.

The realization of her mistake came in a violent rush, like a plunge into icy water, the knowledge that she had been lured into a trap. She saw footprints, not the small tennis shoes and flip-flops she'd seen Sara Farrow wearing over the past few days but the big, unmistakable print of police-issue boots. Amanda had left her gun in the boat. She was so far from the banks now, on a wandering path she'd taken trying to follow a moving sound, that finding her way back would be a guessing game, and there was little chance Superfish would be able to find her even if she screamed.

Joanna Fischer stepped out from behind a tree and Amanda gave a full-body sigh that made the torchlight shift up and down.

"You know, this swampland is two hundred and seventy square kilometers," Amanda moaned. "Couldn't you have found another patch of it to be a creepy bitch in?"

"Where's my partner?" Joanna asked.

"He's off hunting the legendary Australian bunyip." Amanda shined her torch in Joanna's face. "He wants to bag one and sell it to Ripley's."

"He put in for a transfer," Joanna said, wandering out into the light. "He wants out of Holloways Beach and into Crimson Lake department. He wants to be away from me."

"I've never been less surprised by anything in my life," Amanda said. "Being away from you is one of my favorite pastimes."

"Superfish has really been good to me," Joanna said. She looked down at her boots on the sand. "He's had a lot to try to understand with Pip's loss. How what happened to my best friend still haunts me."

Amanda slapped at a mosquito on her arm, sniffed.

"Jesus Christ, you're boring," Amanda said. "Pip didn't even like you. She wasn't your best friend, she was your partner, and she probably put in a request to get away from you just like Superfish did."

"She was promoted."

"Yeah." Amanda rolled her eyes. "I bet she was devastated, too."

"You're wrong." Joanna inhaled unsteadily. "She was my friend, and you took her. You ruined me. You ruined everything I could have been. I had someone in my life to look up to. A guide. Look at what you did to me. I've killed a man because of you. An innocent man."

"Oh, come on," Amanda said. "You loved it. You loved it when Pip died, because that gave your already unhealthy fixation a tremendous bump into psychosis territory. You're so interesting now, aren't you, Joanna? The grieving, traumatized friend. People are falling all over each other trying to defend you. Suddenly you're surrounded by friends!"

"No one is grieving for Pip," Joanna said. "And no one recognizes my grief. They've forgotten all about her. They're all just so consumed by you."

"Well," Amanda said, "who could blame them?"

"I need to do something," Joanna said. "I expected you to go. I pushed you and pushed you. You should have understood that you're not welcome here anymore. You like the attention too much, I think. Well, let's end the story for them, Amanda. Let's give it a nice poetic finish, and then people can forget you altogether."

She took a knife from her back pocket and threw it at Amanda's feet. The tattooed woman didn't flinch. The blade stuck in the sand, then flopped slowly onto its side. It was short and thin, like a folding knife.

"This is what happens when you get too close to Amanda Pharrell," Joanna said.

"What?" Amanda laughed.

"You're a killer." Joanna took another knife from

her back pocket, though it was bigger than the one lying on the sand. "You came at me, as you have before. I defended myself."

"I'm not doing this." Amanda turned away. "I'm not giving you—"

The knife was badly thrown, hitting Amanda in the back and only penetrating the skin a couple of centimeters before the weight of the handle dragged it out. Before she could turn and grab the weapon from the sand, Joanna was there, sweeping upward with her shoulder, barging into Amanda hard so that she fell in the damp mangroves. Joanna's body was hot, her breath coming in furious pants, the way a man's had that fateful night when Amanda killed for the first time.

"I'm not—" Amanda tried to say. "I'm not—"

It was working, Joanna's plan. She was taking her back. All the way back to when she was seventeen, the first time she had killed. She was hopelessly enslaved to it, the memories of Lauren Freeman in the rainforest that night impossibly accessible, even after all these years. Amanda remembered the girl's desperate, wide eyes, the same as Joanna's now, so shocked by the wounds in her back as she rolled over on the ground, gripped Amanda's arms. She remembered the roar of the cicadas in the trees all around them, the way her own heartbeat seemed to trip, skip, hammer in turns.

She remembered the second time she'd killed. Pip appearing at the glass doors to the little house just as Amanda raised her gun too late, firing and hitting one of the men who had attacked her. Defending herself.

Taking a life. Ruining everything Pip could have been. Taking Pip from the world simply by being, marking her with the touch of death as soon as she'd laid eyes on the other woman. She had to kill again now. Make Joanna part of it. She had no choice.

Joanna's knife was coming down, teasing wounds in Amanda's chest and forearms, tiny pricks and slashes, goading her. Amanda grabbed for the other knife in the sand, gathered it up, slashed wildly and caught Joanna across the chest, tearing fabric, the knife knocking over plastic buttons. There was blood. Joanna got off Amanda, stumbled back, examined the blood on her hand in the moonlight.

Amanda staggered to her feet, wiped the blade of the knife on her denim shorts. She hadn't wanted to give in, to surrender to Joanna's will. But her body was burning and bleeding and the rage that was usually so fleeting, so hard to access, was roaring out of her now.

"Remember." Amanda waggled the blade at Joanna. "You asked for this."

The two ran at each other. Amanda slipped sideways at the last second, palmed Joanna in the jaw, knocked her off balance, and dug the knife into the soft flesh under her arm. The tip penetrated the back of her shirt, shallow, wounding. She didn't see Joanna's move coming, tried to shove the woman down onto the sand but got the edge of a boot scraping down her shin bone. The scream caught in Amanda's throat. Joanna came for her again, halfhearted slashes and jabs, baiting Amanda into another entanglement. She went willingly, trying to get enough swing to ram the handle of the blade into Joanna's temple. They fell, Joanna giving Amanda three quick jabs with the knife in the ribs, wounds Amanda knew would bleed well but never threaten her life.

This is it, Amanda thought. *You die by a thousand cuts or you give her what she wants.* There was no winning. She could see Joanna telling one story, those dramatic tears, the twisted tale of Amanda Pharrell's vicious attack on her in the dark night. Avenging her friend by taking Amanda's life and refusing to give up her own, a bittersweet ending to a long and traumatic tale. The hero's journey from victim to predator. Amanda's frantic brain was also flashing visions of Joanna's other purpose, the end she wanted even more. Joanna's death by Amanda's hand.

The only way to win was to give her neither. Survive somehow. Flip the game board and scatter the pieces.

Amanda rolled and tried to scramble away, but Joanna had her hair in her fist and the knife at her neck.

The breath left Amanda as another body slammed into them, Superfish wrapping his arms around Joanna, trying to haul her backward, fumbling for the knife.

"Don't!" His voice was high, desperate. "Don't! Don't!"

Joanna twisted, swung the knife, missed him as he fell away. This wasn't in her plan. Her story included three people—herself, Amanda, and her dead friend. Amanda could see the rage and excitement in Joanna's face fall from her features like lead. Superfish had to be dealt with quickly. He was not part of her script. He lay watching, eyes wide, as she came for him.

Joanna's advance toward Superfish was halted when he slid the gun on his belt from its holster, lifted his arm, and shot her in the face.

Amanda and Superfish lay in the dark for what seemed an eternity, Superfish on his elbows, feet sprawled, the gun still in his hand. Amanda had turned to pounce on Joanna from behind, but the sound of the shot had stopped her. She sat, flopped on her side, looked at the body of her nemesis curled on the earth. It seemed to Amanda that if she lay there long enough, Joanna's chest would start to rise and fall again with breath. She looked at Superfish, and he looked back at her, the two of them marking the seconds since Joanna had died silently in the night. In the distance, boats puttered toward them, voices calling and no one answering. Somewhere a chopper thumped through the heavy air.

When Superfish spoke, Amanda realized she had almost been dozing, lying bleeding and exhausted, curious crabs beginning to emerge and wander at the edge of her torch beam.

"I told her to stop," Superfish said. "I've been telling her for months."

It was clear to Amanda that this was Superfish's first kill. She was too tired to assure him that he'd get used to it, all of it: the stares, the whispers, the strange sudden memories of his victim through the coming years. Amanda was wet, wounded, covered in mud and mosquito bites, and she was pretty sure she'd broken a finger somehow in the fight. She could comfort Superfish later, or, ideally, not at all.

Amanda held her hand up to the moonlight, appreciating the interesting new angle her right pinkie finger now took from the second knuckle. It was then that she noticed the strange shape in the tree near them.

She stood and walked over to the tree and looked up at the shape in the dark, stood as still as she could to measure if it moved.

In time, she put her hands on her hips.

"Well, fuck me," she said.

Richie Farrow had spent the day in the sunshine. It was a beautiful, blue, sunshiny day from the moment he opened his eyes in the hotel room, rolled out of bed, and saw the aquamarine sea beyond the white strip of sand across the road. A day full of brilliant colors—vibrant orange egg yolks at the hotel buffet breakfast and a thousand shades of green in the rainforest as they drove out to the crocodile farm. Richie couldn't believe it was actually happening. Ever since he'd spied a brochure with a grinning croc on a stand in the hotel lobby he'd been whining and complaining and poking and prodding at his mother about visiting the farm. She'd promised she would take him there. Richie had wanted to go that very second, but it hadn't been "practical," and it wasn't in the next day's plans, either. Richie remembered once on a group trip to Dubbo in the Outback, his mother promising that he could sleep on the top bunk in the kids' room on the third night—the bigger kids got the top bunk first. But they'd only stayed two nights. Richie had learned of her betrayal in the car on the drive home. So it was possible that when his mum said—*promised*—they were going to the croc farm that in fact another Top Bunk Lie was at play. Richie had been skeptical until he saw the gates of the park.

He tried to rein in his excitement, but he did all the things he wasn't supposed to do. He whooped and squealed and kicked the seat in front of him in the car, banged on the windows, went "hyper." His mother usually screamed at him when he went hyper. He'd tried to learn to control it, let it out only when it was safe, when he was at his dad's. But his mum didn't seem to mind it today. She smiled as he ran up to the gates of the park, high-fived him. So weird. She was in such a good mood. He didn't have time to wonder why she was being so cool. He was too excited.

It was great. So great. Richie could see himself being a crocodile wrangler. He liked the khaki uniforms and the utility belts the men wore, liked their sun-tanned faces and hairy arms. Richie imagined he'd be an awesome crocodile trainer—he was awesome at most things. He'd wear a big knife on his belt, get it out and chop the crocs if any of them tried to attack him. He'd be able to train the best crocs to accept pats along the nose, perhaps be bridled like a horse and ridden around. Richie's crocodile training skills would be world-renowned. He'd watched the crocodile feeding display, trying to ignore his mother's odd questions.

Since his parents had decided to live in separate

houses, the weird questions happened quite a bit, from both of them. Mostly they were about the other parent—his mum wanted to know if he loved his dad more than he loved her, and his dad wanted to know if his mum seemed happy. Today the questions were coming hard and fast and they weren't about his dad at all. Did Richie think he'd had a good life so far? Had he always had fun, felt loved, felt safe? Did Richie really love his mother—love her no matter if she did bad things sometimes, or if she would do bad things in the future? Richie couldn't figure out what had got his mother into this strange, thoughtful mood and tried to show her the crocodiles and how amazing they were and get her to stop with the crazy wonderings before they had to leave and she would have missed all the great animals. His mum was a bit silly sometimes.

It was after the park that things got strange.

Richie had asked if they were going for ice cream— she'd promised that they would—but his mum wouldn't answer and wouldn't take her eyes off the road to look at him. They drove and drove, with him asking questions and his mum not answering, and eventually Richie just assumed she was tired or still suffering whatever weirdness had come over her at the park and would shake it off soon. Richie's mum got into strange moods sometimes, and they could last for days, but they always went away in time. He went to sleep. When he'd awakened they'd been bumbling along a dirt track into the forest, and it sure didn't seem like they were heading for an ice cream shop but Richie liked the look of the place anyway. He saw water, and eventually they parked on a strip of firm sand.

"Are there crocs around here?" Richie had asked as he wandered in the mangroves, his sneakers squelching in the mud. He saw fish jumping in the water through the trees. "We'd better be careful."

Something happened. Richie wasn't sure what. Later he thought it must have been an explosion, a bomb maybe, hidden in the mangroves nearby. There was a big red flash and a pain in the back of his head that was so bad it made his knees go weak. He hit the sand, and then there was another red flash, and then darkness.

When he opened his eyes, it was dark, and he was alone, lying on the sand with his hand tangled in something around his throat. It was wet and heavy, and in time he pulled it away and realized it was a plastic shopping bag tied at the back of his neck. He pulled the bag off and rolled over but didn't seem to be able to stand. He knew only that he was alone, that the water was higher now and lapping at his sides. There were mosquitoes. The darkness came into his brain again.

He was aware of some things, but not others. Richie knew that the sun went over the top of him once, and that the water came and lifted him, and that when it set him down again he'd walked some way, calling out for his mother and receiving no answer. The night came, and he was tired, and his legs wouldn't work properly. A half-full bottle of red Powerade floated by and he drank some of it. Richie couldn't remember if his mother had said there were crocs in the area or not, but he decided that if his legs did start working again he would climb a tree. The sun went over, blazing on him, and when he woke again it was hammering with rain. He pulled himself to the base of a tree, then pushed and pulled with all his strength until he got up on a branch. His arms hung down, trailing in the water. The sun, when it came again, blistered on his back so badly it was like he was being poked with sticks of fire.

The boy spent the next day pulling himself up onto a higher branch, and then another. He nestled into the tree, sleeping peacefully even while ants walked along his arms and things rustled in the leaves above him. He called out for his mother now and again when he could, but his voice was soft and raspy. Wherever she was, she probably couldn't hear him.

I learned what had happened to Richie Farrow like everyone else did—in frantic, hour-by-hour news bulletins on every available television channel. I sagged in my kitchen chair with a glass of Wild Turkey and listened to the medical reports changing as they came through. Richie had been found by the infamous Amanda Pharrell, sagging in a tree, severely dehydrated, covered in insect bites, and with life-threatening cerebral hemorrhaging from blunt-force trauma to the back of the head.

Over the days after he was discovered, the boy was put into an induced coma while the blood clot in his skull was drained. It was thought that the boy would suffer some long-term paralysis on one side of his body, but he was soon awake and capable of telling his story. Police believed Sara Farrow had bashed her son's head with a rock or other blunt object, placed a plastic bag over his head, and left him to the crocs.

Richie had likely torn the bag off in some autonomic reflex while he was unconscious.

There were lots of headlines about miracles. The miracle of a boy lying unconscious in a mangrove for days and not being approached by a single crocodile when his mother was eaten, it seemed, within minutes of leading me to the same spot to kill me. The miracle of the boy having the strength necessary to rip open the plastic bag his mother had placed over his head after she struck him with a rock. The miracle of the enormous blood clot in Richie's brain settling at the base of his skull and not swelling, not pushing on his spinal cord, not cutting off his small, tenacious life.

Of course, Amanda told me this same story in a phone call, and Val came and visited and discussed it with me, but I wasn't good company in the forty-eight hours after the event. The moment I took Lillian back into my arms after we were abducted, I knew what the responsible thing to do was, and I did it. A part of me wanted to simply lie to Kelly about what had happened, tell her that our child had been perfectly safe for the entire time we spent together and that nothing eventful had occurred. But that wouldn't have been fair. Lillian was her daughter, too. So I had a police officer drive me and the child directly to the mountain-top resort where Kelly and Jett were staying, and I told my ex-wife exactly what had happened in the mangroves.

There was screaming. A bit of shoving from Jett. Kelly snatched a sleeping Lillian from my arms exactly the way I'd snatched her from Amanda: with the desperate, furious, aching relief only a parent with a child fresh out of danger can understand. I listened to their tirade as Lillian cried. I'd risked our child's life. I'd put her in peril for the sake of a case. I was a psychopath. A monster. I'd never see my child again. The whole situation was not aided by Lillian calming down long enough to examine Jett's T-shirt, which he'd obviously bought somewhere local. There was a crocodile on the chest. Lillian pointed directly at him and said, "Tiny cock." The veins in Jett's temples stuck out like noodles on his sweat-slick skin.

I went home and moped for a couple of days, sleeping on the porch with Celine, lying on the lawn with the geese. I sat on the back step and talked to Woman, the mother goose, for hours, trying to find the words to explain to the great white bird how empty and ashamed I felt. I got drunk, seriously drunk, so worryingly drunk that Celine followed me everywhere whimpering and pawing at my chest.

On the third day, I was feeling mildly better about everything when Kelly called me to tell me that Jett had flown home to Sydney. They'd had a fight. He'd taken their scheduled flight, but she'd stayed behind. I was sitting on the couch on the porch with my morning coffee, Celine slumped across my legs, her pointy ears pricked.

"Don't fight about me," I told Kelly. "You're good for each other. I don't want to be an issue between you."

"How arrogant," Kelly said. "We could have been fighting about anything."

I managed a tiny laugh, no more than a snort.

"He knows exactly how he feels about what happened," Kelly said. "And I don't."

"You don't?" I asked.

"No," she said. "I mean, yes, your job endangered our child. You endangered our child by not keeping it away from her. You should have taken the week off and spent time with her. But then again, a boy was missing. And he was found because of you. What am I supposed to think?" She laughed humorlessly. "That's the thing. No one's had an answer for that question since you were arrested. I used to just jump in and feel the first thing that came along. Go with the flow. But I . . . Maybe that's how I lost you. By not giving it time. Trusting you."

I gripped the phone and listened. I could barely hear Lillian singing in the background.

"When are you going back?" I asked.

"Well, that's kind of why I was calling," Kelly said. "You didn't really get your time with her. Proper time. I know it probably doesn't make up for it, but . . . if you have no plans today—"

"I have no plans today," I said. It was a lie. I'd intended to go see Amanda, battered and bruised and cut up the way she always seemed to be at the end of our cases, as though her very skin marked out our journeys, a map of violence in progress. She'd been the one to find Richie Farrow, so I also owed her a cake.

"Let's spend the day together," Kelly said. I could hear the smile in her voice. "It'll be like old times."

Chief Damien Clark finished another report and stretched his neck, hearing cracks and pops in the bones and joints as he rolled his shoulders. He was unsurprised to see that the clock on the wall of his office read nine in the evening. It had been a solid day of reporting on the occurrences that brought Richie Farrow's disappearance to an end. There was still so much more to account for. Constable Joanna Fischer's death was the second duty-related death in the region in less than a year, a score that soared above the national average, and a good part of Clark's morning had been spent trying to relate into the report the actions of one of the officers under his command, Lawrence Supevich, in releasing an arrested suspect against command's orders. In the middle of all the chaos, one of his lead detectives on the Farrow disappearance had to be stood down a day before the boy was discovered. Detective Ng had failed to account for a substantial sum of money missing from the station evidence locker, seized in a drug raid he'd led only a month earlier. It would look to the outside world as though Clark's handling of the Farrow case had been haphazard and chaotic, his staff unreliable and underhanded. Certainly the true crime books that would come out about it would portray it that way. All Clark could do was try to make sense of it all on paper and hand those accounts over to the higher authorities.

As he packed his things into his bag and shut off the light in his office, he tried to decide how he actually felt about the case, and found he was not as down in the dumps as he expected to be. Yes, an officer had lost her life, but he suspected investigations into her passing would reveal that there was more to the Pharrell–Supevich–Fischer incident in the mangroves than simple officer misconduct. Everything about Amanda Pharrell was clouded. Her whole history was impossible to lay out in a straight line—it was more a collection of sharply angled pieces that appeared to fit while held in a certain light, and did not in another.

Clark had reached a point of exhaustion with his involvement with Amanda Pharrell that defied the sadness and anger he'd felt over Pip Sweeney's death. He felt calm. He had given the woman a second chance, and in doing so, a missing boy had been found. Clark had visited the child in the local hospital the previous evening, finding the boy's father asleep in an armchair by the bed. Clark had quietly informed Henry Farrow that his ex-wife's remains had not yet been discovered, but that searches would resume in the morning.

Clark walked out of the station, waving goodbye to the two officers manning it overnight, and slung his bag over his shoulder. The lights in the garden that led to the parking lot were being battered by moths and strange, elongated insects with shimmery blue wings. The sound of a couple of motorbikes roaring off in the distance reminded him of the rumor he'd heard that morning that, during the case, a few of his officers had become involved in a fray with a group of local bikies. Something to do with Pharrell and her disagreement with Fischer. More of Amanda's mysteries, Clark supposed. If he knew one thing about bikies, it was that they didn't let go of grudges, and if there'd been some kind of attack, retribution would have come already. He was skeptical that his own men would be so stupid as to tangle with the local gangs, but he knew there was always some truth to rumors. It might have been that the bikers and his guys had traded insults at a local bar or something. There weren't many of those, so sometimes it was necessary for soldiers of different camps to rub shoulders.

He went to his car in the middle of the long, rectangular lot and unlocked the door.

The first car went off by the gate to the parking lot, fifty meters from where Clark was standing. The explosion came from under the bonnet but quickly engulfed the midsection of the vehicle, blowing the roof off in a huge ball of white and yellow flame. Clark felt the searing breath of the explosion on his face, watched the roof of the patrol car peel back and the red and blue lights splinter on the concrete. By the time the second car went off, this one across the lot from him, directly in line with his own, he was cowering with his hands over his head, wincing as the heat rushed over him, glass and debris falling on his back and arms. In mere seconds, it seemed, every patrol car in the lot had thumped with an internal explosion and burst into flame. Clark stood and looked around him in wonder as the ten cars crackled and ticked and groaned with flames, popping and bursting with secondary explosions as his colleagues rushed into the lot and dragged him away from the danger.

The three officers stood outside the lot and watched the cars burn, their mouths hanging open at the spectacle before them.

The first time I knew of her presence was when Celine perked up at a sound I couldn't hear, rushing off around the side of the house and into the growing darkness. I was sitting on the step with a glass of Wild Turkey on my knee, sunburned and salt-washed and exhausted from my day out with Lillian and my ex-wife. My phone was full of pictures Kelly had taken of Lillian on my shoulders, walking under the sprawling trees by the beach, the two of us sharing ice cream, Lillian asleep in my arms as I carried her back to the car. I had been sitting, remembering my beautiful day, as the sun set. I was thinking of putting the geese away, watching them wander in the grass chasing off cane toads and tugging at the ground, and that got me to thinking about Laney Bass.

She appeared just like I'd dreamed her up, Celine trotting beside her, a happy escort for a decidedly unhappy-looking woman, this time wearing a pale blue dress. I didn't get up, but didn't voice my dismay at the prospect of ending a wonderful day with being shouted down. Since I've lived on the edge of Crimson Lake, people seem to feel as though they can just wander down the side of my house at any time, but I don't blame them. The front of the house, with its boarded-up windows and burns and paint stains from the vigilantes, seemed to have given up its duties as an entrance by virtue of being so ugly.

Laney came and stood not far from me, and I suddenly became fascinated with my drink.

"I'm really sorry," Laney said. She waited for a response, but I didn't have one, so she continued. "I came around here yelling and screaming like a lunatic, when what I should have done is ask you to explain yourself. I just, uh . . . I got caught up in a kind of fantasy, you know? When you meet someone you like . . . You get this idea about them." She gave a gesture, a winding of the hand, like she was trying to find the words. In time she dropped the hand, looked at my eyes. "You know you're probably wrong, but you never think you're *that* wrong."

She gave an awkward little laugh. I sipped my drink.

"So I'm really sorry," she concluded.

"I'm sorry too," I said. "Have you . . . Have you looked at my case at all?"

"A little bit," she said. "I saw that you're no longer a suspect."

I patted Celine.

"I'm going to look at it more," Laney said.

"Why?" I asked.

She thought for a moment. "Because I really had

fun out here." She looked around my property. At the light on the lake. "With you."

"So did I," I said.

I wanted to tell her that I felt the same, but it seemed unfair to put that kind of pressure on her. To tell her that it hurt, the way she'd fluttered in and then stormed out of my life so quickly, a little fantasy I'd also enjoyed.

She turned, seemed to want to go. I thought about walking her up the driveway to her van, but didn't know if she wanted me to. She paused, wringing her hands so that the muscles in her forearms flexed.

"Anyway, I just came to tell you that . . . I think I'm . . . I think I want to have you in my life somehow," she said. "But I don't know how. Yet."

I nodded. She turned to go and almost ran straight into Amanda, who was walking around the corner in her swift, awkward gait, ready to slam into anything she might encounter, the way she generally was in life.

"Don't touch me!" Amanda threw her hands up. "I'm contaminated!"

Laney gave me a puzzled look, only a second's worth, before she disappeared.

Amanda trudged through the grass to my side, flopping down in the gold light.

"What are you doing here?" I asked.

"I came to give you this," she said, and sneezed on my arm. She took a handkerchief from the pocket of her shorts that was covered in little cartoons of bees. She held it to her reddened nose and glared at me over the top of it. "I've caught some disgusting disease from your human spawn and I'm giving it back to you, so help me god. Didn't I tell you how much I hate being sick? Didn't I tell you I was going to catch some lurgy from that gross little pukebag?"

"You did." I smiled. "You did."

"And where's my goddamn cake?" she asked, blowing her nose loudly. Her exposed arms and upper chest were covered in fresh, neat stitches over the wounds she had suffered from Joanna Fischer. "I found Richie Farrow. *Me*. So you owe me a cake. Raspberry cream sponge."

"With hand-tempered chocolate shavings," I said, jerking a thumb toward the kitchen. "I made it this afternoon. It's in there."

"It better be." She stood. "I'll be back in a minute after I've licked all your cutlery and blown my nose on your pillows."

Amanda went and cut herself a slice of the cake, returning to my side with two corners of the handkerchief stuffed up her nose. She sat down with a fork and started shoveling the cake into her mouth, having not brought me a slice or asked if I wanted one. I watched her, feeling a smile creep onto my face, while she smacked and licked her lips.

"I can't even taste this," she said, her words muffled by sponge. "Look at that cream. That raspberry cream. You're a great cook, Ted. If that was the stupid girlfriend I saw just now marching out on you, well, she's nuts, mate. This is probably the best cake ever. But I've gotta tell you, I can't taste it at all. I'm not sure it counts as your case-loser cake."

"I'll make you another one. You can have it when you're better," I said, patting her shoulder.

Amanda looked at me, shoveling another bite of sponge into her mouth.

"Don't touch me," she said.

ACKNOWLEDGMENTS

I have my dream job. I visit serial killers and murder sites, talk to huge audiences, hang out with my hero authors, and travel to the far corners of the Earth in pursuit of new readers. Half my life is spent having adventures with wonderful people who don't actually exist. I get to do all that largely because of four things—hard work, luck, the efforts of great teams of people who work behind the scenes, and the support of loving readers.

The list of people who have believed in me and helped me is growing, and the space on this page to thank them remains the same. But I learned my craft at the University of the Sunshine Coast, the University of Queensland, and the University of Notre Dame, Sydney, from the brilliant teachers and writers I have named in previous novels.

Gaby Naher is indescribably valuable to me as both an agent and a friend. She and Bev Cousins, Nikki

Christer, Jessica Malpass, and Kathryn Knight make up the original Team Fox Australia. Lisa Gallagher champions me in the U.S. with limitless gusto, and in the U.K. Emily Griffin, Selina Walker, Susan Sandon, and others do the same. Kristin Sevick, Linda Quinton, Brian Heller, Alexis Saarela, Robert Allen, and their colleagues are my irreplaceable U.S. team, and Thomas Wortche and his superb people take care of me in Germany.

Thanks to James Patterson and Adrian McKinty for always being willing to lend an ear to a fellow writer.

I'd like to thank the readers and reviewers who have been with me from the beginning, and if this is your first time taking a chance on me, I am very grateful to you, too. My husband, Tim, makes a mean coffee, reads all and reads fast, and doesn't think I'm really that scary despite all my morbid weirdery. He's a real brick.

Read on for a preview of

GATHERING DARK

CANDICE FOX

*Available in March 2021
from Tom Doherty Associates*

A FORGE HARDCOVER

BLAIR

I looked up into the eye of a gun. She'd been that quiet. That fast. At the edge of my vision I'd half-seen a figure pass the front window of the Pump'n'Jump gas station, a shadow-walker blur against the red sunset and silhouetted palm trees. That was it. She stuck the gun in my face before the buzzer had finished the one-note song that announced her, made her real. The gun was shaking, a bad thing made somehow worse. I put down the pen I'd been using to fill out the crossword.

Deep regret: *Remorse*. Maybe the last word I would ever write. One I was familiar with.

I spread my fingers flat on the counter, between the bowl of spotted bananas at a dollar apiece and the two-for-one Clark Bars.

"Don't scream," the girl said.

As I let my eyes move from the gun to her, all I could see was trouble. There was sweat and blood on her hand, on the finger that was sliding down the trigger, trying to find traction. The safety switch was off. The arm that held the weapon was thin and reedy, would soon get tired from holding a gun that clearly wasn't hers, was too heavy. The face beyond the arm was the sickly purple-gray of fresh corpses. She had a nasty gash in her forehead that was so deep I could see bone. Fingerprints in blood on her neck, also too big to be her own.

Screaming would have been a terrible idea. If I startled her, that slippery finger was going to jerk on the trigger and blow my brains all over the cigarette cabinet behind me. I didn't want to be wasted in my stupid uniform, my hat emblazoned with a big pink kangaroo and the badge on my chest that truthfully read "*Blair*" but lied "*I love to serve!*" I had a flash of distracted thought, wondering what my young son, Jamie, would wear to my funeral. I knew he had a suit. He'd worn it to my parole hearing.

"Whoa," I said, both an expression of surprise and a request.

"Empty the register." The girl put out her hand and glanced through the window. The parking lot was empty. "And give me the keys to the car."

"My car?" I touched my chest, making her reel backward, grip the gun tighter. I counseled myself not to move so fast or ask stupid questions. My bashed-up Honda was the only car visible, at the edge of the lot, parked under a billboard. Idris Elba with a watch that cost two college funds.

"Car, cash," the girl said. Her teeth were locked. "Now, bitch."

"Listen," I said slowly. For a moment I commanded

the room. The burrito freezer hummed gently. The lights behind the plastic face of the slushie machine made tinkling noises. "I can help you."

Even as I said the words, I felt like an idiot. Once, I'd been able to help people. Sick children and their terrified parents. I'd worn surgical scrubs and suits; no kangaroos, no bullshit badges. But between then and now I'd worn a prison uniform, and my ability to help anyone had been sucked away.

The girl shuffled on her feet, waved the gun to get me moving. "Fuck you and your help. I don't need it. I need to get out of here."

"If you just—"

My words were cut off by a blast of light. The sound came after, a pop in my eardrums, a whump of pressure in my head as the bullet ripped past me, too close. She'd blown a hole in the Marlboro dispenser, just over my right shoulder. Burned tobacco and melted plastic in the air. My ears ringing. The gun came back to me.

"Okay," I said. "Okay."

I went to the register, snuck a sideways look at her. Gold curls. A small, almost button nose. There was something vaguely familiar about her, but during my time in prison I'd probably cast my eye over a thousand troubled, edgy, angry kids who knew their way around a handgun. I took the keys from the cup beside the machine.

"This is a cartel-owned gas station," I said. I realized my hands were shaking. Soon I'd be sweating, panting, teeth chattering. My terror came on slowly. I'd trained it that way. "You should know that. You hit a place like this and they'll come for you and your family. You can take the car, but—"

"Shut up."

"They'll come after you," I said. I unlocked the register. She laughed. I glanced sideways at her as I scooped out stacks of cash. The laugh wasn't humor, it was ironic scorn. Something sliced through me, icy and sharp. I looked at the windows before me, at our reflections. She was looking out there, too, into the gathering dark. No one else was visible. We seemed suddenly, achingly alone together and yet terrifyingly not alone. I handed her the cash.

"Someone's already after you," I surmised. She gave a single, stiff nod. I slowly took my car keys from my pocket and dropped them into her hand. When the barrel of the gun swept away from me, it was like a clamp loosening from around my windpipe.

I watched her turn and run out of the shop, get in the car, and drive away.

Through the windows, Koreatown at night seemed to breathe a sigh of relief, to become unpaused. Long-haired youths knocked each other around on the corner. A man returning home from work let the newspaper box slap closed, his paper tucked under his arm. The malignant presence I'd felt out there when the girl had been in the store was gone.

I could have called the police. If not to report the robbery, to report a girl running from something or someone with the furious desperation of a hunted animal, a girl out there in the dark, pursued, surviving for who knew how long. But Los Angeles was full of people like that; always had been. A jungle, prey fleeing predators. I'd give the girl a little head start with my car before I reported it missing. I lifted my shirt and wiped the sweat from my face on the hem, trying to regulate my breathing.

My addiction pulsed, a short, sharp desire that made me pick up my phone beside the register, my finger hovering, ready to dial. I forced myself to put the phone down. The clock on the wall said I had an hour left of my shift. I thought about calling Jamie but knew he'd be asleep.

Instead I went to the ATM in the corner of the store. I slipped my card into the machine and extracted four hundred dollars, about the amount I knew the girl had taken. I went back and put the notes in the register. Though I'd never met the gas station's true owners, I'd known cartel women in the can, and had picked up enough Spanish over the years to eavesdrop on their stories. The girl, whoever she was, didn't need the San Marino 13s on her tail. Neither did I.

I hardly looked at the ATM receipt before I crumpled it and let it fall into the bin. It was going to be a long walk home.

JESSICA

"Here's what I don't understand," Wallert said. He'd been saying it all day. Listing things he didn't get. Waiting for people to explain them to him. Jessica guessed they were probably into the triple digits now of things Wallert couldn't comprehend. "What the hell did you do on the Silver Lake case that I didn't do?"

She didn't answer, just looked at Detective Wallert's bloodshot eyes in the rearview mirror. Jessica hated the back seat of the police cruiser, didn't belong there. She was used to the side of Wallert's ugly head, not the back. A biohazard company gave the back seat a proper clean out every month or so, but everybody knew that it never really got clean. The texture of the leather wasn't right. Gritty in places. But Wallert was looking at her more than he was driving. Combined with the frequent sips of bourbon-spiked coffee from his paper coffee cup, he was eyeing the road about one in every fifteen seconds. In this case, she was in the dirtiest but likely the safest place in the car. Detective Vizchen, who they were babysitting for the night, sniffed in the front passenger seat when Jessica didn't answer Wallert, as if her silence was insolence.

"I was there," Wallert continued. They cruised by a bunch of kids standing outside a house pumping music into the night. "I was *in* the case. I was available to the guy whenever he needed me. Day or night. He knew that. It was me who came up with the lead about the trucker."

"A lead that went nowhere," Jessica finally said. "A lead I *told* you would go nowhere before you began half-heartedly pursuing it. You weren't of much assistance to Stan Beauvoir the few times he called on you."

"This. Is. Bull. Shit," Wallert snarled. He slammed the steering wheel with his palm to the beat of his words. Jessica said nothing. To say that Wallert wasn't of much assistance on the Silver Lake case was an understatement. The nearly decade-old case had been handed to her and Wallert as a "hobby" job, a spare-time filler, something Wallert hadn't taken seriously from the beginning. The series of abductions and murders of young women taken from parking lots in the Silver Lake area had ended as suddenly and mysteriously as it had begun, four women dead within the space of three months in 2007. Wallert was sure that the killer had been a long-haul trucker, someone who probably carried on their killing spree in another state, making it someone else's problem. He'd looked at the photographs of the four young women who'd gone missing when Jessica first handed them to him and yawned, then remarked on Bernice Beauvoir's full, pouty lips. "You don't get lips like that from suckin' jawbreakers," he'd said. The picture was of Bernice's head sitting like a trophy on a tree stump in the wooded area where she had been found.

"House like that," Vizchen broke the silence. "Gotta be—what? Five million dollars?"

"You don't just give a five-million-dollar house to someone who worked on a case for you." Wallert's eyes seared into Jessica in the rearview mirror. "Just say you sucked his dick, Jess. It would make me feel better."

Jessica felt her teeth lock together.

"I'd suck a dick for five million dollars," Vizchen mused.

"Vizchen, you shut your mouth or I'll stick my gun in it. See how you like the taste of that," she snapped.

They pulled in to Lonscote Place. Blackened houses, perfect stillness. Wallert kept the emergency lights off but gunned it to number 4652, where the sighting had occurred, and slammed the car into park. He wanted to get this over with so he could go back to his pity party.

Jessica got out of the car, checked her weapon, called in the 459—possible burglary—and told the operator they were responding as the nearest unit to the scene. She looked at the moonlight reflecting off the stucco walls of the houses around her, dancing through diamond wire onto bare yards. No dogs barking. Wallert's hand on her shoulder was like a hammer swinging down.

"You're going to take the house, aren't you?" He

turned her too roughly. "Is it just like that? They just give you the keys?"

"Get your fucking hands off me, Wally." Jessica shoved him in the chest. "I've had one phone call about this mess. *One*. I know as much as you do. I've got to meet with the executor of the guy's will and see what it's all about. This could all be a stupid goddamn mistake, you know that? You're treating me like I've taken the inheritance and moved to Brentwood already, and all I've got so far is—"

"Every house in Brentwood has a pool," Vizchen said. He was leaning against the car, his arms folded. "Place has got a pool, right?"

"If there was any justice"—Wallert poked her in the chest—"you'd split the house with me. It's only fair. I was on that case, too."

"You didn't work it! You—"

"I don't see any goddamn prowler." Wallert stormed back toward the car and flung a hand at the surrounding neighborhood. "It's a false alarm. Let's get out of here. I need a proper drink." He leaned on the car rather than getting in, big hands spread on the roof, his round belly pressed against the window. He looked at Vizchen. "Even if she gave me a quarter of what it's worth, I'd be set for life."

"Set for life," Vizchen agreed, nodding, smiling at Jessica in the dark like an asshole.

Jessica heard the whimper.

She thought it was Wallert crying and was about to blast him for a day's covert drinking ending in a mewling, slobbering, pitiful mess. But some instinct told her it was a sound carried on the wind, something distant, half-heard. Sound bounces around the poorer neighborhoods. All the concrete. She looked right, toward the silhouette of the mountains.

"Doesn't Harrison Ford live over there?" Vizchen wondered aloud. "I know Arnie does."

"Did you guys hear that?"

"She got on pretty damn well with the guy. The father. Beauvoir," Wallert grumbled to Vizchen. "I mean, if you'd seen them together. She spent hours at his place. Just 'talking about the case,' about the dead daughter. Yeah, right. Now we know the truth."

"Shut the fuck up, both of you." Jessica flipped her flashlight on. "I heard something. That way. We gotta go. We gotta check this out."

"You check it out." Vizchen jutted his chin at her. "You're the hero cop."

The sound returned, faintly this time, no more than a whisper on the breeze. Vizchen smirked at her as Wallert fished in the car for his cup.

Jessica headed east along the curve of the road, waiting for the sound to come again. Between the houses she caught a slice of gold light. Movement. Rather than continuing to follow the road around, she walked down the side of a quiet house, brushed past wet palm fronds as she found the gate leading into the yard. She vaulted it, jogged across the earth in case of dogs, vaulted the next fence. The house in Brentwood and Wallert's rage were forgotten now. She could feel the heat. The danger. Like electricity in the air. She hit the ground and grabbed her radio as she headed for the garage of a large brick home.

A body. She knew the instant her boot made contact with it in the driveway, the sag of weight forward with the impact and then back against the front of her foot. It was still warm. Damp. She bent down and felt around in the shadows of a sprawling aloe vera bush that was growing over the low front fence. Belly, chest. Ragged, wet throat. No pulse. Jessica's heart was hammering as she grabbed her radio.

"Wally, I've got a code two here," she said. "Repeat. Code two at 4699 Lonscote Place."

A sound in the garage ahead of her, up the driveway. The roller door was raised a foot or so, and from its blindingly bright interior she heard the whimper come again. A thump. A growl.

"Wallert, are you there? Vizchen?" she whispered into her radio.

Nothing.

"Wallert, Vizchen, respond!" She squeezed the receiver so that the plastic squeaked and crackled in her hand. Static. "Fuck. Fuck. Fuck."

Jessica pulled her gun and headed for the garage. Stopped at the corner of the building to radio command.

"Detective Jessica Sanchez, badge 260719. I've got a 10–54 and code three at 4699 Lonscote Place, Baldwin Village. Repeat, code three."

There was a flash in her mind of Wallert and Vizchen laughing. Another officer might have wondered about the two of them, why they weren't responding. If they were in danger. But not Jessica, not today. She'd heard Vizchen's words, knew she would hear them again in the coming weeks, from her brethren at the station. *You're the hero cop.* No one was coming to help her.

She'd betrayed them all with the Brentwood inheritance. She'd marked herself as a traitor.

She sank to the ground, flattened, and rolled under the garage door, rose and held the gun on him. He was a big man, even crouching as he was, a heaving lump of flesh, bent back straining. At first she thought the old woman and the young man were kissing on the ground. Intimate. Mouth to throat. But then she saw the blood on his hands, all over his face, her neck. Jessica thought of vampires and zombies, of magical, impossible things, and had to steady herself against a pool table. Her mind split as the full force of terror hit it, half of it wailing and screaming at her to flee. The other half assessing what this was. A vicious assault in progress. Assailant likely under the influence of drugs. Bath salts—they'd been hitting the streets hard in the past few weeks, making kids do crazy things: gouge their own eyes out, kill animals, ride their bikes off cliffs. She was watching a man eat a woman alive.

"Drop her!" she shouted. An absurd part of her brain noted she was talking as if to a dog. A wolf. A werewolf. "Drop her! Stand back!"

The man raised his bloody face. The old woman in his hands bucked, tried to shift away. Too weak. Almost dead. Every vein in the man's body was sticking out like a slick blue rope on his sweat-soaked skin. He wasn't seeing Jessica. He was trapped in his fantasy.

"Back up now or I'll shoot!"

The man lifted the woman to his lips. Jessica fired over his head, hit a dart board hanging on the wall, sending it clanging to the ground. He got up, staggered away from the noise. She fired again and hit him in the left shoulder. The bullet flecked his shirt with blood, embedded itself in the muscle. He didn't flinch. The man came for her, gathering speed in three long strides. She fired again, a double tap in the chest. A kill shot. He kept coming. A big hand seized her face and shoved her into the wall, then dragged her toward him with the strength of an inhuman thing.

She thought of Wallert as the man's teeth bit down into the flesh of her bicep. Her partner out there, somewhere in the dark, laughing at her.

Jessica grabbed at the man's rock-hard shoulders and landed a knee in his crotch. They went to the ground, rolled on the floor together. He pinned her on her front, his belt buckle jutting into her hip. Another bite on her left shoulder blade, the *pop* sound of the fabric as his teeth cut clean through her shirt. Jessica pushed off the ground the few inches she could manage and smacked her elbow into the man's face. The crunch of his nasal bone. He bit her left shoulder. Clamping down, trying to tear the flesh away, a good mouthful. She looked into the eyes of the now-dead old woman only feet away from her and thought again about how no one was coming.

He tried to get on top of her, accidentally nudging her dropped gun within reach. Jessica grabbed the weapon and twisted under him, put the gun to his forehead as the teeth came down again toward her.

She fired.